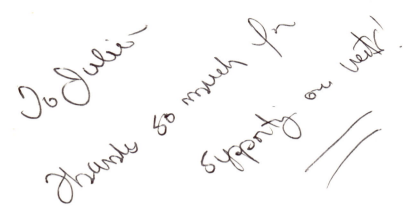

Also by Jeanette Vaughan

Flying Solo
Angel of Mercy

Solo Vietnam

Jeanette Vaughan

AgeView Press

Blue Ridge, TX MMXIII

All main characters appearing in this work are fictitious. Any resemblance to real persons, living or dead, is purely coincidental.

Cover photo credit: US Navy NL 306 of VA-153
http://a4skyhawk.org

Copyright © 2013 Jeanette Vaughan

All rights reserved.
ISBN: 978-0-9892078-1-2

Published in the U.S.A.

DEDICATION

This book was written to honor the extraordinary men and women who serve in our U.S. Armed Forces, most endearingly to those who served during the Vietnam War. God bless those who safely returned home and especially those who didn't.

ACKNOWLEDGMENTS

The Vietnam War has always fascinated me. I remember as a young girl donning a copper POW bracelet. I wore it proudly and prayed every day that the brave man taken prisoner made it home. It was an honor to interview the men and women who helped make this book a reality. Pilots, nurses, and infantry gave texture to the sights and sounds of a foreign land. I am especially grateful to the pilots willing to share their stories. It was a time that was difficult and very misunderstood. For some, excruciatingly painful to remember.

First off, I would like to acknowledge Captain Robert Lathrop, USMC. The many missions in this book were based on his manuscript memoir *Eternally at War* which he wrote as therapy and which is now housed in the Texas Tech University Vietnam Center and Archive. The center is home to a vast collection of oral histories, photographs, and written documents giving vivid insight to a chaotic war.

I would also like to acknowledge several pilots and USN officers who have become friends. Chief Petty Officer Pete Wasmund, an HC-1 helicopter aviation tech who was onboard the *USS Coral Sea* for the July 67 to April 68 cruise. He shared his precious cruise book with me to help add substance and reality to the tale told here.

In addition, I would like to thank Tom Burdick, an agricultural flying ace who crop dusts over the Deep South. His personal descriptions of what it's like in the cockpit were invaluable to Nora's experience. He's promised me a ride.

Finally, I would like to thank two pilots who flew in Vietnam. Stan Thompson flew the A-4 Skyhawk during two tours during the war. His read for accuracy and performance of the aircraft was second to none. The other pilot flew Blackhawk helos. Dr. William Reeder was taken as prisoner of war near the Laotian border just like Steve. His riveting accounts and description of conditions were gold in bringing forth insight to the barbaric conditions under which many of men suffered. He not only survived his ordeal, but went on to become a PhD who now lectures and teaches on the subject.

I am humbled and forever grateful for their time, attention to detail and generous lend of their materials and literary works. As Americans we should forever be indebted to their bravery and service.

Solo Vietnam

Map of Vietnam

Chapter 1
∞ February 8, 1967 New Orleans, Louisiana ∞

Everyone wears masks. Some real, some masquerade. Colorful, sometimes provocative, they often depict inverse juxtapositions of expression. When donned, they become clever deceptions to hide a person's true emotions.

Mardi Gras in New Orleans was in full swing; a myriad of parades, beads, costumes, and, of course, masks. Six weeks of overt revelry and salacious debauchery marked the celebration. Kings, queens, and cotillion festivities prompted even the most well-to-do to get downright bawdy. Lent, a forty day period of fasting and prayer, followed Mardi Gras. But Fat Tuesday, the day before Lent began, was the last blow out. Twenty-four hours of raucous, non-stop excess

For Nora Broussard, a native Cajun from The French Quarter, it had become absolute torture. Her mask was an emotional one, not one of flashy, colored, paper-mache. Despite putting on her mask, which she intrinsically did, nothing could erase the pain of what this season had come to represent. In March, five years ago, she was forced to make the most difficult decision of her life; giving her youngest baby, a daughter, up for adoption.

Wearing her mask as the colorful floats passed by, Nora gaily celebrated the festivities with her friends, family, and children in uptown New Orleans. She enjoyed what time she could with them, for later, she had to work at the club. They shouted from the rooftops, "Throw me something. Throw me something Mister," to gain the multi-colored doubloons and beads. Green for good luck, gold for riches, and purple for royalty. Her outward mask was one of fun, but inside, her heart was ripping open again. Ash Wednesday became a day of reprieve from her pain. The day the Mardi Gras festivities and her memories could be shelved for another year.

It was now early morning and the tug boat whistles on barges pushing up the Mississippi rang out in asynchronous melodies. The bells for early mass at St. Louis Cathedral were chiming. Nora swore she could smell the balsam scent from burning incense from the thurible being swung about. Trucks lined the narrow, empty streets of The French Quarter. Stale beer, partially eaten *muffalattas*, and beads lined Bourbon and Toulouse.

A lone reveler hanging over the wrought iron rails called out to her as she passed. "Hey baby, I'm still up. *Les bon temp roulles*."

Nora continued to walk, nonplussed at his hung-over advances. It was hard to imagine that only hours before, the streets had been packed with thousands of tourists, krewes, and revelers.

Fat Tuesday had been a good night for her at the Blue Room of the Roosevelt Hotel. The one good thing about Mardi Gras was the enormous amount of tips she raked in as she crooned each set of bluesy, jazz tunes. Exceptionally intoxicated patrons were easy targets for excessive gratuity.

Returning home to The Quarter, after the baby debacle in Dallas, Nora had been able to secure her previous job as a torch singer at the club. The manager remembered her and her voice well. He was happy to re-sign her, knowing the effect her deep, silky voice had on his patrons. The Roosevelt had become one of New Orleans' most elegant and eclectic French Quarter hotels. Frequented by Louis Armstrong, Count Basie and in the past, Huey P. Long, one never knew what VIPs might be seen there.

For Nora, what had started as an easy, albeit temporary fix, to start a flow of cash and recovery for her re-entry to the Crescent City had become a position of substance. She had now sung seasonally at the Blue Room for over six years. The only downside was the hours. Her sets often lasted into the wee hours of the morning.

Once she wrapped up each morning, she would take time for a quick stop into Morning Call for a *beignet* and coffee. She read over the headlines in the early edition of the *Times Picayune*, sipping her *café au lait*, before walking two blocks to the street car which ferried her to her uptown bungalow.

Upon her return from the sojourn to Texas, Nora and her four children initially moved into The French Quarter apartment of her mother, on Dauphine Street. With grace and forgiveness, her mother had taken them in. This accommodation allowed Nora to save on monthly expenses, slowly but surely rebuilding her savings account from pennies to a sizable sum. The tiny apartment, however, was cramped with her and her children in it. It had taken about three years, but Nora's proud moment of independence, as a Catholic divorcee, came when she signed the mortgage note on her own duplex on Dante Street, two blocks off Carrollton Avenue.

From the shambles that her life had become after divorce from wealthy, but ruthless, Franklin Greenwood, owning her own place was immensely gratifying. She had sole custody of her children. It was a stalwart testament to surviving domestic abuse and thriving in autonomy. Nora didn't care if she was alone. She was free. And a landlord to boot. The Dubois' rented the other half of her pink Victorian, double shotgun with the tall black shutters. It was a far cry from the mansion in which she had lived on Woodvine in Metairie, but it was hers. All hers.

As she walked the few blocks from the olive colored streetcar, that dropped her off at Carrollton and Birch, she thought about everything she had been through. The illicit affair with the love of her life, her pilot instructor, Steve Novak. Their crazy temporary living arrangement, where she served as caregiver to his sickly wife, Marci. Their star crossed love affair, which had produced her baby daughter, now living in Texas somewhere. The ill-fated goodbye on the steps of the train station in downtown Dallas. It was a time from which Nora thought she could never recover. Yet, here she was, a sultry, moderately popular, New Orleans night singer. A pilot. A woman with her own place, freedom, and independence.

Her children, now ranging in age from eleven to seventeen were all teenagers. Well, all but one, Iggy. Her lone son, the youngest, was a precocious, pre-pubescent teen. For the briefest moment, she reminded herself that he was not the youngest; that would be the baby she gave away, now age five. Ugh, too painful. No. She would not think about that at all. Mardi Gras was over. Time for Lent.

Ready to take on the commotion of getting the children off to school, Nora creaked open the black-faced wrought iron gate to her home. As she climbed the five stairs up to the raised, single floor duplex, she could tell something was amiss. The normal chaos of the early morning was frenetic.

Cathy, already dressed in her long, navy blue, wool uniform skirt and white blouse slammed open the front filigree screen door. "Thank goodness you are finally home. Kayce's gone!" she exclaimed.

"Kayce's gone? Whatever do you mean?" Nora queried.

"She's gone. Kaput." Cathy histrionically bellowed.

As Nora entered the parlor, Leisel bounded in. "Yep. Cathy's right, Mama. Kayce is missing. She musta left before we even got up," she hurriedly explained.

Nora dropped the two grocery bags she was carrying and clambered back to the girls' shared bedroom. Then, she checked the bathroom off the middle bedroom and the kitchen. Kayce was nowhere to be found. Opening the back screen porch door, she scanned the red brick patio surrounded by azalea bushes and large backyard with its towering oak trees. Nothing. No trace of her.

Iggy, who had followed Nora into the kitchen, noted a hand-written card propped next to Nora's coffee pot on the stove. Nora could tell it was Kayce's handwriting. It simply read,

> *Mother. I've tired of the calamity of your life and your choices. I have gone to seek my own life and happiness. I am against the war, the establishment and especially you. I have left the pain of New Orleans forever. You can find me and my people in Haight-Ashbury.*

"Oh my God. Christ almighty. Kayce has run off to be a flower-child," Nora rolled her eyes. "Good Lord."

"What?" asked Iggy confused, pausing from chomps on a bowl of Captain Crunch.

"A hippie. Kayce's run away to be a hippy, stupid." Leisel retorted to her brother, still naive of the anti-establishment movement. The groups of Vietnam War protestors were in full swing in the spring of 1967, especially in San Francisco.

"Heavens to Betsy. I need to sit down. Pour me a cup of coffee, Cathy. You all will be late to school today. Get Grandma Nellie on the phone. See if Kayce's over there." Nora was adept at delegation.

Normally, Nora walked the children to the streetcar and packed them off to Catholic school. Iggy attended Mater Dolorosa in the neighborhood. Leisel, Cathy, and Kayce attended Dominican, which required a streetcar ride down Carrollton, past Claiborne.

"You girls. Walk Iggy to school, then take the street car. I'll give you a note for why you are late." Nora took a deep breath as she contemplated the mess that Kayce's latest escape had incurred.

In the hallway, she could hear Leisel, on the telephone, explaining to Grandma Nellie the saga of Kayce's disappearance. As she sipped her cup of strong brewed Community coffee with chicory, fatigue was temporarily staved. Nora gritted her teeth as Leisel brought her the phone.

SOLO VIETNAM

"Yes, Mama. I am sure she's gone. I know, Mama. I, know. It's risky to leave the children here sleeping while I work." Nellie laid in an extra special dose of Catholic guilt on this particular moment. "I do the best I can, Mama. I'll call you when I know something." Glad to end that barrage, as soon as Nora heard the phone call end with a click, she knew the one person she needed to dial to sort out this latest fiasco. Charlene, her best friend.

Chapter 2

Nora placed the receiver down for the fourth time. She had phoned and phoned and phoned. Where in God's name was Charlene? She took another deep drag of her cigarette. She was down to her last of the pack. With the onset of the Kayce debacle, Nora just couldn't sleep. Damn it. Where was she?

Nora grabbed her purse and walked a block and a half back down Dante to the corner grocery. "Forget something, Ms. Broussard?" the friendly Italian owner of Ruli's mini-mart asked?

"Just another pack of my bad habit. That's all. Benson and Hedges 100s, thanks."

"*Ciao*. Happy to see *mi amici. Bellissima*."

"*Gratzietante*, Paulo." Nora returned his kindness. He knew Nora and her four children well. Just outside the door, Nora quickly unwrapped the package and lit up. She dashed back to the house to ring Charlene again.

Charlene Hebert was Nora's best friend. A member of the Metairie Country Club set, from which Nora was excluded after her salacious divorce, Charlene was her lifeline. True blue compatriot, Charlene had always been there for Nora, although now, their social strata were eons apart. There was simply nothing that the two did not share.

"Hello there," Charlene finally picked up.

"Where have you been, doll?" Nora asked frantically?

"Just running a few errands after morning mass. It's Ash Wednesday you know."

"Yes, Charlene. I know." Nora still did not attend mass after her perceived, emotional, ex-communication from the church post-divorce.

"What's up?" Charlene questioned.

"Oh you just won't believe it. It's Kayce. She's run away. This time to be a flower child!"

"A what? Oh, my stars. That child. Nora, are you sure?"

"That's what her note says." Nora's nerves were fried. She began to sob softly.

SOLO VIETNAM

"Oh, goodness gracious. Nora. Come on over," Charlene beckoned. "I'd come to you, but I have the new maid here. I have to make sure she is going to work out. You know?"

"Okay. I will be right over. I haven't had any sleep. I had a late set last night with Mardi Gras. And I have another one tonight. But we just have to talk. I'll be there in a bit."

Nora raised the green tin garage door and fired up her used VW bus. With four children, it was the most economical vehicle she could afford. Heading down S. Carrollton, she then took Palmetto to Metairie. Charlene still lived in her stately home on Iona. As Nora pulled her VW into the driveway, a chill went up her spine, remembering the harrowing times with her ex, Frank, at her home on Woodvine. She purposely avoided that street, knowing he still lived there.

Charlene greeted her at the door with a big hug. "Nora! Come on in, honey. Good Lord, what has gotten into that Kayce girl?" she exclaimed.

"Oh, I don't know. She's been spouting about protesting the war for months. Her room is papered with anti-Vietnam pamphlets. I just took it to be her normal storm of rebellion. That and being a teenager. Nothing serious."

Charlene poured Nora a cup of coffee. She put out a silver tray of delectable *petits-fours* from Gambino's. "Did you have any idea? That she was thinking about going"

"Again, I don't know. Not really. I mean, she's been talking smack about it at dinner. When she's out of her school uniform, she's wearing tie-dyed this or that, just like everyone else. Headbands and beads. I honestly didn't think too much of it." Nora stirred her coffee with milk.

"Do you think this is a threat? Or that she's really gone?" asked Charlene. "Maybe she went over to Frank's or Nellie's place in The Quarter."

"We've already checked. Knowing Kayce? I have no doubt. She's gone for real. I checked her dresser drawers and closet. Most of her 'groovy' outfits are gone. I think she has really done it."

"Oh dear, Nora. I just don't know what to say. You know she's never forgiven you for the affair. Even though you did give up the baby. I've seen the resentment building for years. She hates it that she goes to Dominican, not Ursuline."

"I know. I've tried everything with her. Counseling. Catholic school. She was just old enough for that drama to have a major impact. The others seem to cope. Mainly because I don't think they really knew or understood what was happening. We've all gotten on with our lives. Just not Kayce."

"Nora, when does she turn eighteen? Isn't it soon?"

"Yep. Next month, in fact." Nora could see where Charlene was going.

"You know. Once she gets there, there's nothing you can do. Legally she is considered an adult."

"I know. That's why I am just sick about it. God almighty, I hope she survives her venture out into the world. Who knows what could happen to her out there? The drug scene at Haight-Ashbury is just rampant."

"I've been reading about it in the *Picayune*. Apparently there is some movement going on. They are expecting a surge of hippies and young people to converge on that area of San Francisco. It's like The French Quarter on steroids. 'The Summer of Love,' it's being dubbed."

"Oh, brother," smirked Nora, rolling her eyes.

Charlene went over to hug her friend and wrapped her arms tightly around her. "I'm so sorry, Nora. So sorry. Just as things have finally started coming together." Charlene sighed deeply, knowing the times her own teenagers were facing. Race riots in New Orleans. War protests. Hurricane Betsy in '65. Psychedelic rock and roll. The growing surge of weed. It was all almost too much with which the average teen had to cope.

On the one hand, America was all about the Space Race. Women's lib was surging. But there was a dichotomy brewing amidst the youth. Those that grew their hair long and experimented in the psychedelic anti-establishment and others who stayed true to their 1960s right wing conservative, nuclear families. There seemed to be no middle ground. Even the most popular band in recent history, The Beatles, who initially dressed in matching slim legged suits had morphed. Their music had now become defiant; a rock and roll which skirted exploration of Eastern ways and mind altering drugs.

"Let's get in the car and check the bus terminal. Surely, she didn't have enough money to fly to San Francisco." Charlene grabbed her purse and they got into Nora's VW bus and drove towards downtown. The Grey Hound bus terminal was in a more seedy part of town.

Approaching the ticket counter, Nora asked the agent if he had seen a long-haired, strawberry blond teen in tie-died clothing. The agent had only been on duty since 7:00 AM. Negative. No sign of Kayce.

"It was a futile idea. I am sure she is long gone," Nora sighed dejectedly.

SOLO VIETNAM

"Well. It was worth a try," Charlene benignly comforted. "Now what?"

"For once? I'm just not sure. I'm convinced this was it for her. I think she's really gone."

Charlene reached out and cupped her dear friend's hand. "You can't blame yourself you know. She just never got over that whole Bacchus princess mess. It wasn't entirely your fault. Her father was an ogre. You had to do what you had to do."

"I know. In time, I hope she realizes that too. Life isn't about what Mardi Gras parade you are princess in." Nora drove the VW up to the levy, beyond Jackson Square and parked along the Mississippi, so they could talk.

Charlene believed Nora was the most courageous woman she had ever met. Nerves of steel. Independence that left most women speechless. It was for that reason that Charlene admired her so. Yet often, Charlene was panged to see the results that Nora's assertion of independence brought upon her. It beguiled her.

"Oh, I almost forgot to tell you," Charlene giddily exclaimed.

"Charlene. I haven't seen that gleam in your eye since we bought you those how-to sex books in The Quarter. Give it up."

Charlene reached into her large Channel purse to pull out some papers. "You just won't believe what you have inspired me to do."

"Try me," Nora gave her a smirk.

"I've applied to go to nursing school."

"For real?" Nora sounded doubtful.

"For real. Just looky here and see. You're not the only suburban housewife that can shake up the norm!" Charlene pulled out her admission letter from Touro.

"Well, I'll be darned. What made you want to do that?" Nora could only think of Nellie, her long hours and shifts at Hotel Dieu. It was hard to imagine Charlene's pretty, manicured nails all calloused and worked over.

"You did. I've been thinking about how meaningless my volunteer work with the Junior League has become. I've crocheted one too many booties. I love when we volunteer rocking the orphan babies at the hospital. Every time I do, I think of yours, somewhere in Texas." Charlene teared up and knew mentioning the baby would make Nora tear up too.

"I'm only mentioning it, because you know I pray for her and say a rosary each and every day during Mardi Gras and lent."

"I know, Charlene. I must be the only person in New Orleans who hates Mardi Gras."

"Eh, it can be overrated." Charlene laughed nervously to break the tension. "You hide your pain well."

"I have too. There's no other way I could cope. I can't think about it all the time. So, I only allow myself to think about it during the season. As soon as Ash Wednesday hits. I'm done," Nora gazed out the window at the swirls of the mighty Mississippi. The river was full of tug boats pushing their barges up the river. "So, tell me about this nursing school thing."

"Well, Touro Infirmary has a program that they were recruiting for. They took most of my previous college. When I'm not doing my Junior League stuff, I've been taking correspondence courses to complete the sciences that I didn't have. I finished the pre-requisites two months ago and applied. I just got my acceptance letter today!"

"Charlene Hebert. Do you mean to tell me that you have kept this a secret. All this time?"

"Yes. Aren't you proud?"

"The first time those lips have been sealed. Ever! This momentous event deserves a celebration. Let's go over to the Camellia Grill and have lunch."

"So you don't think I'm being silly? A country club wife becoming a nurse? My mother said I was going to do 'nigger' work. That it was the dirtiest job I could ever choose. I hate it when she uses that derogatory, racist term."

"That sounds like something she would say. Heavens no. You're doing something you were called to do. All on your own. I'm terribly proud of you."

"I just knew you would be."

"How did Max take it?" Nora asked, referring to Charlene's dear husband who had adored Charlene for almost twenty years of married life.

"He's been a dreamboat. Feeding the kids when I had to study. He couldn't believe I could keep it a secret, but he wanted me to surprise you."

They pulled into the Camellia Grill, took a seat in one of the red leather booths and were greeted by one of the long-time waiters, Harry Tervalon. Harry had been there since the place opened in 1946. Nora and Charlene agreed on a giant omelet to split, coffee and a slice of the restaurant's famous pecan pie warmed on the grill.

"You're gonna make a great nurse. I just know it." Nora assured her. "Now. Let's get back to figuring out what we need to do about Kayce."

Chapter 3
∞ May, 1967 ∞

The spring months slowly ebbed into late May. What should have been the time of Kayce's graduation from Dominican, just wasn't going to happen. No one had heard a word from her. For Nora, it was time to resume her other job, as a crop duster for Wyatt Aerial Spraying. During the winter months, Nora did what she had to, sing at the Blue Room to pay the bills. But come summer; Nora took to the skies.

Wyatt Aviation was a small crop dusting firm located in Vacherie, Louisiana. They owned two planes, both Boeing-Stearman PT-17s. They were World War II surplus conversions. As such, they were capable of dynamic, aeronautical moves.

It was the time of year Nora relished because, once again, she was liberated in the skies. No one questioned her ability to fly. She was brilliant. Spot on in laying down the pesticides and ripening agents. She was handed her schedule of plantations to spray and she went after them with gusto.

During late spring, it was time to put down 2-4-5TP herbicide, otherwise known as Agent Orange, which treated and prevented grass overtake of the cane. Later in the summer, she would lay down Guthion to prevent cane bores. Cane bores were tiny worms which if allowed to burrow into the cane root meant devastation to the crops grown along the River Road. Failure to protect a crop resulted in negligent yield. Devastating to plantation production.

Pre-flight, Nora made her preparations for the day's work as if it were any other normal day at the office. But her office was a cockpit. Going over maps, figuring acres and payload, pre-flighting, and inspecting her aircraft. She was diligently focused.

With an approaching storm, this day was anything but normal. What didn't get done would surely result in loss of revenue. It might be days before she would have the opportunity to eradicate the highly destructive weeds. Timing was critical. Huge financial losses to the farmer affected Nora's ability to support her need to fly.

Nora had to push the envelope. She felt a sense of responsibility, a duty to complete the mission for the fall harvest. Once in the cockpit, a sense of calm came over her within the familiar environment she'd spent so many hours. The sun was beginning to light the horizon. Nora saw the humidity beginning to condense as the atmosphere warmed. She detected a heavy haze reducing visibility to only a couple of miles. Bringing the engine to life, she hoped she could see through the soupy atmosphere well enough to navigate to her first field.

As the engine warmed to normal operating temperature, Nora scanned the instrument panel, checking for abnormalities. She verified the oil temp, oil pressure, fuel pressure, and altimeter. She noticed the barometric pressure dropping, reminding her why this day would not be a typical day at the office.

The runway was nothing more than a sandy, dirt swath about 500 yards long. Nora taxied her plane, which had been loaded with 250 gallons of liquid pesticide. She sprayed using a Swath Master. There was no tower to radio. No flight plan to file. It was just up and away.

Nora felt committed. Taxiing to the end of the runway to complete her final run up, she made sure the nine cylinder workhorse was making power. She looked down the runway, easing the power forward, the instrument panel blurred with vibration. She felt her body being forced firmly against the seat back.

The wings were rocking side to side as the speed built on the uneven turf runway. Half of the runway length had passed as aerodynamics began to work on the airframe. Nora's forward stick pressure lifted the tail, increasing efficiency. Another fifty feet passed when she felt the wings lightening the load from the gear. More slight back pressure as the plane left the ground. Nora felt a positive climb.

As Nora passed through 100 feet, the scant visibility got uncomfortably low. She felt like she was flying in a bowl of pea soup. Time to make a decision. Nora now saw the glow of the sun through the clouds. Should she stay down below in this scud? Or aim for the sun and climb through to clear air?

Adding back pressure, by increasing her elevation, her decision was made. A few moments of zero visibility. Then she felt a sense of relief as the sun brightened and the air cleared. Nora could see fragmented pieces of the ground through the broken layers of clouds as she concentrated on keeping her orientation, searching for the field to be treated.

Nora loved flying out over the rows and rows of sugar cane, rice and cotton. These were the crops which made the low lands resting next to the giant Mississippi famous. Large thirty foot levies lined the river and protected the low lying fields as the Mississippi snaked up from New Orleans to Baton Rouge. The tiny, two lane highway which ran up alongside the river aptly named, The River Road, helped her find her bearings.

Once airborne, Nora could see the long rectangular fields which fronted the levies. Each plantation owner treasured the narrow strip of land which they owned along the river bank. For those lucky enough to own a swatch where the river curved, silt collected. Once dredged and drained, it was turned into sand providing another source of revenue from the generous Mississippi. From the barrier of the levy, each plantation then stretched back in a narrow rectangle for about a mile or so, planted with uniform long rows of crops. There were a few stately plantation homes that remained standing, having survived decades of hurricanes, levee breeching floods or fire. *Amelie* was one of them.

Amelie was built by Valcour Aime around 1846 as a wedding gift to his daughter, Amelie Emma and her spouse, Septime Saucier. The plantation had changed hands several times between its construction and the 1890s. At that time, it was purchased by Saturnine Wyatt. In 1901, Wyatt combined *Amelie* with the St. Jude plantation to form St. Jude Plantation and Manufacturing Company. Louis Wyatt, Sr., his eldest son, headed the corporation. Margaret was Saturnine's first born daughter. Married to Bernard Arceneaux, she now lived in uptown.

Approaching the bridge at Lutcher, Nora got her visual. *Amelie* was easily recognizable through a break in the clouds. A tall, stately three story home with tall, square pillars across its front. It had a single gable in the front, and two gables on its left and right sides on the roof. She also spotted its large azaleas and large birdbath in the front. It was painted brilliant white and had ten foot, dark green shutters alongside each window. Plantation majesty at its best.

Minutes after arrival, Nora circled the field preparing for her descent into the soup again. Flying on the edge was totally her nature and she pushed through the cloud deck without hesitation. The challenge of reduced visibility was adding to the inherent risks of the job. Any other pilot would have called it a day. But not Nora. Lined up for her first pass, she anticipated the field entry.

As Nora lowered her Stearman over the extensive acres of sugarcane, she couldn't help but think about the slaves that used to be housed in the shanties just at the edge of the fields she was spraying. Now, paid workers lived in them. When she flew, she had a fan club. Today was no different. Sure enough, at the edge of the cane fields, a group of six Negro children hooted and hollered as she approached the field. They were fascinated at the aerodynamic stunts that each crop duster performed as a perfunctory requirement of their job. For the land bound voyeur, crop dusting was like watching a ballet in the sky.

Nora approached the 2000 acres of *Amelie* plantation with precisely plotted calculation. Entering airspace at the edge of the fields from the south, she would target the rows of cane in rectangular geometric patterns, flying with the wind, which maximized fuel consumption. As the plane cleared the wire along the edge of the field, Nora aggressively pushed the stick and dove towards the crop.

Nora's flare was a mere four feet above the crop. At the same time, she opened the dispersal door. At the other end of the field, the sixty foot trees were barely visible in the haze. As heavy as she was, fully loaded, Nora knew she would have to anticipate the pull up over the tall obstacles. The familiar feel of three Gs came quickly as she pulled on the elevator stick while making a hard right turn. Nora swung her head around in the same direction of the turn, fighting to keep sight of the field. The nose of the plane pointed toward the clouds in a hard banking turn.

Briskly, Nora banked the old bird hard in the opposite direction. Again swinging her head in the direction of the turn, still trying to keep sight of the field. Giving it a little rudder the airplane skidded into a tighter radius, the nose passing through level flight and gracefully falling toward the next pass. Making each barrel loop turn, the plane each time coming to a near stall, she would fly down low over the cane, dangerously close to ground and release the spray jets saturating the stalks with chemicals.

As she completed each section of cane, she pulled back on the throttle and pointed the nose of her plane skyward, pulling two or three Gs. Craning her neck to look backward attempting to see her flag spotters, she completed a wing over. Each sharp 180 degree turn almost put the plane in a stall, as the airflow over and under her wings became minimal. This was the magic of the duster. Flying as one with her plane, Nora knew the exact moment to complete the turn and head nose down toward the field. It was brilliance in motion. Nora absolutely adored it.

SOLO VIETNAM

After repeating this process twenty times, Nora climbed back through the clouds seeking clear air for her return to base. On top once again, she could see an ominous line of dark, grey clouds way off in the distance. Nora felt the turbulence of the approaching storm. She hoped she would still have enough time for at least one or two more flights to complete St. Jude or Oak Alley.

Nora got a charge out of flying the old World War II biplane, as it was able to do loops, barrels and rolls quite easily. Watching her fuel levels, she sometimes took an extra roll or two skyward as she made her turns, just for the sheer exhilaration of hurling toward the clouds. For Nora, this wasn't work, it was paid bliss.

Amelie was owned by the St. Jude Plantation Company, also part owners of Wyatt Aviation. Nora had jumped at the chance to fly for this particular firm, because she remembered the stories about the plantation from her old maid, Justine. Justine had grown up on this plantation as a small girl. Nora fortuitously got the opportunity when she met her neighbor, Margaret Arceneaux. Having grown up on the plantation, Margaret was one of the descendent offspring.

Mrs. Arceneaux lived in a large, stately, modified shotgun home across the street from Nora on Dante. All of Mrs. Arceneaux's six children were now grown and she resided there with her retired husband. Mr. and Mrs. Arceneaux drove their Cadillac each day to mass. Once a week, they followed that trip with a visit to Whitney bank.

One day, their car was on the blink. Being stuck at the bank, they were quite in a dither. Nora, also taking care of bank business, gave them a lift back home from Oak Street. Through Margaret's stories, Nora had come to know the owners of the plantation to be kind, honest and fair individuals. They had run the family business since the late 1890s.

Rumor had it, that at one time, Huey P. Long used to have meetings in the country grocery store located on-site near the River Road. Some of the original thirteen children of the plantation, now in their older years, still lived there. There was a long standing family pride in the fact that the plantation was still a working operation. *Amelie* was not open to the public, like Oak Alley. Little did Nora realize, but she was connected to this plantation in more ways than one.

Chapter 4

Completing her dusting for the day, Nora drove back into the city. It took about an hour down the River Road to Highway 91. During a quick stop to Ruli's for some milk, Nora ran into Mrs. Arceneaux's maid.

"Ms. Nora, how u be?" the old, colored maid greeted her warmly.

"Fine, just fine, Merrybelle. I just finished crop dusting Mrs. Arceneaux's family place, out in Vacherie."

"Did you now? Mrs. Arceneaux's done sent me on a run to get some ham and cheese for her company. Her daughter from Texas is coming in."

"You don't say. I thought all her children lived in New Orleans."

"No Ma'am. One of her daughters and her two sons do, but she gots one that lives at Waveland and another at Biloxi, over in Mississippi. Then this third girl, she live in Texas."

Nora grabbed some milk, still packed in glass bottles, and a loaf of French bread. Despite being an Italian grocery, Ruli's made it the best. "Well, I know you'll be busy getting ready for her guests."

"Yes Ma'am. You know Mrs. Arceneaux. Everything gotsta look nice. Must be a long drive from Texas to 'Nawlins. And her daughter, Ms. Odile, gots two children in tow wid her."

"She has quite a few grandchildren, doesn't she?"

"Yes Ma'am. Twenty-six in all. I sure nuff stay busy, cuz some of them twenty some odd be visiting all the time."

Nora paid Paulo for her groceries. She was anxious to get home and check the mail. "Good to see you again, Merrybelle. Tell Mrs. Arceneaux hello for me."

"Same to you, Ms. Nora."

It was only a few blocks back home. Nora didn't know why that day she was so anxious to check the mail. Day after day, there was no word from Kayce. But Nora held out hope.

SOLO VIETNAM

Opening the mailbox, she thumbed through the ads and bills. There at the bottom of the stack was a colorful postcard of the Golden Gate Bridge. Quickly flipping it over, Nora recognized Kayce's handwriting straight away.

> *I made it to San Fran. I'm living in a commune working with ten others. I bake the bread. Wanted you to know I was safe.*
> *Kayce*

That was all, no details. But at least Nora knew she was alive. Thank God. After putting up the groceries, Nora sat out on her porch with a cup of coffee, a piece of pecan *brioche* she had made and a smoke. Mr. Dubois was out too. They often sat and smoked together on the porch. Mr. Dubois had a daughter that lived in Texas, too. Some town called Fort Worth. Nora enjoyed the times she could kick back at her own place and just unwind.

While they smoked, an early model red Cadillac hardtop stopped in front of the Arceneaux's silver short, wrought iron gate. A tall, handsome, dark haired man got out to open it. Curiously, Nora watched as the Cadillac pulled in. Mrs. Arceneaux always made whoever visited close the gate and latch it. She thought parts of the neighborhood were getting a little rough.

Nora knew it was because some Blacks had moved into some of the cheaper duplexes a few blocks down. Nellie and Mrs. Arceneaux still used the term colored folks. Although she was sweet, Mrs. Arceneaux had grown up in a time where Blacks were not seen as equal to whites. Some ideology was hard to change. The South remained very much divided when it came to color.

Mrs. Arceneaux poked her head out of the side doorway. "Hey, you made dat long trip fast," she called out in her French accent waving to her daughter Odile.

A very attractive, dark brunette haired woman got out of the car. She was impeccably dressed. Her hair was done up in a braided French chignon with a ribbon matching the green of her outfit. She was followed by two children, a rough and tumble three year old girl with a blond pixie haircut and an olive complected five or six year old girl with brown, shoulder-length hair. They were both dressed in matching outfits. The smaller one in blue, the older one in pink. Solid palazzo, double knit pants and matching print pinafores.

"Hi, Mama. Yes, we finally made it," Odile climbed the stairs to hug her mother for the longest time. Odile, although happy with her life in Texas, missed New Orleans and her siblings terribly. Mr.

Arceneaux, still smoking his cigar, was now out in the yard too. He reached out to hug the grandchildren. Nora noticed that the visitors had a little beige Chihuahua.

Watching the blissful scene, Nora was briefly reminded of her own five year old daughter. But she quickly eschewed that thought from her mind. Not the right season to dwell on that, she reminded herself. Nora wondered if Mrs. Arceneaux's daughters knew Mr. Dubois' only girl.

"Mr. Dubois, does your daughter Vera know Odile, Mrs. Arceneaux's daughter?" she wondered out loud.

"I don' know. Could be. My daughter was friends wid da older girl. Rosalyn. She livin in Mississippi now. My daughter lives over in Fort Worth. Texas."

"So does Mrs. Arceneaux's. Hmph."

"Next time I talk wid Vera, I'll mention it."

Mr. Dubois's memory sometimes wasn't always that good. She wondered if he would even remember. What a small world, Nora thought. New Orleans was a microcosm of mish-mashed cultures. French, German, Italian, and African-American. Its melting pot of residents, as well as artists, musicians, Southern belles, and average Joes is what made it interesting.

Nora took another drag on her cigarette, pondering the twists and turns her life had taken. French Market brat. Ursuline graduate. Married socialite. Catholic divorcee. Pilot. Single mother. Survivor. Little did she know that her own baby girl, the one that she had given up for adoption five years earlier, had just entered the home of her grandmother by adoption, a mere twenty five yards away.

SOLO VIETNAM

Chapter 5
∞ July, 1967 NAS Lemoore, California ∞

Steve Novak was a pilot with extensive experience. Not only had he flown the Vought Corsair in Korea, but he owned his own aviation service, Novak Aviation at Lakefront Airport in New Orleans. Most recently, he had flown oil execs around in a Lear jet for Humble Oil based out of Tyler, Texas. Always a naval aviator at heart, he remained active in the naval reserves, which ensured his competency in combat aviation. Jet aircraft had now replaced turbo-props and seemed to evolve into faster, more maneuverable machines on a monthly basis. With a war on, defense contractors like General Dynamics, McDonnell Douglas and Grumman continued to push the envelope for speed and precision.

Steve had been called up to return to active duty to fly in Vietnam. Uncle Sam's decision had not gone well with Marci. She had lived the life of a war "widow" without her husband and was not pleased to have to do it again. But she knew she had no say in it. Steve was committed to his country and his country was at war.

He was no virgin to being struck by war. Unlike most enlisted or young Ensigns or Lt. JGs, who were barely twenty-one, and inexperienced in the military and life in general, Steve knew just what he was getting into. He was older than many of the officers and had survived many traumatic experiences, both in life and on the flight line. Just prior to leaving for service, Steve had seen the extensive news coverage of the battles around Hue and Khe Sanh, near the DMZ. Flying an A-4 Skyhawk, he would be making ground level bombing and strafing runs. Since there was no end in sight to the offensive, he had a pretty good overview of what was going to be expected.

When Steve accepted his commission for active duty, he negotiated with the recruiter for an upgrade to jets. He loved the speed and agility of his Corsair, as well as the Learjet he had been flying. He was going to tailhook or nothing. The recruiter acquiesced, happy to have a pilot with wartime hours. Going from a propeller background to a jet required that he go through the RAG at VA-125 in Lemoore Naval Air Station, located a few miles west of Lemoore, CA.

It meant going back to school. Anxious to get him to the carrier, the CO of NAS Lemoore required that Steve work through a modified version of the RAG's syllabus. This entailed hours of field carrier landing practice both day and night at the air station. The left runway had carrier lights installed. At night, when the LSO was at the end of the runway, the tower turned the runway lights off. The pilots then saw only the small area lights that duplicated what the carrier would look like.

The pilot had to practice over and over; many times into the wee hours of early morning before daybreak, catching the wire on the ground, just like they would do on the carrier. When first learning to tailhook, it was a helluva lot safer to miss the slope and take out a landing gear then crash off the end of a carrier into the ocean. Steve's first night time pass did not go well.

He had already made four traps or arrested landings during the day. On his first pass at midnight, he "took a cut." Meaning he reduced his airspeed to land, which was what he remembered from flying the Corsair. But when landing a jet on a carrier, he was supposed to maintain power to touchdown, firewalling it after contact with the deck. Which was literally flying the aircraft to a controlled crash with power on. So when Steve cut his power, like he had been used to with the Corsair, the A-4 sank rapidly below the glide slope.

On the radio, he heard the controlling LSO calling "Power! Power," flashing the red wave-off lights that were on top of the Fresnel lens.

Steve dreaded the scrape he was about to hear as his aircraft struck the tarmac hard, crunching his landing gear and scraping the empty centerline fuel tank mounted on the belly of the aircraft. Mortified, he was determined to never make that mistake again.

"You're not flying a damned tank. Use your machine, man!" the LSO chastised.

Being a student pilot again was nerve wracking and demeaning. But he knew it was a necessary evil if he was to upgrade to jets. As such, he wondered if the instructor pilots were not tougher on him. It sure felt like it. He gritted his teeth, dug in his heels and was determined to succeed.

After qualifying at the field, Steve was then ready to attempt actual carrier landings, called carqual. Most refresher pilots got four day traps and two night traps. Sometimes, they were joined by marines,

SOLO VIETNAM

but the flyboys had their own LSOs that would fly out to the carrier to wave control their own pilots during refresher landings. The naval aviators considered themselves superior pilots and LSOs all around.

The carrier *USS Kitty Hawk* was coming into port at San Diego. Steve was sent there to qual. If he passed those traps, he would be off to Vietnam. The worst part of carrier quals was watching the mandatory film in the ready room. It was a sixty minute documentary of the dangers of flying off and landing on a carrier.

The film began with crash, after crash, after crash of planes striking the round-down, or tail end of the carrier. Then exploding and falling into the ocean. Others failed to elicit enough power on the throttle to jettison off the deck. Most of the time, pilots that stalled off the deck or crashed into the carrier were not recovered. Others would misjudge the slope. They would poorly strike or miss the wire and skid awkwardly along the angle decks sometimes falling off into the ocean. Naval Flight Ops wanted to make sure that each tailhook pilot knew exactly what risks he was to face with each flight.

When out to sea, the deck of the carrier would change in altitude anywhere from six to twelve feet per second. With day traps, the pilot had a much better visual, unless a low cloud cover or fog inhibited the view until the pilot broke under the deck. But night traps were an entirely different story. Steve felt it was like looking for a barely lit cigar in a mire of darkness.

But as he knew he would, Steve qualled. After SERE training, which was required by all pilots, it was time to join the ship. SERE involved indoctrination on how to survive, evade, resist, and escape the enemy if a serviceman was captured. Although Steve had already undergone some SERE, he was required to attend a course sarcastically known as JEST, jungle escape and survival training for the conditions of Vietnam.

All pilots were assigned escape and evade codes during the Vietnam War. Most, if not all, went through repeat JEST training at great effort and expense to the military. Should a pilot go down behind enemy lines, the skills taught at JEST training would buy them time to evade the enemy. The codes were a way of assuring the government the time it would take, in unusual, guerilla combat conditions for a rescue to be successfully executed.

After JEST, Steve was assigned to VA-153 and was to join the A-4 Skyhawk attack squadron when the *USS Coral Sea* arrived in San Francisco. He would be shipping out for a eight month cruise to Vietnam.

Chapter 6
∞ September, 1967 New Orleans ∞

Nora continued to dust throughout the summer. She completed runs on Laura, Glendale, and St. Jude Plantation also owned by one of the Wyatt's, as well as Palo Alto near Donaldsonville and even Oak Alley, in Vacherie. For Nora, taking to the skies were her most happy moments. As she hurled towards the sky, she felt liberated, self-actualized, and totally herself. She had mastered the art and skills of dusting.

Many considered dusters the hotshots of the aviation industry. Flying mostly uncharted and unfiled flight paths under the altitude of most commuter and commercial flights, they were free to dance and twirl in the skies. Flying the old WWII biplanes and newer, lighter single wing planes, the sky was the limit to their aerodynamics.

Sometimes when Nora flew, she couldn't help but think about Steve. He had been the love of her life. But remembering the intense chemistry between them was simply too painful. Nora had reframed it. Looking at Steve as a flight mentor, she considered him the catalyst who had helped her gain the skills she needed to be doing what she loved now.

Nora was one of only a handful of female crop dusters in the South. It was largely a man's world. But Nora didn't care. They were good people. Often, when the pilots were through for the day, they would meet at Nobile's, a local bar at Lutcher, before catching the ferry back to Highway 91 for the drive back into New Orleans.

Nora was living a life in two realms. One, in the city, during the late fall and winter months, torch singing for the hotel guests at the Roosevelt. The other, doing what she loved during the months required for crop dusting. But it suited her. Each day was different. She never knew who she might meet at the Roosevelt. Nora had sung for the famed Louis Armstrong, the test pilot Chuck Yeager, even civil rights leader Malcolm X. The crowd changed with whatever delegation, convention group, or military were in town. New Orleans tourism rained strong. Everyone loved The French Quarter. For Nora, this job suited her desire to meet interesting people.

The crowd was ever-changing. During the late sixties, so was the music and fashion. Nora's most requested tune was Nancy Sinatra's *These Boots were Made for Walking*. Probably because many nights, Nora donned her white, patent leather knee high boots and short mini-skirts. There was something men loved about a woman's legs in boots. Nora was glad to oblige, as her legs still looked great. Heck, the practice generated large tips. Thanks to Twiggy for the trend setting styles.

Nora's crop dusting position afforded her the luxury to fly without the expense of owning her own plane. That privilege was reserved for those with money. Which for Nora, paying Catholic school tuition and a mortgage on her own place, was an echelon to which she no longer belonged.

Charlene was nice enough to extend Nora the occasional social invitation. As long as the event assured that Nora would not intersect with her ex, Frank Greenwood, she often accepted. It felt nice to dress up and mingle with some of her old friends. Although many had not a clue how to relate to her. Nora was a unique and quirky woman. She was a divorced Catholic. Single and gorgeous. A working mother. A torch singer by night in The Quarter. A pilot by day. Still quite an anomaly for the time.

It was at one of those Charlene events, a backyard Labor Day BBQ, that Nora ran into Chet, who had taken over Steve Novak's aviation program. He was there with some of his navy buddies. In New Orleans, a party was a party. Many times, friends of friends turned up. All the talk was about the Vietnam War, which was in full force. Nora greeted him warmly. It had been a several years since their paths had crossed. For Nora, it was just too damned painful to go out to Lakefront Airport. Every foot of the tarmac reminded Nora of Steve.

"Chet, sweet Chet . . . my Piper instructor. How the heck are you?" Nora greeted him with a hug.

"Wow, Nora. You look stunning," Chet replied.

He was right. Nora did. Her figure was still a slender hourglass. Tall. Sultry. Exuding sexuality to the core. Her auburn hair was swept up and stylishly adorned with a pearlescent comb. Her slim burgundy skirt was short, above her knees, as was the style; which only served to accentuate her long, shapely legs. Gawd, she was still a knock out.

"So how are things out at Lakefront?" Nora queried.

"Good. Still training lots of private pilots. It's always busy."

"That's great," Nora said politely taking a sip of her dirty martini.

"So, I heard you were still flying?" Chet asked her.

"Yep. I am crop dusting for Wyatt Aviation. I fly every day, just about. From May through August. Stearman bi-plane."

"That's super, Nora. You were always great on the rolls and barrels."

Nora felt flattered that he complimented her skills. She took a sip of her martini. "Chet, You realize why I haven't been out to Lakefront?"

"I think I can guess," Chet responded referring to Steve.

"So what is Steve flying these days?" she asked with curiosity.

"Oh, I thought you'd have heard. Steve hasn't been out at Lakefront for a while. He re-upped for the navy. He's over in Vietnam."

Nora almost spit out her martini. "What?" she asked incredulously.

"Yep. He was in the reserves and the navy called him up. He was pretty pumped about it. But after his wife died, about a month ago, he was pretty lost."

"His wife passed away?"

"Yeah, real sad. I thought he might come back. Her family, they were a piece of work. Had her in the ground before he could even get back." Chet took a swig of his beer.

"Where are his kids?" Nora asked incredulously.

"He sent the kids up to stay with her parents in Chicago area. The navy was happy to have him. I believe he's over there flying the A-4 Skyhawk, last I heard."

Nora was stunned beyond belief. Marci, dead? Steve over in Vietnam? How did she not know? How did Charlene not know? Such stunning revelations where almost more than she could handle. God, the news was filled everyday about helo and fixed wing pilots being shot down, listed MIA or taken as POWs. Her own daughters, Cathy and Leisel, wore copper POW bracelets in support of the men lost.

Charlene noticed the shell-shocked look on Nora's face. Coming over to her friend, ever the consummate host, she put an arm around Nora's waist. "What's cooking over here guys?"

Nora briefly recovered. "Charlene, you remember Chet don't you? He took over Novak Aviation for Steve. When Steve moved to Tyler?" Nora took a long, hard swallow and downed her dirty martini. She motioned to the bartender for another.

"Why yes, of course I remember you Chet. You were quite the instructor for Nora," Charlene reached out to shake his hand. "So strange how life is just changing all around us," Charlene made small talk. "I'm so glad you could be here tonight. Great to see you, again

Chet." Charlene flashed her smile. "Nora, honey. There is someone I want you to meet," Charlene guided her friend away from Chet and out of the crowd to the powder room.

Once inside, she began her interrogation. "Okay. Out with it. You look like you have seen a ghost."

"I think I just did," Nora looked into the mirror. The color had drained from her face. Turning around, she faced her dearest friend in the world and relayed the story. Marci dead. Steve in Vietnam. Charlene was beside herself hearing the shocking news.

"What is going on in that head of yours, Nora?" Charlene was almost afraid to ask.

"I dunno. It is all just so . . . incredible. I had no idea that her multiple sclerosis would take her so soon? Good God . . . she must have only been what . . . thirty-seven? I am just reeling. Marci. Dead. I declare."

"I declare, indeed. And what about all his children? Good golly, he had what . . . six?"

"Seven, including the one we gave up."

"Nora. It's a lot to take in. But remember. You let him go. You have moved on with your life. What you had back then. It probably would never be the same. So much water has gone under the Huey P. Long Bridge. You know?" Charlene hoped Nora was listening. But something in Nora's eyes told her different.

"I know you are probably right. I just can't imagine how rough it is over there right now. In Nam. With Marci gone. Poor Steve. I'm sure he is heartbroken. At least he has his flying." Nora knew what a palliative salve that hours with the yolk could provide.

"What another crazy 'Nawlins night this has turned out to be," Charlene admitted. "Come on. Let's go have some strong coffee. And maybe some late night *beignets*. It's a lot to think about."

That was an understatement. Nora had long ago processed what happened with Steve, grieved it, and let it go. She had placed all of her heartache into a neatly wrapped package, wrapped it up tightly with twine and put it up on a mental shelf. Far, far away from her conscious daily existence. She had to. It was the only way she could have survived.

Now, that package had been taken off the shelf and unwrapped. All of the feelings she had stuffed away were at the surface. Love. Elation. Frustration at not having him. The excruciating pain of giving up her daughter. Abject depression, and ultimately, resolute survival. A jumble of cosmic force emotions had now resurfaced and shaken her to the core.

Nora left her VW parked at Charlene's. She took a taxi to The French Quarter. She needed to walk to ground herself. She walked and walked and walked. It was now in the early hours of the morning. She headed for the one place that she knew she could unwind. The Ryder Coffeehouse where Gia worked. Gia was Nora's birth-mother.

Chapter 7

"Long time no see," Gia greeted Nora with slight trepidation. Since the revelation that Gia was Nora's actual birth-mother, Nora' presence in the coffee house had been scarce. "Sit down. Relax. You look like you've been through a hurricane."

"You could say that," Nora admitted. She took a seat at one of the tables in the back corner. The coffee house had not changed. Still dark. Jazzy. A small trio of blues musicians were playing acoustically in the background.

Without even asking what she wanted, Gia brought out some herbal tea and shortbread cookies. She knew Nora had been drinking and thought the tea and light shortbread would soothe her soul. "So tell me. What has life brought you lately?"

"Triumph. Heartache. It seems to come in waves. The moment I think things are turning out okay, some chaos intervenes to tear that success down," Nora explained.

"I see. My 'chile of chaos. So what I said was true den? Da baby you had to give up?" Gia questioned knowingly. She had predicted as such, from her Tarot cards.

"Yes. You were right. In the end, it was the best thing. But it nearly killed me. To hold that baby. Feel its skin. To know it was mine. And then have to turn it over to those nuns. Hoping and praying that they found a good home for her," tears began to well in Nora's eyes.

"My darling girl. You know I know what you feel. Dat's right?" Gia comforted Nora, holding her hand. Stroking her arm. "Tis what I was trying to tell you. Giving that gift. So hard. I tink a woman never gets over da crevasse in her heart."

Nora sat in silence. She just let the soft tears roll down her cheeks. It felt good to have someone comforting her who knew exactly what she had been through, having done it herself.

"But in time. It will pass. Life will take its turns. In my cards, I see happiness for dis 'chile. She be happy, Nora. Twas a good ting you did. You will see. Dat happiness will come back to you. At some time."

Nora took her at her word. She wasn't sure she believed in all of the voodoo and psychic messages that, in Gia's world, were truth. But she had to admit, so far Gia had been right. About almost everything.

"So what else?" Gia queried. "I know dat you are still flying planes."

"How do you know that?" Nora was surprised.

"I have my ways," Gia chuckled slightly, belying her wide grin. She was missing several teeth. Even so, Gia remained ethereally beautiful. Lines of age graced her eyes and mouth. Her skin was the most marvelous shade of caramel. Looking into her eyes, Nora felt understanding, acceptance and warmth.

"So how are you udder children den? Dey must be near grown."

"Okay. They are all back in Catholic school. Mostly teens, except Iggy. He is almost eleven. The girls all go to Dominican. Well, except for Kayce. She has run away."

"Yes. I know. She came here. Before she left. I would have told you, but I promised her, I would not. She had to work dis out herself. The anger she has for you still lingers. I tink it will be good. Her far away. She will see what she had."

Nora was a bit miffed that Gia had not told her of Kayce coming to the club. But, they had been estranged. "Can you tell, from reading your cards. Will she be safe?"

"I dunno. Let's see," Gia got our her Tarot cards. She shuffled them. Then said some incantation and began to lay them out. Turning over the first card, she predicted, "Journeys. I see journeys. Not just with Kayce." Gia's face was intense.

"Yes . . . " Nora was intrigued. "Go on." Nora stared at the large cards with various images on them.

Gia turned over another card. "Dis is da card of well-being, Gia continued. But da next card shows danger. "Kayce will be safe, but shown a scary part of life. Intense. Some heartbreak. But safe."

Nora was concerned, but relieved that Gia's prediction was that Kayce would come through okay. She speculated how much faith she should place in the voodoo traditions of The Quarter. Nora took another sip of her tea. Gia was still turning cards.

"Dere is so much. More happiness amidst grief. Journeys. Far away." Suddenly, Gia gathered all the cards together quickly. Just after turning over a particular card, which Nora could not see. "Enough.

Tis enough for today." Gia appeared slightly shaken. "We can visit more about dis again." Gia poured herself a cup of tea from the brass tea pot. She was visibly troubled, but tried to mask it from Nora. The Tarot cards did not lie.

"What's wrong?" Nora asked her.

"Nuting. Dere were many messages in da cards today."

"Why do you give them so much credence?" Nora shook her head. "Do you really believe in all that voodoo stuff?"

"Not everything is as it seems. Dere are other truths."

"Black magic ones," Nora remarked. "I dunno. I'm just not sure I believe in all that stuff."

"You believe what you believe, den."

After Nora had finished her tea, she bade goodbye to Gia. So strange, to know Gia and she were related. In many ways they shared their Cajun culture, a rebellious streak running within both. Gia was a friend. A confidant. But that was all. It was just too much for Nora to consider Gia, her mother. Despite their differences, that was Nellie's role. It was a boundary that Nora set for her own emotional sanity.

She walked down the narrow streets of The Quarter. Growing up here, the wrought iron filigree balconies and brightly colored buildings made her feel like herself. Her life had taken so many unexpected diversions from what she had imagined it would be as a young girl. Now, Kayce, her oldest daughter, was lost to her due to blame and disillusionment. And at the other end of the spectrum, another daughter, her youngest; lost to her because of the only choice that could be made at the time. Adoption. Life could be cruel.

Nora found herself in the pews of St. Louis Cathedral. Seated at the back in the rich, oak seats, Nora gazed up at the crucifix. Did God understand? Did he get her anguish? Did Jesus? If they did, why was she still not allowed to find solace within her own faith? Despite knowing she was not allowed full participation, she was still drawn to the faith that she knew. It was ingrained as a part of her. More than anything else, Nora prayed for forgiveness. Forgiveness for what she had not provided Kayce; and forgiveness for changing the life path of her youngest.

Chapter 8
∞ September, 1967 Yankee Station, South China Sea ∞

Today was like any other aboard the *USS Coral Sea*. Steve arrived on the flight line deck for preflight of his Douglas A-4E. Another day of flying sorties for VA-153 to disable key transportation routes for the North Vietnamese by dropping ordnance. His targets would be major highways, bridges and railroad lines. Steve's mission was to bomb the port of Haiphong, on the heels of strikes carried out earlier in the week on the country's third largest port, Cam Pha. The veteran carrier's pilots dropped a highway bridge and rendered a rail bridge unusable in the teeth of heavy antiaircraft fire.

He checked the wings, flaps, tires, and fuselage of his scooter. It was all routine, as he knew the brown-shirt naval aircraft support teams aboard the *Coral Sea* were second to none. It was difficult to focus on his mission after hearing about the funeral for his wife in Chicago for just weeks before. He had not been present when Marci had lost her life to respiratory complications after a bout of pneumonia.

Multiple sclerosis had finally taken its tragic toll. The pneumonia occurred after yet another flood of their home in New Orleans. The illness had set in quickly. Her family requested that her funeral take place at her birthplace, Hyde Park, an upscale neighborhood of Chicago's community. They never liked that Steve had taken their baby girl to the bawdy city of New Orleans.

Much of New Orleans was under sea level. Many of the neighborhoods flooded after heavy rains, despite the valiant efforts of the Corps of Engineers and their levy systems. Marci and Steve's three story home on Galvez had flooded at least four times. The Red Cross telegrammed the ship. Upon notification of her death, by the on-board Catholic chaplain, Steve was overcome with grief.

Steve protested the location of the funeral, knowing that he had established their life in New Orleans, with his business Novak aviation. But with his deployment to Vietnam, Marci's family had overruled.

SOLO VIETNAM

They buried her so quickly, Steve didn't even have time to make it back. The legal officer on-board helped arrange a power of attorney for Marci's parents to care for the children, who now ranged in age from eight to seventeen.

It was horrific to not have been at Marci's bedside. Much less her burial, but he was thousands of miles away in the Pacific. The navy would have made arrangements for him to leave the ship had Marci's family given them time. The fact that they didn't was heinous. It infuriated him.

The chaplain arranged for Steve to talk to his grief-stricken six children, now without a parent, on the mainland by radio. He gave what comfort he could. As Steve climbed into the cockpit for today's mission, the conversation he had with his children kept playing in his head.

The radio transmission was sketchy at best. Communication from the middle of the South China sea was difficult. There were cracks and pops and interference.

"Hey, you all. It's Daddy. Can you hear me? Over."

Crack. Crackle. Bzzz. "Daddy . . .you?" Words were lost. He knew that was his youngest daughter.

"Yes. It's me. I want you to know, I love . . ." crackle. Bzz.

"We love you, too, Dad. Please come home soon." Steve recognize the voice of his oldest son. "It's tough, Dad." Bzzzz. ". . .tough."

He couldn't imagine what they must be going through. Their mother dead and their father thousands of miles away. He could hear a younger one crying. "Please, my darlings. Don't cry. Daddy will be home soon." Bzzz bzzzz. ". . . promise. Over."

"We . . ." Bzzz "Mommy."

"I know you do. I miss . . ." Bzzz. "too. Over." Crackle. Crackle. And then it went dead. Steve's heart felt broken. But duty called.

Yankee Station was a point in the Gulf of Tonkin off the coast of Vietnam used by the U.S. Navy aircraft carriers of the Seventh Fleet to launch strikes in the Vietnam War. While its official designation was "Point Yankee," it was universally referred to as Yankee Station. Carriers conducting air operations at Yankee Station were said to be "on the line." At any given time, there were three carriers at work on various twelve hours shifts.

The name came from it being the geographic reference point "Y", pronounced "Yankee" in the NATO phonetic alphabet. Starting in 1964 aerial reconnaissance missions initially conducted over Laos were launched by "Yankee Team" and sent from a particular point. Thus the name for the spot became "Yankee Station." The exact location of Yankee Station was about 190 km due east of Dong Hoi, at map points of 17° 30' N and 108° 30' E.

During a period of sustained air operations against North Vietnam from March 2, 1965 to October 31, 1968, each carrier on the line conducted air operations for twelve hours, then off for twelve hours. One of the carriers would operate from noon to midnight, another from midnight to noon, and one additional during daylight hours. This gave the US twenty-four hour air coverage. Additional sorties were flown during daylight hours when efforts were most effective. Although rare on the *Coral Sea*, this evening was a night mission for Steve.

The A-4 was designed as a delivery vehicle for the atomic bomb, but with Vietnam, its functionality changed. Although considerably light weight at 14,000 pounds it could carry a significant payload of rockets and bombs. Normally, each carrier transported two or three squadrons of attack fighters, a squadron of heavy bombers, and a smattering of sky warriors. Usually A3-Bs were also onboard to be used as early warning spotters and weather planes. In addition there was a squadron of H-2 helos for transport and rescue near the *Coral Sea*.

During the missions, a forward aircraft controller, an OV-10 would mark targets with colored flares at night or smoke during the day. This guided the attack pilots to drop their ordinances with precise, destructive accuracy. Much of their payloads were 500 pound, Mark 82, snake-eye, low drag bombs which were designed with metal fins to slow them down. This type of delivery ensured that the aircraft dropping them gained separation from the explosion so as not to get shot down by their own ordnance. Occasionally, a unit would require strafing, which was ground coverage with 20mm cannon. The pilot would fire his gun pod in the same direction the aircraft was flying to hit ground targets of the enemy who were firing continual anti-aircraft ammunition.

Steve clipped himself into the snug cockpit of the A-4. Two straps held his integrated harness attached to the seat pan of the plane. The other two straps connected to the parachute on his back. In addition, Steve wore a G-suit which partially covered his lower body. The anti-gravity apparatus was there to prevent him from passing out due the G-forces incurred during the aeronautical maneuvers the A-4 was capable of achieving. On top of his green, fire-retardant Nomex flight suit was a survival vest complete with flotation device and pockets, which contained a portable radio, pistol, and survival gear. Some pilots even carried their smokes.

SOLO VIETNAM

Most navy pilots hated the steel toed boots required due to their ejection seats. Not wearing them would mean they might lose toes if required to eject. Steve dutifully wore his. After putting on his helmet, Steve attached the rigid oxygen mask. The naval aviators hated them. Oft times, the pilots would switch over to the Air Force masks. They were softer and more flexible. Flying in Nam was life-threatening on any given day. Survival was utmost. As such, flying so many hours at a time, some pilots defied the regs and donned helmets with boom mikes instead. This meant not using the oxygen masks so that they could better maneuver their heads and avoid anti-enemy air ammo.

Steve always experienced a brief moment of anxiety and then steady calm, as the flight ops crew hooked this catapult bridle onto his jet. He always clipped two pictures to his instrument panel, one of his wife and one of the best female pilots he had ever met, Nora. Sadly, on this day there was only one picture. He had put the picture of his wife to rest, packed away in his duffle bag in his state room.

Steam rose from the deck of the carrier as the Skyhawk was ready to launch. Yellow shirts gave signal and in one blast, Steve's plane was catapulted off the deck. Once away from the ship and over the ocean, he could see the coastal plain by looking past the lead aircraft. It was clear enough in the fall haze to almost see the mountains. They quickly gained altitude to 10,000 feet. Even at that altitude, it was possible to see the ground which was torn up from the coast inland. There were scattered bomb craters, smoldering artillery shells and smoke from places where napalm fires still burned. Some villages were desecrated.

There was constant chatter on the radio, both on Red Crown and the Guard frequency, supposedly used for emergency broadcasts and monitored by all aircraft. A sharp left bank brought him in formation with the other Skyhawks. They were off to another mission near Haiphong.

VA-153 flew for nearly half an hour, tanking on the way. Then he turned inland just south of the DMZ towards the target. Steve kept the lead in sight, but still couldn't help but look at what was below. At 10,000 feet, on a clear day, which was rare, you could see almost the entire zone of I Corps. The land was battered beyond belief. Bomb craters overlapped, there was almost nothing that hadn't been desecrated. But Steve didn't have time to look long, suddenly, he got word on the radio from the Red Crown network that they were being tailed by North Vietnamese MiG-17s.

Steve's wingman reported seeing four, and shot off an air-to-air missile. At the time of the explosion, however, the pilot was already in a banking turn to fire at a second MiG. But Steve could see the hit to the right wing of the MiG, confirming that the strike sent the North Vietnamese plane tails-spinning into the ocean. Steve hard rolled his scooter to the right and followed up on his wingman's left. After another brief engagement, the MiGs peeled off and it was back to business as usual.

Red crown radioed to switch to a coded frequency. "Dash 1 up," Steve responded. He heard the lead call out.

"Fingerprint 12, this is Blue Tail 224 inbound with delta two and delta nines for your control." Which meant 500 pound bombs and napalm.

Immediately, there was a reply from the OV-10 target spotter, call sign Fingerprint. "Proceed inbound to the 090 radial and Channel 109, Blue Tail, and hold."

Dash 2, the wingman moved Steve into a trail. Steve set all the armament switches he could while moving back into position. He now could see Khe Sanh, which was a base under siege by the NVA. Steve dropped back and set his flaps at one quarter to give himself a little more lift and surveyed the scene below.

The first thing that caught his eye was how small the base was. It looked like a piece of tape, red and torn and laid across a small ridge surrounded by taller mountains. There were wrecked aircraft on the mat and rounds were impacting inside the perimeter.

The rings of trenches were blown apart and separated from each by almost interlocking bomb craters. The hills around the base to the north, hills 881 and 861, appeared to be in US possession, which had been shown to Steve in the briefing. Mount Coroc in Laos, overlooked the base. From about five miles out, it seemed to have caves in which large artillery pieces could be located.

There were airstrikes being conducted by more than one air controller and the impact of bombs could be seen for miles west toward Laos from where Steve was orbiting. He could see the flames from shitters burning, and the mottled layout of the base. Bunkers were covered with unrecognizable bits of debris. Trenches went as far as Steve could see, with a bombed out road west of Khe Sanh.

The orbits over South Vietnam had planes stacked like pancakes from about 10,000 to 30,000 feet. The controllers would pull sections of two or flights of four out of the bottom of the stack, assign a target and away one would go.

"Blue Tail Flies 304 and playmate 311, another mission, you ready to copy?" The voice of the controller boomed, self-assured and commanding.

"Roger," Dash 1 replied before Steve could answer.

"Run in heading zero six zero, with a left hand pull. Friendly forces will be at your eleven o'clock at five hundred meters at Khe Sanh. Ground fire is expected to be heavy."

Dash 1 read back the brief as it had been given. He was descending and maneuvering to a position so that he would be at the roll in point when permission was given to roll in.

"Do you see my mark, 304?" Fingerprint had shot a smoke marker between the base of one of the mountains and Khe Sanh. Steve saw Dash 1 turn toward the smoke, call "Roger, Dash one in hot," and start down the chute and toward the target, with all switches armed. The plan was to drop all the rest of the bombs and napalm on a single run.

Steve was too far behind to roll in on the target as he called off. Dash 1 rolled inverted, did a double half roll entry, leveled out and released over the target.

The orange winking of ground fire was coming from Steve's nine o'clock position abeam the target. He turned in on the run in line, rolled inverted, holding the gun sight rings above the smoke and moving 100 meters to the right as the controller had indicated.

Steve had turned on his master armament switch. As he pulled up on the run in line to target, time suddenly seemed to slow to a crawl, like slow motion.

The smoke and fire of Dash 1's ordnance drop was drifting toward Khe Sanh slowly. The target was big and too hard to miss. Steve pulled the gunsight ring down below it and started rolling back into a wings level upright position. The smoke got bigger and bigger in the gunsight picture. Steve never noticed the ground fire being aimed at his plane; he was too intensely focused on hitting the target.

He pressed the target, until it looked like he was going to impact it with the aircraft, hit the button on the top of the stick and pulled up and to the left. Khe Sanh was now above him about a hundred feet or more. He kicked his rudder hard left and craned to see what was happening behind him. He just caught the napalm and flame in the mirror on the right side of the canopy.

Fingerprint was reading off the bomb assessment. But Steve couldn't get his armament switches off, try to find his wingman in the haze toward the coast near Dong Ha, and write the bomb damage assessment all at the same time. Quickly, he scribbled the bomb damage assessment, just as his own Dash 2 called to ask if Steve had him in sight. Luckily, Steve just caught sight of him at his one o'clock, a little above and called, "Tally ho."

There was a big black F-100 flying in the same area, in the same direction. There was safety flying in tandem. The A-4s flew alongside him for a minute or two until they saw some other Skyhawks flying down the coast. Steve and Dash 2 moved away from the F-100 and joined their lead.

At ten miles out, the A-4s began descending from 8000 feet, were given signal to drop back and follow the lead toward the carrier. Catching the wire, Steve trapped landing safely. There was not much of a debrief. There wasn't enough time. Before Steve had a change to get out of his torso harness and G-suit, a Commander came over and asked Steve, "Are you ready to brief Lt. Jackson?" Jackson was a newbie to the squadron, having returned from bingoing off at Danang. "You're going back over Khe Sanh for another run to take out a bridge."

And they did. That was the way many of the missions went. Flying run after run, to the point of exhaustion. If you were on day flights, you looked forward to the setting sun. On nights, for the sunrise. The twelve hour shifts of missions were exhausting. Luckily, the newer *USS Forrestal* and *Kitty Hawk* took most of the night missions.

Steve maneuvered his scooter back to the *Coral Sea* for a second time. As it became dark, the sea and land began to look as one. He was glad to have clear skies for once, which allowed him to visually determine sky and sea. The lights of the runway aboard the carrier came into view. Despite it pitching some six feet per second in the relatively calm waters of the early evening, Steve expertly flew his slope, keeping the meatball centered and came in to catch his tailhook safely in the wire. Another mission complete.

Upon returning, Steve took off his flight gear, went to the ready room, got a Coca-Cola, and walked around to the office of the intelligence clerk, Petty Officer Jones. Steve introduced himself as the new Intelligence Officer and asked him to show what was expected on the job. On the carriers, the naval officers didn't just fly, there were other responsibilities too

There were five days of such attacks during which the A-4s of the *Coral Sea* struck the Haiphong rail and highway bridges, dropping the southern section and demolishing the last span of passage linking the city with the mainland. Each and every flight, both day and night involved flying through heavy flak and dodging numerous surface to air missiles. But the *Coral Sea* lost not one plane or pilot.

SOLO VIETNAM

Chapter 9

In late September, the *USS Coral Sea* departed Yankee Station headed for a brief rest and upkeep at Subic Bay in the Philippines. Cubi Point Naval Air Station was an aerial facility located at the edge of Subic Bay Naval Base and abutted the Bataan Peninsula. NAS Cubi served as the primary maintenance, repair and supply center for the 400 carrier-based aircraft of the Seventh Fleet's carrier force. During the Vietnam War, its jet engine shop turned out two jet engines a day to keep pace with demand.

The Cubi Point Officer's Club was a place where war-weary navy and marine corps aviators, marines and sailors could let off a little steam after flying and supporting combat missions over Vietnam. The club was forever tasked with devising new and challenging ways of keeping the warriors entertained. More often than not, the pilots became a bit raucous and caused havoc within the club with their antics.

This night was no different. Throughout the Vietnam conflict, NAS Cubi Point O club was legend. It was a marvelous mix of American efficiency and Filipino hospitality. One of its bars, known as the Plaque Bar, had become infamous to all transitioning squadrons. NAS Cubi was the landing and departing station for all carriers deployed to Vietnam. As each new squadron arrived, the retiring squadron would retire their plaque and commission a new one to commemorate each WestPac tour.

As Steve sat with the other pilots chugging down his beer, he stared at the colorful wall full of naval and marine squadron plaques. Each one was a colorful piece of art, depicting the squadron's number, mascot and slogan. Each represented yet another group of men hurling through the clouds in their aircraft, bombing roads, railways, and villages to strategically protect the interests of the US ground troops below. Steve wondered how many pilots with their names inscribed on the plaques never returned. Although losses in naval air squadrons were occasional, they were far less common than the loss of life and limb for the ground troops. For that, Steve was glad.

There was a raucous celebration underway for a Chief Petty Officer from HC-1. He recently advanced from First Class and had become chief of the helo detachment. It was a nice promotion and some fellow officers had taken him out to the Cubi Point O club.

A young, tall newbie Lt. from VF-161 having had one too many beers, made the comment, "HC-1. So you're the helo unit that has never made a rescue of any of our pilots."

"You sonofabitch asshole." the newly promoted detachment officer came unglued. No one was going to insult the rescue work of his unit. He reached back and took a swing at the six foot four inch, young pilot.

"Settle down boys, settle down." Steve attempted to intervene. He ended up getting clocked hard on his jaw by one of the punches. He knew that HC-1 did great work. But many times, when calls came in to rescue a downed pilot, the downed craft was either too far away or had submerged too quickly into the ocean before the pilot had egressed. Despite valiant efforts, the helos just couldn't get to them. "The *Coral Sea* hasn't lost a pilot yet from failed rescue on this cruise," Steve reminded the crowd.

Being a senior officer, the juniors listened and backed off. Such was the testosterone level and ego of air wings that flew off carriers. They were an arrogant sort. Get them liquored up and all chaos broke out at the bar.

Local girls from Olangapo, the town adjacent to Naval Station Subic Bay and NAS Cubi point were allowed to work in the Officer's Club, the Chief's Club called Top Of The Mark, and the enlisted clubs. They were dressed in short, colorful mini-skirts and tight, sleeveless sweater tops. You'd never know they were not American, accept for their wide flat faces, slanted eyes, and jet black hair. Girls were made up to the hilt in heavy eye liner, bright lipstick and beehive hairdos. They were a lovely sight to see, as opposed to weeks of khaki and green military garb.

Hanging with the females was fun, but the girls had to be off the base by curfew; either 11:00 PM weeknight or 12:00 AM on weekends. The naval club managers were quite strict on the girl's activities with military personnel for one reason. As local proprietors themselves, they would lose their license to work on the base if any of the rules were broken. The girls were forbidden to linger with any individual for long. Often, they served as dance partners.

It was late in the evening. Having had their fill at the O club, several of the officers decided to walk over the bridge to hop a jeepney into Olangapo. NAS Cubi Pt. was adjacent to Subic Bay NS. They had to pass through Subic Bay NS to get into town from Cubi Pt. The town was just outside the gates of Subic Bay NS. There was a river which separated the base from the town. The river had a very strong, distinct odor. Basically, it was an open cesspool. Most of the enlisted and officers couldn't tell you the correct name for the river, but designated it Shit River, due to the horrific smell.

There were some pilings near the bridge. Young Filipino boys would climb on top of the pilings and beg for money. Many people crossing the bridge would throw their change into the stinky river just to watch the boys dive in to retrieve the money. It was twisted entertainment to be sure. It wasn't uncommon for hookers to be on the bridge and throughout the streets and nightclubs of Olangapo.

The jeepney was none other than a large, rebuilt WWII US military jeep with a roof put on and repainted in bright colors. Many had been left behind after WWII. The owner of the jeepney would drive slowly up and down the main streets of the city. People, both locals and military would jump on and off even while it was moving. It was cheap transportation, about one or two pesos per person. The Filipino exchange rate was one US dollar to seven pesos. If a group of sailors jumped onboard when a single Filipino lady was aboard who wasn't a working girl, she would jump off. There was a heavy stigma on those who got too close to an American service man.

Once in the local bar, one after another, hookers approached the tables, trying to coax a willing aviator into submission. "Come on Joe. Let's have good time. Okay?"

With each invitation, Steve politely declined. His heart still felt empty with the loss of Marci. Plus, he had no idea where in the world Nora might be, or if she would even see him.

"You not like, Joe? I not your type?" the hooker continued to pester, running her hands up and down her slim, curvy frame. She was pretty enough with her slanted, dark eyes and straight, jet black hair. Lips ruby red. Despite their military affiliations, the girls called everyone from the base Joe. She seemed perturbed that Steve continued to pass up her lurid invitations. "Here, I get girl you like. Okay?" The young Asian woman motioned for another. "Here you go, Joe. Nice girl, you like?" She touched the other, very young girl, her black hair done up in curls. "She your type. You like?"

Steve was getting tired of their beleaguering. Knowing it would just continue, he let the young girl sit down at the table. She must have been no more than sixteen. He thought of his daughters back home. He looked into her dark, almond shaped eyes. She was lovely, but way too young to be selling herself. Many of the hookers spoke broken English, so he questioned her about her situation.

"So, where are you from?"

"New Banicain, near Olangapo," she said in her small, delicate voice.

Steve knew that to be a village near by on Subic Bay. "Would you like something to drink?" he offered.

"Sure, Joe. Coca-Cola."

Steve went to the bar. "A coke and a beer please."

Although he had no intentions of letting things go further than just a drink, it was nice to have someone to talk to that didn't wear a flight suit. While at the bar, he noticed a young boy who kept approaching her at the table. She would shoo him away in terse, abrupt Filipino language.

When Steve returned he asked about the boy. "So who is he? Your little brother?" It was surprising to see such a young boy in the bar. Clearly, he was around four years old. At first, the young girl hesitated and looked down. "It's okay. I won't tell anyone," Steve assured.

"He Liling's boy. She gone," the girl explained.

Steve assumed that she meant that his mother was dead. Taking another sip of his beer, he contemplated asking anything further. He was stunned to the core at what he heard next.

"Liling. She tell Joe, she pure. Never touched. Joe fall in love with Liling. They marry. Joe take her to United States. Liling bad. She never tell Joe about boy."

All of the emotion Steve had been stuffing down since the funeral came bubbling up. Tears rolled down his cheeks. Tears that he couldn't stop. He grabbed for a handkerchief from the pocket of his flight suit. "Oh, God" he sobbed.

The young girl was taken aback by his tears. GIs didn't cry. She slid off the bar stool and went to pursue another potential customer.

Not wanting the other officers to see him broken up, Steve downed the rest of the beer and went outside the night club. He jumped into the first jeepney he saw for transportation back to the ship. All he could think about were his own children, now alone in the states with their grandparents, their mother dead. But not only them, the baby that he had seen and held six years ago. The baby that he had encouraged Nora to give up for adoption. His heart was full of sadness and remorse.

This war was senseless. Worse than Korea. He had wanted to serve. But there was something different about Vietnam. He would never admit it to his aviation buddies. Steve dutifully and silently followed the orders given to him, as a rock solid officer should.

But this war had no direction. No purpose. It dragged on and on, with senseless killing. Orphaned children. Destroyed villages. War ravaged soldiers in the jungle, gritty and grimy awaiting the next bamboo spikes. Hueys cutting the air with their loud propellers, transporting thousands of burned and severely wounded to evac hospitals. He would finish his tour and be done. The people of the nation that he represented did not support this war. Long-haired protesters with beads were burning the flag and carrying anti-Vietnam signs on the steps of the capitol.

Before her death, Marci had written to him about the hundreds of soldiers returning to the states with mental and emotional problems. They were poorly received back home. Their heartbreak centered upon returning to a nation who seemed not to care about their efforts. In fact, many had been told to be silent about their service. Others were verbally assaulted and slandered; characterized as "drug using, glassy eyed baby killers." This was not a war with honor.

Because he processed all this with a sense of patriotic duty to his nation, Steve was determined to carry on. In order to do so, he existed by not thinking at all. Each day, he took his assignment with steel nerves. Day missions, night missions. Steve knew from the first week flying in Vietnam, that he was different than most of the other, younger Lt. JG pilots. Their devil-may-care, tomorrow-we-may-die attitude explained their cocky naivety. They laughed more than he did, were more open and cavalier, and just seemed to take things less seriously than Steve thought they should.

Steve, however, had flown during wartime before. What seemed unreal to them, was reality for Steve. When one of the Captains was shot down and escaped, it came as a big surprise to them. But it wasn't to Steve, he had experienced that in Korea, having been shot down at night and not rescued until morning.

The pilot of a jet powered, fighter bomber in combat, was flying nothing more than a blow torch within a fuel tank, loaded with explosives. The attitude a pilot took depended upon his experiences; ranging from the probability of something happening, to the reality of something happening. When a pilot was rescued, the information about the incident was given to the other pilots in the ready room. But when one was not rescued, determined to have been killed, captured, or worse, MIA, the name was just erased on the duty roster and the person ceased to exist. Not a word was spoken among the pilots. Recently, when one of the Lt JG newbies to the squadron replaced a pilot that had snapped a wire and run off the end of the carrier, no one talked about him at all. Talking about the loss made it too real.

Flying in wartime was a dangerous business. Day after day, when Steve saw those he flew out with, shot down in attacks or lost in various accidents, he had developed a hard line in his jaw. His eyes didn't laugh anymore. Reality had replaced probability.

Chapter 10
∞ October, 1967 New Orleans ∞

The coastal winds turned chilly as fall finally arrived in NOLA. Nora had flown her final passages over the huge expanse of sugarcane, putting down ripening agents in late August and early September. Timing of these agents was just as important as eradicating the cane bores. For if the ripening agents were put down too late, the reap of the harvest was severely affected. The climate in the Deep South required hurrying of cane ripening, to assure a bountiful crop. Harvesting of the cane had begun.

Timing for harvest was also critical. September and October were peak months for hurricanes. Hurricane Betsy of '65 had nearly wiped out all of the crops due to mass flooding. During hurricane season, weather watchers were constantly watching the gulf.

For Nora, it meant hanging up her flight suit. Time to don her evening wear for more rounds of singing at the Roosevelt. Her manager had taken to marketing her return as a homecoming, for Nora had gained quite a following. Scads of locals came on Friday and Saturday nights to hear her croon their favorites.

On this crisp October evening, Nora couldn't help but notice the number of navy whites in the crowd. Seamen and officers crowded the bar and tables. The brilliant gleam of their whites almost blinding to the eye. During her breaks, she could hear their conversations. Many were on leave or celebrating the end to their tours in Vietnam. Nora noticed that at one table there were pilots. Obvious, with their gold navy wings adorning their crisp uniforms. Nora made her way to their table.

"Congrats, boys. Welcome home. If "Nawlins is your home. But then again . . . 'Nawlins makes a home for everyone," Nora used her most sultry voice.

Cheers went up. Hip, hip hoorahs. Nora heard that many Vietnam Vets were not readily accepted, once arriving home to the US. She wanted to make sure that was not the case for these military men. Not in the club where she sang in, anyway.

After her set, Nora had a chance to sit down with some of the pilots. They bought her martinis and began to talk aviation. She was fascinated to hear their frustrations about this war. Lots of frustrated aviators were held on deck and prevented from striking. Others were required to napalm. It was heart-wrenching. They were tired, shell-shocked and disillusioned. Many were anxious to get home and out of their uniforms. Vietnam had not been like Korea or World War II. The atrocities from guerilla warfare, both on the villages and the soldiers were horrendous.

Nora brought up Steve, and asked if they knew anyone from the VA-153 division. Unfortunately they said no. But one of the officers asked about her singing.

"With a voice smooth as silk, you outta go over there. Sing for the USO," he encouraged.

"Me? Nah. 'A' I'm not famous enough and 'B' I'm too old," Nora laughed and tossed back her head. She touched his shoulder, "but thanks. You know what to say to make a girl feel good. I needed that." Nora took the last sips of her martini. "You boys stay safe going home. Okay, now?" She wished them well.

"Nora, baby. Stay, just a little bit longer" one of them crooned. "Ooooooo . . .stay. . . just a little bit long. Yeah, yeah, yeah," they sang their version of The Hollies hit.

"Good night flyboys," Nora waved. As she walked across the street to the street car, she couldn't stop thinking about what the naval officer had suggested. The USO. Nora planned to check into it the next day. One of the pilots from the group had followed her.

"Nora, please. Stop," a dashing, dark haired aviator with piercing green eyes pursued her.

Nora turned and looked at him. "Yes?"

"I couldn't help but notice. The interest in aviation. In Nam, in general."

Nora tried to look away. Talking so much about Vietnam, she was temporarily overcome by a surge of emotions. Bittersweet love, devotion, pride, and survival. It was almost more than she could bear, yet strangely she needed to know more.

The pilot reached up and put his hands on her chin. He reached around her pulling her close for a kiss. His lips were soft and sensuous. The dashing aviator in white obviously knew what he was doing. Nora initially melted into him, kissing him back. It felt good to have a man's hands run down her back.

SOLO VIETNAM

But suddenly, she pulled away. "I can't. I'm sorry. I just can't." The tears were flowing.

"Saya babe, I didn't mean to make you cry. Guess your heart is still on your sleeve for him aye?"

"Yes. You can say that," Nora dabbed her eyes not wanting her liner to run. "We were lovers. Before the war."

"Lucky guy," the aviator remarked. "It's a bitch out there. In Nam. Worst assignment of my life. I'm glad to be outta gookville. Some bad stuff over there," he started talking. "Here, I'll walk you where you're going." He offered her his strong arm.

Nora was glad to take it. She felt weak in the knees thinking about Steve. The heart that she had so carefully wrapped and protected, was now open and vulnerable having heard the news that he was widowed. She couldn't imagine what horrors he might be enduring in Vietnam. "If you can, tell me more," Nora begged the strong, sinewy pilot accompanying her.

"I'll try. It's just . . . so hard," he looked off into the neon lights in the distance as they neared Canal Street. "I lost some buddies. Great guys. Shot down over the jungle, never to be heard from again. They're listed as MIA. Missing in action. Some were taken prisoners. Those Commie gooks are doin' some unspeakable acts of torture. Stuff that's against all the rules of engagement."

Nora stroked his arm. She couldn't stop listening. Even though they were at the streetcar stop, she let several cars pass. They sat down on the bench under the gas street lamps. They could still hear the jazzy tunes and saxes of Bourbon Street in the distance. "I've heard it was horrific. I don't think the nightly news is giving us the true story."

"No. I'm sure they aren't. Suburban America couldn't handle it. I don't wanna go back, myself. But I'm scheduled for another cruise. I dread every moment across the Pacific, knowing I'm one step closer to hell. But being navy, we're luckier than the marines and army. At least part of the time, were on a boat. Those poor dudes are on the ground and at risk from dawn until dusk. It's really a fucked up war. Not like Korea or the big one."

Nora had heard as much from various reporters that landed at the Roosevelt. Just like the bartenders, she often overheard much of their gossip. She wondered when it would all stop. "Say," Nora paused realizing she didn't even know this guy's name. "You look like you could use a cup of coffee. Why don't you just tag along with me? I'm going home. To uptown. But I often brew a pot when I get there. Whaddaya say?"

"Sure, why not? A home is a home. Better than a bar."

Just to make sure he didn't get the wrong idea, Nora added, "But just coffee okay? I know what a late night invitation means to most guys."

"Just coffee. And conversation. You're easy to talk to, Nora. And I haven't had a chance to do that with a pretty girl in a long time. He looked intently at her. "By the way, my name is Dave," he wryly smiled. "Dave Gillett, VF-74."

Chuckling, Nora realized how friendly she had gotten with someone whose name she didn't even know. "Nice to meet you, Dave Gillett," she extended out her lovely hand. Dave took it and kissed it, but Nora politely returned it to her lap

Nora was flattered and endeared by Dave. Had she not known about Steve, Nora would certainly have been more flirty. Dave was at least six feet tall, had piercing green eyes, and a thick head of short, wavy dark hair, cropped navy style. He was dreamy to be sure. But as he identified, Nora was wearing her heart on her sleeve for another pilot thousands of miles away.

As the street car rumbled down St. Charles and made its way toward Carrollton, Nora pointed out some of the sites. Audubon Park. The stately mansions on St. Charles, one of which she used to live in. As the street car whirred along, its brass bell ringing, her pilot talked and talked. Nora pulled the black cord to signal the car to stop right at Hickory. She explained that her house was just another two short blocks.

The front porch was quiet, as Nora opened her wrought iron gate. Only the porch light remained lit. The rest of the house was dark. Mr. Dubois' side was dark too. Nora and Dave tip-toed up the stairs and into the duplex.

"Do you rent?" Dave queried.

"Nope. I own the place. Both sides," Nora proudly explained.

"Well good on you. Pretty and pennywise. You're something else, Nora," her aviator guest whispered.

They made their way to the kitchen, turning on a hurricane lamp, and Nora started the coffee. Within minutes, the rich aroma of strong coffee with chicory filled the tiny kitchen.

Nora listened intently, taking some notes on the strange names of the bases and locations that Dave spoke about. She wasn't even sure she was spelling them all correctly. But she was determined to go to the Nix Public Library and look up some maps to understand the logistics of Vietnam. She had to know more about where Steve might be.

Dave continued to talk about all of the fixed-wing aircraft. He mostly flew F4 Phantoms off the *USS Forrestal*. Many were lost to ground fire from antiaircraft artillery, surface-to-air missiles, or fighter interceptor MiGs. After several hours, despite all the coffee Dave was getting sleepy. Nora gave him a blanket and a pillow and he laid down on the couch for a sleep. It was already into the wee hours of the morning. Nora knew her children would be up soon. She was so tired herself, she trudged off to bed.

At about seven AM, she awoke to calamity. Cathy was standing over Nora who was still wearing her night eye covers. "Mother, really. One of your boyfriends is still laying on the couch. What are the neighbors going to think?"

"What?" Nora asked in sleep deprived stupor.

"That navy man. Mother how embarrassing. We have to get ready for school."

Nora groggily answered. "Cathy don't jump to conclusions. He's a Vietnam War vet. Not a boyfriend. Go get ready for school," Nora mumbled and rolled over for another twenty minutes sleep.

Cathy threw her arms up in frustration. Another morning where she was forced to be in charge. Cabinet doors in the kitchen were slammed open as she took three cereal bowls down and put out boxes of Raisin Bran, Chex, and Captain Crunch for breakfast. Cathy noted the time and called out to her sister and brother, giving them their D-day departure time. "Iggy, Leisel. Twenty minutes and we're leaving."

Nora could no longer sleep with the racket, so she got up and put a robe on heading out to the living room. Dave was just waking up. "How about some breakfast and coffee?" Nora offered.

"Naw. I've troubled you too much. I'll be on my way. It's an excuse to get one of those *beignets* I've been hearing about," Dave smiled wryly.

"Try Morning Call," Nora suggested.

"Nora, I want to thank you. Thank you for listening. It really helped," he reached out his hand to shake hers. She moved over to him, hugged him and gave him a kiss on the cheek instead.

"The pleasure was mine, Dave. Talking to you somehow made me feel closer to Steve. Just hearing about it all. I wish you all the best. You go and be careful out there."

Dave grabbed his naval officer's cover and jacket. He put it on and was buttoning it as he left. "If you're ever over there. Look me up. I'm sure I'll be deployed out for another cruise. The war is far from being over." Dave smiled as he headed down the stairs. "You're really something else, Nora. My kinda girl." Dave turned and waved goodbye.

Nora stood on the porch and waved back from her screen door. As she turned to go back inside, she didn't notice that Mr. Arceneaux was out on his front porch getting the morning paper. The scandalous divorcee was bidding a man goodbye in the wee hours. That certainly was something to be noticed.

Chapter 11

The USO office was located inside Moisant Airport. There wasn't much too it. Just a small waiting room and another office. Some posters with the blue and white USO logo. A picture of Uncle Sam pointing his finger and saying "We Want You."

Nora dressed in a smart navy blue suit with matching navy pumps and purse. Her auburn hair was coiffed in a respectable bun. Reaching out to shake the hand of the recruiter, she introduced herself. "Hello, there. My name is Nora Jean Broussard. I'd like to volunteer my services for the USO. I'm a singer."

It was only then Nora noticed she was the oldest woman in the room. The others were all young girls. About age twenty. They all looked up from their magazines and two of them sniggered. Nora raised her eyebrows and shot them an disdainful look.

"I'm very qualified. I headline at the Blue Room at the Roosevelt hotel," she handed the recruiter a recent flier.

The female recruiter, about aged forty herself, gave Nora the once over. "Hmm. Come into my office. Let's talk."

As Nora followed the recruiter, she smiled at the young girls she was bypassing in the cue. Some of them had waited for an interview for hours.

"So what can I do for you?" the recruiter asked.

"Look, I'm a great singer. Just name a tune and I can belt it out for you right here."

"No need for that. If you headline the Roosevelt, I know your voice must be good. But why do you want to do this? Don't you have children and responsibilities?"

"Sure, I have four children," she knew the woman meant husband. "But they're almost all grown. I'm divorced. I feel strongly that I want to do my duty to serve for this war." Nora wanted to add but they won't let me fly as a pilot, but knew better.

"As you can see, most recruits for the floor shows and tours are in their twenties. The USO gets quality girls. Fresh outta school from some of the best colleges."

Clearing her throat, Nora attempted to make her case. "I realize that I'm older," she began.

The recruiter held up her hand. "No need to explain. I pulled you in the office, because I have something else in mind. The regional office is looking for a house mother of sorts."

Nora looked intrigued. "A house mother?"

"Yes. Most of our recruits are just young girls. They wouldn't have a clue how to manage themselves outside of New Orleans, much less a foreign country," she explained. Nora listened intently. "Do you have references?"

"Impeccable ones. Yes."

"No police involvement of any kind?" the recruiter asked ticking off the requirements.

Nora thought back to her escape in stealing Frank's plane to regain custody of her children. She was never charged with anything. "No. No criminal record."

"Good. So, I was thinking. You might be just the right candidate to fill that position."

"Please, do tell." Nora requested.

"It's still only a volunteer position. You would run a USO club and manage the recruits. It would be an eighteen month long contract."

"Eighteen months?" Nora repeated. She wasn't sure what she was thinking when she came in. A year and a half away from her children. And no pay? She wasn't sure going over to Vietnam was sounding so good now. Pondering, she characteristically bit her lower lip.

"Listen, it's a lot to take in. I'm sure regional will find someone. But think it over and if you are interested, let me know," the administrator offered, handing Nora some paperwork. "I don't know if the boss would go for ya. A middle aged woman on a USO performing tour probably wouldn't work. I mean, it's not like you're Doris Day or Nancy Sinatra," the recruiter offered. "But as manager of a club? Maybe. I'll need those references and for you to complete the job application. I think they will be interviewing next week."

"Okay, I'll mull it over. It sounds like a wonderful opportunity." Eighteen months was all that was swimming around in Nora's head.

"I'll warn you, it's a challenge. It's a shame that the USO is all volunteer. But that's the way we operate. We are a subsidiary of the government you know. Women's positions don't quite get the ranking that men's do."

SOLO VIETNAM

Boy, didn't Nora know it. Yet another battle for Gloria Steinem and the women's liberation movement. "Thank you very much. I'll get back with you by the end of the week," Nora reached out her hand to shake. As she exited the office, she looked at the row of young women, some of whom she would manage. Hmph. I'm barely good enough with my own children, could I possibly be housemother to these silly girls? Lots to process.

Chapter 12
∞ October, 1967 Tonkin Gulf ∞

An aircraft carrier is none other than a floating military base. Runways, commissaries, an on-board hospital complete with a dental labs and an operating room. Gray on the outside, white on the inside. Over 4500 sailors, airmen and pilots carrying out missions from the middle of the ocean, who also have to live, eat and sleep on a moving flotilla of war planes.

Also onboard were thousands of pounds of ordnance and artillery. All of which were explosive. Although thousands of sorties were flown during a cruise, October was not a good month for safety aboard the *Coral Sea*.

The first situation occurred during an unrep operation on October 11. In order to carry out the navy's mission effectively, fleet units had to be capable of remaining at sea for prolonged periods of time. Sometimes they sailed into areas of the world where friendly re-supply ports were not available. Carriers had to be equipped to replenish combatants underway with fuel, ammunition, provisions, and spare parts. As a result of underway replenishment techniques, or unreps, the *US Coral Sea* could remain mission ready to carry out military action anywhere in the world.

While receiving supplies from *USS Mount Katmai*, an ammunition ship, a collision occurred. The sea state was relatively heavy and the two ships rolled into each other which knocked two of the *Coral Sea*'s elevators loose. Elevators were large hydraulic plates of metal which transported planes and ammunition between the hangar deck and the flight deck. They lifted the planes from protected storage below deck onto the flight deck. Only the aft port elevator was working.

All three elevators were used heavily during flight ops. Despite being down two, the *Coral Sea* remained on station. Instead, orders were given to bingo off all aircraft that would require heavy maintenance to either Danang or Chu Lai. The ship managed to retain her capability of combat effectiveness by extensive modification of operational techniques through experimentation and coordination between the air wing, general operations and air departments.

In fact, during that time no missions were missed and the carrier operated with extreme efficiency, even participating in implementation of the MiGCAP plan for positive control of the combat air patrol in direct support of the strike groups. This plan was devised by ComCarDiv Seven, the Commander Carrier Division while embarked in the ship.

One good thing that occurred in October happened during one of Steve's night missions. Steve was flying lead when one of the Lt.'s radioed urgently. "This is Blue Tail 227. Over." Lt. Cook transmitted.

"Blue Tail 227, copy."

"I've got a fleet of VC boats embedded in some sampans." Lt. Cook detected six N. Viet patrol boats, cleverly screened by a sampan fleet about a mile east of Thang Hoa harbor. Sampans were Vietnamese fishing boats with large, beige, unusually shaped sails. They would fish early in the predawn morning and go out again in the evening. It was almost first light.

"Roger that, 227. How do you plan to proceed?" Steve queried.

"Bomb the crap outta them, sir."

Chuckling, Steve responded. "Roger that, Lt. Execute a shallow dive. That'll get them in sight for both of us. Bomb's away."

Assisted by his wingman, Lt. JG Watson, they released their bombs and squarely impacted the middle of the formation of enemy boats, sinking four and severely damaging the other two. The *Coral Sea* gained her first "PT-boat-Ace" and Cook received a Distinguished Flying Cross for his airmanship, revolutionary tactics, and courage in the face of a determined enemy.

Celebrations were often short lived, however. Two days later the *Coral Sea* suffered fatalities among its 'black shoes,' 'brown shoes' and 'gators.' An SH-3A helicopter from the *USS Kearsarge* lost control and hit the carrier causing a significant loss of life.

But duty called the next day. Surface-to-air missiles and anti-aircraft fire were always the biggest risks to pilots flying their missions. Steve was given a large tactical sortie. Air wing CVW-15 and VA-153 were to coordinate efforts with several other naval and air force attack wings to pound N. Vietnam's largest and previously unstruck MiG base at Phuc Yen, which was eleven miles north of the capital of Hanoi.

Any tailhook pilot knew, the war from the air and from the ground were two different things. The night was clear and for that Steve was glad. As he approached the coast from such a high altitude, Steve could see almost all of I Corps lit up. The moonlight was reflecting off the sandy beaches and the stars were bright over the sea. It was almost pretty, until he realized that just inland were two and one half marine divisions, two army divisions, several ARVN units, and hundreds of aircraft fighting in an area that averaged forty miles in width and was only 140 miles long.

In the darkness, Steve could see the other aircraft expending their ordnance, the ships on the coast firing inland, and artillery being fired here and there from ground units in contact, flares marking their positions. There must have been three hundred thousand combatants in a small area of only 600 square miles.

During this evening's flights, the air wings were under control of Vice Squad until they got near the ASRAT, a radar site which turned them over to a ground controller.

"Ground to air. Please give your BuNo for receipt of vector and target." One by one, each plane airborne then gave their identification. "Blue Tail 224. Vector 180 at 30 degrees. Mark at 5,000 meters to target. Over."

"Blue Tail 224. Roger that," Steve responded.

When he was within 5,000 meters he heard, "Mark. Mark."

On cue, Steve released his bombs. He could see a bright, white, flash of the explosions visible out of the cockpit. Having no idea what he had just struck, his mission was complete. Orders followed. Back to the carrier.

North Vietnam was black and void at night by order. There were no lights anywhere. South Vietnam had lights in the cities and larger villages and over the ocean. Fishermen fished in small round boats, no larger than a washtub and each one had a light. In North Vietnam, under certain conditions, the ocean and the sky looked the same, and vertigo was a possibility if you didn't keep scanning your instruments or watch the coastline.

Along a vector from Dong Ha, Steve was watching the coastline upon his return. Suddenly, he caught the glimmer of a flicker in his canopy. There had been reports of numerous SAMs being launched during the massive attack. Steve checked his instruments to see if his generator was going out, as that was a symptom of that happening. That wasn't it.

He saw nothing wrong until he looked out and realized he was being perfectly tracked, not on radar, but from the visually controlled explosions nearby of a 57mm gun or larger tracing him. Steve switched off the master lights on his plane and made a hard turn toward the

SOLO VIETNAM

South China Sea. The orange balls of flame passed through the position he had been at just after he turned. Near miss.

When the N. Vietnamese opened up with ground fire at night, it wasn't piecemeal. During this mission, Steve could see an F-8 photo plane being marked by extremely bright flashes, one after the other, like a continuous dotted line of fire. It was triggering all the guns in sight and thousands of them seemed to be shooting at the straight line of fireballs as they flew south.

There had been at least thirty SAMs in the air tonight, as both air wings from the *Coral Sea* battered the revetment area and taxiways with their 500 and 750 pound bombs. Once they were called off, Steve relaxed as he flew back. Coming out of N. Vietnam and flying back to the carrier, light from the bright flashes of bombs and various flares gave him a chance just to watch the lightshow of the massive and destructive war.

The next morning was chaos, as tragedy again struck the *Coral Sea*. Steve was down in his berthing space reading a letter from his children when he felt a heavy compression and muffled explosion. Poking his head out, he heard shouting and mass confusion.

"What the hell was that?" he asked a passing sailor.

"Explosion, sir. Down below."

A few seconds later, alarms sounded and he heard instructions given over the 1MC. "All personnel. Code Red. Code Red. Please follow your designated evacuation route."

As Steve exited his berth to evacuate, he could see flames shooting out of the hatch with great force. When Steve got to safety, evac'ing with the other sailors they heard the details.

In a forward assembly area, a Zuni rocket had exploded during a routine test. The men had been checking the firing circuits of several dozen rocket tubes that had been returned for refilling. One of the rockets had not been fired and remained in the tube. When the sailors applied the tester to the firing circuit, the rocket ignited and became imbedded in the bulkhead several feet in front of the rocket tube.

The warhead penetrated the bulkhead and stopped inches in front of the face of a first class petty officer in first class mess, who was relaxing and watching TV. Although the warhead didn't explode, unfortunately, the rocket's motor expended its burning fuel in the ordnance work space killing the man who straddled the tube to apply the tester. His two fellow workers were treated in the on-board hospital, but died later.

The *Coral Sea* left Yankee Station to head south. All personnel not immediately involved in the damage control were moved to the aft end of the ship, as were all aircraft in the forward hanger bay. All equipment that could not be moved immediately was dumped over the side, including a million dollar tester for the AEW, early warning aircraft aboard. The massive fire curtain doors between the hangar bays were shut. The fire spread down into some of the engineering spaces and into the ordnance storage areas where the bombs were sorted prior to being prepped for use.

Many sailors donned heavy gloves and man-handled the hot bombs up several decks and tossed them over the side to avoid further explosions. The ship burned for several hours before the fire was put out. But true to form, Steve, his fellow pilots and the deck crews were back on station and launching planes the next day.

There were fires on board almost every day, but normally they were small trash or electrical fires which were handled quickly. The entire crew came close to becoming an exploding mushroom cloud with this incident. In the privacy of his new berth, Steve got out his rosary and thanked his lucky stars. His children sure didn't need to be orphaned now.

Chapter 13
∞ November, 1967 New Orleans ∞

Nora used to relish her days off because she spent them mostly with Charlene. It was a time that she could catch up on the latest gossip and just girl talk. Now that Charlene was in nursing school, most days she was knee-deep in study. Although Nora had the utmost respect and admiration for her friend's endeavor, she missed the mornings they used to share. Especially the gossip.

Charlene was so excited about her entry into nursing school; she had invited Nora over for lunch once she got a day off, to model her uniforms. As Nora drove to Metairie, she heard an announcement on the radio that would change New Orleans forever.

Pete Rozelle, Commissioner for the NFL was reporting that New Orleans now had an NFL football team. As of today, November 1st, the New Orleans Saints football franchise was born. Aptly announced on All Saints Day as recognized by the Catholic Church.

As Nora drove up in the driveway, Charlene ran out on the porch to greet her. "Did you hear? Did you hear the news?" she proclaimed, waving to Nora.

"About the football team? For New Orleans?" Nora asked getting out of the VW bus.

"Yep. Isn't it going to be fun? 'Nawlins and football. We'll be the best fans ever. We already have the song. 'Oh when the saints. Oh when the saints come marchin' in'" Charlene paraded. They made their way to the dining room, where Charlene had set the table for lunch. "Wait," she told Nora heading down the hall, "I want to show you something," Charlene giddily chirped.

Oh, how Nora had missed her. "Pretty crazy. Mardi Gras. Jazz festivals. And now NFL football."

"I wonder where they came up with the name? It's perfect, don't you think?" Charlene called out from her bedroom. "Wait in the hall. Don't peek."

Nora leaned against the hallway. She wondered what Charlene was up to. "Funny that you ask, but I heard Mrs. Arceneaux telling me something about this last week. She said her oldest son, Bernard Jr., won a contest to name them. His picture was in the *Times Picayune* this morning. Not a coincidence that they waited until November 1st to announce the team."

"That family has the Midas touch. Everything they touch seems to turn to gold. A plantation. Star athlete at Loyola. Almost done, keep your eyes closed." Charlene wriggled into an outfit. "Didn't you tell me that your daughter Leisel was working for the youngest son, Mat? Selling wax or something?"

"Yep. Mat's wax. She's making a killing, but spending it all on clothes."

"Speaking of clothes, take a look at this!" Charlene popped out of her bedroom. She looked adorable in her starch white uniform with the pink pinafore, indicating she was a student. "Like it?" She twirled around like a model.

"You look so professional," Nora complimented. She knew her friend was proud.

Charlene showed Nora her stethoscope, pen light and scissors. "I couldn't wait to show you. We started clinical rotations in the hospital this week. I'm at Charity, on the orthopedics ward," Charlene gushed.

"So how is it? Is it what you thought?" Nora couldn't wait to hear.

"Yes. And no. It's a lot harder than I thought it would be. Not just the class work. What you see with some of the patients is heartbreaking. I've seen some stuff that would make your hair curl. Ya know?"

"I can only imagine, Char."

"Some days, my back is just aching and my feet dead tired when I get home. I change beds, help lift patients. Empty urinals. Last week, I got to give my first shot. I was so nervous. My hands were shaking like I was having a seizure. But I got it in there. Right in the butt!" Charlene was beaming from ear to ear. "You'd be so proud of me, Nora Jean."

"I'm very proud. I wonder if you'll run into Nellie. I hear she runs her units with an iron fist," Nora laughed.

"I might. We go to Hotel Dieu next. For labor and delivery. Come on, let's go eat!" Charlene led Nora back into the dining room.

"Well, I hope you're nicer to your patients than those nun crones were at St. Paul in Dallas. They were downright evil," Nora recalled, remembering her birth experience there. "They never did let me do Lamaze, like I wanted."

"I've never forgotten that story, Nora. I'll never be a nurse like that. I am always going to advocate for the rights of my patients," Charlene assured. "So enough about me. What's going on with you? You seemed to have been very pre-occupied lately," Charlene remarked as she set the table for lunch. "Do tell."

Charlene listened as she put out the large shrimp she had boiled up and then chilled for shrimp cocktail. In true Charlene form, the table was set with china and tall parfait glasses for the shrimp. She filled each glass with the spicy, red cocktail sauce and arranged the large shrimp all the way around. Placing each glass over a large Romaine lettuce leaf on the plate. Hostess with the most-est, Charlene Hebert.

"One night, after getting off at the club, I met this navy pilot," Nora told her of her encounter. "He had just finished his cruise in Vietnams and was on leave. His stories. What he had seen was horrific," Nora said taking a big bite of her shrimp.

"I've taken care of some of those Vietnam vets at Touro," Charlene relayed.

"Oh, yeah?"

"Yeah. I had some trouble relating to some of their emotional tales. My instructors told me it was because they had anxiety disorder. It really messed some of them up bad."

"What the heck is that?"

"Some post war thing. They just can't cope. It's bad."

"It doesn't help that people treat them like crap when they come home. I just don't understand that."

"Some of the nurses told me it was like no other war they'd ever heard about. Whatever's going on over there sounds pretty wicked."

Near the end of lunch, Nora told Charlene about her visit to the USO and the job they offered. Charlene was a bit taken aback.

"You aren't considering going are you?" Again, Nora managed to shock her.

"I'm seriously thinking about it, Charlene. I can't shake it. There is just something calling me. Some force."

"I just can't see how you could do it. Your kids are still at home. Well, at least three of them. How would they manage?"

"They are teens. Doing their own thing. Nellie is about to retire. She could move in and watch over them. It would only be for eighteen months," Nora explained.

"That over a year! Oh, Nora. I dunno. It's so far away. Texas was one thing. But Vietnam? Are you going to fly?"

"Heck no. They don't allow women to fly into combat zones. In fact, it's a big controversy at the moment. Jackie Cochran is causing all kinds of heck about it. Women were used in World War II all the time, as transporters and test pilots. But the service won't have anything to do with them now. Which is really hacking off legions of women pilots."

"Well, then. As what?"

"Don't' laugh, but I'd be managing a USO club. Basically I'll be going as a den mother to a bunch of young USO girls. But at least I'd be going."

"Nora Jean. The ideas that you come up with just blow me away. Here I think I'm little Miss Women's libber, doing my nursing thing," Charlene said shaking her head. "But somehow you always manage to trump me." With that, Charlene poured them each another class of chilled Pinot Grigio. "Well, honey. I guess you gotta do what 'cha gotta do. I can't wait to see the expression on Nellie's face when you drop this bomb."

That was something Nora was not looking forward to. Nellie was never happy at having to cope with Nora's escapades. She was quite ready for Nora to settle down. Be still and just enjoy life. But that just wasn't how Nora operated. As luck would have it, fate intervened.

Chapter 14

A week later, Nora received a frantic phone call. It was late in the evening, luckily on a night that Nora had off from the club. Nellie was nearly hysterical.

"Nora. Nora Jean is that you?" Nellie's normally soft voice was shrill. "Oh, Nora. It's just awful. There's been a fire. In The Quarter."

"Mama, are you okay?" Nora was alarmed.

"Yes. I'm fine. I got out, just as the flames were coming. But my home. It's gone. All gone," Nellie began to weep.

"It's okay, Mama. Where are you?"

"I . . . I dunno. The firemen. They hurried us out."

"Go to a corner, Mama. Look at the street sign. Tell me where you are," Nora commanded with calm resolution.

"Okay. Okay. I'm walking," Nellie answered. She dropped the pay phone and hurried to the nearest corner to look at the street sign. The seconds ticked by as Nora awaited her return.

"Dauphine. Dauphine and Governor Nicholls St.," Nellie said gasping for breath.

"Stay there, Mama. Stay there. I'm coming for you right now."

"Okay. Okay Nora. I'll stay right here. I have nothing. No clothes. All my things. Up in flames," Nellie started crying hysterically.

"Stop. Mama. Just hold yourself together. I will be right there. Do you hear me, Mama?"

"Yes. Yes, Nora Jean. Oh, dear. Thank God for you," Nellie balled.

"I'll be right there Mama. Do you have your rosary?"

"Yes, Nora Jean. That was the one thing I grabbed."

Somehow Nora knew she would have. "I'm coming, Mama. Just say your Rosary. I'll be there in just a few minutes."

Nora threw a sweat shirt over her nightgown, slipped into some flats and dashed for the door. Before she left, she woke Cathy.

"Cathy, sorry to wake you. There's been a fire at Grandma Nellies," Nora effused.

"What?" Cathy was still half asleep.

"Just stay put. I am going to Grandma Nellie. I'll be right back."

"Okay, Grandma Nellie. Okay," Cathy answered in a daze.

Nora kissed her goodbye and dashed for the door. The VW bus started right up. She drove as quickly as she could. There was no traffic at almost 3:00 AM. Nora took Carrollton all the way to City Park and took a right on Esplanade. It was the fastest way to the side of The Quarter where Nora grew up and where Nellie still lived. Nora could see the flames spiraling into the sky as she approached. Luckily, she chose the right route, as the fire department had many of the other blocks of The Quarter blocked off.

Just a few more streets. Broad. Miro. Rampart. She was almost there. Just as she had instructed, there was Nellie. Frantic and shivering in her nightgown. No shoes. Just clutching her rosary. As she recognized the VW bus, Nellie started to run. "Nora. Nora," she cried out.

"It's okay, Mama. I'm here." Nora pulled over to the curb. Getting out, she wrapped her arms around Nellie. "Oh, Mama. I'm so sorry."

"It's all gone. Up in embers. The fire. It started down the block. Just raged through everything in its path," Nellie related through sobs.

Nora just held her there. "There, there, Mama. It's okay. I'm here. I'm here. You're okay, thank God. You're okay. It's all just stuff, Mama. But you are okay."

"Roux. Where's my Roux?" Nellie suddenly cried out.

Nora had forgotten about Nellie's kitty, Roux. He was a large grey-brown tabby, named after the base of flour and bacon grease that formed the foundation for nearly every New Orleans dish. Nellie had him for years. He roamed The Quarter like a fat cat. "I'll drive around, Mama. You call for him."

After helping Nellie into the VW bus, Nora rolled down the windows. Slowly, Nora made her way through the streets that she could. They were both calling for him. "Roux. Roux. Here kitty, kitty, kitty." Nora knew it was probably a lost cause. But she was determined to try. "Roux. Roux. Here kitty, kitty."

Making a few more turns, Nora was about to give up. But just as she turned into St. Phillip for one last pass, she thought she saw some green eyes in the darkness. "Mama, is that him?" Nora pointed out.

"I think so, Nora. Yes. Yes, that's him." The poor cat looked horrific. His brown-grey hair was singed and part of his tail was burnt.

SOLO VIETNAM

But the minute Nellie got out of the VW, Roux ran into her arms. Nellie burrowed her head into him. Rubbing and stroking him. "Roux. Roux, my baby. My sweet kitty. Oh, you poor thing."

"Let's get him home. Mama. We'll have to get him used to a new home."

"But where, Nora? Where am I going to live?" Nellie continued to sob.

It was evident that it would no longer be in her apartment. Half of the block was nothing more that blackened rubble.

"I've lost everything," Nellie fretted. "Furniture. Pots and pans. After all these years, I've lost everything." It dawned on Nellie that she had also lost all of her photos. She began to weep harder now. "All your baby pictures. My wedding pictures. Jack. It's all gone."

Nora thought about how all of the memorabilia from her eclectic father was now lost. He had been quite a rogue character. All she had now were her memories of him from when she was a child. It was a stunning revelation. Nora suddenly felt very sad. How much tragedy was her family to endure? The murder of her father. Her divorce. Now this. But it was just too much. She couldn't think about it now.

"I know, Mama. It's awful. But you have me. And you have Roux. It's going to be okay." They drove the rest of the way in silence. Nora handed her mother some Kleenex to blow her nose. She could hear Nellie's broken-hearted sobs. Nora had never seen her mother like this. Not since that dreadful day at the above ground cemetery, when they put her father's body in the crypt.

It was almost 4:00 AM when then pulled into the gate on Dante. Nora made a pot of coffee and added some brandy to Nellie's. After she got Nellie calmed down, she moved one of the girls, Leisel, onto the couch. She bedded Nellie down in the girls' room. Cathy woke with the commotion.

She got out of bed to give Grandma Nellie a hug. "Grandma, I love you. It will be okay. You can have one of our rooms," Cathy offered. Stroking Roux, the kitty, which Nellie would not turn loose of, Cathy then returned to bed.

JEANETTE VAUGHAN

Chapter 15
∞ November, 1967 Yankee Station ∞

The *Coral Sea* avoided typhoon Emma, in late October, by putting out to sea for evasive steaming via Hong Kong. She then altered course for an international sojourn to assist the Liberian flag freighter Loyal Fortunes at Pratas Reef about 170 miles southeast of the British crown colony. On November 7, two HC-1 helicopters shuttled between the two ships bringing off thirty-seven Chinese crewmen, where they were disembarked upon the carrier's brief return to Hong Kong.

During a break in the monsoon weather, *Coral Sea* aviators kept up a relentless pressure on the N. Vietnamese transportation system with strikes on multiple airfields, rail yards, and highways around Haiphong. Missions were extremely treacherous as pilots braved increasing barrage of devastating SAMs. For three days, pilots flew continuous missions night and day.

As luck would have it, Steve was assigned to several more night sorties. Although the monsoons were gone, one night a very pesky thunderstorm lingered. Loaded with six, five hundred pound bombs, Steve cat'd without incident. As he climbed north and penetrated the clouds, he climbed to his assigned altitude. Due to the overcast, Steve was focused on his instruments, as well as the climb schedule of airspeed and altitudes.

Suddenly, he felt a presence in the cockpit that he hadn't experienced before. He was halfway to his target and was being vectored between spotty thunderstorms when the strange feeling overpowered his need to keep his instrument scan going. He looked away from the instrument panel and forward over the nose probe on the right side of the fuselage and saw it glowing blue.

For a moment, Steve's mind disconnected from his hand holding the stick. "What the fuck?" was all Steve could manage. For the next thirty seconds, the plane flew itself while Steve, mesmerized, gazed at the blue glowing wings, the blue cone around the nose and the nose probe, and the blue drops of water on his canopy in the boundary layer that did not move.

The plane looked like it was irradiated. Steve was about to call on the radio, but was afraid of making a fool of himself. He thought he might be in some kind of bereavement-induced haze. So, he flew another thirty seconds looking out at the incandescent, blue glowing light. The plane was flying well without any commands. Suddenly, the A-4 was being banged around by the vertical air currents and Steve took control. He made a hard turn out of the storm, finished his mission and trapped back safely on the deck of the carrier.

In the ready room, several other pilots, checking out the greenie-board were gabbing on about the same thing.

"Holy, moly. Did ya see it?" asked a Lt. JG.

"Shit ya. My bird was glowing like a blue flame," exclaimed another. "What about you? Lt. Commander Novak?"

"For about half a minute, I didn't know what was going on. My SA blew the coop. I'd heard about St. Elmo's fire, but sure hadn't ever experienced it," explained Steve.

"Bizarro. Just freaking bizarre," the JG shook his head.

What they had just experienced was none other than St. Elmo's fire, which was a weather phenomenon that occurred when a mixture of gas and luminous plasma forms created by a coronal discharge from a sharp of pointed objects, such as a plane's nose or wings in a strong electric field in the atmosphere. The perfect conditions for such an occurrence were during a storm.

As Steve returned to the privacy of his stateroom, he took time to write home, describing the many strange events he was witnessing during his flights. He wasn't sure if it was the grief he intermittently experienced or the effects of war, but this time, when he took out his pen, he could not fight the impulse to describe the anecdotes to the one person who would understand. Nora.

On Nov 25th, the perils of war again struck the *Coral Sea*. A deck accident claimed the life of a Skyhawk pilot when the jet blast from another aircraft taxiing forward knocked Commander W.H. Searfus' plane into the sea. The wake of white water off the fan tail of a carrier is a about a mile long. HC-1 helos immediately were launched, but the A-4 sank, carrying Searfus with it.

Chapter 16
∞ November, 1967 New Orleans ∞

It was rare that Nora had a Friday night off, but as luck would have it, The Roosevelt booked a special guest. Arlo Guthrie of Alice's Restaurant Massacree fame. Nora was relieved to spend the weekend at home. The complete destruction of Nellie's home by fire had taken it out of her.

Time for comfort food. Nora took some garlic and onion and bell pepper and sautéed them in butter. The triad of veggies in any New Orleans dish. Then she added some flour and made a white sauce. Finally, she added some crawfish tail meat. Next, she prepared some white rice. Nothing provided more comfort than some Crawfish Etoufee. Leisel helped her by buttering some French bread. Iggy was away at a football game with friends, watching LSU play Tulane.

Cathy set the table. It was an all-girls night for dinner, but Cathy and Leisel had dates later for their football games. Their dates were from Jesuit and they were doubling. For that, Nora was glad.

After dinner, Nora had time to just unwind and prepare for the inevitable conversation about where Nellie would live. She knew it would be painful. Nora served her mother a slice of the pound cake that Cathy had made. One thing was for sure, Nora had taught all of her girls how to cook.

Nellie sat quietly in the living room sipping her *café au lait* after dinner. Nora poured herself a demitasse, but all black. It was time to confront the inevitable.

"Mama. I'm so sorry for what has happened. I know you must feel devastated losing your home."

"That's the least of it. I've worked so hard, Nora. All my life. After Jack died, I had no one but myself. To provide for you. Send you to Ursuline. I worked myself to the bone," Nellie defended weakly.

"I know, Mama. I know," Nora comforted.

"I've survived hurricanes. Jack's death. World War II. But now this," Nellie started to sob. Nora wanted to hug her mother, but Nellie was just not that affectionate. "I never was blessed with your looks, Nora. Your vamp and spirit. My one chance at love, with your father Jack, was all I had. And it wasn't perfect."

Nora was not sure where this was going. She sipped more of her coffee wishing it had bourbon in it.

"There are things you do not know. Things then. They were different. I wanted to have a baby with Jack. But that never was possible. We tried and tried. I knew I was not the most attractive woman. And the riverboats, there were many *belle de catin*."

For once, Nora sat spellbound. For Nellie had never spoken to her about the intimacies of her life. She was riveted.

"What I never expected, was that Jack would fall in love. With one in particular. She was exotic. Beautiful. She offered Jack in bed what I could not. And soon, she was with child."

Nora sat still. She just let Nellie talk.

"I had just suffered yet another miscarriage. I was heartbroken. And so, Jack arranged with this woman. For her to give us her baby. And that baby was you," Nellie then looked Nora in the eyes.

"Mama. Oh dear, Mama. I am so sorry for all that you have been through. But, I knew. I found out about five years ago. In a strange circumstance. This woman, Gia is her name. She works at a coffee house in The Quarter."

"But how, how did you know?" Nellie looked surprised.

"One night, when I had been cast out by Frank, I ended up there. As it turns out, Big Daddy, also worked there. You know, Mabel's husband? It's a long story. But, yes. I met her. She told me. About Jack."

Nellie rose and came over to Nora. She knelt by her side. Nora buried her mother's head into her chest. For once. Maybe for the first time. They connected, now that the truth had been revealed. Veritas. Truth to one's self. It was truly healing. Such profound revelations were now out in the open.

"But Mama. Remember. I only have one mother. The mother who raised me. Loved me. Fed me. And that mother is you."

Nellie again sobbed quietly. "Do you ever think of that baby? The one that was born in Texas?"

Nora wasn't sure if she could endure the pain of this conversation. "Yes, Mama. I do. But I force myself to only think about it once a year."

"Near Easter," Nellie revealed. She knew Nora better than Nora thought. "The front you put on isn't transparent to me. A Mother knows."

Boy that was the truth, Nora knew. She knew what her children were thinking even before they said anything.

"I know it's painful. But think of the gift you gave to a woman just like me, who couldn't have any children." Nellie dabbed her eyes and blew into her Kleenex. "Nora Jean, you are all I have in this world. Promise me, you will never leave me."

"Mama. I'll always be there for you," Nora told what she knew was sort of a white lie. Nora knew that through the tragic and strange twist of fate with Nellie losing her home, she would probably have to live at Nora's. Which, in turn, allowed Nora the freedom to go to Vietnam. There was now someone to reside at her duplex and supervise her children. She just had absolutely no idea how she was going to tell her. Now was just not the time.

SOLO VIETNAM

Chapter 17
∞ December, 1967 ∞

Before Nora had time to formulate a plan to tell her family about Vietnam, the gig was up. Nora received some astonishing news when she went to finalize her paperwork at the USO office.

"Ms. Broussard. I'm so glad you came in today. There has been a change in plans," the Associate Director piped, shuffling some papers around on her desk. "But you're going to be so excited," she giddily exclaimed. "Your group was chosen to tour Vietnam with Bob Hope!"

"Oh my God. Bob Hope? Are you serious?" Nora was astounded.

"Yes. Bob Hope. You lucky girl. He's doing his Christmas tour and our USO girls were chosen to accompany him."

"Christmas tour? For next year?"

"Oh, no, no, no. This year."

Nora felt her heart sink to her stomach. "But that's in a couple of weeks. I . . . I'm . . . I mean I haven't . . ."

"Packed? I'm sure. So you'll have lots to do in the next few days. You leave outta here in two weeks."

"But I . . ." Nora just stammered. She had to think fast. Bob Hope. She might never get this opportunity again. But what about her children. Christmas. The news was overwhelming. "I see."

"It's all arranged. You'll fly out to Los Angeles. There, you'll join up with Bob Hope's entourage. Be fitted for costumes. And then take off for the Philippines on December 14th. Can you believe it? Bob Hope. I'm so jealous."

"Gosh. It's pretty amazing."

"After the tour, which will last a couple of weeks with Mr. Hope, you and the girls will head to Chu Lai. There, you're assigned to manage a USO club."

"I'll be in one spot? What about the rest of the girls?"

"Well," the woman babbled. "That's the military for you. They changed the assignment. Had some kind of incident at that club. So they needed to get a manager in there real soon. The tour arm of the USO and the USO Club are two different things. There was a snafu with some group that was to tour with Mr. Hope. You got lucky and get to fill in. Some of the girls will continue on and join up with another tour. But you'll get to keep five or six to help you work the club at Chu Lai. You'll be in charge."

"I see. Thank you for letting me know. Here is the paperwork you needed. I got all of the shots required. I can still barely move my right arm."

"As manager, I want to make sure you understand the rules. We are very strict about what our purpose is in running these clubs. They are vital to the mental well-being of our troops. You have one goal: to bring a touch of home to our boys whatever they've been through and wherever they are. Is that clear?"

"Yes, Ma'am."

"Oh, and some other things. Civilian clothes only. There are no uniforms. Make sure the girls bring lots of mini-skirts. No slacks are allowed. If they didn't pack enough, you can order them some from R and R's in Bangkok. When you get there, make sure you hold an orientation. No matter what happens, the men are never, and I mean never to see you cry. Your job and the girls' is to be happy."

"Of course, I understand." Paste on a mask. No matter what. At that, Nora was an expert. "What are our hours?"

"Pretty much every day. Whatever the clubs hours are. USO club staffers get a week of R and R every three months. Other than that, you are on duty. Just like our men."

"Do we live or have rooms at the club?"

"Oh, no. Each base is different. Depending on how much artillery it has taken. In Saigon there is a BOQ. A bachelor's officer's quarters with special provisions for USO staffers. But, hmm . . . I believe in Chu Lai," she shuffled some more papers on her desk. "Right. It says here that in Chu Lai, there are some small Quonset huts with bunks."

Nora wanted to say sarcastically, "Sounds divine." But she donned her mask. "Great," and smiled gracefully.

"Looks like you are good to go. I'll see you in a few weeks. Guess you won't have to worry about Christmas shopping," the sprightly Associate Director chirped.

Nora walked out of the USO office in a daze. Two weeks. Good Lord. What was she going to tell her children? She took out a cigarette and lit up for a smoke to calm her nerves. Note to self, pack cartons of cigarettes. She was sure she was going to need them.

SOLO VIETNAM

When she arrived back home, Charlene's car was parked alongside the gate. "Hey, girlfriend," Charlene called out from the screen door. "I haven't seen you in ages. What's cooking?"

"You'll want to have a drink when I tell you," Nora explained as she climbed the stairs.

"You're all dressed up like the bees knees. I've got the coffee on. Just been chit chatting nurse stuff with Nellie. So do tell."

Nora's children were home. All the significant people in her life, save the errant daughter at Haight-Ashbury, were present. Summoning up her courage, she gathered them into the living room. She took a big breath, bit her lower lip, and began. "I have something tell y'all. You know how concerned I am about the war in Vietnam. Well, I'm going over there. With Bob Hope."

"Bob Hope!" they all exclaimed.

"Mama, are you pulling our leg?" Leisel asked.

"No. I am certainly not. I'm going on a USO tour to sing with Bob Hope."

Nellie looked like she was going to faint. "But Nora, when did you get this crazy idea? The USO girls are all young. They don't have families."

"I'm insulted that you don't think I can compete with some twenty-somethings," Nora chuffed, putting her hand on her hip.

"My stars, Nora. You never cease to amaze me darlin' girl." Even Charlene was shocked at this news.

Iggy just sat there speechless. He wasn't sure what to think about another crazy adventure his mother dreamed up.

"So when do you leave?" Cathy asked pensively.

"That's the exciting part. It's a Christmas tour and I leave in about two weeks."

Nellie burst into tears and went to her room. Iggy, Cathy, and Leisel's eyes were round and wide as saucers.

"You're leaving before Christmas? Mother, how could you?" Cathy got up, went to her shared bedroom and slammed the door.

"I'm happy for you, Mama." Liesel offered, coming over to Nora and kissing her on the cheek. "Even though Christmas won't be the same. I bet Bob Hope has a good Christmas tree." Leisel returned to the girls' room to get ready for her study date with the youngest Arceneaux son, across the street. Iggy just shrugged and went back to watching TV.

"Oh, Nora. Right before Christmas?" Even Charlene sounded dismayed. "I just don't know what to say. Singing with Bob Hope would be wonderful. But your mother. The children. Nora, are you sure this is a good thing?"

"I know, Charlene. I'm pretty flabbergasted too. But I was planning to go anyway. Just not so soon."

"And not at Christmas."

Returning from her room, finally, Nellie spoke. "Nora Jean. You promised. Not to leave me."

"Mama. Please try to understand."

"Oh, I understand. First the flying lessons. Then stealing that plane. Now this. You're just like your father, Jack. Born with the wanderlust. Never content to stay in one place and just enjoy life."

Both Nora and Charlene knew that to be true. Nora was always involved in something outside the box. She wasn't like most other women of the sixties. It was unsettling and sometimes just downright selfish. But there was usually no way to change her mind once it was made up.

"Mama, I can't do it without your support. I was hoping that you would consider staying here. On Dante Street. To supervise the kids."

"I see. You had this all figured out did you?"

"No, not at all. But I would really appreciate it, Mama."

Nellie had her jaw set tight. Her lips pursed. Nora knew that stern look well. "I suppose someone has to stay here and look after your children." Disgruntled, Nellie went into the kitchen to look after the supper that she was preparing on the stove.

Nora could finally breathe. Thank God, Nellie was going to do it.

Charlene was still shaking her head. "Two weeks. I just can't believe it. I'm always having to say goodbye to you. I don't guess TWA flies to Vietnam."

"Not during a war," Nora smirked and laughed. The good friends hugged tight. "I'm gonna miss the heck outta ya, Charlene."

"You better! Hey, I almost forget. I had something to tell you too."

"What's that? You're full of surprises."

"I have an interview. To work at the VA in New Orleans when I graduate."

"Charlene, that's great. I'm so proud of you."

"You're my motivation. Hey, this way I'll have some way to get insider scoop from the government. I'll keep tabs on where you might be."

Nora laughed. "You're a pretty pickle. But I'm awfully glad to have you as my best friend. Forever."

"Forever, indeed. I'm going to the library to make a Xerox of a map of Vietnam. Where is it you are gonna be?"

"The USO club at Chu Lai. It's on a beach somewhere in South Vietnam."

"When are you going to tell Nellie you'll be gone for eighteen months?" Charlene queried.

"I have no idea. I think I'll leave that for another day."

* * * * * *

The next fourteen days zoomed by with an endless array of business. Notice to the Roosevelt. Notice to Wyatt Aviation. Power of attorney for the kids to Nellie. Packing and repacking to meet the weight limits on luggage for the overseas flight. The selection of outfits, including no pants. Almost. Nora packed one pair just for herself. At least Nora was used to dressing for humid weather.

On December 13th, in the middle of the week, Nora, Nellie and her three teenagers still at home celebrated Christmas early. Nora and Nellie made turkey. Dressing with oyster stuffing. Cranberry sauce. And Nora's specialty, cheesecake with strawberry topping. They lit the second candle on the advent wreath.

The Christmas tree had been up since the week after Thanksgiving, complete with nativity scene. They opened presents, and shared some eggnog. Nora and Nellie spiked theirs with a little bourbon. Nellie assured the children that they would attend midnight mass at Mater Dolorosa. Just as they always did.

Nora couldn't sleep the night before she was to leave. Sitting out on the porch on Dante Street, she was having last minute second thoughts. Was what she was about to do crazy? But in her heart, she knew unless she did it, she couldn't rest.

Earlier in the week, Nora had driven out to Lakefront. Her trips there were rare. Just way too painful, due to the memories of Steve. Her purpose for this visit was to see if Chet had heard anything from Steve.

Chet had only received one letter, since Charlene's shrimp boil. The letter said he was flying the A-4E Skyhawk onboard the *Coral Sea*. Somewhere, amidst the tropical rainforests of Vietnam and the vast South China Sea was a widowed Steve.

Chapter 18
∞ December, 1967 Tonkin Gulf ∞

Departing Subic Bay after a period of maintenance upkeep in early December, the *Coral Sea* returned to Yankee Station. The purpose of the missions had not changed for VA-153. More attacks on transportation links to disrupt the N. Vietnamese. On Dec 17th, Steve participated in four major attacks at the outset against two major highway ferries. One was near Thai Binh, the other south of Nam Dinh in conjunction with other CVW-15 attack and fighter squadrons. The barrage inflicted heavy damage to major passageways.

While carrying on the operations, Steve was monitoring Guard frequency, the universal emergency frequency used to transmit during a crisis. Normally, "Moonbeam," a C-130, served as an orbiting command post which assigned fighter air command control missions to Yankee Station aircraft. Guard frequency was used to transmit all manner of instructions and warnings. Most of the time, when in the target area, it was necessary to turn off the frequency in order to conduct sorties. But this was not the case on this mission.

While watching the second wave of attacks come in, a Mayday came over Guard frequency from an Air Force RF4. It was a reconnaissance plane flying a photo journalist from well up in Laos. It had taken some ground fire and was coming into South Vietnam, near the DMZ. The pilot was trying desperately to get away from the Laos area where if they went down, capture was certain.

Instead of going to another frequency, the RF4 Phantom stayed on Guard with a continuous relay of information to other aircraft in the area which were vectoring in to help them if they could. Steve had to turn off his emergency frequency so that he remained in contact with his own mission. He would turn back to Guard when he could since he had the ordnance to cover a Rescap. He knew the bases available for the Air Force pilot if he wanted to land. Rescap was a term used for rescue and was the acronym for Rescue Combat Air Patrol. Steve had personally brought in wingmen with battle damage to bases before.

As the injured bird came down near the DMZ, Steve could tell that something was different because the pilot was being deferred to by the other Air Force planes. The beleaguered aviator kept up his running commentary on Guard.

"Hellborne 331. Vector 090. I believe I'm south of the DMZ."

Steve could only follow part of it due to mission transmissions. The pilot was now near South Vietnam deciding to land on the beach. He must have still had some altitude, because he kept talking for some time.

"See a long strip of beach. North of a cove."

Steve didn't recognize exactly where he was or the beach he was talking about because of the need to periodically turn off the frequency.

Knowing he was going to try to land on the beach, Steve desperately tried to figure out the location, wanting to radio in Rescap helos. It seemed that the plane was being escorted by someone who knew I Corps. Steve was running low on fuel, so he departed the area, switching on Guard again after he had confirmed position with his wingman.

Steve had seen half a dozen planes after they had ditched. The biggest piece of any of them that he had seen afterward was a tail, burned out beyond recognition. Although the A-4 aircraft were not like the heavy F-4 Phantoms, structurally they were just as strong.

When Steve turned back on Guard, the plane had crashed and had been destroyed, with one crewman ejecting. After yet another round of missions, Steve returned safely to the deck of the carrier. He heard details in the ready room.

"The plane crashed near the Hue/Phu Bai air station."

"Damn, that's just a few mile from where I was orbiting. I felt so damned helpless listening on Guard," Steve revealed.

"Nothing you could do, man," another aviator remarked.

"But I just don't get it. Seemed like he was being deferred to."

"He was man. Cuz he was a General."

"No kidding?" Steve questioned.

The chatter on the radio was explained. The pilot, an Air Force General, had been killed. Hearing the situation in detail, Steve knew he could not have prevented his death. But he would never ride in a jet in which he wouldn't eject, and he certainly would never have bypassed the runways the General had.

Steve was one of the older pilots aboard the *Coral Sea*. He had seen older, highly ranking pilots killed several times doing just what had happened to the General. A jet aircraft was different than the older prop fighters. On the props, fuel was in the wings. The moving parts of the engine were enclosed in an engine block with high temperatures and the engine ahead of them. As such, these planes carried way less fuel.

But a jet was different. That's why there were ejection seats in them. The pilot sat in front of the engine. The engine had vanes that came apart and ran through the fuselage at 450 degrees centigrade or more. Both the fuselage and the wings were all fuel, hydraulic fluid, and integral parts of the aircraft's flight control system. If a jet struck anything, it started to come apart. The engine would come forward and the vanes would go through the fuel tanks. The jet itself was essentially an airborne bomb.

Steve was more affected by this useless tragedy than others. Over two hundred airborne craft in the area all had heard this happen. The co-pilot, in this case ejecting, made the better decision. The talk in the ready room continued to be tough.

"He shoulda ejected. Why the hell didn't he?" One of the young pilots asked.

"Who knows? It's mandatory in that kinda situation," remarked a Lt.

"Guys, he was a pilot, not the Captain of a damned ship," remarked Steve.

"Definitely woulda had a chance had he bailed," another argued.

"He was a General. Ain't no junior who's gonna contradict his decision to ride it in," a cocky, young pilot, clearly from the South based on his accent, remarked.

Steve got a Coca-Cola and continued to listen to the discussion. People he knew in other divisions and of all ranks were being killed every day. When seeing someone killed so uselessly, it bothered him more than the combat casualties. Especially when so many pilots in the area, who knew what to do, were not able to prevent the tragedy from happening.

"Say, I got wind of your accent," he addressed the southern pilot.

"Yep. Pete Watterman. From Tennessee," the young man said, chugging his soda. "I'm with HC-1, the helo unit."

"Steve. I'm from down South too. 'Nawlins."

"Nice to meet ya, Steve," he extended a hand. It was refreshing to meet a guy who still understood Southern charm.

"You guys do some good Rescap out there," Steve mentioned.

"Thanks, man. Despite what your fellow pilots say."

"Naw. Good work. Good work. It can't be easy searching for a needle in a haystack."

"Nope. Sure not. Say, you got some good looking women from 'Nawlins."

"Yep. Sure do." Steve's thoughts went immediately to Nora. Little did he know, but she was onboard Southern Airlines in route to Hong Kong and then Saigon.

* * * * * *

Four major attacks by CVW-15 and VA-153 took place in mid-December taking out two important highway ferries. One near Thai Binh and the other south of Nam Dinh inflicting heavy damage. These attacks occurred just before the controversial twenty-four hour truce announced by President Johnson. Just minutes after the truce ended, *Coral Sea* planes streaked through the airspace over N. Vietnam and bombed streams of trucks headed south, laden with war supplies. The grand total was 455 such vehicles.

One of the Lt. JGs returning on deck said, "It looked like a mass pile up on the freaking New Jersey turnpike."

But death to *Coral Sea* pilots was not done for the year. Three days before Christmas, Lt. Wilmer Cook, the one who had previously been awarded the Distinguished Flying Cross, died when attempting to take out a pontoon bridge in his A-4E.

The somber mood aboard the *Coral Sea* needed some rapid reversal. That same day, sailors received word that a special visitor was coming aboard. Bob Hope. He would be arriving to give a special Christmas performance, even while they were still off the coast of Vietnam.

Chapter 19
∞ South Vietnam ∞

At 10:05 AM, a large four engine US Air Force jet took off from Los Angeles, California for Thailand, eight thousand miles away. On board were Bob Hope, Raquel Welch, Elaine Dunn, Phil Crosby, son of Bing, Earl Wilson, Barbara McNair, Les Brown and his Band of Renown, Miss World Madeleine Hartog Bell, as well as Nora Broussard and her entourage of thirteen babbling USO beauties recruited from some of the top colleges in the South.

Nora couldn't believe that she was onboard with such an illustrious gang. During rehearsals in Los Angeles, she and her crew had to learn all of the main numbers. Just in case one of the principle performers became ill. In addition, they were to be back-up singers and dancers. Nora looked pretty good among these younger girls. She could definitely hold her own in the mini-skirted outfits and flowing, chiffon, low cut V-neck after five dresses.

The celebrities were seated up front, near Mr. Hope. But Nora, seated in coach with the girls could overhear some of their conversation.

Raquel Welch was sipping on a mimosa, "Barbara, when did you decide to join the tour?"

"Decide to join? I was thrilled to be asked, why?" she replied.

"Bob has been having some trouble in recent years getting performers to sign up. I mean, I knew I wanted to do it. He needed someone first rate to help make it "star quality," she explained.

Elaine Dunn piped in. "Mr. Hope has a deep respect for the men and women who serve. He's gone just about everywhere in the world during each war."

"Yes, that's true. But this war is different. Anti-war feelings are high. It's made him the target of a lot of criticism. He's just so pro-war," Raquel stated.

"I hope we don't get booed off the stage," Barbara expressed.

"No, way," assured Elaine. "Even if we do, we're performing for our boys. We're reminding them that we are one-hundred percent behind them. It's gonna be on TV, broadcast all over America on NBC. How could anyone look into the faces of those young men and not have some kind of sympathy."

"Yeah, Bob will carry it off like it's nothing. He probably already has his writers poking fun at the protestors," acknowledged Raquel. Barbara seemed satisfied with the confidence of Elaine and Raquel. She knew they had plenty of show biz experience under their belts.

Nora had heard much of the same. Nellie warned her that many considered him an enabler of the war and as such, part of the system that was responsible for the US involvement.

Peering out the windows of the plane, all Nora could see was water, water, everywhere. Deep, rich, navy blue. Raquel, Elaine, and Barbara each had on their eye covers and were falling asleep, their mimosas having taken effect. But Nora couldn't sleep. In the back of the plane were the band members, the hairdresser, the wardrobe woman, the camera and sound technicians, as well as her USO girls. There simply was just too much chatter. The sixteen hour flight was long, but her mind was full of anticipation regarding the adventure that was about to begin.

* * * * * *

Their first stop was Ubahn, Thailand at the Royal Thailand Air Base to perform for the 8th Tactical Fighter Wing. They were also to do a command performance at the Royal Palace for the King of Thailand. The stage was large and outdoors. The white backdrop had two sets of stairs leading up to it. Two large classic USO tour signs donned either side of the backdrop, classic with their bright red letters and royal blue borders with stars.

Les Brown and his band, about fourteen members, were seated center stage and remained such for the performance. Bob Hope was at his raucous best. He was dressed in a white golf shirt, with an Air Force baseball cap and carrying his classic wood tipped golf club. He never performed without it. The show lasted two and half hours. Nora got her girls ready in their outfits to sing and dance. She was not to perform in this one. Raquel was dressed in a light purple ball gown. She was breathtakingly gorgeous, with huge breasts and the widest, sweet smile.

Despite not being head liners of the show, the USO girls were nervous. But Nora calmed them down. She reminded them of why they were there. To bring those men a little bit of home.

From the corner of the stage, Nora could peek out. There were hundreds of men. Each and every one of them had the biggest smiles on their faces. So happy to just have a bit of Americana in front of them. Bob Hope knew how to entertain the troops. His jokes were pointed and clever, focusing on the tribulations they faced and making them poignantly sardonic.

Nora heard one of them. "Have you heard about those peaceniks burning draft cards? Well, they should come over here 'n Charlie'll burn em for em."

There were huge roars of laughter and applause. Mr. Hope sure had a knack for knowing what tugged at a GIs heart. So many young men. So far away from their families at Christmas time. It was tough to see.

The next stop was Udorn. Again, hundreds of men turned out to see the show. Today Mr. Hope was bedecked in fatigues. He brought out Miss World in her long, flowing yellow evening gown and false, long, black fall hairdo. They joked about her "vital statistics" being 35-26-35 and how she only weighed eight stones. Bob Hope could make a joke about anything. His wry wit brought joy to the troops.

"At home, everything's going up. Prices, taxes, and mini-skirts. But I'm sure you guys don't mind that" he quipped as the troop of USO dancers came out to go-go.

Danang was next. Nora wasn't quite ready for what she saw there. The massive expanse of the war became apparent, as their group arrived via Hueys. The stage was set below some large hilltops. Seas of green amassed the hillsides. Thousands and thousands of GIs had turned out. Some were atop the telephone poles, just to get a glimpse. It broke Nora's heart to see the fresh, young, youthful faces full of life in such a terrible place.

It was at Danang, performing for the Third Marines, that Nora was required to sing due to an unexpected highlight of the show. It seemed that the zipper of Elaine Dunn's one piece sequined bathing suit style costume had broken. What a site to see some awkward support officers attempting to reclose it on stage. As she went off, a signal was given to Nora.

Dressed in an orange mini-dress and white high heeled boots, Nora went on stage and sang what she knew best. Sinatra. Cheers and screams erupted from the crowd as Nora crooned out *These Boots were Made for Walking*. Nora bowed when she finished and was escorted off stage by a handsome young marine. As she exited, she got the highest compliment ever when Mr. Hope approached her.

"Girl. You gotta voice like spun sugar. Damn. You ought to tour with me more often."

Nora blushed and hurried back to the dressing room to help her girls change for the next numbers. The Christmas special was always filmed. Each and every show was shot by cameras at each base they stopped. But Nora was sure none of the non-famous performers would make it off the cutting room floor once it was edited. And she was right.

The tour itinerary was arduous. Twenty-two bases in fifteen days. They performed at Camp Bearcat, home to the 9th Infantry Division, 20 miles east of Saigon. Next was Pleiku, up in the hills only twenty-five miles from the front. To get there they had to fly in choppers only twelve feet from the ground to avoid sniper fire. At Pleiku, there had been so much loss of life, that a memorial had been erected. It read:

I cannot think of them as dead, who walk with me no more,
Along the path of life I tread, they have but gone before.

There was not a dry eye among the USO group. It was a somber sign of what they were amidst in this strange land. Some of it was tropical jungle. There were mountains. Other parts semi-arid hills.

Then, they arrived at Chu Lai. When driving in, they were warned about land mines. In jest, Bob Hope called it "the Malibu Beach for losers."

At Chu Lai, there were naval aviators, army, air force, seabees and marines. Bob joked, "At Chu Lai, as a GI you had your choice of five wars." He introduced sixty-nine year old navy Chief Stephen Cotellis, as "just about the oldest active duty officer aboard the *Coral Sea*."

Nora paid close attention to the surroundings at Chu Lai; for she knew she would be returning there for the duration of her eighteen months of service. The road leading to it was pretty barren, filled with lots of dust and sand. Razor edged curls of barbed-wire surrounded the perimeter. Stacks of ammo and bunkers lined the road. Raquel and Barbara wrapped scarves around their heads and faces not to choke on the dust from the convoy.

Raquel Welch seemed to be the favorite act. Her white sequined V-neck with purple sequined mini-skirt and knee high boots seemed to rock the crowds. That and the way her pelvis gyrated when she would dance on stage with several GIs. It was one of the highlights of the show.

Next was Li Che. Then Nakhon, a large air force squadron in secret near Laos. Bob quipped, "Nakhon - the only place where you can get your backside filled with lead and then be sent home as a classified incident."

During that performance, a disgruntled Private got the treat of a lifetime. It seemed he was asked to guard the ladies' dressing room, which was behind the stage. He put up a fuss to his Sergeant. "But I'm not gonna be able to see the show," he argued. "I've waited all year."

The Sergeant gave him a look which immediately put him in his place. He was under direct orders to keep any man from entering the dressing room. "It's an important job," the Sergeant barked. "It's an order."

While the show was going on, the Private was approached by several officers and press people begging to speak to one of the ladies. The Private stuck out his chest, raised his M-16 and cheekily responded, "Sir, my orders are to shoot to kill anyone with unauthorized entrance." Miffed, the officers backed down, not sure if the Private was serious.

During the performance, Miss World swished by in her beige, bejeweled gown and said, "Hello there." The Private blushed bright red. Then, Barbara McNair practiced her song right next to him. The Private was star struck, but kept his post. But the highlight was Raquel.

Stopping on the steps that lead to the stage, she leaned on the Private. "Sorry, darling. Help me out. I have to pull up these darn fishnets."

The young grunt nearly fainted. "Um. Certainly, Miss Welch." He could smell her Channel No. 5.

"How long have you been here honey?" she asked, raising her skirt up to her thigh and pulling on the hose.

"Nine months, Ma'am," he barely could get out.

"Well, be safe out there, okay?" she kissed him on the cheek.

Suddenly, the Private was the envy of every guy in his platoon. When the show ended, Mr. Hope and his entourage passed the Private's post. During one of the breaks, Nora told him of the kiss.

Mr. Hope extended his hand to the Private and said, "You're doing better with Raquel than I am." Laughing heartily, he moved on.

They were moments the Private would never forget. To be kissed by any beautiful woman was memorable, but by Raquel Welch? And not only that, but shaking Bob Hope's hand? It was beyond his wildest dreams.

The show and all its trappings were transported across the interior of Vietnam by choppers or a C-4. There where shows at Phukat and

SOLO VIETNAM

Phan Rang, which was one of their largest. Phan Rang, just inland of the coast of South Vietnam, was home to a large collection of Air Force Tactical Fighter Squadrons. Hundreds of F-100 Super Sabres and F-4 Phantoms lined the tarmac. Nora saw one of the largest bomber planes she had ever seen in the B-57s positioned there. South Vietnam was certainly not short of American air power.

At Cu Chi, they were held on the runway in their C-130 transport plane for a half hour as snipers took shots at them. The danger of performing in a war zone became apparently clear. Bullets could be heard pinging off the fuselage of the plane. Combat patrols were sent out to chase off the enemy. Next it was out to Yankee Station. The first ocean performance was aboard the USS Ranger.

It was a harrowing experience to land via arrestment on the deck of the huge carrier. The stage was set up on the flight deck. There were sailors everywhere. On every aspect of the bridge, atop helicopters, even sitting on top of planes. The white back drop of the stage was festooned with red and blue streamers. Mr. Hope brought irreverent hilarity to the crowds of seamen by playing the role of an apprentice sailor. He managed to make the troops laugh by poking fun at their everyday lives.

Next was the stop that Nora was waiting for, the *USS Coral Sea*. If she was going to see Steve, this would be her chance.

Chapter 20
∞ Yankee Station ∞

It was quite an ordeal for a turbo-prop plane to land on a carrier deck in an arresting gear. The carrier-on-demand, COD plane was approaching the *Coral Sea* in the late afternoon. For the Bob Hope entourage it was a hair-raising experience. But Nora was exhilarated. Even though it wasn't in a jet, she was getting to see what Steve did every day.

The huge ship was nothing more than a narrow strip of grey floating in a brilliantly blue sea. She couldn't imagine how the pilot could target the deck. There were shrieks of anxiety from the cabin as the plane got closer and closer. Seconds before it contacted the deck, Nora held on tightly to her armrests. Bam, they were down and had trapped in the gear.

As Nora disembarked, she was stunned at the sheer magnitude of the ship. There was a buzz of activity by the yellow shirted arresting crew and the green shirted ground crew. This was a special arrival to be sure.

Captain Sharcross and the Commanding Officers for each division formed a welcome reception line. Every sailor not on duty was out. Either on the deck or bridge, they cheered and shouted with glee at the special guests' arrival. After months without seeing many women, watching twenty pairs of bare legs and short skirts walking down a metal staircase from the plane was not a site to be missed.

Nora felt like a movie star as she shook hands with all of the smartly dressed officers. Now that she was off the plane, she could hear the whistles and cat-calls coming from the bridge.

"Hope you don't mind," said Commander Woolcock. "It's been quite some time since most of them have seen a woman. Much less women with such legs."

"No, sir. It's lovely." Nora responded shaking his hand. She noticed he had on aviator wings. She didn't know it, but he was actually the skipper of Steve's attack squadron.

Mr. Hope and the girls were shown to their berths where they could freshen up. Nora was surprised to see how small the quarters were. They would be spending the night onboard the ship. Within an hour, several of the USO girls had to be taken to the infirmary for sea sickness. Nora attended to them as they puked their guts up. "Come on girls. Mind over matter. Let's get it together. We have a show to put on," she encouraged. But it was clear, one or two, despite being medicated by the navy docs on board, were not going to perform this evening.

Nora couldn't keep focused on the performance. All she could think about was where Steve might be on-board this massive, floating city. At this point, he had no idea she was even aboard.

Because it was a night show, the stage had been moved into one of the large hangar decks for safety. Thousands of sailors sat in the darkened area to watch the performance. Red and white curtains streamers be-decked the stage at which 2500 enlisted and 400 officers tried to get a good view.

As the Les Brown band struck up the familiar opening bars, Bob Hope came out to a thunderous applause. He was wearing a yellow T-shirt which read *Hot Air Boss USS Coral Sea*, a black navy cap, and of course had his golf club. He called the *Coral Sea* "the 51st state of the union," as the crowd was so large.

Barbara McNair had a bout of laryngitis, which meant that Nora was called up to sing. She was the one person who not only could fit into Barbara's dress, but torch sing *For Once in my Life*. Nora quickly shimmied into the beautiful gown. The hairdresser coiffed up Nora's locks and applied extra eyeliner, false lashes and lipstick. Nora looked stunning; every bit the part of a star.

Steve had just gotten off duty and made his way down to the hangar deck. Logging flight data, he had missed the arrival of the VIPs. He sat with some other pilots on top of one of the stacks of ammo crates stored there. He noticed the familiar face of the helo pilot he had met.

"Hey, there Pete."

"Lt. Cmdr." Pete saluted. "Good to see ya."

Steve returned the salute, but then stuck out his hand for a shake. "Same. Damned glad I'm not on duty."

"No doubt" Pete smiled.

"Been waitin' to see the Bob Hope Christmas show since it was announced. I'm overdue for some diversion from the war."

"Yep. Pretty rare to get USO entertainment of this magnitude transported aboard a carrier."

As each number was performed, Steve remembered what it had been like to hear Nora sing. She had the velvety smooth voice of an angel. But he put those thoughts away, as they made him too melancholy. Steve and his shipmates laughed hard at Bob Hope's acerbic humor. It was the Christmas morale booster that they sorely needed after the recent death of Lt. Cook.

Raquel Welch was every bit as hot as he remembered, shaking her long, brown bouffant hair and hips. She was dressed in a multi-colored rainbow mini-dress and white go-go boots. The men loved it as she gyrated her pelvis with her trademark go-go dancing. Next was a soft shoe routine with Elaine Dunn and Bob himself. Then the announcer made an apologetic announcement about a substitute for Barbara McNair.

Steve nearly hit the floor when he heard the name of the next performer, Nora Jean Broussard. His eyes were mesmerized to the stage as drop dead gorgeous Nora took her place. She was dressed in a gold lame round necked gown with a copper lace overlay. She was a vision of loveliness to behold.

Once Nora was onstage, the bright lights made it impossible to see anyone in the audience. Cat-calls broke out as the Les Brown band began the opening bars of the tune. Nora reminded herself not to squint in the bright spot lights. Hearing her cue, she raised her mike began to belt out the tune. She only hoped that Steve saw her.

For once in my life I have someone who needs me
Someone I've needed so long
For once, unafraid, I can go where life leads me
And somehow I know I'll be strong

For once I can touch what my heart used to dream of
Long before I knew
Someone warm like you
Would make my dreams come true

With each word, Steve felt she was singing directly to him. His heart melted on the spot. He borrowed some binoculars from one of the pilots to get a better view. Yep, that was her alright; the pilot he had fallen in love with six years ago. His heart was beating so fast, he thought it would leap out of his chest.

"She's pretty good for a sub. Someone you know?" Pete questioned at the crazed look on Steve's face.

"Yeah. You could say that."

Steve catapulted off the crates and into the crowd below. He pushed and shoved his way forward to the edge of the stage, just as Nora finished up, took a bow and prepared to exit. There were enlisted guards at the edge of the stage, to keep the crowd controlled. One of them blocked the entrance to the backstage.

"Heya, Seaman. Lt. Commander Steve Novak, here." Steve had to think fast. He folded his program over to appear like a telegram. "I've just come from the bridge with an urgent classified message for one of the USO girls." The E-3 raised his eye brows, surveyed the gold oak leaf insignia on the collar of Steve's khakis, and reluctantly lowered his M-16 to let Steve through.

Since the show was in the hangar, the dressing rooms were ammo storage compartments and aircraft maintenance part areas that had been temporarily vacated. Steve frantically searched from door to door until he recognized the voice of his beloved Nora. He recognized that laugh anywhere. He knocked on the partially opened door.

"Come in," Nora's voice beckoned.

Steve slowly opened the door. Seeing a high ranking officer in uniform up close, the two younger girls assisting her were agog. Nora, left leg propped up on a chair, looked up from un-buttoning her fish net hose.

"Miss. I'd recognize that leg anywhere," Steve exuded.

"Oh my God. Steve!" Nora exclaimed. Then she caught herself. "I mean, Lt. Commander Novak." Nora lowered her shapely leg. She extended her hand. "So nice of you to drop by the show," she remarked coyly. She motioned to the girls. "Girls. See if you can help Ms. Welch get ready for her number. I'm fine."

Both girls left with the most sheepish looks on their faces. Nora knew she would have to explain later.

As soon as the door closed, Steve grabbed Nora around the waist and pulled her close. His lips sought hers hungrily for a long, ardent kiss. "Damn woman. I've wanted to do that for five years."

Nora melted into his body, returning his kiss and probing his mouth with her tongue. Their exchange was hot and passionate. Steve's hands ran down her spine and over her ass, pulling her pelvis into his groin. She could immediately feel his hard-on.

Steve kissed down her neck and cupped her left breast. "God, I've wanted you for so long," he moaned.

"Me too, baby. Me too," Nora whispered. They continued to embrace and just feel one another. The cataclysmic chemistry that they had shared five years before, even when Nora was nine months pregnant, was still there. It was like time had stood still.

Finally pulling away from each other, Steve was bewildered. "But how? How in the hell did you end up over here?"

Nora tossed her head back and laughed. "Well it wasn't easy."

"Nora. You crazy woman," Steve still couldn't believe he was with her in the middle of the South China Sea; in the middle of a war. "You must have gotten my letter."

"What letter?" Nora asked.

"I wrote you. Over a month ago. One night when I had a rough time on a mission," Steve remembered St. Elmo's fire. "Didn't you ever get it?"

"No. I'm sorry. I must have shipped out before it arrived."

"Oh, God. Nora. I . . . there's so much to talk about."

"I know. That's why I'm here."

"But you're on tour. I'm sure you all will be leaving in the morning," the thought downed his elation, like a kid whose Christmas toy was taken away.

"Just for a bit. I'm technically not with the tour. My assignment will be at the USO club in Chu Lai."

"Chu Lai? But that base was just under siege."

"I know. That's why they are without a manager for the club. And you are looking at the new one." She gave him one of her characteristic brow poses.

"Oh my God, this is just so much to take in," Steve ran his hands through his short cropped hair. Nora thought he was dreamy in his uniform.

There was a knock on the door. "Miss Broussard. The girls need you for the next number."

"Steve. Stay here. I'll be back in a few minutes. Please?"

Steve debated whether he should risk being caught in what was to be a secured area. But only for a moment. He wasn't going anywhere. To hell with protocol.

The show wrapped up and Steve could hear the thunderous applause. As they did for every show, the cast began to sing *Silent Night*. It was very moving to hear 3000 sailors sing the verses of the famous Christmas spiritual. It nearly brought tears to his eyes. What a Christmas. Nora, onboard the *Coral Sea*.

In a few minutes, she returned. She had told her girls that they were on their own, that she had a special guest. They had such profound respect for Nora and all that she had done for them, they didn't rat her out.

The minute she closed the door, Steve wrapped his arms around her, kissing her ardently. Their tongues intertwined like serpents in heat. All the chemistry they had once shared was set aflame. Steve kissed her slowly down her neck, kiss by kiss, setting Nora on fire. She ran her hands up his back and pulled his head towards her breasts. The rounded neck of her evening gown prevented him from kissing further, but he cupped her breasts with his hands, remembering their shape and wanting so much more.

"Gawd, Nora, I've fought this for so long," he uttered.

"I know. Me too," she massaged his head against her bosom, holding him close.

"I love you so much, despite everything. I've never stopped," he gushed.

"I love you too, Steve. Desperately."

They briefly pulled apart, gazing into each other's eyes. Her huge brown eyes were pools of deep understanding. Each was awed by the power as they saw into each other's souls.

"We can't get by with much else, here," Steve pointed out.

"I figured as much. God knows where our quarters are on this huge boat," Nora wondered.

"I can't risk getting caught in a forbidden area," he explained.

Nora pulled a small bottle of whiskey from her bag and poured them a drink in the plastic cups that had been provided. She raised her glass to him. "To past and future encounters," she toasted.

"Especially future," he joined her.

"I'm going to be stationed at club for quite some time," she began to tell him.

"Oh yeah?" he asked incredulously.

"I've signed up. To serve for eighteen months."

"Holy shit. Nora, that's insane. The war on the ground is a helluva lot different than from the air. It's barbaric down there."

"I know the risks," she hesitated and looked at him intently. "But I had to do it. To get over here. To see you."

He took her back into his arms. "You crazy woman. But why?"

"You know why. I heard about Marci. You were over here, alone."

"Alone with thousands of other sailors," he cracked a smile.

"You know what I mean. I had to see you."

"To see if it was still real," he continued for her.

"Yes," she acknowledged.

"Does this answer your question?" he lowered his head to kiss her again. He was powerless in her presence. All the decorum and discipline he lived as an officer flew out the window. He again tasted her with his tongue. Steve sucked her lower lip with his kisses. Their mouths melded. He pressed himself up against her. Reaching around her he lifted the long flowing skirt and ran his hands up her inner thigh. She moaned as he cupped her mound and slipped his fingers inside her. "Baby, I want you so much," he nuzzled his face into her neck.

"I want you too, Steve." She kissed his head and held him there as he touched her. His deft movements sent her into an ecstasy she had not felt in years. She wanted so much more than his fingers inside her.

There was a rap on the door. "Two minutes for escort to the bridge. Two minutes 'til Hope."

"Steve. I have to get ready," she pulled away from him. "Mr. Hope walks us all to meet the CO."

"When can I see you?" he questioned. "How?"
She scribbled the FPO address the USO had given her for the club. "I'll be finishing up the Christmas tour on December 31st. Then, they'll fly me and the girls to Chu Lai. Maybe you can get some R and R?"

"Or if I'm lucky, get bingoed off before. It was wonderful to see you, again Nora."

"For me too. Here. A New Orleans tradition. Merry Christmas, darling," she handed him the small bottle of Southern Comfort. "Even if it is a few days before."

"Close enough for me. Merry Christmas," he smiled. He was going to enjoy something that wasn't Scotch, the drink of navy pilots.

She checked her hair in the mirror and applied a dash of lipstick before waving goodbye. He sat in awe in the small ammo room, still stunned at what had just happened. He heard her high heels clicking down the metal of the floor as she dashed for the stage.

Drinking while on Yankee Station wasn't allowed. That was the official word. So the whiskey they just downed was sweet relief from the stress he had been under. Steve poured another small swig and tucked the bottle away under his bomber jacket. In reality, most of the officers had a bottle of Scotch or whatever locked away in their stateroom safe. Drinking was only done after flight ops and then only sparingly. He had no idea when or how he was going to see Nora again. But he knew that somehow, some way, he would.

Chapter 21

The next morning, after breakfast with the sailors, the USO troop visited the on-board hospital. As a bit of a prank organized by the navy docs, the girls were told to hop in bed and cuddle some patients who had recently had surgery. There was a big push going to have all men onboard circumcised. Unfortunately for these poor sailors, it must have been a painful experience. Mr. Hope seemed to get just as tickled about it as the navy docs did.

Nora didn't take place in that bit of revelry. She was too busy scanning the onlookers that had gathered on the flight deck and bridge to see if she saw Steve. But, to no avail. Unbeknownst to her, Steve was again on duty. After the hospital visit, it was time for the USO troop to depart.

Steve took a break and watched from his post high atop primary flight control of the carrier as the USO troop boarded the C-2A Greyhound. His thoughts were on nothing but Nora, and how he might get to see her again. As they each climbed the ramp to enter the rear of the plane, they turned and waved good-bye, including Nora. Her normally huge smile was smaller this day, knowing that somewhere among the scads of khaki clad officers and blue shirted navy personnel was Steve. She looked radiant in a red mini-shirt, black high heeled patent leather boots and V-neck sweater.

The C-2A was towed to the catapult and loaded. Engines whirred on the propellers and in seconds they were launched out over the deep blue ocean into clear, aquamarine skies. Nora felt her insides wrench and her back was jammed against the seat from the force of the catapult launch. It was like no amusement park ride she had ever experienced. She wondered what it would feel like to be in a jet, like Steve flew, going twice the speed and was jealous.

The next stop was Cam Rahn Bay, where 27,000 GI's from the 1st Logistical Command turned out for the performance. Cam Rahn Bay was probably the most desolate base they had seen. Acres and acres of sand.

Hope came out onto the outdoor stage wearing jungle fatigues which had every medal awarded for every conflict that the U.S. military forces have been in dangling from this jacket. There must have been hundreds of them. He thanked the thousands for turning out and joked that Cam Rahn Bay was nothing more than "a zillion dollar cat box" to howls of laughter.

Raquel and Hope took a piss out of Bob's age by doing a mixed rendition of a soft shoe with intermittent spurts of go-go dancing. The GI's loved it. As he always did, Mr. Hope brought some GI's up on stage to meet Raquel. They danced the latest dance craze, the twist. She was always the highlight of the show.

Near the end, he brought on stage a twenty-three year old Sergeant, who was out-processing from Vietnam at Cam Rahn Bay on his way to ETS, expiration of term of service, with the army at Fort Lewis, Washington. He was completing an eleven month tour of duty and had heard that Bob Hope would be coming. Winning a hand in poker, he got the privilege to see the show near the front row.

Mr. Hope called him up on stage. "I want to thank you son, for your service to your country. Here's a little Christmas gift for ya." Raquel Welch came over and kissed him on the lips. Mr. Hope said, "That was a little gift from your fiancé that you're gonna see in two days." The crowd erupted in cheers. Then, he turned to the thousands sitting on the sand dunes. "Have a Merry Christmas and God Bless you all!"

Hope's hawkish stance on the war brought its own controversy in the growing discontent back home over the war. But attending one of the Christmas tour performances, you would never know it. Nora could see that without a doubt, his visits boosted morale to the lonely servicemen fighting a difficult war in a strange and hostile land. Just one look at any of the soldier's faces revealed that.

Nora and her girl's time with the USO tour ended. As Hope and his starlets prepared to return to Thailand to close the show at Korat, she and the girls were loaded onto a military C-117 plane headed for Chu Lai. The plane, used for night flare drops when not for transport, was delivering cargo. The C-117 was a converted C-47 with longer wings, bigger engines, and a stretched fuselage. During her first weeks in Vietnam, Nora saw more types of military aircraft than she knew existed.

On the way to Chu Lai, the plane made at stop at Danang. It was during the first days of the Tet Offensive. Multiple airstrikes were being run. Planes were taking off continuously to the north from the seaward runway and also from the south from the landward runway. Crazy air traffic patterns. There was no way for the pilots to make a radio call to land, as the strikes were being run on tower frequency. Instead of feeling the plane descend, Nora felt the plane gain elevation as it was denied clearance to land. The C-117 should have just continued to circle around awaiting clearance. But suddenly, the plane plummeted, as the pilot just cut into the flight pattern and landed without clearance from the tower. Nora had never experienced the bedlam of air activity that was characteristic of Danang.

While the plane was being unloaded, Nora got up to take a look at the airfield from the small round windows aft. She could see a C-123 unloading casualties having been removed from the northern part of the battles at I Corps. There must have been seventy casualties, some carried on stretchers. Most were covered with white bandages, some missing limbs. Some were ambulatory. Suddenly, Nora was filled with fear at the stark reality of war. Momentarily, she questioned what she had done in deciding to come to a war zone.

Nora thought she would get some fresh air as the doors of the C-117 opened, but the heat from inside the aircraft, which was not air-conditioned when stationary, was augmented by the jet blast of Phantoms and A-6 Intruders taxiing into and out of the flight line. Their spray blowing through the opening, added another thirty or forty degrees and deafened the passengers within.

Within minutes, just before the doors to the C-117 were closed and she was instructed to return to her bench seat, a group of rowdy marines were boarded. "Hey asshole, get that motherfucking bag outta my way," one grunted to the other.

"Fuck you, cocksucker. I was here first. You want it moved, move it yourself sonofabitch," the other marine replied back.

The girl's eyes were big as saucers. You could smell the war on their greased, dirty bodies.

"Just smile, girls. Just smile." Nora motioned to the girls to move down on the bench. "Let's get everyone buckled in safely." She made sure the girls had their harness straps attached securely as they prepared to take-off.

Taking her seat, she could feel the power of the engines rev up as the aircraft taxied down the crowded runway. It frustrated her that she could not see much out of the few tiny windows. Air travel by basic military standard, without the VIP trappings of the Bob Hope entourage, was a metaphor for how their USO experience would shift. It was back to reality.

On the short forty-three mile flight south, she caught glimpses of the yellow-beige sandy beaches along the coast and the coastal planes inland. The ground was torn up from various combat actions. Flying at barely 1500 feet, it was possible to see both jet aircraft and helicopters flying to and from targets possibly attacking them. She could also see some details of the villages, roads and small Vietnamese fishing boats along the shore.

Chu Lai stood out from the surrounding green mountains and yellow fields by its color. It looked like a big sand box. There were tin roofed, brown buildings scattered in clusters along the main concrete runway that ran parallel to the coast. A matting runway ran crosswind and perpendicular to the main one. Beyond the airstrip, there were some more tropically forested mountains. Nora saw some black smoke rising from some structures.

One of the marines noticed the smoke and said, "They got the shitters burning."

It took a minute for Nora to understand that he was referring to the latrines. As they landed, Nora noticed the hangers and metal roof revetments for the Phantoms and Skyhawks. There were some remains of several cannibalized planes, their parts burned and broken with sand dunes built up near their broken fuselages.

Once the plane landed, the duty NCO radioed for a jeep. While they were waiting, Nora watched the flight operations. There was a plane taking off or landing every ten or fifteen seconds. All were totally loaded with ordnance. Interspersed in the fighter jet patterns were an occasional C-1A aircraft or C-46. It was frenetic and chaotic. Nora had no idea how the tower could control all of the aircraft taking off from just a couple of small runways.

Nora and the girls unloaded their personal baggage and were taken by jeep to their hooch. One hangar they passed had just been hit by a bomb during the ongoing Tet. Its roof was hanging down in the back and it was barely protecting the A-4s within.

The USO quarters consisted of a Quonset hut built up on stilts. It looked bizarre elevated eight feet above the sand.

Pilar, one of the girls, made the remark, "That's weird. It's up in the air."

"I hope it isn't for the same reason that New Orleans homes are elevated," Nora raised her eyebrows.

"It floods Ma'am. During the monsoon season," the driver answered.

"Lovely, just like home," Nora smirked. Even though it was January, it was a hot and sticky eighty-five degrees. Nora noticed that several of the girls were perspiring. But it was not unlike the weather Nora was used too.

Chu-Lai was home to over eighty A-4 Skyhawks flown by the marines, as well as three F-4 Phantom units. In addition, there were naval supply units and infantry from the 23rd Americal Division. Fatigues, fatigues everywhere the eye could see. Very few women were housed at Chu Lai. Dressed in their short skirts, as directed by the USO standards, they felt bizarrely out of place.

The hooch was sparsely furnished. There was a row of cots and some stacks of open cubbies. There was single, silver rack like from a dress shop, shoved against a wall. Nora guessed correctly that was to be their closet. Upon seeing the interior of the hut, two of the girls burst into tears. The trip had been arduous. Coming off the high of flying around with celebrities, the harsh surroundings of a real USO assignment during the middle of a war became apparent.

As Pilar sat down on one of the cots, she began to cry. "That'll be enough of that. No tears, remember?" Nora fussed at the girls, reminding them that the men were never to see them cry.

She assigned each one of them a cot and a cubby. She took the one nearest the door. There was a desk and chair near it and she felt she was somehow protecting the girls by positioning herself between them and the door. A few of the girls collapsed on the cots for a nap. Nora hadn't slept in about twenty hours and was running on reserve energy. But she was buzzed with anticipation at seeing the club. Quickly unpacking her things, she freshened up her makeup and made her way across the sandy walk to the entrance of the club.

The USO club was a double sided blue-grey shack with a white roof. A white traditional USO sign with red letters, blue edges and white stars was mounted and propped on the tin roof. The structure had a breezeway that looked out onto Chu Lai beach. The light beige-white sands of the beach were gorgeous. There was a volleyball net set up. The azure blue of the water was simply exquisite. Nora had never seen anything quite that color. One side was the bar and the other, a café of sorts, with tables and chairs. It was an unranked club, meaning that both officers and enlisted could hang out together. Several marines were playing cards and dominoes on the bar side. All heads turned as Nora appeared in the doorway, several of the guys started whistling and winking.

"That's enough," one of the marine aviators called out. "Sorry about that. They don't get to see many pairs of legs in skirts."

"I get it," Nora smiled. "Hello there," she said sticking out her hand. "I'm Nora Broussard, from the USO. I'll be the new manager of the club."

"Nice to meet you, Ms. Broussard. You'll have your work cut out for you here," the pilot chuckled. "We're a rogue, mixed group of war fatigued hooligans."

"I see," Nora looked around. There were pinups of the latest topless tarts from Playboy. Some of the furniture looked pretty beat up. The bar was made out of bamboo. There was a cracked Budweiser mirror with neon behind it hanging from the wall. Nora had her work cut out for her.

"Where might I find the Duty Officer?" Nora asked.

"That would be Lt. Commander Watson. He's in the SDO office across the yard," the pilot explained.

"Thank you," Nora turned to exit and walk over.

"No, no, Miss. I'll get someone to drive you over. With Tet going on, there's snipers everywhere."

"Tet?" Nora asked.

"Yep, the Tet Offensive. The Viet Cong are attacking like crazy. Happens every January, but this year's worse than ever. You'd risk getting shot on your first day walking over."

Nora shuddered for a moment. Shot. By gunfire. It was worse than she thought. How would she ever keep her young entourage safe? The pilot motioned for a jeep nearby. A young marine in fatigues helped her up and into the seat and handed her a green metal helmet to wear. Good Lord, she mused. And this was day one.

The Operations Duty Officer was located in another Southeast Asia hut with a metal roof, open at the sides and screened with windows. There were four desks inside. It was stifling hot. The officer, seated at one of the desks, looked up.

"Ah, the USO has arrived. Great news, great news," he rose and went over to a rusted out filing cabinet. He pulled out some papers. "Here's the specs on the club. You've got a cook and cleaner. Local folks from the village. They know how to make some American stuff, but not much. You'll need some girls to run the bar, wait tables. You'll be responsible for picking up the locals' pay in this office and booking entertainment. I'll send the requests I get from singers, bands, and acts as I get them over to you. That's about it. We're glad you're finally here. The club's been a mess since the previous manager bailed."

"My name is Nora. Nora Broussard. Nice to meet you?" Nora said shaking her head.

"Sorry Ma'am. Forgot my manners. You tend to do that with the muck we deal with every day." He took a drag from the cigar he was smoking. He looked far too young to be smoking a stogie. "I'm Bill. Have any trouble? Just talk to me. Overseeing the ops of the club is just one of my hundred duties, but I'll try to help you out."

"Where do we get and receive mail?" Nora thought to ask.

"Mail call. It's about once a week or whenever it gets delivered. You'll hear it called out."

"I see. Well, thank you Lt. Commander Watson," she started out formally. He raised his head up. "I mean, Bill," she continued. "I'm sure we'll figure it all out."

"Yes, Ma'am," he turned to the radio mike and barked out some orders.

Exhausted, Nora returned to her hooch. Time to try and get something to eat and rest before the evening shift. As they were leaving, she noticed the sign, mounted near the main gate. It read, *Curfew 2000 to 0600 hours until further notice.*

"Do they really stick to that? Curfew at eight PM?" Nora asked her driver.

"Yes, Ma'am. Snipers."

"That will certainly make for some early evenings at the club." Nora thought of her long shifts until 2:00 AM at the Roosevelt.

"Yep. We gotta get her done. Then, it's back to the hooch until morning," her driver remarked nonchalantly.

Nora, as manager of the club, was given the ranking of GS-10 or Captain. She asked the driver where the Officer's mess was, but it was suffocating hot and she was being devoured by mosquitoes. Soaking with sweat and covered in a fine red dust from the roads of the base, she decided to forgo food for the moment.

Arriving at her hut, she laid down on the cot. The girls had made the beds with the sheets and blankets they had been given. The blankets were more to fend off the rats, bugs and mosquitoes more than for warmth. Nora tried to fall asleep to the sound of afterburners.

Chapter 22
∞ Chu Lai, South Vietnam ∞

A few hours later, Nora awoke just as the sun was setting. She couldn't tell any difference in the flight operations from earlier in the day. They never seemed to stop. Determined to rid herself temporarily from the sand grit caked to her body, she took a shower from the rigged water collection tank that had water piped down a tube and into the small bathroom. The latrine had the waste syphoned down into a common septic tank. It felt good, even with cool, barely tepid water heated from the sun, to wash off the grime of the base.

After she finished, Nora woke up the girls and instructed them to get ready. They would go to the Officer's mess together. Work would begin in the morning. The officers had built a grass-roofed, tile floored mess and club that looked like a large Vietnamese hut. It was less than a hundred yards from the South China Sea and had an uncovered veranda where you could sit and look out over the water. The marine engineers had taken the advice of the Vietnamese and thatched the roof, to keep out the rain.

The mess was filled with pilots who talked shop about the missions they had flown. Nora couldn't completely understand all of their jargon. She caught wind of a story they were telling.

"Dude, I'm tellin' ya. He was fully loaded with no airspeed at fucking midfield."

"Naw, seriously?" questioned another pilot.

"Shit, ya. Aborted his take-off. Couldn't slow the freaking Skyhawk enough with the brakes. Missed every damned arresting gear."

"Christ almighty."

"Yep. Ejected into the exploding plane, man."

Although the pilot had ejected, the plane left the overrun and he died in the explosion that followed. Nora noticed that they talked about the incident, but curiously never mentioned the pilot by name.

It was difficult to hear the GIs talking about so much death. She realized she was in a war zone, but just wasn't used to hearing it.

Nora had never eaten military rations. Most of the food tasted bland, compared to the spice of New Orleans to which she was accustomed. Some of the girls didn't want to eat, but Nora encouraged them. They needed their energy to get to work on the club in the morning. After putting up her plate on the tray line, Nora went out to the veranda.

"Look at the color of the water," remarked Pilar.

"At least we have that," said Marsha one of the older girls.

"Do we get to swim, Mrs. Broussard?"

"That's Captain Broussard," Marsha corrected. Nora still wasn't used to being called by her rank.

"Righto. Captain Broussard. Do we get to?"

"I'm sure when you have time off. It's at your own risk. I mean, there are some lifeguards on duty." Nora was pleased that they were looking on a brighter side of things. Seeing the beach that they would be responsible for, they were in better spirits.

Nora made out a duty roster on a legal pad. There were already two girls who wanted to go home. If the girls left their post before their contract was up, they were required to pay their airfare back to the states.

There was so much to learn. The club was decent enough, but had really deteriorated with no management. Nora's first job would be to meet with the Supply Duty Officer, the SDO, and learn how provisions for the club were ordered and obtained. She thought she would never figure out all of the military jargon. There were abbreviations for everything.

Following the task list given to her from Operations, she went through the papers submitted by local acts wishing to perform. Some of them sounded pretty lame, but she was reminded that without them, the men would have next to nothing. The one thing the club did have was an old juke box.

Feeling she had worked enough for one day, Nora took out her pen and the stationary she had packed and wrote a letter home.

Dear Mom, Cathy, Leisel and Iggy:
We arrived safely at Chu Lai today. The club is nice enough and set alongside a pretty beach. The water of the South China Sea is an amazing color blue. I am living in a hut with the girls. It is elevated like the homes along the Biloxi coast, to pre-

> vent flooding. Right now, it is not too hot in January, but I understand that will change.
>
> There are planes that take off and land here at all times of the night. I sure wish I was flying, instead of singing. I enjoyed my time with Bob Hope. A couple of times, I actually got to sing when one of the leads had laryngitis. On another occasion, one had some food poisoning and felt ill.
>
> I sure miss our New Orleans seafood. There's lots of fish here, but they sure don't fix it like we do. I miss you all so much. I carry you around with me in my heart. Be sure to write. Especially if you hear from Kayce.
>
> All my love,
> Mom
> P.S. Please send some Community Coffee ASAP

Next, she decided to pen a note to Steve. She wasn't sure he would get it, but thought she would try. Letter writing was just about the only form of communication possible.

> *My dearest Steve:*
> *Seeing you again has filled my heart with joy. All the love I felt for you has returned. Seeing you just once, served only to fuel the desire to spend more time with you. I pray that you are safe on your missions. Please know that I think of you every moment of every day. Just one touch was all it took to bring it all back. Be well, my love.*
> *Nora*

Returning to the hut before curfew, Nora showed the girls how the make-shift shower worked. Donna, one of the younger girls tried to get a signal of any kind on her transistor radio. Stephanie and Maria lay down on the cots to read. Joan and Pilar did each other's nails. Marsha appeared to be the most self-actualized and mature of the group. She might have assistant manager potential, Nora thought. Their emotions had settled down. Nora hoped that some good old fashioned work at the club would keep their doubting minds occupied. Day one. It was going to be a long eighteen months. Holy moly. Eighteen months.

SOLO VIETNAM

Chapter 23
∞ January, 1968 Yankee Station ∞

After having spent Christmas day in port at Hong Kong, the *Coral Sea* departed once again to Yankee Station. Early missions in January involved numerous strikes on significant military targets of the N. Vietnamese. Successions of railway and highway bridges connecting Haiphong with the mainland were destroyed.

The Tet offensive was in full swing. During one of Steve's preplanned missions, he and his wingman got word from Red Crown to divert on emergency to cover a Rescap of a downed pilot in the Ashau Valley. Steve switched frequency to get on with Rescap and heard them talking about the downed scooter, a plane from VMA 311 at Chu Lai. The pilot, who was alive, could be seen in a meadow near his chute. At the moment, no rescue aircraft or controller was available.

"Blue Tails, we gotta pilot down. He's on the Laotian side of Ashau Valley. Look for a clearing near the Ho Chi Minh trail. Over."

"Blue Tail 224, roger that." Steve flew just east of the mountains west of Danang and switched to Red Crown, the airborne rescue coordinator who flew into the area of downed aircraft and coordinated Rescap.

Steve could tell things were not going well, as they heard aircraft rolling in on the flak suppression.

"This is Blue Tail 331. We're getting heavy ground fire here. Difficult to get to target," the pilot called to Red Crown.

"Roger, Blue Tail. Do what you can."

"Holy shit, we gotta jolly green going down," the pilot called to the controller.

A jolly green giant rescue helicopter was in the process of being shot down and crashed into the ground, taking all of its crew with it, as Steve and his wingman approached. A second Jolly green was orbiting

-- 101 --

five miles west of the downed pilot, and reported the downed chopper and heavy ground fire.

Steve and his wingman split up, so that they could each analyze the site. Dropping back, Steve looked down to see if he could tell where the pilot was and where the ground fire was coming from. The rescue helo needed a place to land.

The pilot was in a clearing above a road that led to the Ho Chi Minh trail to the floor of the valley. Steve could see his parachute in the middle of the clearing, about twenty yards from the tree line. The jolly green was orbiting in Laos and ground fire was being shot at him from every direction.

Red Crown was trying to coordinate aircraft that could suppress the anti-aircraft artillery. "Blue tails. Vector 180 over. Do what you can."

Steve thought it would take a massive effort to clear what he could see. As he orbited at 10,000 feet, two Air Force Phantoms rolled in and dropped west of the parachute and the Jolly green. Dropping ordnance, they didn't even dent the amount of ground fire. There were also some big guns being fired, typical of the N. Vietnamese. There had to be thousands of troops in the area to be launching that much anti-aircraft. The jolly green pulled up and out, not able to sustain his position.

The lead and Steve rolled in to do what they could. The lead dropped his load of Zuni five inch rockets into the overall pattern of flashes that were covering the ground. Steve salvoed his just to the right, running south. Steve skimmed the ground, just above the valley floor at more than 500 knots and unloaded the rest. Steve saw his lead above him six or eight thousand feet and pulled into a steep climb, joining up over the mountains. Clearing the area, they flew straight out to sea and then up the coast toward the carrier. As they did so, they heard the Rescap being terminated.

"Mission aborted. Repeat. Mission aborted." The pilot had no chance of being rescued from the time he was shot down.

After trapping, Steve inspected the plane, sure he would find holes somewhere, but was surprised that he didn't. "How is it we were able to fly through so much triple A at the altitudes we were at and not get hit?" Steve asked his passing wingman.

"I dunno, man. I dunno. Lucky I guess," he remarked heading for the ready room. "Say, we just made it back in time for the movie."

It was Steve's birthday. But there was no recognition of it. He joined the pilot in the ready room for the nightly 7:00 PM movie. Tonight was *The Graduate*. As Steve sat there, watching sexy Ann

Bancroft, he thought of Nora. She occupied much of his mind. He hoped she was safe with South Vietnam under siege.

CVW-15, which included VA-153, carried out more strikes against the Dong Phong Thuong railway and highway bridges. A significant change to the war came on January 20th. N. Vietnamese troops, who had been missing near the 17th parallel in South Laos, infiltrated the I Corps area south of the DMZ under cover of the monsoon rains. N. Vietnam army forces overran the Lang Vei special forces camp and laid siege to Khe Sanh taking control of the main infiltration route, Highway Nine in I Corps.

Missions for CVW-15 were designed to attack artillery positions, supply routes and troop concentrations in Laos and the western I Corps area. Sometimes these attacks were while friendly forces were entrenched within the Khe Sanh perimeter, making it difficult to protect their own, while fighting off the Viet Cong. Such were the frustrations of the air war pilots. They wanted to take out the air bases of MiG's which they flew over constantly.

On Jan 25th, SAMs downed Commander Thomas Woolcock of VA-153. He had been flying a strike against a N. Vietnamese coastal defense site that had taken the Australian guided missile destroyer *HMAS Perth* under fire. Woolcock ejected safely and was recovered off the enemy shore by helicopter. Lt. Myers, his plane damaged by the same exploding SAM that claimed Woolcock's, managed to nurse his crippled bird back to the deck of the *Coral Sea*. He re-fueled continuously by a KA-3B tanker from VAH-10 and executed a barricade arrestment, emerging from the plane unhurt.

As the Tet offensive continued, the burden of the air war fell upon the navy's shoulders, since many air force and marine corps units were disabled from mortar attacks on key air fields. Carrier sorties were diverted to targets in South Vietnam and Laos, closing in on the support line of the Third Marine Division forces in Operation Niagra, a counter offensive aimed at the major infiltration routes of the Laotian border.

Several weeks later, intelligence reports revealed that a second Jolly green and crew had landed in a mine field near Khe Sanh. The pilot was listed as MIA, one of a number of pilots shot down over or near Laos that were never heard from again after being captured.

Chapter 24
∞ Chu Lai ∞

New Year's at the USO club at Chu Lai came and went. Nora did her best to make do with the scant decorations. The club still had a small artificial Christmas tree up and some multi-colored lights. It was bittersweet for most, being away from home. Nora and some of the USO girls had attended a multi-denominational Christmas service at the base chapel. The holidays for Nora, being abroad, were lack-luster. Getting to know the ropes of just how things worked on the base was her main objective.

New Year's eve at the club had been more raucous. Everyone that wasn't on duty was at the club. It was packed. The girls were all on duty as GIs waited for the cue to kiss on the stroke of midnight after *Auld Lang Syn*e. Nora realized it didn't take much to arrange a party. There was a desperate need for escape from the realities of war.

On January 31st, Nora and the girls were roused out of their sleep by the sound of mortar attack. The North Vietnamese were bombing Chu Lai. Air raid sirens were going off. At first Nora wasn't sure what to do. Running for a bunker, they would be targets for snipers.

"Get under the beds. Under the beds, now!" she commanded them. Several of the girls were hysterical and Nora tried to calm them down.

The deafening sound of incoming rockets shook the hut. Two pilots from VMA-311 were injured near the flight line and four of that squadron's A-4s were taken out, as well as part of the bomb dump. Loud explosions could be heard which shook the buildings of the base as the bomb dump exploded.

The attack was severe. The Tet offensive was in full swing. It was almost more than Nora could take. After the initial barrage, there were a few more isolated rockets and mortars. The crackle of gunfire pierced through the dark of night.

"Holy shit. What in the world?" Nora shouted.

"We're going to die. Right here," one of the girls shrieked.

SOLO VIETNAM

"Stop it. Just stay quiet and under the beds. We are going to be fine."

"Yes, Captain Broussard," several of the girls answered obediently.

The blasts shook them to the bones. She and the girls cowered under their bunks; holding hands until the last of the in-coming mortar ceased. After it was finally over, they climbed back into their beds. Several of them slept together in the same bunks.

In the morning, there was rising black, oily smoke everywhere. Fires where all around. Emergency vehicles were screaming across the dusty roads taking casualties to one of the field hospitals. One of the young officers, who had not kept his head down during the attacks, had been shot in the throat from the top of the building he lived in. Several marines had been struck by the exploding rockets while attempting to save the large trucks loaded with US rockets.

Just having begun to serve at USO Chu Lai, the attack nearly did Nora and girls in. But they woke, dusted off and began their jobs as if nothing had happened, albeit a little more quiet than usual. Nora warned the girls to stay away from the barbed wire perimeters of the base. There were nearby villages which appeared peaceful enough, but the Operations Officer had told her that many times snipers took shots at passersby. The worst of these villages was one that the marines called Dog Patch.

Nora was sure it was delusional, but somehow, inside the USO club and so close to the beach, she felt safe. All the men seemed relaxed and at ease there, hearing the sounds of music from home, downing some liquid refreshment and dancing with some of the girls from the club. When the club was open, it was almost never empty.

The girls had worked hard to repaint the interior, hanging some lanterns that several marines had commandeered while on R and R. They polished the tables and repaired the legs on the chairs. Nora revamped the menu based on what she could obtain from the NASU. Several cooking classes were held with the Vietnamese cook, nicknamed "Peanuts." He got the name from the peanuts he craved and bought from soldiers.

On a rainy Thursday, Nora finally got the mail she had been hoping for, a letter from Steve. Finishing her work at the club, she took a stroll out to beach to read the letter in private.

> *My love, my one and only, Nora:*
> *My focus on my mission here has been completely fragmented. It's hard to focus on conquering the enemy, when all I can think about is how I'd love to bail somewhere, just to see you. The*

few glorious moments we had onboard have rocked my world. I knew in my heart, that destiny would somehow win the day. You looked as gorgeous as ever. Voice like velvet, just like I remember. I'll never forget this Christmas. You were the best present a guy could hope for. I don't know when I can see you again. Our cruise is coming to an end. We are due to ship out for home in March. And you will be stuck in the country I can't wait to leave. What a fuck up! Just know, I will do anything in my power to get to Chu Lai, at least once before I go. God speed, my aviator angel.
Love, Steve

Nora read and re-read his note to her again and again. It was ridiculous. Here she was in Vietnam for eighteen months. And in three, Steve was going home. Now that she was here, however, she felt she had a purpose. She knew she was making a difference. That effect on her was profound.

Tucking the letter in the pocket of her scooter skirt, Nora walked over the plank bridge from the beach to the club to begin another shift. There was a larger crowd than usual. One of the girls had a gotten a spider bite which abscessed and was sent to *USS Providence* hospital ship for IV antibiotics. So, Nora was waiting tables.

A local Vietnamese band with singers was performing on the outdoor "stage" which was no more than a wooden porch which faced the beach. They were attempting some renditions of Beatles tunes, but they really weren't very good. The guys didn't mind however, as some of the dancers wore no more than sequined bikini's. Thin and almost flat without much for breasts, the guys didn't care. The girls could still shake their asses and turn them on.

As Nora brought a round of drinks to one of the tables, she noticed an officer seated at a table by himself. He was one of the marine aviators. "Hey there, buddy. You look like you could use someone to talk to."

The pilot looked up at her with sadness in his eyes. "Is it that bad?"

Nora sat down beside him and introduced herself. They exchanged some small talk about what he flew. As soon as Nora heard it was the Skyhawk, she wanted to know more. She brought the Captain a Budweiser on the house.

Captain Robert Lathrop was married and a pilot from Washington State. He was a forester by trade. He'd been in Vietnam only for a couple of weeks, but already looked battle weary. He explained that he hadn't gotten much sleep. Due to Tet, he'd flown continuous missions, both day and night for days. He had just lost a buddy in the recent bombing raid, the mechanic for his plane. In addition to his flight duties, Robert was assigned the additional duty of being base intelligence officer.

"No wonder you're tired. Good God, isn't flying enough?" Nora asked incredulously.

"Not for jarhead flyboys. But it's not too bad. No one else wanted the job."

"What's a jarhead?" Nora asked curiously.

"Slang, my dear. It means we have a propensity to follow orders. No matter what. Regardless of the consequences or our safety. Duty before yourself."

"I see," Nora continued to chat. "I learn some new term every day, here."

"You'll get the hang of it soon. Doesn't take long. Some people think jarhead means hard on the outside and empty on the inside. But that's a bunch of baloney. Ya gotta love what ya do and I love to fly."

"Has it been pretty tough, over here?"

"You're gonna see just how much, with Tet."

"And the intelligence work. That must be interesting."

"A reality check for sure. I'm weird, I kinda like it. It's like getting insider scoop on what's going on with the war. You know?"

"Groovy," Nora said and it made Robert smile.

"They were just starting to use that word. When I left," he took a sip of his beer.

"So what are you doing here, sitting alone?" she asked.

"I'm kind of a loner, I guess you could say. Just doing the job. Staying the course. And already looking forward to some R and R."

"Already huh?"

"Yep, believe me. Like I said, it won't take you long."

"I get 'cha. Like this morning with the mortar attacks."

Robert smiled wryly. "Exactly."

"Say, I'm just learning all the different ranks. Are you a Lt.?"

"Nope. Made Captain."

"I know a naval aviator. He's a Lt. Commander."

"Oh, yeah? Off one of the carriers?"

"Yes. The *USS Coral Sea*. So is Captain similar to that?"

"Sorta. But a marine's ranking is like the army's. Strange, since we're a division of the navy. The main thing is officers and enlisted. That's the big break."

"I see. They actually gave us a ranking in the USO. I'm a Captain too. Of whatever." Nora laughed. "So tell me about some of your missions over here. I'd like to hear it." Her work could wait. He looked like he could use some company.

Nora listened as he told her about the intelligence work. There were two parts to the job, keeping track of the classified documents as they came in, registering them, and disposing of them when they were no longer needed. There was as stiff penalty for losing a classified document, a permanent black mark on your record. The mindless paperwork kept Robert from thinking about the war. When he took over, the system at Chu Lai was a mess. He worked with a corporal assigned to him and culled and burned the outdated documents. There were summaries of what happened on the base perimeter and analyses of actions in I Corps.

Flying the area, seeing the combat, talking to those engaged on the ground and then having access to the reports from the Third Marine Amphibious Force gave him a keen overview of what was actually happening in the war. Unlike most of the pilots with which he flew, who only flew their missions.

"There's all kind of crap that happens, that few know about. Some of it is so bizarre, you don't even wanna know." Nora could sense that Robert had the big picture.

The duty truck driver, Frenchy, popped into the club. Robert knew what that meant, duty called.

"Thanks for the brewski, Nora."

"Anytime, Captain Lathrop."

Nora watched as the duty officer briefed Robert about his mission. They took off for the flight line in a jeep, leaving a cloud of dusty sand behind them. Nora hoped she would get to see Robert again. It would be nice to have a buddy. Especially one with insider information. She felt an instant connection with him as a friend. He was genuine and slightly sardonic. He might be helpful in knowing what was going on with the *Coral Sea*.

SOLO VIETNAM

Chapter 25
∞ February, 1968 Tonkin Gulf ∞

Change was a word ubiquitous with the military. Just when you thought you knew the plan, the plan was changed. Such was the situation when Steve arrived back on board the *Coral Sea* after flying another day sortie over I Corps. Khe Sanh had become the epic battle ground for ground-air actions during the war. It was perilously close to falling, thousands of marines and army losing their lives in trying to hold on. As such, up to sixty missions a day were being flown off each of the three carriers now positioned at Yankee Station.

Steve had been briefed for his mission in the dark. It was 0400 and lightly drizzling as he heard the specs. The sky was overcast, but it was too early to tell whether flights were under instrument conditions or not. Despite meteorologists aboard, it was often the reports of the returning pilots that determined flight conditions which existed in the narrow margin of 160 x 70 miles of the area flown.

Still wet from the drizzle, Steve's fingers were zapped electrically going over the switches in the cockpit during his pre-flight. He was going to be number four on an instrument take-off it was revealed. Steve watched as the three planes before him disappeared after their cat at six or seven hundred feet into the low hanging clouds. He would have to take off and join the group on top, making a TACAN, the main navigation instrument in tactical fighter bomber aircraft, which gave bearings and distance to a station. The brief had included information on how to do that, if necessary. But in doing so, it was like flying in a beehive. They were briefed that there'd be about eighty other aircraft within the vicinity doing the same thing.

The section leader reported that he was on the roll, and Steve gave him thirty-five seconds and followed, noticing that the two other A-4s were already in position to roll when he did. The landing gear was up in the well as Steve turned into the clouds at 400 feet. It was a low

- - 109 - -

overcast in which to be flying and recovering, even with a radar controlled approach to target.

Steve was flying north, the world outside as white as the inside of milk bottle, yet dim for the early morning. He was climbing through eight thousand feet, and had heard no one call on top, yet should have. He wasn't sure what to expect next. The target information and the rendezvous were only given to the section leader, and for this mission that wasn't Steve. He had no idea where he was hooked up with the flight or at what altitude. While he was flying at reduced throttle and 300 knots, the following radio transmission came over the departure frequency.

"Vice Squad, this is Beetlebug 301, out of Danang, over."

"Go ahead, Beetlebug 301."

"Roger, Vice Squad, this is 301 at 32,000 feet and we have no tops in sight."

"All aircraft in the Danang vicinity, be advised that the Danang radar is down. This is Danang tower on Guard."

"All aircraft airborne in the Danang and Chu Lai areas, this is Vice Squad on Guard, hold within forty nautical miles of your base and deck."

One flight of eighty had just become eighty flights of one. Steve knew it was a good thing that the radar controller didn't have his radar on for the next hour. The appearance would have been a hive of bees, having all the bees orbiting around the hive while blind, all carrying loads of explosive and all coming back to the same hole at the same time.

Steve didn't hear a sound on the radio for a full fifteen minutes, as he flew five miles off the coast, maintaining his position by TACAN radials and distances. He stayed low so that he would stay away from the Phantoms and A-6s who would be orbiting higher with their more powerful engines and greater fuel load.

Suddenly, an F-4 came up. "Danang departure, this is Beetlebug 323, requesting clearance to the ordnance dump area, over."

"This is Danang departure, 323, be advised the ordnance dump area is closed due to friendly vessels in the area."

Another fifteen minutes pause while all eighty aircraft found some place they felt safe. Amazingly, all 40,000 pounds of bombs were dropped randomly into the South China Sea. Such was the business of war. Sheer insanity on any given day.

Steve knew about where he was, set his ordnance to drop and unarmed and salvoed the entire load into the ocean, 12 miles NW of Danang and hoped he didn't hit anything. He had plenty of fuel left in his A-4, as compared to some of the other aircraft. His group was one of the first airborne and decided to be one of the first ones back.

When he got down to 4000 pounds of fuel, well over what he felt he would need, he called out in the blind that he was coming down the 100 degree radial, starting at fifteen miles from the deck. He opened his speed brakes, slowed to 220 knots, put them back in and started a gentle guide slope to visual conditions or five hundred feet, whichever came first. The overcast remained thick and he had to watch his instruments carefully, as he was descending into unknown conditions. At two thousand feet, the soup was just as dense as before. He eased his descent to five hundred feet per minute and slowly passed one thousand feet at seven miles, starting his turn over a wild gray ocean, whipping up with whitecaps. The carrier would be pitching like mad.

Steve stayed on the five mile arc, unable to see the deck. There was only a one mile visibility. He then moved into a three mile arc from the deck TACAN and approached the runway heading, turning to his final landing heading, still not seeing the deck in the soup. He was now down to 300 feet under a constantly lowering overcast, but got the deck in sight when he looked up and saw the wheel of an F-4 Phantom over him.

The carrier's radar kicked in. There was a hawk circle forming. Steve heard the LSO radio, "Abort, abort."

Steve immediately turned right and went into a 360 degree turn, letting the Phantom trap. When he got back on the runway heading, he saw that the Phantom was in the first arresting gear. Steve decided to circle and take the second.

Once the Phantom was towed off, Steve adjusted his slope and took the second wire, the mid-deck morest. While he was in the morest, a third aircraft, another Skyhawk, lowered and then aborted the trap. No doubt hearing the screaming LSO. Gunning his engines, he barely missing whacking the tail of his Skyhawk on the end of the carrier deck as he ascended back into the air. Steve was glad to clear the deck, as the mass of planes were now landing. The red shirts were scrambling to re-load the wires as quickly as possible, as one after another plane approached to trap. All were coming in out of the soup with no ground control to separate them.

It said something of the experience of the pilots at the time. A crisis situation was handled with no more difficulty than a change in combat mission because they were conditioned to make such decisions rapidly and with success. Each had made a decision on how to recover, and did so without major consequence. They did so because of a confidence level developed by the constant challenges of daily carrier flight ops.

As Steve descended into the ready room, he was approached by his CO, Commander Woolcock. "Good work out there."

"Thank you sir," Steve said as he saluted.

Handing Steve a set of papers, the miniboss announced, "There's been a change of plans. Khe Sanh is still under siege. Your orders have been changed. You'll COD to the *Bonnie Dick* and join VA-212, the Rampant Raiders flying the A-4F."

"Yes, Sir," Steve answered. Unsure whether to be disappointed or intrigued. His cruise wasn't going to be over in April as planned. The rest of his squadron would be sailing for home, but this change in orders bought him some more time in Vietnam to see Nora.

"You'll COD with the next helo. Stand at the ready." With that, Commander Woolcock departed.

A new air wing. New personalities. New plane. Yep, change was the name of the game for the Seventh Fleet during the WESTPAC of 1968.

SOLO VIETNAM

Chapter 26
∞ February, 1968 New Orleans ∞

Jana Charbonnet, age six, was mortified to be riding in the early model red Cadillac Coupe de Ville hardtop along Highway 1 in Louisiana. She wasn't sure what made her cringe more, the big red fins, the red leather interior, or the fact that her father, Stew was standing in front it, with the hood raised, as the 1961 car over heated yet again.

She hated that car, from the moment her mother, Odile had wanted to buy it. It was so pretentious. Fire engine red. Jana turned her attentions to her baby sister, Stacy riding alongside her in the back seat. Stacy was three and a half; a most obnoxious preschooler, crawling all over the seats, and nearly crushing their little Chihuahua, Poncho. Stacy was still too little to play games, so on these long car trips to New Orleans, Jana was left to count cars, play the ABC game with her mother finding letters of the alphabet on signs, or read her Dr. Seuss books.

They were on their way to New Orleans for Mardi Gras. Her mother had explained that is was a big party with lots of parades featuring people in colorful costumes. They planned to attend one of the parades, Endymion, because it was scheduled to go right by her aunt's house off Napoleon Ave. Jana had practiced calling out, "Throw me something. Throw me something Mister." She planned to get as many beads and doubloons possible. No one in Texas had a party like this.

Her daddy finally got the car running and put down the hood. She knew they tried to skimp and save money, but Jana didn't understand why they couldn't just buy a nice station wagon like everyone else. As she watched the swamps go by, she reminded herself that the trip was a diversion from school. Kids in Texas didn't have Mardi Gras days off, but Jana's mother was determined to go this year, as one of her

-- 113 --

brothers was King of Bacchus. Her mother was thrilled to have gotten an invite to the ball.

"What are you so deep in thought about back there?" Jana's mother asked.

"Nothing. Just thinking about how many beads I'm gonna get."

"Do you want to practice again?" her mother beleaguered.

"No. I know what to say."

"Stew. Maybe it's time to say the Rosary," Jana's mother suggested. They always said a full rosary on each leg of the trip. Jane got hers out of her Smiley face purse. Saying them so often, she knew the prayers well.

Odile began with a citation. She always did. "In the name of the Father, the Son, and the Holy Spirit. This Rosary is being offered for a safe trip to New Orleans and a happy time at Mardi Gras," Odile prayed. "But also, for the penance for Jana who visited the principal's office this week."

Jana was embarrassed. Her mother said she would never talk about it again. Normally Jana was a well behaved, young lady in the second grade at St. Peter's Catholic school. She completed all her work, studied her spelling words, and aced math. On the playground, she had several friends. Sonia Fuentes, Maryanne Murphy, and Paula Urbanovski. But a couple of days before, her best friend, Yvonne Aguilar had caused Jana to end up in Sister Joseph's office.

All over a kafuffle about Jana's mother. Or really, as Jana came to know, her birth mother. Jana had always been raised with the fact that she was adopted. That was no secret. Her parents had always told Jana and her sister Stacy how lucky they were, that God had chosen Odile and Stew, who couldn't have children as their parents.

Odile had repeated the script hundreds of times. "Let's say a prayer for the nice lady who gave birth to you and brought you into this world, so that your Daddy and I would have babies of our own to love and take care of." To Jana, her mother was her mother. There was no question of that. Odile may not have given birth to her, but in Jana's young mind, that didn't matter. Her Daddy was her daddy and her Mother was her mother. Case closed.

But last week, while on the playground, Yvonne threw a wrench into Jana's idyllic thinking. Jana had been happily swinging on the swing set. She liked going as high as she could go. Dressed in her Brownie uniform, she proudly wore her brown beanie and numbers of her troop to which she belonged. Yvonne wasn't a Brownie, she was a Camp Fire girl. Jana thought belonging to Brownies was better. As Brownies, they would become Girl Scouts. To Jana, that was like Boy

Scouts, only girls. Camp Fire girls certainly didn't have that kind of equal.

Jana liked to swing. With her powerful legs, she could pump and pump gaining as much height with each swing as she could. When she could absolutely go no higher, Jana would launch herself out of the swing, feeling the wind in her hair, and for the briefest moment, dream she was flying. At least until her legs caught the ground, sometimes sending her into a tumble.

Yvonne had been swinging next to her. "See? I can swing higher than you," Yvonne boasted as she pumped her legs faster and faster.

"No you can't" called Jana from the ground.

"Oh, yes I can," challenged Yvonne. "Just like I'm better at tap dance than you. And better at gymnastics than you."

Jana quipped back, "Oh, yeah? Well my Mom's the Brownie leader. So I have a better Mommy than you."

Yvonne's face turned into smirk. "You don't have a real Mommy. She's your fake Mommy. That's what my Mommy said."

"My Mommy is too real. She's my Mommy!" Jana screamed at her best friend.

Just then, Yvonne launched herself out of the swing and landed on her two feet. Jana was right there, ready for battle.

"You take that back. My Mommy is not fake."

"Is too. Is too. Jana has a fake Mommy," Yvonne began dancing around the playground, taunting her.

"Shut up, Yvonne. Just shut up."

But Yvonne was relentless. "Fake Mommy. Fake Mommy. Jana has a fake Mommy."

That was all Jana could take. She ran over to Yvonne and yanked her ponytails so hard, she pulled her to the ground. Then, she kicked her.

Just then, Sister Margaret approached. "Jana Charbonnet. That is quite enough. How unladylike. Sit on the steps this instant. You and I are going to Sister Joseph's office as soon as the recess is over."

Yvonne got up and dusted herself off. But first, made sure she stuck out her tongue at Jana, who was now punished on the steps. A pariah. Headed to the principal.

As the recess bell rang, all of the other children lined up and marched back to their classroom. Jana was led by hand to Sister Joseph's office. Her face was ashen. She listened to the tale of her crime as described by Sister Margaret. After a few minutes, she was summoned into the interior chamber of the principal.

Sister Joseph was a large women, standing about five foot ten inches in her black habit with the squared off black and white cover over her head. Her face was round and her green eyes intense. "Young lady, it has come to my attention that you hurt another child in your class. Is that true?"

Jana thought for a minute about lying, but decided to tell the truth. One sin was better than two. "Yes, but I had a good reason."

"And what, may I ask was that?" the bombastic nun queried as Jana stood shaking in her saddle oxfords.

"She told a lie. She said I had a fake Mommy," Jana defended.

"Well, that is just ludicrous. There is no such thing as a fake Mother. Are your parents real, Miss Charbonnet? Do they eat and breathe?"

"Yes, Sister," Jana dutifully answered.

"Then, Miss Charbonnet, they are not fake."

"No, Sister. That's what I tried to tell her," Jana thought this was going well. Maybe she would get leniency. But she was wrong.

"So even though you were simply being taunted, you lost your temper and broke one of God's Ten Commandments."

Jana was silent. Her head was hanging low.

"Look at me when I am speaking to you. Can you tell me, young lady, which one?"

Jana raised her head and racked her young brain. Which one? Which one? She really didn't know them by heart. "Um. I think maybe the one that you shouldn't kick other people?"

The principal cleared her throat. "Miss Charbonnet, you are referring to Commandment number nine. Thou shall not bear false witness against thy neighbor. In addition, you have broken Jesus's heart. He asked us to love one another, as he loves us."

Jana was not sure how pulling Yvonne's pigtails and kicking her was bearing false witness. She wasn't even sure what that meant. But she wasn't going to argue.

"Your punishment is two paddles," Sister Joseph explained. "And a call to your parents, letting them know how naughty you have been today."

Paddles? Jana eyed the wooden board mounted on Sister Joseph's wall. She wasn't sure which was going to be worse, getting whacked on the behind or having to listen to her mother and daddy tell how disappointed they were in her actions. She knew either way, it was going to be painful.

"Bend over, Miss Charbonnet," Sister Joseph commanded, motioning for Jana to bend over the large oak chair. Sister Joseph raised the paddle. Jana closed her eyes.

Whack. Whack. Jana could feel a searing pain on her buttocks underneath her Brownie uniform. She certainly was not being a good Brownie on this day. A couple of tears rolled down Jana's eyes as she stood up. Part one of her agony was done.

"Miss Charbonnet, you will report to my office every day for two weeks. I will monitor your behavior on my behavior chart. If you go two weeks without incident, you will no longer have to come."

With that, Jana allowed to return to class. She took her normal seat on the front row, careful not to return the glaring looks she was getting from her stunned classmates. Jana Charbonnet was now a marked student. Gone was her perfect behavior. Jana was mortified.

The pain on her buttocks was not nearly as difficult to bear as the humiliation she felt. What did her classmates think? None of her other girlfriends had ever been to the principal's office. Only boys.

Jana vowed never to let herself lose that kind of control again. At least not at school. She would never give rise for anyone to send her to the Principal's office again. School she could handle. Jana tried so hard to be good. To prove herself. But now, she dreaded facing the disappointment and guilt trips over the incident from her mother.

Chapter 27
∞ February 1967 Chu Lai ∞

Nora was quickly learning the lay of the land when it came to the base at Chu Lai. With ground forces, it was the officer's rank that defined command, but not necessarily local power. As a volunteer, Nora was ranked Captain, but many of the men on base didn't consider the women of the USO seriously. After all, they were not required to wear a uniform or fatigues.

The pecking order was clear at Chu Lai. The army considered themselves the most important. The navy was not there in great enough presence to count for much, although Nora knew different, as they were the support units for supplies and aircraft maintenance. The marines? In Nora's eyes, they worked the hardest. Were yelled at the most. And definitely were dealt the worst, in terms of access to supplies, workloads, and overall temperament by their officers. Indeed, the marines had to be jarheads, as they were treated as grunts.

Add to this mix, the USO. Not belonging to any real service, yet providing plenty of service to all branches, Nora had to figure out the political land mines required in order to get what she needed to run the club well.

As luck would have it, one day, as she was headed to Base Ops to negotiate the supplies she was going to need, fortuitously she was picked up by a navy jeep. It was being driven by a Chief Petty Officer. Since Nora thought the only navy personnel on base were medical, she asked him what he did.

"Chief Woody Woodson. I'm with the Seabees," he proudly boasted. "We're responsible for the base water system, the roads, and unloading ships, Ma'am."

"Your mother named you Woody with a last name of Woodson? I see." Nora's mind was in overdrive. This young man could be an asset to her supply problem. "We're not so lucky. The USO club is being supplied by the army. And in some situations, by no one."

"Yep." Chief Woodson smiled. This lady had a sense of humor.

Nora had seen some of the marines come into the club in tattered fatigues and flight suits. The sheets and blankets she had been given had been dissolved by the Vietnamese laundry, as well as some of their best lingerie. She and the girls had learned their lesson. Nora's hut had recently had an air-conditioner installed. The girls learned quickly to collect any water from the window mounted air conditioning unit in used ammunition cans that they placed below the air conditioner. They used that water to wash their finer things. As Chief Woodson drove her up to the office, he handed her a pad of paper.

"Write down what you need. I'll see what I can do. We gotta take care of our girls that take care of our boys."

"Thank you, will do."

Nora got through the meaningless weekly request meeting with the SDO. When the meeting was over, there was the Chief, ready and waiting to take her back to the club.

"Say, doll. You know how it works. Catch as catch can. I have a favor to ask."

"What's that?" Nora dreaded the response.

"Well, it's like this. I want a good meatloaf. Savory. Like my Momma used to make back home."

"Meat loaf? That's it?" Nora broke out into laughter. "Sure, Chief. I can certainly do up a Mom's meatloaf for ya. It'll be the best you've ever tasted." Nora smiled all the way back to the club. When she got there, she immediately went in and wrote out a recipe for her cook. That evening, Chief Woodson came and enjoyed several helpings at the club.

The next week, Nora found a gross of new sheets and blankets, light globes, paint, a case of bourbon and the address of the Seabees unit in case they needed anything else. On top of the bar, was a package that contained three new sets of Clairol hair rollers, brushes, and some makeup. Nora had just been introduced to the military supply system, black market style. Commonly known within military ranks as cumshaw, something procured without official payment, it operated continuously at all levels and was piracy at the highest level of proficiency.

The mail truck came, and a large manila envelope and another letter had come for Nora. Nora recognized the handwriting on the smaller envelope. It was from Steve. She planned to save that for later. The large envelope contained several letters. They had all been placed into one. The return address was her own, at home.

JEANETTE VAUGHAN

Nora poured herself a cup of horrid club coffee and sat down at one of the tables to read them. There was a gossipy, newsy letter from Charlene. Another post card from Kayce and a long, two page letter from Nellie. Wanting to get the latest information about her children first, Nora read Nellies hand written post.

My daughter Nora

Where do I begin? It has been such an adjustment trying to manage three teens. I don't know how I ever did it with you. They are always running here or there. I hardly keep up. Cathy has been a dream helping me learn how everything is set up in a home that is not mine. She seems to be in charge of the other two. We've kept all the bills paid. Kept the house looking nice.

I'm worried about Leisel and all the time she spends studying with that Matt Arceneaux. I hope he is not just using her to sell his wax. Iggy's grades have suffered this term. He is turning more and more away from athletics and is interested in the arts. I included a post card sent by Kayce. She is your biggest worry at the moment. It sounds like she has hooked up with some hippie in San Francisco. I just hope she doesn't get herself knocked up.

I had the strangest experience recently. I was at Ruli's getting some milk and bread, when an urgent order came in for Mrs. Arceneaux. She wanted it filled right away. Some aspirin, some Pepto Bismal, honey and some Community Coffee. Since I was right there and overheard Mr. Ruli, I offered to take it to her. When I got there, she was nice as could be. Seems Mr. Arceneaux had the flu. She was busy making him some chicken Gumbo. He was in bed. The honey was for some tea she was brewing. The coffee for her. She started a pot brewing and asked if I would like to stay and have a cup. I said yes, and waited in the kitchen while it percolated.

Well, here is the strange part. While I was there, she showed me some pictures of her grandchildren from Texas. They were coming for Mardi Gras, but these pictures were from when they were there at Easter, last year. Nora, it was so odd. When I looked at this little girl, age five, she had big brown eyes and high cheek bones with a round face. Nora, she looked just like one of your pictures from when you were a little girl. Isn't that strange? This little girl lives in Texas I think. I never knew you looked so much like your neighbors.

We all miss you. I sure don't understand why you felt the need to go all the way over to Vietnam when your children are here. I think they feel you abandoned them. I wish you could have just served by volunteering at the VFW, I am sure they would have enjoyed you singing just as much. I'm telling you this because I love you, Nora. You will always be my daughter. But if you don't hurry and come home, I think two of your children are going to go live with their father in Metairie. God forbid. Leisel and Iggy have been talking to Frank lately. I think Cathy will stay with me. Just do what you can, Nora. But remember, your family is at home. We need you too.
Love, your Mama Nellie

Nora felt like she needed something stronger than coffee after reading Nellie's letter. Her children? Talking about living with Frank? She felt her stomach turn over as she mulched on the effect her coming to Vietnam was having on her family back home. Her face told it all.

Just then, Captain Lathrop dropped by the club. "Hey there, girl. Now it's you that's looking glum."

"Letters from home," Nora pointed to the pile.

"I know the feeling. After being over here. Life over there seems like some *Leave it to Beaver* episode." They both laughed.

"Here," she gestured. "Pull up a chair. I could use the company."

Robert sat down at the table and Nora had one of the girls bring him a strong cup of coffee. It seemed that Robert had his tribulations too.

"Where've you been lately? I haven't seen you in a bit."

"R and R, which was a bust. The wife's pretty ticked that she didn't get to come over. I was overdue and just got sent. So, there was no time to book her over."

"I'm sure she was disappointed."

"Yep. That's the military. Little regard for family. Maybe next time."

"It's strange, isn't it? When you're away, you just sort of lose touch and control of what happens at home." Nora wondered if that was the effect that war and deployment had on all families.

"Yep. And I hear, re-entry is hell."

Nora sat with Robert for about an hour. He loved hearing the story about how she had commandeered supplies. He applauded her efforts. Nora was the one person on base that Robert felt he could talk too. For one, she was not only a woman, but a pilot. He could tell about her missions and she understood, but added a woman's point of view. Whomever she was wearing her heart on her sleeve for was one lucky guy. There was never any romantic interest between them, as Robert was married. Nora was simply just a great friend. God knows, in Vietnam, that was an asset of gold.

Nora hugged Robert as he left. She knew he put his life in his hands with each mission he flew. Although he flew the same plane as Steve, being ground based at Chu Lai and flying over some of the most active war zones, definitely seemed to put him more at risk.

This night was going to be a big one at the club. Nora decided to bring a bit of Mardi Gras to Chu Lai. She had the girls decorate the club with yellow, green and purple streamers that she had ordered from Hong Kong. She booked a band for the evening that knew how to play jazz. Getting some local fish and crustaceans from the local fisherman, she instructed the cook on how to make a roux and Gumbo.

Time to forget about your troubles. At this, Nora excelled. Tonight, was going to be Fat Tuesday at club USO Chu Lai. *Les bon temps roulles.*

SOLO VIETNAM

Chapter 28
∞ Tonkin Gulf ∞

Steve packed his B-4 bag in silence. He expected that like the rest of the crew onboard the *Coral Sea*, he had only a few weeks before they set sail toward home. He wasn't the only A-4 pilot being reassigned to the *USS Bon Homme Richard*. Because of a fire on the *Bonnie Dick* back in the fall, they were short of pilots. There were several others scheduled to serve in the Tonkin Gulf until October. Once on deck to await his COD helo, Steve ran into Pete Watterman, the helo pilot he had met before.

"Lt. Commander," Pete saluted.

"Lt." Steve saluted back. "At ease."

"Hey man, how's it going?" Pete asked.

"Being relo'd. To the *Bonnie Dick*," Steve replied.

"Yep, I'm taking some of the pilots over now. COD."

"Aren't I included on that manifest?"

"No, man. You're orders must have changed again. Sorry."

"What?" For a moment, Steve was confused.

Before Pete turned to make his way to his helo he offered, "Hey Lt. Commander Novak. You're an alright guy. Nice to have met another man from Dixie land. Good luck out there."

"Same to you," Steve responded.

About three other pilots and their bags were loaded. Pete geared up his propellers, kicking up some salty mist. About that time, Steve was approached by Commander Woolcock, the skipper from his squadron.

"Sir," Steve saluted.

"Sorry to jerk you around, buddy. But there's been a change in plans. You're to bingo off to Chu Lai, taking one of our scooters for hand-off to VMA-311. She's seen her days on the decks of the *Coral Sea*. Commander Nelson from Air Ops is fazing her out."

"Gotcha," Steve acknowledged. Chu Lai? How lucky could he get?

"But that's not all. Your recent service bought you some R and R. After you hand off the plane, you've got three days before you report to the *Bon Homme*. Here's your pay advance."

Steve was handed an envelope containing the customary $200 given to pilots for spending money during their brief time off. He couldn't believe his luck. Chu Lai, Nora and R and R. It couldn't possibly get better.

Often, when the navy felt an A-4 had seen its days on the carrier, they would send the plane to one of the marine VMA stations for repair and refit. The marines would patch it up, repaint their own VMA call signs and numbers and the plane would be used for another hundred missions or so. Second hand.

After pre-flighting the Skyhawk, Steve was given signal from the LSO to cat. One last look at the deck of the *Coral Sea*. She had been good to him. As he gained altitude, he saw the lights on the deck become a small line of white, amidst a black sea.

He would be flying under night cover to transport the plane. Another chance to see the war in action at night, from 10,000 feet. By now, he knew the coast well. He could see stars out everywhere on this clear night.

Despite flying over a war zone, it was relaxing, in a way, to be flying a plane for delivery instead of a mission. On shore, he intermittently caught site of flares being dropped. There were white hot lights of anti-aircraft fire launched skyward. It was a short flight from the deck of the carrier to Chu Lai, a mere ninety miles. Before long he saw the lights at Danang. The moonlight was shining on the pristine, yellow-white sands of China Beach.

Soon, he visualized the river at Chu Lai. As he descended, he saw the sampans out in the water. No attacks for tonight. He radioed Chu Lai ground and got clearance to land.

"Chu Lai tower, this is Blue Tail NL-317 requesting to land, over."

"Bingo in, NL-317. Keep your eye on the meatball. Clear to ground."

The runway at Chu Lai was fairly short. He positioned the plane such that his slope would contact the arresting gear. Lowering his speed and putting down his landing gear, with a small bump and scrape, Steve touched down at Chu Lai at 1930 hours.

There was no one to meet him on the tarmac. For a moment, he wasn't sure where to go. But then, a marine flight crew approached. Haggard and covered in dust and grease, they were a site. One of them radioed for a jeep. Steve took a moment to take the flight line in. It was sure a far cry from the organized symmetry of the *Coral Sea*. There were bunkers and razor-edged barbed wire everywhere. It looked like the tarmac as well as the flight line had taken some substantial mortar attacks. Airplane parts, partially burned out made it a metallic graveyard.

A six by six jeep transport pulled up with three other pilots in it. "Where to, Lt. Commander?" beckoned the driver.

"The USO club. I hear they've got a great singer there," Steve said.

"Yeah. Righto. Tonight's a Mardi Gras party. But you've only got about twenty minutes to curfew."

"Then step on it," Steve chided as he threw his bag in the back.

"Right on, Sir," the jeep took off and sped toward the beach and the club. As it neared, Steve could hear the sounds of jazz emanating from inside. He could hardly contain himself and nearly jumped out of the jeep before it pulled adjacent to the make-shift arched bridge over a trench to the entrance.

Homesick for New Orleans, Nora arranged through her black market connections with Woody, to get the adornments for a Mardi Gras celebration. Doubloons, beads, and plenty of seafood. She booked a Vietnamese band that could play some jazz. One more way to bring a little bit of the U.S. to Vietnam.

The place was packed. Bar and restaurant were almost standing room only. GIs were bedecked in vibrant Mardi Gras beads. Some had on colorful masks. The distinctive spicy smell of Zatarain's filled the air from boiled shrimp and "bugs," a crustacean native to the South China Sea. Steve traced the sounds of jazz to the porch along the backside. Sure enough, Nora was crooning out one of her favorites, *Moon River*. He stood in the breezeway out of her sight.

She looked amazing, as always. Radiant smile. Bright pink lipstick. Long, sensuous legs and high heels. Her skirt had to be at least eight inches above her knees. Damn, she was hot.

The crowd cheered as Nora wrapped up her song. "Thank you all for coming tonight. *Les bon temp roulles*." The GIs hooted and hollered. As she finished replacing the mike in its stand, Steve came up from behind her.

"Say gorgeous, I'd know that voice anywhere," he whispered in her ear. Nora felt her knees grow weak hearing his voice.

Whipping around, she exclaimed, "What the heck? Steve, where the devil did you come from?"

"About a hundred miles north of here. Just to see my gal," he couldn't resist and in front of everyone grabbed her and planted a big kiss on her lips. Catcalls erupted from every corner of the bar.

Nora was a mass of emotion. Joy, tears, and pent up libido just hearing his voice. Taken aback at first, she quickly recovered. "I can't. Not here. Let me wrap things up and make sure everyone clears curfew. Then," she pulled him close and whispered in her sultry voice, "I'm all yours."

Directing her cook, dishwasher and one of her girls running the bar, she quickly wrapped things up for the evening. The books and tabs could wait till the morning. She thanked everyone for the great job they did. Within a few minutes, due to curfew, it was just Steve and herself left in the bar.

"What on earth are you doing in Chu Lai?"

"Had to deliver a Skyhawk for refurb to VMA-311. How's that for luck?"

"Brilliant," she said throwing her arms around him. "I'm just tickled pink you are here."

"Nice place you got going," he said referring to the club.

"The girls and I have really worked it over. It was a dump. But I've learned to make, uh, well, let's just say connections."

"That's the navy way. Way to go girl," he could hardly keep his hands off of her. "I'm about as randy as ever. But where can we go?"

"I've been thinking about that," she had a gleam in her eye.

"Certainly not to your hooch,"

"Nope. The girls are there and curfew's on. But we might be able to sneak out back under the decks. There's a small, unused elevated tent. It was the original officer's mess, near the beach."

"Sounds great, doll. Let's go," he said taking her hand. Nora locked the place up and they quietly snuck out down the back steps of the club. They walked close to the jungle line of trees, so as not to be seen by the sentry guards. Clearing through some brush, they came to a clearing with the tent. It was dank, dark, and sandy, but they didn't care. They were finally alone.

The flap of the tent barely went down before he had his hands all over her. The fact that there was dust everywhere and cob webs didn't bother them. They finally had a secluded, stolen moment alone. He kissed her passionately, relinquishing the pent up sexual tension between them. She darted her tongue in around his mouth, long, slow and ardent.

Pulling her close into him, she felt his desire for her. He was rock hard. He stopped kissing her for a moment and looked deeply into her eyes. Without saying a word, he unzipped the back of her dress, exposing her shoulders. He lowered his head and began kissing along her collar bone, starting on her left. Small, wet kisses across the notch in her neck to the other side. Nora felt herself get wet. She was on fire, remembering his touch.

He lowered the dress completely and it fell to the floor. There was a lone chair there. Gently, he pushed her shoulders down, guiding her to sit. Then, he removed the dress from around her ankles. Briefly, he stood up, un-zipped his flight suit and took off his skivvies. Hard, athletic, and muscular, she remembered his physique.

Kneeling before her, he again lowered his head to her chest. He kissed along the rim of her red lace bra, running his fingers along the other breast. Reaching around, he deftly unfastened it. Her breasts were full and supple, just like he remembered.

Taking her left breast into his mouth he suckled her, hearing her moan in delight. Next, he took the right, circling his tongue around her nipple. Nora was in ecstasy.

"Steve, God I want you," she moaned. He knew she did, but wanted to take his time.

Slipping his fingers into the edges of her panties, he lowered them off her buttocks and removed them. Then, he spread her legs and positioned himself between them. Starting from the nape of her neck, he kissed and licked her downward, pausing at her navel and tickling her there with the tip of his tongue. He could tell she was on fire. When he could wait no longer, he took his penis in his hands and gently put it inside her, pulling her hips closer to him. She gasped as he entered her and began to intensify his thrusts. Long, slow, and full, he rocked her hips as he plunged deeper inside. Nora arched her body into him, wrapping her legs around his waist. She was close to climax. He could tell by the way she moaned with his thrusts.

"Steve. Oh, God. Steve," she cried out.

He quickened his strokes, knowing he was about to cum. When he could no longer hold back, he exploded inside of her.

"Glorious, woman. Just. So. Glorious," he gasped.

Totally spent, he held her close to him, his head resting on her chest. Nora ran her fingers through his hair and held his head to her chest. She had tears in her eyes.

"I've missed you. God, I've missed you so much."

"Me too," was all that he said. Then, after a few sweet moments with him still inside her, he took her face in his hands. "I want you to know. I never stopped loving you," he said and gently kissed her lips.

She looked into his eyes, staring into his soul. "I love you too, Steve. More than anything in this world."

Steve slowly removed himself from her, rose and they began to gather their clothes. Nora had brought along a bottle of bourbon and two plastic cups. "Here ya go, my naval aviator. You look like you could use a drink." She put on his cover and was standing there, naked before him in her high heels.

Steve laughed. "What the hell? God, Nora, now I'll just have to fuck you all over again." He was hard as rock. She drove him nuts.

"Down boy, stand down. There'll be more time for that. Let's have a quick drink before I have to get back." She poured them both a shot of bourbon. The stress of the war made most hard core drinkers. "So, how long can you stay?" she feared the answer.

"How many days can you take off?" he asked.

"You've got R and R? Fantastic."

"Yeah, but I sure don't wanna spend it at Chu Lai. I was thinking Saigon, or Hong Kong. Do you think you can get away?"

"I dunno. We're only supposed to get a week off every three months. I'm a bit early for that, but I'll see what I can do. What bliss that would be. There's no way I'm gonna let this chance to be with you slip by," she moved up closer to him, putting her arms around his waist.

"Do you know how much I've missed you? Over the past five years?" he asked.

"About as much as I've missed you. It was agony, putting my feelings away in a box. It was all I could do, just to carry on. I wasn't sure if you felt the same."

"Watching you leave that day, on the train. It nearly killed me. I ran after you."

"I saw you. But I pulled down the shade. I just couldn't take looking at your face. It was breaking my heart."

"You understand why, don't you? That it had to be that way."

"Yes, of course."

"The consequences we created left us with no choice," he explained.

"But I don't want to talk about that now," Nora countered. "You're here. That's all that matters." At that moment, that's all that did.

Chapter 29
∞ Chu Lai ∞

Both Steve and Nora could hardly sleep a wink that night, knowing that they were separated by decorum several Quonset huts away. Fighting the mosquitoes, sandy bed, and the sticky heat, Steve couldn't imagine how Nora was making it here. Her tenacity never ceased to amaze him. He sat out on the steps and puffed on a cigar one of the marine pilots had given him as a welcome. Only a few more hours till morning.

Nora was up at the crack of dawn. She quickly showered, put on some makeup and woke up one of her girls. She explained to Marsha that she was going to take her leave early. "Can you manage everything for a few days? I really need this favor."

"Sure, no problem. God only knows you've been here for us," Marsha agreed.

Steve arranged for them to catch a hop on the next cargo plane out to Saigon. There were only two other passengers, both displaced Vietnamese who needed transport back to the city. Inside the hull of the C-117, Nora and Steve finally got a chance to just talk.

She started first, "So tell me. About what you've been doing? What's it like out there?"

"Hell in a cockpit. I've flown nearly a hundred missions. Some during the day. Others at night. I fucking hate the night ones." Nora listened glued to every word. "But we've got it a helluva lot better than the marines. Those poor buggars never stop. Two or three missions a day. Smacking down in arresting gear. I've been in some pretty hairy situations. But nothing like I've heard them tell."

"I know what you're talking about. Sorta. I've been talking to an A-4 pilot. Robert Lathrop. He comes into the club," she explained.

"Should I be jealous?" he raised his eyebrows at her.

"Nah. Robert and I are just buddies. He loves his wife."

"And doesn't fuck around on her? Good for him. Okay then. Go on," he smiled wryly.

"It was only to understand what you do. Or at least part of what you do. It's so damned frustrating seeing all these pilots and wanting to fly myself."

"That's my girl. But honestly, Nora. You might not wanna know what we see. It's ugly out there." He told her about the bombed out villages. The napalm. The villagers that were burned and scarred for life. When he told her the story of bar at Cubi, and the little boy there, tears were rolling down her cheeks. She thought she saw one in the corner of his eye too.

"I had no idea," she said shaking her head in dismay. "How bad it was. I mean, I hear bits and pieces of stories. Some of the guys come into the club looking so shell-shocked. You can tell when it's been a day of routine flying and a day when stuff went really south."

"We all have this calendar, where we mark off days to the end of the cruise. I was nearly there. Till I got bounced to the *Bonnie Dick*. At least it meant I got to see you," he touched her hand next to his thigh for a brief moment. Being in uniform, PDA was strictly prohibited. "How are you making it here?"

"Day by day. I can't think of how long I'll be here. I just do what I gotta do. Bringing a little bit of sunshine and home to the men. It probably wasn't the best decision. But I just had to do it. I had to do something. To see you."

"Crazy woman. Vietnam. You oughta have your head examined," he laughed. "The problem is, after my time on the *Bonnie Dick*, I'll be shipping out for home before you do."

"I've thought about that. I dunno how I could get out of it. But in a way, I feel I'm doing something. For the boys. I want to see it through."

"Right," he was bothered that she would be over here alone. Impulsivity had again outweighed common sense. "This freaking war is never gonna end. Hey, feels like we're on the descent," he told her as they both felt the plane getting into position to land.

Tan San Nhut, Saigon was a busy, international airport. One half of the airfield was occupied by military. The C-117 taxied toward the hangar. Once they were out, a jeep took them to the terminal. They were two white specks in a sea of Asians. Nora held Steve's hand tightly as they navigated their way to the street.

Saigon was like nothing she had ever seen before. There were lots of Vietnamese women dressed in traditional *ao dai*. The *ao dai* was a tightly fitting, long sleeved silk tunic with mandarin color. It was long, past their knees, but split up to just below the hip. Traditionally worn over white or black, loose fitting pants. It accentuated their slight frames. Most of the women had thick black hair, some long, some short. Several of them carried brightly colored parasols to protect them from the sun. Nora saw sunglasses just like in the U.S.

Other young women were dressed in mini-shirts and dresses of the day. Some older women were wearing the traditional cotton loose fitting top with three-quarter lengths sleeves, usually in pale pink, beige or white and boxy, black peddle pusher length trousers with the cone shaped straw hats. There were motor bikes and bicycles that wove dangerously close out of street traffic. Many people were walking outside the rows of shops. It was rare to see an Anglo woman in the city. The only other women besides the USO and Red Cross donut dollies were nurses serving. Mostly, however, there were only male GIs on the street. Nora tried not to let the stares from the other women bother her. She clearly stuck out with her height and auburn hair.

Steve hailed a pedi cab. Nora was glad to tuck inside and view the city from within. With the ferns and palms surrounding them, some of the architecture of the larger buildings was similar to New Orleans. Steve had booked them into the Continental Palace, one of the nicest hotels in Saigon. It had arched white windows and large arched passageways on the first floor. Standing about four stories tall, a long white sign with green letters spelled out the name. There were balconettas with pink flowers hanging from the top level.

Inside, it was opulent; in contrast to the war ravaged city. Some buildings had never been repaired following the recent Tet offensive and several other bombings. The large hotel took up a whole block. The hotel was shaped in a square which surrounded a large, tile interior courtyard with tables, chairs and a fountain.

"What do you think?" Steve asked her. "Did I get it right?"

"It's lovely. Just lovely. Such a far cry from the base. I had almost forgotten what nice looked like. It reminds me of the Roosevelt."

"Yeah, I thought you'd like it. Wait until you see where we're going for dinner."

Nora took a long, luxurious hot bath. Steve enjoyed watching her in the bubbles. It was rare to get hot water in Chu Lai. He came over and sponged her back. Not missing an opportunity to sneak in a couple of kisses to the back of her neck. Seeing the steam rise off her bare shoulders was driving him wild. When she was finished, he handed her a thick, plush white towel. Nora was in heaven. The towels, her only two, were thread bare at the hooch. She quickly swept up her hair, applied the remainder of what make-up she had left, and put on some lipstick.

She planned to do some desperately needed shopping in the markets of Saigon. The girls had given her a list. Grabbing her handbag, she announced to Steve, "Ready to go."

"You look gorgeous as ever, Nora. Watching you take a bath made me think about our last weekend together at the Melrose," he sighed.

"I was big as a barn. Nine months pregnant with our baby."

"And every bit as ravishing as you are now," he handed her his arm.

Steve rented a motorcycle. He hopped on and had Nora sit behind him. It felt great to wear pants again. She had on a V-neck sweater and some slim fitting black slacks. She was going to enjoy wearing pants while she could. Steve guided the motorcycle through the streets of Saigon. They passed Notre Dame Cathedral which looked like any other Catholic church one might see in the U.S. But she was quickly reminded this was Vietnam, as they passed Buddhist temples nearby. The city was filled with exotic buildings. Many of the structures were not more than two stories high. There were some major streets, but lots of tiny, jam packed ones too.

Heading out to the waterfront, Steve pulled up in front of a popular spot, My Canh was a floating restaurant. You had to cross over to it on a small, covered bridge. Nora loved it.

Waiters dressed in white tunics and traditional boxy black trousers greeted them and sat them near a table over-looking the water. The menu was printed in French, English and Vietnamese.

"I have no idea what to order," I've never eaten Vietnamese food.

"Don't worry. I'll order for us," he motioned for the waiter. "We'll start out with some *Pho sate*," Steve said. The waiter nodded, bowed and was off to the kitchen.

"What is that?" Nora was intrigued.

"It's a spicy noodle soup with thinly sliced, rare beef steak, hot chili sauce, sliced cucumber, tomatoes, and peanuts. You'll love it."

"I'll take your word for it," Nora smiled. It felt good to be with him again, letting him just take charge. She was game for anything.

They feasted on *Com tam* and *Bo luc lac*, followed by some *Bahn cuon* pork stuffed rice paper rolls. Steve topped the meal off with some *Rau cau*, a popular gelatin cake made with agar and flavored with coconut milk and pandan. It was layered and shaped into an intricate cake. Then, they shared some strong iced Vietnamese coffee *Ca phe sua da* which had sweetened condensed milk at the bottom to be stirred in. It was a popular beverage among the Vietnamese.

Nora ate so much, she thought she would pop. It was a far cry from the food served at the officer's mess. "Oh, I'm stuffed."

"Pretty decent grub, huh? Half the time, I'm afraid to know exactly what it is. But it tastes good."

Nora laughed. "I tasted some unusual spice, maybe coriander? And coconut."

"Yep, coconut milk is in lots of the dishes, blended with hot curries."

"Now what? I'm game for some adventure."

Steve paid up and they took off on the motor cycle to see the city at night. Some of the markets were still open. They were jam packed together, offering fabrics, mats, lanterns, jewelry and pottery. The noisy streets were crowded with young people amidst the obvious GIs, unmistakable in their drab olive green. Nights in Saigon were spent in the speak-easies with go-go dancers, scantily clad singers and women of the night.

Steve parked the motorcycle outside the Son Ca Bar. Nora and he entered the smoke filled room for a night-cap. He ordered one *Ruou de*, a distilled liquor made of rice and a *Bia hoi*, a locally brewed Vietnamese beer, just in case Nora didn't like the other. Nora noticed that many of the singers sang with a nasal quality to their voices, no matter what the tune. She and Steve danced a few tunes and then settled in to watch the floor show. The costumes were elaborate with sequined dragons and demons. As it always did, the show ended with female performers in heavy eye make-up stripping down to nothing more than sequined bikinis.

After hopping to several bars, at 2:00 AM in the morning, Steve and Nora called it a night. Back in their hotel room, Steve again made love to her. It was slow and sweet. This time, with her on top. As she fell into his arms, after another climax, she snuggled into his shoulder falling fast asleep.

The next morning, she awoke startled to find that Steve was not in the bed with her. Slipping on a robe, she looked around the hotel room. At first, she was worried, but then he entered the door bringing her some coffee and some Vietnamese donuts.

"Hey. Good morning, gorgeous."

"Steve," she ran to him, almost knocking the coffee out of his hands.

"It's okay, babe. I'm not going anywhere," he said tickled that she was worried. "Here, have some coffee."

"I know it's silly. But I was just worried." Now that they were finally together, she just didn't want to be away from him.

Nora and Steve spent the rest of the day taking in more of the sights. In 1968 it was the cultural center and the capital of South

JEANETTE VAUGHAN

Vietnam. Heavily influenced by the French in terms of culture and style, Saigon had an air of a French provincial town with a Vietnamese twist. The city was dubbed the "Pearl of the Orient" by the foreign press, alive with activities and diversity that rivaled any Asian city at the time.

The Cho Ben Thanh shopping area was where Nora purchased some of the luxuries that were scarce at Chu Lai. Lipstick, eye liner, eye shadow, face makeup and rouge. She also obtained several pairs of fish net stockings, some ladies panties and some new white boots for one of the girls who had broken a heel. Steve had done some shopping on his own.

Their plans for the evening included a nice, private dinner at the hotel, followed by cocktails out on the enclosed courtyard. Nora looked stunning, in a chartreuse mini-dress with a green, jeweled belt. The time spent with Steve had been magical and she didn't want it to end. They were due to fly out in the morning.

Steve looked serious as he finished his Seven and Seven. "Nora, there's something I been wanting to talk to you about. Have you ever thought about where our daughter might be?"

"Somewhere in Texas, I suppose. I try not to. Just too damned painful. I just hope she is happy and loved."

"Would you ever want to find out?" Steve asked tenuously.

"Honestly? No. She has a mother and father, who I hope love her. I think it would shatter the world she lives in. You can't go back." Nora had built up a protective wall around that subject. She wished Steve would drop it.

"I understand. I just wanted to know how you felt about it," Steve was twirling his lighter with the naval crest. Nora remembered it from long ago.

"I remember that lighter," she picked it up.

"I've had it forever. I had it on our first date."

"At Lafitte's. Yes. That seems like so long ago," Nora's voice trailed off.

"Nora. There is something else."

Nora couldn't imagine what. About that time, a waiter appeared with a silver tray covered by a silver dome. He placed the tray down the table.

"What's this?" Nora asked, anxious to find out the surprise.

"Open it and see," Steve was beaming, his crystal, cerulean eyes dancing.

Nora pulled up the silver dome. On the tray was an indigo velvet box. Nora's hands began to shake. Steve stood up and came over to her. He dropped to his knees taking her hands in his.

"Nora. I have loved you from the moment we met. Life and circumstances just got in the way. But now, finally, I can be true to my heart. Nora Jean Broussard, would you make me the happiest pilot in the world and marry me?"

Nora was stunned. It was a moment she thought she would never experience. For a split second, she couldn't speak. She placed her hand on her heart. Tears rolled down her cheeks.

"Yes, Steve. Of course I will. Yes. Yes. Yes," she cried out. She threw her arms around his neck.

"Wait, we have to make it official," he said pulling away. He got the beautiful marquis cut, three quarter carat diamond out of the box and placed it on her left ring finger. "Now for that hug."

She stood up with him and held him for the longest time. "I love you, Steve. With all my heart. But you know, I can't marry you in the Catholic church."

"Nora. We're in a war zone. Do you think I give a damn about that?"

It had finally happened. Nora was to become Steve's wife. Her head was swimming in joy. On the flight back, Nora could not stop looking at her ring. She was in another world. Exuberant joy filled her entire being. They laughed and told more stories to each other about their experiences. Steve talked about several serious incidents that happened aboard the *Coral Sea*.

* * * * * *

All too quickly, their C-130 transport plane back landed at Chu Lai. Nora was going to have to say good-bye to Steve almost immediately, as there was only one plane headed for Yankee Station. They shared their last thirty minutes together near the hangars, stealing quick kisses whenever they could.

"Your letters take so long to get here. I never even got the last one you said you sent, before you arrived," Nora fretted.

"I'll try to write more often. Every day if I can," he offered. He was so happy to have spent the last three days with her. They were sheer bliss. "It'll only be a short time on the *Bonnie Dick*. Just three months," he tried to comfort her.

"And then what? I'm stuck here. Good God, Steve. What have I done?" her voice was becoming frantic.

"Hey there. Hold it together. We'll figure out something. I'll be back before you know. Hell, we can get married at the club," he chuckled. Nora shot him one of her looks. "Kidding, just kidding. Maybe Hong Kong or Tokyo. I'm gonna find a way to take you home as my wife."

It was killing Nora to see him go. But duty was duty. The minutes ticked by way too fast. They heard the engines of the Phantom rev up. Steve would be riding back seat. Forgetting all protocol, Steve grabbed Nora around the waist and pulled her in for one last kiss. It was long, slow and sweet. He didn't give a rat's ass about rules at that point. Turning to leave, he called out to her, "I love you, Nora. From now, until eternity. We are destiny."

"Just be safe out there, Steve. Just be safe," Nora waved him off, blowing him kisses into the air. She stood on the tarmac and watched as he climbed up into the Phantom and it was pulled out by the crew into position to taxi. The planes had to be pulled out manually, as they were parked so tightly together. Once out on the taxi-way, they were pulled out of the trailer by the flight crew and allowed to taxi on their own.

The jet wash was strong, as the engines whirred for taxi. The Phantom made its way to the end of the runway. Within seconds, it raced down the short stretch and soared into a steep climb. Nora stood there motionless watching it climb and bank a sharp left over the sea northward. Her moments with Steve were over. For now, anyway. Her gut was twisted in sadness. Three months. Three months. I can do anything for three months, she told herself. Ninety days. She would now start marking her calendar.

SOLO VIETNAM

Chapter 30
∞ April, 1968 New Orleans ∞

The small duplex on Dante Street was in chaos. Without any warning at all, Kayce had come home. Nellie was overjoyed to open the door and see her, but Kayce looked frightful. Her hair was long, stringy and dirty. Her clothes disheveled. The strap on her right sandal was torn. She had a tattoo on her wrist, which read *Truth and Justice*. She was a site for sore eyes, but she was home.

Nellie frantically tried to get in touch with the Red Cross, such that they could message Nora, that her runaway teen was home. But she wasn't having much luck.

"Hell's bells, why won't they answer their emergency call line?" she carried on. "Cathy, go run Kayce a hot bath. And get her some clothes and some shoes. Hurry now," Nellie took charge.

"Where is Mother?" Kayce asked. "Is it one of her nights to sing? Why are you calling the Red Cross?"

It dawned on Nellie that Kayce had no idea that Nora had gone to Vietnam. She put down the receiver. "Kayce darling. We need to talk. After your bath, come into the kitchen. I'm going to make you something good to eat. You're skin and bones."

Kayce was gaunt and thin. Living in the commune, she hadn't had much to eat. That and the profound morning sickness she had while carrying the baby with which she had become pregnant. There was lots she had to tell, too.

Nellie went into the kitchen and pulled out some red beans and rice that she had made the night before. It was Kayce's favorite. She put the rice on to steam and reheated the beans in their brand new Amana Radarange.

Kayce entered the kitchen, brushing her hair which was still wet. "So, Grandma. What is the news you have to tell me?"

Nellie was nervous, her hands shaking as she made Kayce a cup of *café au lait*. "My dear. We are so happy to have you home. We were worried sick.' Nellie stalled. Kayce sat there silently. Waiting on Nellie to continue. "Kayce, please just promise me that you won't get mad. Or storm off."

Kayce's eyes narrowed. This didn't sound good at all. She knew it probably had to do with her mother.

"Your mother. Well, she was very concerned about the war. She wanted to do something to help."

"Help. She's the only person on the planet who is supporting the war then. Have you been watching TV?" Nellie's words had struck a nerve.

"Now Kayce calm down. Please just give me a chance to get it all out," Nellie pleaded.

"Go on," Kayce now sat with her arms crossed and a pout on her lips.

"Your mother joined the USO. As a club manager. She went over on tour with Bob Hope. To Vietnam. She'll be over there for a little over a year."

"What?" Kayce asked incredulously. "Has she lost her mind? The war is wrong. Everyone knows it. And yet she goes over there?"

"She is providing a service, Kayce. To our troops over there. She went with a group of young girls, recruited to work the USO clubs. She is their manager."

"So she just abandons her own kids? To take care of other people? Freaking unbelievable. She's just unbelievable. History repeating itself. She's the most selfish woman I have ever known," Kayce was now screaming. Cathy entered the room hearing the commotion. Kayce glared at her. 'Did you know about this?"

Cathy nodded. "But what was I supposed to do? You know how she is. No one's gonna talk her out of something once she makes up her mind."

"This is just outrageous," Kayce raged. It was getting late in the evening. "And where are Iggy and Leisel?" she demanded, just noticing that they were not at home yet.

Nellie wasn't sure how to start that one. "That's the thing, Kayce. They went to live with your father. Just for a while, until your mother gets back." With that news, Kayce became livid. She ran out of the kitchen to the front door onto the porch.

Nellie was in pursuit. "Kayce, please. Kayce. Don't leave, not again," Nellie plead with her. Kayce stopped short on the porch. She had nowhere else to go. She had never forgiven her father for not coming to her aid the first time she had run away, when Nora had taken them from their father during the divorce. "This is just so fucked up," Kayce began to cry.

Cathy came out onto the porch and put her arms around her sister. "I know it is, Kayce. I know. But you are home now. Please stay. It's been hard, me just living here with Nellie. She drives me nuts."

Kayce hugged her sister. At least they had each other. They had always been close, when not at war with each other. "But why? Why Vietnam? It's not like they were going to let her fly there."

"I don't know. She weirded out when the war started. Then, after going to one of Ms. Hebert's parties, she just wasn't the same. She just detached and didn't talk to us anymore. Then, at Christmas, she told us she was leaving. In two weeks. And she did." That was the story.

"I just don't get her. Why isn't she just happy being our mother? Why aren't we enough?"

"I dunno," Cathy pondered. "Maybe it's some kind of women's lib thing."

"It's just not right. She's just the most selfish person in the world. It's always about her," Kayce fumed. "She makes us feel like we don't even matter. That's just like her, to not be here when I finally made it home."

"Why did you come back? Was it awful?"

"At first it wasn't. The summer was great. Lots of teenagers from all over the country came. All wanting to make a difference. Let our voices be heard. We joined groups, participated in protests. We all were living together and working for the cause," Kayce explained. Cathy listened intently hanging to every word. "But then," Kayce continued. "It was like . . . it all changed. After the summer was over. Everything just went kaput. The work was hard. Money was scarce. There were days that I didn't even get a meal. Our commune got run down. Filthy even. Some people really started spacing out on drugs. They started using things with needles. I didn't like it."

"You did drugs?" Cathy was shocked.

"Some. Everyone smoked pot. I dropped a little acid. But it really screwed with my head," Kayce looked down. "Things. Happened. Things that weren't supposed to."

Cathy wasn't sure what she meant. She wasn't even sure what to ask her. But Kayce continued talking.

"I met this guy. Doug. He was from Seattle. Doug was sort of the leader of our group. He just couldn't figure out what was happening. Why it was all falling apart. We kept trying to rally the group, but they were just flaking out. Some of our money, that we had gotten from baking our bread was stolen. They used it for drugs. Some girls were prostituting, to get money. It wasn't supposed to be that way. One night, we dropped some acid, to just escape from it all. You know?"

Cathy really didn't, Kayce realized. She was just stunned to hear that Kayce had actually used drugs. "Weren't you afraid? Of being arrested?"

"Not really. None of us were afraid of the pigs. We really didn't care about anything, except the cause. But that night," Kayce suddenly became sullen. Her lip went into that pout again. "I woke up the next day and couldn't remember where I was. Doug was gone. There was some guy lying next to me. I didn't even know who he was. Something didn't feel right. Down here," she pointed to her vagina.

Cathy's eyes were huge. What Kayce was telling her was so far off her radar screen. She felt like her sister was someone she didn't even know anymore. Kayce continued her story.

"I started getting sick. Morning, noon, and night. Throwing up. I thought maybe some of our food went bad, so I went to the doctor. But it wasn't that. I was pregnant."

"Pregnant? Kayce." Cathy was shocked to the core.

Kayce was silent for the longest time. She looked away from her sister. She wasn't sure she could tell her.

"Kayce," Cathy rose and turned towards her. "Where is the baby?" her anxiety was escalating.

"They wanted me to give it up," Kayce said softly.

"You didn't have an abortion did you?"

"No. I could never do that. Mother may not be anymore, but I'm still Catholic," she explained. "I called Catholic Charities. They wanted to come and get me. I would have been living in a home, until the baby was born. But that was just it, I did want that. I wasn't sure where I wanted to go, but not some maternity home. I rode the bus as far as I could go on the money I had. Then, I hitched the rest of the way."

"How long ago was that?" Cathy wanted to know.

"About a month ago. At first, I went to Seattle, to try and find Doug. I did, but he didn't wanna see me anymore. He thinks I cheated on him with that guy. Hell, I didn't even know what happened. But Doug wouldn't forgive me. What a creep. He didn't even care about the baby."

"That's pathetic. So then you left?"

"Yeah. I didn't care anymore. I got to Denver and worked as a waitress. But I got fired when I served alcohol under-aged. Then, I hitched to Amarillo. But I didn't work there. Just hung out at the shelter and served soup. One day, I found a two twenty dollar bills near the gutter. I kept them, bought another bus ticket, and here I am."

"Kayce. So, you're still pregnant? Geez," was all Cathy could manage. She hugged her sister again. She smelt better now that she had a bath.

"Come on. You can go through my clothes. Some of them are yours anyway."

"So, you don't think I'm terrible?"

"At least you didn't have it sucked into a sink. That would have been terrible."

They both went back into the house. Cathy was still a bit out of sorts at hearing all the sordid details of what had happened to her oldest sister. But she was glad to have her home.

JEANETTE VAUGHAN

Chapter 31
∞ April, 1968 Tonkin Gulf ∞

The *USS Bon Homme Richard* CVA-31 was one of 24 Essex-class aircraft carriers completed shortly after World War II for the United States Navy. She was the named after John Paul Jones's famous Revolutionary War frigate by the same name. Jones named that ship to honor Benjamin Franklin, who was an American Commissioner in Paris at the time. Franklin's *Poor Richard's Almanac* had been published in France under the title *Les Maximes du Bonhomme Richard*.

Steve joined VA-212, the Rampant Raiders, an attack squadron of A-4Es. He was glad that they were busy with combat air support missions for the marines still under siege at Khe Sanh. As such, they had no time for newbies to go through their "Pollywog" initiation for new crew members. The Raiders were infamous for the initiation rite which involved a new crew member slithering through some very smelly pollywogs.

The navy loved time honored traditions. Pollywog to shellback was an example of one tradition no sailor ever forgot. With few exceptions, those who had been inducted into the "mysteries of the deep" by Neptunus Rex and his Royal Court, count the experience as a highlight of their naval career. Original members of Neptunus Rex's party usually included Davy Jones. Current crew members, both officers and enlisted, role played the characters for newbie pollywogs.

Officially recognized by service record entries indicating date, time, latitude and longitude, the crossing of the equator involved elaborate preparations. The "shellbacks," those who had crossed the equator before, ensured the "pollywogs," those who are about to cross the for the first time, were properly indoctrinated. All pollywogs, even the Commanding Officer of the ship, if he had not crossed before, were required to participate. A Golden Shellback was one who had crossed the equator at the 180th meridian.

The Shellbacks constructed the "Royal Bath" which was a pool about four feet deep and about seven by seven feet square. A handy billy was then rigged and sea water was pumped into the 'Royal Bath' and mixed with diesel oil.

The 'Jolly Roger,' a black pirate flag with skull and crossbones, was hoisted. This meant that the hazing was underway. Steak and eggs was the meal for Shellbacks. Pollywogs had hard tack and coffee made with salt water. Various charges were levied against the Pollywogs. Officers were dealt with more harshly than enlisted men. Some had to kiss the royal baby, which was the ugliest sailor on board. Others had to eat an Irish apple, which was a soured onion. Others were treated to the royal barber who had electric clippers that kept shocking as he cut their hair.

After that came the 'Royal Bath' which was when sailors had to yell Shellback three times as they were dunked. Running the gauntlet was the final stage of the exercise. On some ships, a tarp was spread out on deck and greased with graphite, over it about a foot was strung a cargo net. The initiated sailor had to crawl along the tarp for about ten yards with Shellbacks paddling him. At the other end, another Shellback used a fire hose to drive the Pollywog back, just when he thought he was through.

But for the Rampant Raiders, their torture was the 'tube' a canvas sewn into a tub shape and filled with the most retched smelling garbage and shellfish from the ship. When it was all over, a sailor could take a deep breath and with great pride, say he was now a Shellback. Luckily, Steve had crossed the equator many times before. Another couple of RAG pilots were not so lucky and had been initiated when the *Bonnie Dick* crossed. As for this cruise, Vietnam was above the equator. Other forms of revelry besides the pollywog ceremony occupied the hours of stand down.

The missions to support survival at Khe Sanh were almost continuous. One of the pilots remarked to Steve, as they passed each other on deck, "as soon as I walk into the ready room, I meet myself walking out again." As such, many of the aircraft were becoming taxed and requiring repairs.

Steve took off into what was initially a clear, blue sky. He was flying in loose formation and headed toward Khe Sanh. He was comfortable and relaxed, flying about fifty feet back in cruise with little need for constant corrections on the throttle to maintain position. He was passing two small, sandy islands that were between Cubi point and Chu Lai and was on course.

But as they entered into some high stratus clouds, Steve pulled closer into formation and suddenly got a bit of vertigo, which sometimes occurred when flying in clouds and in formation. As the clouds became more dense, Steve flew closer and closer until he was flying in almost parade formation. Parade was the closest formation of all, which only allowed for control from the flight leader.

The flight leader abruptly called out, "Rampant Raider 227, inbound from *Bon Homme*." Then there was nothing. Only static. He passed Steve the lead, his finger on his earphones in his flight helmet, the hand signal for radio failure.

Steve responded, "Damn it," as he knew his plane had no TACAN navigation and didn't know where they were. He knew it should be about ten minutes before reaching Khe Sanh.

"Danang approach, this is Rampant Raider 224 inbound from *Bon Homme* for Khe Sanh, over." Nothing, as Steve had expected. Danang never answered and Steve was headed somewhere at 450 knots. He had to do something, so he called 227-2. "Dash-two, if you can read me, click your mike."

"Bzzt. Bzzt." He could hear Steve.

"If I am on course, click your mike once for yes and two for no."

"Bzzt. Bzzt."

Shit, Steve thought. "For every five degrees I need to turn left, click your mike once."

"Bzzt. Bzzt. Bzzt."

"Shit," Steve muttered. He was way off course for as close as they were. Steve had 227-2 switch to Danang approach and called out, "Danang approach, we have two scooters inbound for a radar pickup and a GCA, over."

Finally Danang responded. "Rampant Raider 2214, this is Danang approach, be advised we are now shut down and in typhoon condition one, you may shoot the TACAN approach to a radar pickup. The approach end is 0/0, but it's more clear on the south runway. Once you obtain visual, circle and land to the south."

Steve passed the lead aircraft and told him to shoot the TACAN and GCA, he would monitor the radio calls. The pilot signaled he had the lead and they started down.

They were flying through what appeared to be a water spout, and Steve could just see his wing when they broke out into the clear over the numbers on the runway. They had been told to go to the other end and circle to land. Steve followed the no radio plane while it flew a circling approach. Normal for visual conditions. The lead plane took the midfield arresting gear, leaving Steve nowhere to land. His mike now unstuck, he called "Dash two, there is no one out here to pull me out. Say your intentions."

Steve rogered his call. "I'm going to have to land at Chu Lai." He turned toward the direction shown on the approach plate to the divert field, pulled his nose up. Climbing out of the mountains he found a hole at 10,000 feet that showed the ground below as being cultivated. Steve began an orbit. When Steve found the frequency for the Chu Lai approach, he found that now his mike was stuck. He started beating on the throttle handle trying to get the radio back, but finally started stacking his maps and other gear that he had in the cockpit to one side.

He was getting quite low on fuel and with no radio or TACAN, had nowhere land. He switched the IFF to emergency and tried one more time to get the mike unstuck. Suddenly, there was static and then, "Aircraft on the 100 radial of Danang, turn right 180 for identification."

When Steve did so, he heard "Radar contact, descend and maintain fifteen hundred feet, you are seven miles on the 092 radial to Danang."

"Danang? I thought I was shooting for Chu Lai." What a fuck-up, Steve thought. Steve acknowledged the approach and shot a ground controlled approach to a final landing. On rolling out, he check his brakes and found he only had one, a left brake with little braking power in it. He called the tower three times and asked if they had an arresting gear set, but they didn't answer.

Steve shut down the engine and slowly drifted left, finally running off the runway right where the arresting gear was hooked. He sank into the mud and settled into a left wing down position as the 14,000 pound aircraft came to an inglorious stop. Steve climbed out of the cockpit, dropped to the ground, and set the pins that locked the wheels. An Air Force Colonel in a dress khaki uniform was watching Steve in his dirty flight suit and his day-old shave. Steve still had his .45 hanging in a holster on his flight vest.

The Colonel was leaning on the point of the aircraft just ahead of the cannon, but it was too late to tell him. Steve pulled his B-4 bag from the forward hell hole where the hydraulic lines were located and carried it over to the tarmac. As the Colonel walked Steve back, he looked at his filthy flight suit and told him, "I guess you did what you had to do" and never spoke another word. Steve smirked, noting the black smudge on the pristine uniform of the Colonel. The Colonel just had no idea.

It took a couple of days for the brakes to be fixed, it was driving Steve nuts that he couldn't just hop into a jeep and head down to Chu

Lai, knowing Nora was so close. Over the course of two days, they would just get one plane fixed and something would go wrong with the other. Three times, they taxied out to takeoff and had to return. Heading back to the *Bon Homme* they had one radio, Steve's that worked correctly. The lead had one TACAN. When they climbed to 36,000 feet heading to Yankee station, the cabin started icing over. Steve scratched a small hole in the ice to again fly formation on the lead. He could see the ocean below and they were below a high overcast, the same as during the first part of the journey.

Steve felt he had survived another combat mission. Those two flights from the *Bon Homme* and back were worse than flying over N. Vietnam.

Chapter 32
∞ May, 1968 Chu Lai ∞

Robert Lathrop was in the club, sipping on a beer. He looked down trodden to Nora as she approached him. He had been reading several letters from his wife. Most people received their letters in bunches. Robert had also been reading his hometown paper, the *Dayton Washington Chronicle*, which he took to keep up with local news. "It seems like there's a world back there that just doesn't exist," he said to Nora.

"I know what you mean. I've only been over here for five months, but it seems like a lifetime. Are those letters from home?"

"If you can call it that. I just am having real trouble identifying with anything that's in them. It's like reading something from a middle class world that I know people from, but don't recognize." Robert shrugged. Despite having been married five years, with two children, one having been born while he was in Vietnam; he felt like he no longer knew her, that they were just dating.

Nora knew that for many of the guys that had been in Nam for any length of time, that home became more and more of a distant memory. When viewed from the lens of daily missions, flares, tracers, bombings, SAMs and the trauma that went with combat flying, thinking of home was like thinking about life on Mars. Most of the fighter pilots lived only for when they flew again, letting little or nothing impact them. They lived for the moment, not allowing the stress of war to bother them. She had seen it in Steve too, to some extent.

People that Nora, Steve, and Robert knew were dying every few days. "Nora, do you realize that one half of my flight class has been injured, are dead, or worse MIA?" Robert mentioned.

"MIA?" Nora asked.

"Yeah. Missing in action. Gone and body not accounted for. They're essentially in limbo."

"God. That's horrific," Nora asserted.

"Yeah. It's like we're not even gaining on the NVA. They strike at will. Constant conflict. I've been flying so much, there's not even time to think about home."

"Hang in there, Robert. Don't lose sight of your count down. You're gonna get outta here and go home. You hear?" Nora tried to give him support.

Robert had been a good friend and confidant to Nora. As an intelligence officer, in addition to flying, he kept her abreast of what was going on with the war, even though he probably shouldn't have. But he found some comfort in unloading to her. She was a great listener. For Nora, it was mutually beneficial, as she could get status reports, sort of, on Steve.

"I tear up all the letters. Do you?" Robert asked her.

"No. I keep mine and sometimes re-read them a hundred times For me? I just hope I didn't make a dreadful mistake, leaving my teenagers back at home."

"Well, you accomplished your mission," Robert pointed out, referring to the ring on her finger.

"That was never my intent, I just wanted to see him," Nora explained referring to Steve. "The proposal was a surprise perk."

"I'm happy for you. You deserve to be with someone who loves you. Who gets you."

"You don't think your wife does anymore?"

"I'm not so sure. It's like were strangers."

"Robert. I'm sorry. I had no idea things were not going well."

"I don't know if they are or aren't. That's just it. Just the damned war," he solemnly replied.

Nora had been writing home regularly, but only getting a few letters here and there. She had heard from Charlene who was now working at the VA. She had also been keeping a diary. At first it had been very descriptive, about all of the new sites and sounds she was experiencing. But after many weeks, there was no emotion in it whatsoever, regardless of what happened. What she supervised for entertainment or a meal at the club was written in the same tone as what she saw after a rocket attack that had hit their NCO area directly, costing lives.

Some GIs were able to call home, but only in the stilted language of the MARS system, a radio that called a ham operator in the states, who called your family. It was possible to speak, but only for three minutes. Due to the restrictions, it was forbidden to talk about anything that was really happening in Vietnam. Sometimes, there even were people from the United States who blocked those conversations. Some GIs were talking to their families maybe for the last time. Nora was infuriated when Robert told her of such activities. If she ever ran into anyone who had prevented a eighteen or nineteen year old soldier from talking to home after surviving the conditions in which they existed, she didn't think she could control her anger.

During mail call today, she had received a couple of letters from Nellie. She wasn't prepared for what she read in the second.

> *Nora, you just aren't going to believe this, but Kayce is home. She got here a week or so ago. She looked dreadful, but is alright. Skin and bones, but I am working to get some weight back on her. Cathy has been her lifeline. It seems that while in San Francisco, Kayce got pregnant. She is about two months along. I didn't know at first, she didn't tell me. But she told Cathy and Cathy let me know. I haven't scheduled an appointment with the doctor yet. Kayce doesn't even know that I am aware. I will keep you posted about her due date. I am just not sure how to handle it. I sure wish you could come home. With love and hugs, your Mama.*

"Now, you're the one who looks like you've seen a ghost," Robert remarked.

It took a moment for his comment to register. "What? Oh, right. It seems that my oldest, the runaway, is home. But she's pregnant."

"Damn. I'm glad she's home. Safe, so to speak."

"Yeah. But good God. Pregnant. She's seventeen."

"Don't guess the guy is going to marry her?"

"It doesn't look like it," Nora replied sullenly.

"What an asshole," Robert commented. "I'm real sorry, Nora. That's hard news to get when you're way over here."

"Yep. It's just like what I was saying. I shouldn't be over here. It was a mistake. But I've got a long time, another year, before I can go back. She will have had the baby by then."

"Mine was born while I was over here too. A boy."

"I just hope my Holy-roller mother doesn't put her in some kind of convent. Good God."

"You don't think she will, do you?"

"I'm not sure what to think. What a mess."

Nora took her letter, tucked it inside her shirt pocket and continued about attending to the business of running the club. It was just like Robert advised, keep working. Working and working and working, in order to not really think about what was happening at home.

"Come on, Nora. Let's take a ride. You need a change of scenery," Robert suggested. He had commandeered a jeep recently as part of his job to stand air base duty from 1800 to 0600 hours, in addition to his flying. The rest of the girls didn't like to venture far from the hooch or the club. But Nora enjoyed getting out and seeing what was happening on the base, especially when Robert would take her near the flight line.

Part of Robert's job was to make sure the lights on the flight line were working and that there were no problems to disrupt flight operations. It was early evening and relatively safe. The sun was just about set. Robert had just checked the tower and GCA shack to make sure they were fully manned.

"You wouldn't believe some of the crap that goes on out here, Nora."

"Yeah? Like what?"

"Most of the time, the Army grunts from Americal are in some kind of scrape with the VC. Right near the perimeter, near the main runway."

"You're kidding. I had no idea."

"The tower never warns us. It just kinda happens. You break out of the clouds at 1200 feet and suddenly, bam. You're blinded by two one-million-candlepower flares, one on either side of the cockpit."

"Holy shit. How can you see to land?"

"That's just it. Your night vision's blinded instantly. You can't even see your instrument panel."

"Geezus, Robert. How can you land?"

"You have to keep your lights on, so you don't get run over by another incoming plane. Makes you a beacon for anti-aircraft. Just a sitting duck until the all clear sounds and the arresting gear crew pulls you clear."

"Good Lord."

"Yeah, your fiancé's got it easy, compared to this. I'd pick trapping over this crap any day."

Robert drove out to Nora's favorite spot, the flight line. On that night, there weren't any skirmishes. "You wouldn't believe what you see out here on patrol. I've seen a tiger on the crosswind."

"No way!"

"Yep, he didn't run, even with the planes coming. Just kept walking at the edge of the lights from my jeep. One night, I ran over a huge black snake. Had to be a cobra."

"I had no idea all that stuff was out here."

"Yep, another reason for the curfew. Just not safe after dark."

He had positioned the jeep at midfield waiting for two Skyhawks to takeoff. Nora could see them running up in the shadowy evening haze some 5000 feet down the runway. Nora was taken aback at what she saw next.

The first plane, on her side of the runway, started rolling. It was accelerating towards her. She watched it approach the midfield marker, raising its nose and pulling up its landing gear to start accelerating. But strangely, it settled back on the runway on its bombs, continuing to skid towards the end of the runway. There was a massive explosion.

"What the hell?" Robert yelled as he released the clutch and in hero mode, drove rapid fire down toward the plane. "We've gotta get that pilot outta there."

Nora held onto to the jeep for dear life. Just then the second plane went by, lifting its nose and retracting its gear, missing them by about twenty feet. "Holy shit," Nora cried out hearing the roar of the engine above her.

Robert and Nora were not the first to the aircraft. Two enlisted Marines had come from the perimeter and were trying to get near the plane, which was now engulfed in flames. The fire was burning dangerously close to the bombs which had been knocked from the plane and were still in their racks. The canopy was still closed and the pilot was still in the cockpit. Robert got out of the jeep and started to go around the wing when all six five-hundred pound bombs went off, all low order with a blast, but not fragments. He was lifted up and set back down about fifteen feet from where he had been. Nora had been shaken in the jeep.

Shaking like leaf, Nora called out to him, "You okay out there, Robert?" She was fearful he had been killed.

But he slowly rose up, ears ringing. "Yep. Yep." He felt like he was floating over the ground rather than standing on it. Robert kept moving towards the cockpit, knowing they had to get the pilot out before he burned to death.

When he got to the front of the plane, he found the canopy gone and no pilot to be seen. Both Nora and he looked around in the dimming dusk, but could barely see a thing. Just then, a shout came out from toward the coast, indicating that the pilot had been found. The explosion had blown the pilot out of the plane, ejecting him a good distance away, relatively uninjured. The marines were in route. They passed a stunned Nora with the pilot resting on a stretcher that had been loaded on top of the jeep they were driving. The severely wounded pilot was taken to the Americal Division Hospital.

"You okay?" Robert called out to her.

"Yeah. I'm still here. Does that happen often?" she asked still a little shaken.

"More than we would like. Loaded with ordnance, we're flying a potential inferno."

"It's crazy. Just crazy," Nora said shaking her head in disbelief. "I just had no idea."

It made Nora even more conscious of why women weren't allowed in combat. She wondered if she could handle that type of impending danger on a daily basis. Robert explained to her that unlike the naval aviators who landed in safety, that often he would land hearing "Chu Lai rockets" over the tower frequency. He was required to sit in the arresting gear while incoming rockets came. It was anything but conducive to peace of mind. Nora shuddered as she thought of the danger Steve flew in nearly every day.

SOLO VIETNAM

Chapter 33
∞ May, 1968 Phu Bai, South Vietnam ∞

There was a clear and present danger in flying, whether taking out bridges in North Vietnam, spotting for the battleship New Jersey in the Tonkin Gulf, or bombing and strafing to protect troops on the ground south of the DMZ. The southern part of North Vietnam was littered with anti-aircraft guns. At any given time, day or night, if they opened fire their missiles could take out planes with effective results.

Flying so many bombing and strafing missions, maneuvering the dynamics of the A-4 had become second nature to Steve. Often, he would make changes to standard flight ops to fit the various ground, weather and enemy conditions. Normally, when strafing an enemy position, a pilot would roll in, keeping the plane upright while approaching the target. As the gunsight got close, the pilot would squeeze off the rounds, pushing or trimming the plane down so that the nose didn't rise when firing and increasing speed. But Steve found he could never hit anything that way.

He developed a technique that worked for him. He'd make the standard upright run, but then would roll into a ninety degree angle of bank, strafe in the angle and roll inverted, continuing to strafe as necessary. By rolling with the gunsight mark over the target, he was pulling positive G forces down to the target rather than staying in a negative G situation all the way down.

With his head seemingly on a swivel, it gave Steve a rush to see the ground target from that position. The ground rushed by so fast, it was a blur. The plane's gunsight coming down on the enemy, Steve saw the bullets impact in groups. However, it was this same type of hot-dogging that got some killed by flying to close to their targets. Steve had to remain totally engaged and alert.

Flying inverted and attempting to strafe with a Hughes gun pod would put the aircraft in a dangerous, slowly moving position, so Steve

-- 153 --

would keep semi-inverted; strafing to the internal guns and rockets, not the gun pod. When he first fired the growling gun pod, hearing the roar of its 1200 round per minute firing rate and seeing the two solid red beams of tracers, each fourth one a tracer; he felt the plane immediately slow from 450 knots to 375 knots. He was exhilarated and filled with awe at the sheer power of the weaponry on board.

The Skyhawk, with its short turn radius and rapid roll rate, made the impossible, possible. When he fired off the five inch Zuni rockets, they sounded like roaring freight trains as they left the wing stations. During some missions, Steve didn't know if he had managed a positive or negative result. But there was sheer joy and validation when flying low. Barely fifty feet above them, ground troops in bunkers would wave their arms wildly in the air, having been protected from the approaching enemy. These kind of missions gave Steve immense confidence and purpose. Some real meaning to the insanity of the war itself.

Early one morning, Steve's squadron had been called in to work with a helicopter controller from the marines. This mission brought them into the Hue/Phu Bai area to support some marines trapped down in a canyon. They were in combat with an enemy NVA unit. Steve knew when he heard the brief, it was going to be challenging.

The squadron would have to attack up the bottom of a blind canyon which had a mountain at the end of it that they could not possibly get over. The canyon was deep and the planes would have to run right up the canyon bottom toward the mountain near the canyon head. It would require some deft aerobatics to climb out one side or the other, fly over into the next canyon and fly down it to recover airspeed for exit.

Once in the next canyon, they would have to descend to its mouth, climb back to altitude and enter the main target area again from the bottom. To mark the target, the Huey popped a smoke, which was a white phosphorous rocket near the terminus of the stream in the bottom of the steep walled canyon.

Steve engaged as soon as he saw the mark, rolling in low at the mouth, noticing that the canyon floor climbed at maybe ten degrees. Steve put his gunsight on the smoke and went level up the canyon, approaching the target. The walls of the canyon closed in. It was freaky seeing a mountain dead ahead and the green jungle racing on either side of him. Steve was getting deeper and deeper, approaching the smoke. The headwall continued to loom larger and larger as he drew near.

Steve fired two salvos with his rockets and then pulled straight up, turning to climb parallel with the slope on the left side of the canyon wall. Steve sharply climbed, turning slightly more steep than the slope, his nose getting higher. But he had to steepen his left bank until he could finally see the nose of the plane over the horizon at the top of the ridge, barely clearing it.

He then rolled into a 120 degree angle of bank and continued so that he was inverted and climbing precariously over the ground, but with the nose just high enough to clear the ridge top. Just as he approached the top, the jungle crown sped by the canopy, and Steve pulled a positive G force and went over the top, inverted, wings level, pulling down into the net canyon, rolling back to the ninety degree angle of bank. As he turned down the canyon toward its mouth, he recovered to the upright, paralleling the bottom of that canyon. Steve had flown a wingover to the inverted position on the ridge top and back to wings level as he accelerated down and out of the mouth of the next canyon.

He found flying the recovery just as thrilling and challenging as the mission, pushing the A-4 to new limits of performance. Steve watched his wingman follow his suit. Watching it was worse than flying it, he thought.

During their second pass, the mark was even farther up the canyon than the first. Steve didn't know if he could make it or not, but he had enough clearance the first time, so he tried to push it for the second. This go round, the mountain was right in front of him, but fell back more than it appeared. He did the same thing again, but this time pulled up a canon to the eleven o'clock so that he didn't have the initial problem of having to clear the ground so soon.

On the final run, Steve was light. The mark was back down the canyon, so Steve ran for it. Faster than normal, he pulled off with heavier G forces than before. Steve had his nose above the horizon early and rolled inverted, paralleling the ground and pulling down, right over the fire base at the top. This time, he rolled into a ninety degree angle of bank, nose level.

Flying missions where he pushed beyond limits without thinking or having ever done it before left one wondering if they were not pushing beyond his own limits or the planes. But Steve flew without reservation, using his gut instincts to guide him. Confidence, skill and guts, however did not prepare him for what happened without warning.

As Steve pulled up he saw a flash of bright light outside the canopy. Within seconds, he heard a deafening loud explosion. His plane had been hit, severely damaging his right wing. Before he knew it, the plane began to spin out. Knowing he was going to crash into the mountain in seconds, Steve hit the eject button.

Still buckled in his seat as he was launched out of the plane, tremendous G forces and heat from the exploding jet fuel caused him to pass out. The parachute deployed causing Steve's almost lifeless body to be cast out over a dense jungle. Two seconds later, his A-4E Skyhawk made impact with the side of the mountain, exploding and lighting up the sky in orange and yellow flames. What he did not know, was that the canyons which they were bombing, were surrounded by hundreds of Viet Cong, just fifty yards away.

SOLO VIETNAM

Chapter 34
∞ Chu Lai ∞

Normally, when Nora woke, at least anywhere but Vietnam, she felt a moment of joy that she was greeting a new day. Back at home, she would put on a pot of her strong coffee with chicory and take a look outside to see what the day was like. Sitting out on the front porch with her cup of coffee, she would think about what she would be going to do for the day. At Chu Lai, Nora would wake and feel the moment of joy for perhaps one-half a second. Then, laying in her sandy bed in the Quonset hut, her mood would slowly sink into a sick feeling in her stomach when she realized where she was.

May 28, dawned semi-humid but clear, much like the climate of her homeland, the coast of southern Louisiana. When she walked out for her first morning coffee, brewing at the USO, she was ready for another average day at the club. The weather was unusually cool for a spring day in Vietnam. Nora stood at the top of the sandy hill where the Quonset hut was built, looking over the South China Sea and took in the beautiful early hour.

It was going to be a lovely day. Her best girls were working, she had a nice local band booked, and her cook was whipping up some Shrimp Creole. The base was quiet as there were no flights. The flight crews were on a six hour stand down, in preparation for some hotpad launches later in the day.

Robert had returned from an earlier 0700 launch to the area around Dong Ha. An attempted insertion by CH-46 Marine Corps helicopters had been a failure. Launch, drop ordnance and return. Simple enough. West of Dong Ha, the target was about seven miles inland on the highway to Khe Sanh. They had been flying support missions for ground troops near there for a couple of days.

He had taken off to the north, the day as clear and bright as any he had seen anywhere. The South China Sea sparkled as did the ships in

Danang harbor. Robert could see the area from his cockpit window as he was passing over Danang. It was possible to see completely across South Vietnam as he continued to fly towards the target.

The purpose of this mission was simply to destroy enemy bunkers housing the shooters. Robert routinely and quickly dropped his ordnance. As he rolled out of the area, he saw the explosions below that his bombs generated. The mission was over minutes after it began. Sad really. It seemed to be too pretty a day for a war.

After the relatively simple mission of dropping ordnance, he returned to his living quarters to don a fresh flight suit for his stand on duty. Robert signed in the log book, got a sandwich and opened the door to air out the eight by forty foot trailer. He prepared for a pleasant afternoon of reading, processing intelligence reports, and doing little else.

The base was almost silent during the afternoon. Robert wondered what had happened to the assault on Dong Ha, because he had thrown so much at it. During the afternoon, he read and sat with the door to the trailer open, letting in the cool air. He looked out across the flight line to the mountains to the west of Chu Lai. They were benign enough in the afternoon, but in actuality, shielded some enemy units that were the size of some U.S. Army divisions that used the area beyond them for rebuilding.

At about 1520, the daily POW, MIA, and KIA list came across the telex. Robert quickly scanned the list, to see if any pilots were lost. His eyes stopped near the bottom.

VA 212 Lt Cdr Steven Novak, USN, *USS Bon Homme*, MIA.

Robert was sure that was Nora's fiancé's name. He read further on the Intel report. Evidently, his plane had been taken out with anti-aircraft fire, crashing into the side of a mountain. Novak ejected. His parachute was found, but no body. He was officially classified MIA. Robert knew it was the worst possible news. Limbo. He had no idea how he was going to tell Nora.

* * * * * *

Nora had been looking forward to her cook's rendition of Shrimp Creole. It was hard to mess it up. She had to admit, after several lessons, her Vietnamese cook could prepare many of her Creole favorites. It was comforting to smell the familiar aromas of Cajun spices, cayenne pepper, bell peppers and onions simmering in butter.

It made her nostalgic for home. She hoped Robert had an early shift and could come to the club for dinner. Just as that thought crossed her mind, the swinging doors of the club opened. Nora looked up briefly and noticed Robert there. She had not seen him in a couple of days.

"Heya, stranger. Thought you'd be around for the Shrimp Creole, but it's not quite ready," Nora laughed, turning her attention back to the books.

At first, Robert was silent and unmoving.

"Have a bad mission? Grab a beer and tell me about it."

Robert moved closer to her. As he did, Nora glanced up and saw the ashen expression on his face. She stood up.

"Robert. What's wrong? Oh my God. What's wrong?" Nora felt a sinking feeling in her stomach.

"Nora. I . . . it's . . . Steve."

Robert could only look down. Nora moved closer to him, taking him by the shoulders.

"I'm so sorry."

"Robert. Robert. What about Steve?" Nora's voice was shrill and full of panic. But without asking, she knew what he was going to say next.

"Steve's plane went down over Hue/Phu Bai. It crashed into the mountain. He ejected."

"Then he's okay. Tell me he's okay," Nora was near yelling. There were two soldiers and a medic at the bar drinking. All activity in the club had stopped. Nora's favorite girl Marsha dropped the tray of mugs she was carrying.

"He's . . . he's . . ." tears were falling from Roberts eyes. "MIA."

"MIA? Oh gawd. Oh holy mother of gawd." Nora sank down to the floor, grabbing Robert's Neoprene flight suit. Her head was at his boots. She was completely gutted. Her body was racked with sobs as she cried out. "No. No. God damn you. No." Her fists were beating his legs in futility. "Oh, gawd."

Marsha came over to her. She sank to the ground and hugged her. "I'm so sorry, Nora. I'm so sorry." Her words could barely be heard over Nora's deep, gut-wrenching sobs.

Robert stood there, helplessly, as Nora clung to his legs. For ten minutes, the world and the war stood silent. Nora continued to weep. Robert helped lift her up, wrapping his arms around her. Marsha hugged her and then stood apart from them.

"Marsha, I'm taking her outta here," Robert took charge.

"Yes. Certainly. I'll watch the club."

Robert guided Nora to the door and walked her out to the beach. He found a table away from the club. The sun was beginning to set. The sampans were headed out to fish. Nora's mascara had run down her cheeks and Robert pulled out a handkerchief and dabbed her face. She had not spoken. She couldn't. In one instant, she felt her entire world crumble.

Robert sat with her quietly, just holding her hands. Her head was down and she could not look at him. She didn't want to see anything. Not the beach. Not the water. Not the club. Not Vietnam. It was cool outside and her body was shaking slightly. Robert grabbed a large beach towel from the lifeguard rack and wrapped it around her shoulders.

They sat this way until the sun was completely down, the stars and moon beginning to shine over the water. Quiet music could be heard coming from the club. Marsha had continued operations as planned, despite wanting to ball herself, every five minutes. She stifled down the tears and carried on as she knew Nora would want her to in support of the troops.

After about an hour, Nora finally looked up. "You work intelligence. Tell me the truth about MIAs." Nora looked Robert directly in the eyes.

He took a huge breath in and sighed. "It isn't good, Nora. Not good at all. The government lists men as MIA when there is no trace of a body or capture. Many times, there's nothing to be found. If the NVA don't list them as POWs officially, and the Viet Cong have them" he hesitated to continue.

"Go on," she sternly prompted.

"We've heard stories. Stories of torture."

"Christ almighty." At that, Nora got up and ran towards the beach and into the water. Robert ran after her. He stopped a few feet from her as he saw her bend over and wretch. She vomited up all of the anger and frustration and bile until she was just dry heaving. Robert put his arms around her waist and held her. He rubbed her back.

"Come on, girl. Come on now. Be strong. It's Steve. You know he's tougher than that." He helped her stand up and turned her to face him. Robert held her there, the water lapping against their legs. He held her as she cried softly. After several minutes, he walked her back toward the club with his arms carefully wrapped around her. She needed his other arm for stability.

Robert guided her back to her hooch, helping her climb the stairs up. He pulled down the sheet on her bed, sat her down, and took off her shoes. Then he helped her lie down, still rubbing her back. He wanted to give her hope, but knew in reality, it was probably to no avail. He had always been truthful to his friends, to his family, and to his fellow officers and subordinates. He would not sugar coat anything.

Ever loyal, Robert stayed with her until he heard her fall asleep from exhaustion and sobs, continually rubbing her back. Her body jerked with each partial heave of her heavy heart. He did not leave her until Marsha had finished at the club.

"Don't leave her alone. Promise," he commanded her.

"No. We won't." Marsha assured.

In the meantime, Frenchy, the driver, had come looking for him. There was another mission to fly. Despite the fact that Robert had been up for twenty-six hours, duty called.

Chapter 35
∞ Hue Province, South Vietnam ∞

When Steve regained consciousness, initially all he sensed was a massive headache. There was blood dripping from his left eyebrow. Evidently, the left side of his head had struck a tree branch on the way down, knocking him completely unconscious for several hours. Steve squinted to clear his blurred vision. It took him several seconds to gain his bearings.

Immediately after, his heart began to race. This was the worst possible outcome, being downed in the Hue Province, heavily occupied since Tet by the NVA. The USMC and US Army had done its due diligence to attempt to regain Hue City. Steve himself had bombed and strafed the region numerous times during the twenty-eight days of the Tet Offensive from late January into February.

The province was known as an area of heavy fighting. As the second most northern province of South Vietnam, it was very close to the DMZ. More soldiers had died in this province than in any other since the war started. Steve recalled the briefings which described how, during the 1968 Tet Offensive, thousands of Vietnamese civilians, Americans and ARVN POWs were slaughtered by the Viet Cong in some kind of divine mission to eliminate resistance to the communist cause.

First and foremost, Steve sought out his radio to use his coded signals for rescue and recovery. Each pilot was given an alpha-numeric code unique to them. They were trained on how to use the code, whether by radio or by using the landscape in such a way that the enemy could not tell they were using it at ground level.

Steve's right hand had been mangled during his parachute down through the jungle canopy of buttressed hopea and mountain cedar trees, some up to 150 feet in height. The brush was thick with garcinia and ferns. Steve checked the deep pockets of his flak jacket to make sure he still had his pistol. Check. Thank God it was still there.

Getting out his radio, Steve sunk low into the brush, to stay hidden and began to emit his rescue signals. He wasn't exactly sure where he was, as during the drift down and afterward he had been out of it. As soon as he got his signal working, he reached for a knife, to cut and pull down his parachute out of the trees. No need to leave a beacon for where he was hidden.

The air hung like a heavy rug of humidity. Steve had seen most of Vietnam only from the air. He was now getting a grunts view of the hellish conditions described by the ground troops. The jungle was a mass of overgrown vines, ferns, and bush. He knew better than to seek out any type of trail. It would be littered with bamboo spikes and traps set by the Viet Cong.

His compass had been crushed. With the thick overhead canopy of trees, he was having trouble detecting the position of the sun which would help him gain a position on north and south. He knew the most important thing would be to keep hydrated, as he had no idea how long it would take evading the enemy before he was rescued. If he was rescued at all. His worst nightmares about flying missions over Vietnam were all coming to fruition. It was time to enact every tenant of SERE training if he was going to make it out alive.

Overhead, Steve heard the rustling in the leaves. Numerous monkeys were scattering as if running from something. Seconds later, Steve heard the rumble of helicopters flying low over the canopy. But his chute was now down, and he was unable to be seen. Steve hoped that they heard his secret signals. After several minutes, he realized they had not. He would have to keep moving. Without any better alternatives, Steve began to make his way through the jungle brush in the direction the choppers were flying by using his knife.

After several hours, he was exhausted. He took refuge under a large palm tree. Noting the terrain, Steve could tell that he was in near one of the mountain's bottom edges, as he could see elevated terrain on his left. He knew that mountains covered more than half of the Hue province. For all that it was worth, he realized he could be merely hundreds of yards from the Laotian border. That would most certainly mean death and torture if he was captured.

While he was sitting under the tree, it began to rain. Sweet relief. Steve quickly scrambled to form a make-shift cup with his hands. It was a heavy, short and sudden burst, typical of the area. But it meant water. Steve sucked up each gulp with gratitude. The pain in his head had not abated. Although Steve certainly had no medical training, he knew that sign and symptom could mean a concussion or worse.

Once the rain stopped, Steve knew it was again time to move. The rain would cover any tracks he had left. For that he was relieved. The jungle was getting dark quickly. Night was approaching. It would be a long one and without sleep. Too dangerous to close ones eyes in the midst of enemy territory.

Steve returned to the slashing of vines. Hack, hack, whack. At one point, a large green snake about six feet in length slithered rapidly across his arm, causing him to gasp. Round head. Not poisonous. Or so he hoped.

He reached a grove of lychee evergreen trees and quickly tore off as many berries as he could eat. The rest, he stockpiled in a pocket of his vest for later. They would serve as energy, for now. He came to a tall tree, full of durian, which looked like spiked coconuts. One or two had fallen on the ground. Using his knife, he hacked one open and sucked out the pulp.

Despite keeping his energy up with the berries and durian juice, having to break his way through the jungle was exhausting. The pain in his head seemed to be increasing, not subsiding. All of a sudden, Steve had a massive headache, the worst in his life. And then, the jungle turned black as he fell to the ground.

Chapter 36
∞ Yankee Station ∞

Frustration and helplessness were the only terms to describe what a Rescap helo pilot felt knowing one of his aviators was down. When Pete heard the news that Steve had been shot down near Laos, he was sickened. He instinctively wanted to run up on deck, fire up his bird and head out to search for Steve's signal code. But that was not to be.

Pete was assigned to HC-1 which was a lighter helo bird squadron. They weren't equipped with enough heavy duty artillery, nor were they long range capable for inland navigation. He did the next best thing and contacted another bird pilot from a search and rescue, SAR squadron aboard that flew the H3.

Luckily, during this period the squadron was operating off the *Coral Sea*. Most of the guys attached to the squad were enlisted. A few of them could have posed for an old pirate picture with very little touch up. With shaggy hair, un-shaven faces, and unlaced flight boots, much of the time, they looked very tired and drawn out. SAR chopper squadrons were either making repairs to their helos or flying in them as rescue crewmen and gunners. The pace of their operations never stopped.

When the ship was scheduled to be relieved from being on station in the gulf, these SAR squadrons would fly over to the next available ship and continue to operate. Their stats weren't good. One of the SAR squadrons rescued about a dozen or so downed aviators but lost twelve helos and more than half a dozen of their own men in the process. It wasn't a choice assignment.

At that pace, no one was sure of the validity of the rescue process. It probably only helped the moral of the attack and fighter pilots. But in the days of 'full speed ahead and damn the torpedo's' it was as duty called.

Pete met one of pilots following an incident that happened off the deck of the *Coral Sea* a few days before Steve's MIA status was posted.

He was up on the flight deck when the SAR rescue squadron left the *Coral Sea* to operate off another carrier. One of the helicopters was very heavily loaded. He noticed it by the amount of upward arc of the main rotor blades as the bird was straining to lift off the edge of the ship. The flight deck was so jammed up that all the departing helo could do was lift a few feet in the air and then slide sidewise to clear the ship.

As soon as the heavily loaded helo got a little more than half way over the edge of the flight deck, it lost its ground cushion. Dropping like a rock, it hit the side of the flight deck and catwalk. Pieces of rotor blades careened across the flight deck. Pete scrambled down into a tie down pad to escape the flying pieces of metal. The turbine engines came apart with the rotor rocketing forward a couple hundred feet into the air.

Upon impact with the sea, the helo was inverted. About a minute later, after launching his helo, Pete could see it in the water as he got to the edge of the flight deck. He could visualize heads popping above the water, as the men inside the helo made their escape. There were probably about eight or nine guys.

Pete's detachment 43 rescue crew scrambled to try and get over the inverted helo in the water. They desperately tried to lower one of their rescue crewmen into the water to investigate the inside of the inverted helo. But invariably, they were edged out by the other helos. All launchable rescaps had formed a circle of about five aircraft around the downed helo. One of the five would move in and pick up a survivor then move back out. Then, the next helo would move in and make a rescue the same way. It was a tedious process. Roter blades dangerously close to one another in the swirling, dark, cobalt sea.

Apparently one of the crewmen who was not strapped in and sitting on loose cruise boxes full of maintenance equipment got trapped under them when the helo was inverted. The SAR squadron never sent a rescue crewman in to see if the downed helo was clear, which Pete simply didn't understand. They apparently did not want anyone else to rescue one of their own. The trapped crewman was not recovered and went down with the helo.

The next morning, Pete got a bit of heartburn over the lack of 'can do' spirit that he had experienced the day before. He would go to the ends of the earth to rescue one of their own, which is why he approached one of the SARs pilots

"Sorry about the loss, we lost one too. Yesterday," Pete explained.

SOLO VIETNAM

"Oh, yeah? Whereabouts?" asked the airman.
"Laos. Near the border."
"Did they get a signal?"
"Not that I know of. Do they ever?"
"Sometimes. Sometimes. You'd be surprised. But, it's pretty random."
"That's what I hear," Pete sounded dismayed.
The SAR pilot noted the flatness in his voice.
"Dude, I saw ya out there in your bird. Thanks for trying to help."
"It's my job. Frustrating as hell on any given day."
The pilot gave a single nod. He eyed Pete ever. "Say, man. I'll keep my ears to the radio. Laos ain't good. But if I hear anything, I'll let ya know."
Pete noted some Ensign collar devices on the table. "Planning a promotion?" he chuckled.
"No, dude. Out there, ya gotta be prepared. If I went down as an enlisted AN, I'd be toast. Put some of these on and I'm money to the VC."
"Gotcha," Pete was amused at the train of thought of the pilot. But then again, he didn't put his life on the line every day flying inland over a war zone.
Pete stuck out his hand for a shake. "Thanks, man. Anything you can do." He knew it was pretty desperate, but at least it was something. He had come to know Lt. Cmdr. Novak as an alright kind of guy.

JEANETTE VAUGHAN

Chapter 37
∞ June 1968, New Orleans ∞

Charlene relished the job she had taken working at the VA hospital in New Orleans. Located on Perdido Street, near the medical center of downtown, it stood twelve stories tall and had 492 beds. Charlene was assigned as a nurse's aide to the out-patient orthopedic clinic serving veterans returning from Vietnam.

Often, her duties involved completing vital signs and working with mobility technicians who outfitted the returning soldiers with prosthesis for limbs lost during combat. Many young nurses, much less students, simply didn't have the moxie for it. Some of the vets were rude or crass. Angry at the condition the war had left their ravaged bodies. But Charlene felt it was a calling.

Her chipper, positive attitude, and yet sharp tongue, made her just the right nurse's aide to respond to their bitter, sarcastic jabs. Through letters from Nora, Charlene knew the back story. Unlike most of suburbia, she had some idea of the hell that they had been through. Charlene was riveted at the horrors Nora described about the actual conditions of North and South Vietnam.

Charlene was never offended by the vet's rancor. Many times, she had them smiling as she laughed at their jeers and jokes. While unwrapping and re-wrapping their stumps, she attempted to restore their dignity and self-worth. Charlene encouraged them away from alcohol and toward the hope of a better tomorrow and end to the war.

When they were able, Charlene would encourage them to talk about what they saw there. Their stories were horrific and shocking, but she knew that in sharing them, the vets would relieve themselves of the heavy burden they carried inside. Hopefully, lightening their load toward better mental health.

Charlene still had Nora's latest letter in her pocket. This letter had been different from the rest, filled with the joy and elation of Nora's engagement to Steve. A smile crossed Charlene's face as she imagined the expression on Nora's face when her long, lost love had not only

SOLO VIETNAM

hooked up with her, but proposed. War indeed produced bizarre twists and turns to life.

As a part of her job, Charlene had to update and review the wounded/casualty list, denoting what progress the nurse's patients were making in their recovery. Within this data, one page that she checked each day was the POW, MIA and KIA lists. To assist clerically, she was required to scan it to see if anyone from the Greater New Orleans area was on there. Knowing so many people in the community, Charlene also perused the list for relatives of families she recognized.

Sadly, at least once every week, appeared the name of someone she or her husband knew. More often than not, it was a young man with whom her children had gone to school. They were no more than eighteen or nineteen years old. Fresh faced young boys, schooled at only the best New Orleans Catholic institutions, hopeful and full of life. Their families members of local parishes.

Having access to insider information, Charlene was put in tune to the real damage, both emotional and physical that the Vietnam War unleashed. Charlene finished up her last clinic patient and began charting the vital signs she had taken in the records. She was proud to use her newly learned nursing skills.

On this shift, she had taken care of a twenty-two year old First Lieutenant. He had lost his left leg, just above his knee to a land mine. He was leading his platoon out of the jungle and away from the impending drop of napalm. As they entered a clearing, the lieutenant stepped on a land mine. Luckily, only his leg was lost. A private first class, PFC Winters, also from New Orleans, picked up the lieutenant and carried him the three miles back to their base camp.

Charlene was about to wrap up her work for the day. Another young nurse working the clinic approached her. "Mrs. Hebert, don't forget to check your POW, MIA list."

"Thanks, Nurse Sherri. I just nearly would have. My son's baccalaureate at Jesuit is tonight." Charlene quickly scanned the list. Boudreaux, Dubois, Genereaux, Peralta, Prejean, Romano. "'Hmm. I wonder if that Dubois is any kin to Mr. Dubois, my friend's neighbor?" Charlene muttered mostly to herself. She had been to one too many funerals lately.

The color drained out of her face when she got near the end. In the MIA column, in black and white blocked letters it read:

LTCDR STEVEN NOVAK

"No, no, no, no!" she screamed out.

"Mrs. Hebert," the young nurse came over. "What's wrong?"

"This name. This can't be right." Charlene was nearly hysterical.

"I'm so sorry. Did you know someone on the list?"

Charlene began to sob. "Damn it. God, how could you? Damn it."

The young RN held her nurse's aide tight. She knew it had to be extremely bad for Mrs. Hebert to curse in public. Tears streamed down Charlene's face as she sank into her chair. Her heart was breaking for Nora. Steve, MIA. It was just too much. Nora had sounded so happy in her last letter. She wondered if Nora even knew? She wished she could phone her. To hear her voice. To hug her. To hold her in what must be the most tragic news she could imagine. Poor Nora.

"I am so very sorry for your loss, Mrs. Hebert. So terribly, sorry." The nurse brought her some Kleenex.

Charlene sat in her chair for the longest time. She felt hopeless and helpless. Her hands were shaking as she was holding the white paper with Steve's name. Through her tears, she squinted to see the date he was listed as missing. It was marked May 27, 1968.

Chapter 38
∞ June 1968, Hue Province ∞

A searing pain to his back was the next thing that Lt. Commander Steven Novak felt on the morning of June 2. That, and the sound of a foreign voice, yelling in a foreign tongue. Steve's hands were bound, as were his feet. He struggled to open his eyes, the left one now almost swollen shut. He had been struck in the face. Blood had now dripped down onto his eye lids.

"Dậy. Dậy bẩn thỉu Mỹ GI," the Vietnamese voice commanded, which meant 'Get up. Get up, filthy American GI.' "Dậy. Dậy bẩn."

Steve rolled over and attempted to get up. As soon as he did, another Viet Cong struck him in the face with the cane. Causing him to drop again to his knees. "Trí thức Nhận." The VC screamed at him, "No. Get up."

Not willing to be struck again, Steve complied. One of the VC used a large machete and without warning swung it towards Steve in between his ankles severing the lower binding on his feet. His boots had been removed. He had been stripped of all his gear, including his pistol. Steve began to move in the direction the cane-wielding VC was pointing. Gritting his jaw, Steve inwardly winced as his feet struck the reeds and pointed leaves along the jungle floor. But he was damned if he was going to let the VC know he was in pain.

After about a hundred yards, they reached a trail and clearing. Without lifting his head much, Steve tried to take in the visual surroundings of where they were headed. It was obviously up in elevation. Turning for a split second, Steve could see a huge body of water in the distance behind them. He knew it to be Tam Gian-Cau Hai, the largest lagoon in Southeast Asia. At least he now had his bearings.

Steve knew that to survive after capture, he needed to appear compliant to the VC's demands. But inside, as would any GI, he looked for an opportunity to escape. Forefront in his mind were his children and Nora. There was no way he was going out as a prisoner.

His feet were now blistered and bloody. Honor, courage, commitment. Honor, courage, commitment. The naval aviator's ideals were the only words going through his head with each excruciating step. After several hours of walking, the VC stopped to break camp. Steve was chained to a tree. He was given some despicable food, offered to him on a stick. Reluctantly, he choked it down in a pure means to survive.

Fuck the VC. Fuck the pain. Fuck this war. Stand tall. Don't give up. Steve was using every possible means of motivation he could find within himself. He waited until he saw all of the VC except the guard asleep; it was time to get some rest himself. Rest was inherent to keen thinking. Steve managed to get a few hours of much needed recovery.

In the wee hours of the morning, Steve again felt the cane. But this time, on his feet. The VC guard was beating him awake. Steve was instantly jolted into full mental power. Day two of making it.

The VC made their way up one side of the mountain and down the other. It was as Steve predicted. They were headed for Laos. Certain doom. He knew it was now or never. Steve plotted in his head the best method for escape. He decided that when they broke camp for the night, he would make a break for it.

Coming down the other side of the mountain, they reached a valley. In the middle was a dark, murky stream. The VC crossed. The guard poked and prodded Steve. There was no telling what was in the hip high water. Gritting his teeth, Steve entered the stream. He could feel slimy creatures slithering past his feet. When he jumped up on shore, his feet were covered in leeches.

The VC were laughing. Initially, they let him be, suffering miserably as he could feel the leeches literally sucking out his life blood. But one of the guerilla militiamen grabbed a canister. It was filled with sea salt. He sprinkled it over Steve's feet and ankles. Slowly but surely, the leeches fell away, leaving open wounds in which the salt entered. Steve called out in agony, to which many of the VC only jeered.

They had entered a rice patty field. It was submerged in about six inches of water. There were workers making approval gestures toward the VC, noticing the prisoner they had in tow. All of the water from crossing the stream had loosened the ligatures around Steve's hands, but he never let on.

Once across the rice patty, the VC reached their temporary camp. It was a Laotian village which they had overrun. Steve was placed into a dugout bunker, with cane bars securing it. He was not the only prisoner. A skeletal American, surely near death, was chained to a series of metal rings. Initially, Steve did not speak to him, knowing that any communication would surely bring a beating.

The VC guards were exchanging words. Then, there was only one guard remaining on duty. He broke out a cigarette and began to smoke. Steve, not in chains, moved closer to the other prisoner.

"Lt. Commander Steve Novak, USN," Steve whispered.

Attempting to speak, the prisoner at first could only cough. His voice was raspy. "Sgt. Major, Jeff Edwards. USMC."

"We're gonna get outta here, soldier. Mark my words," Steve assured.

"Yessir," the prisoner whispered and then coughed harshly, clearly exhausted from any verbal exchange.

It was obvious to Steve that Jeff had been severely beaten. His arm hung in an unusual angle, indicating that it had been broken. Jeff motioned with the other one to be quiet.

Steve couldn't understand the conversation of the guards above him, but what they were talking about was Steve's rank. Because of his elevated position and status as an officer, they planned to use him as some kind of ransom.

The guards interrogated Steve, pretty brutally for a couple of days. Afterwards, he was a frightful site. His back felt broken from the strikes of the canes. His arm wound had continued to bleed and that blood was now dried solid and collecting flies. His feet, now grossly swollen and looking like a piece of meat, had been nibbled by rats. He was three days unshaven. Unfortunately, during and after the beatings, Steve had lost consciousness and thus had no control over his bowels or bladder. He had soiled himself badly.

During questioning, Steve was threatened with his life. The VC had tied his arms behind his back; the ropes increasingly tightened with each interrogation session. As a result, both his shoulders dislocated. Having elbows pulled together against his seemingly broken spine, was almost more than he could bear.

But he would give up nothing. No information. Sticking to code he gave only name, rank and serial number. Disgruntled and frustrated the VC finally ceased the interrogations. Steve and the other prisoner, barely clinging to life were marched for three days to another jungle prison camp. The buzz of the flies and gnats were still ringing in Steve's ears.

Every night, rats scurried through the cages and nibbled on Steve's arm wound. With it broken, Steve couldn't move it and keep them away. He was a human piece of cheese.

The only time Steve was allowed out of his cell was to take a piss in the jungle. Since this was a temporary camp, there were no latrines. Jeff was just too weak to be let out. There were only a few occasions when he was given water, but it was putrid. Food was also a problem and consisted only of a retched, sour cabbage soup.

As the third evening progressed, Steve regained some presence of mind. He noticed the fatigue of the guard. It was clear that Jeff may not make it through the night. His color was ashen and his breathing had become shallow and raspy. The VC had really done a number on him. Steve knelt beside Jeff and made the sign of the cross.

"I'm no priest, but I'd like to say some prayers for you, Jeff. Remember you are not alone. I'm here with you and so is God. As hellish as it may seem, if you leave this earth, your soul will surely be taken to heaven." Steve grabbed Jeff's hands and began to say the *Our Father*.

Near the end of the prayer, Jeff took a big breath and gasped. It was his last. Steve dropped his head and made the sign of the cross over Jeff's head, his lips, and his heart. "Unto you Lord, please accept Sgt. Major Jeff Edwards."

Steve felt badly about promising Jeff that he would get them out, but Jeff had been more far gone than he first surmised. Jeff's death however, gave Steve an idea. He went over to the wrought iron gate opening which sealed the bunker prison. Rattling the gate, he cried out, "Hey. Hey gook."

The guard, sound asleep, suddenly jolted awake. He began screaming Vietnamese obscenities. Steve motioned towards Jeff's lifeless body, making a noose motion and a sliding his fingers across his neck, indicating death.

Unlocking the gate, the guard opened the hatch. As he entered to see what Steve was talking about, Steve grabbed his rifle and swung it with all his might. Whack. The guerilla fighter fell to the ground. Steve knew better than to shoot him, the noise might attract attention. As soon as the guard was down, Steve removed his worn combat boots. They probably wouldn't fit, but he figured that cramped boots were better than nothing. As it turned out, they were American boots, likely stolen off another prisoner, only half a size too small.

Steve laced them only half up, grabbed the rifle and peered carefully out of the tin roofed, make-shift prison. He could see some smoke from a camp fire about fifteen yards away, but no one on patrol, as best as he could tell. He hated leaving the body of Jeff behind, but he knew if he tried to carry it, it would attract too much attention.

SOLO VIETNAM

Making sure the coast was clear, Steve got down on his hands and knees and slowly crawled out of his holding cell and into the brush of the jungle. Trained with survival instincts like any other soldier, he would do anything to escape. Steve stayed down in a low position as he moved further and further away from the VC encampment. His flight suit was ripped and torn, exposing his right knee. Ignoring the pain from his head wound and multiple bruises on his flanks from the beatings by the guards, crawl by crawl, Steve moved deeper into the jungle; slithering over foliage that had been saturated with Agent Orange.

He now had no way to signal for help. His only hope was to keep moving until he could possibly encounter friendly forces. Steve had absolutely no idea which direction to try. There was no way to see the stars or the moon in the thick, overhanging jungle canopy. This time, he would keep moving. No sleep. Hopefully, no passing out. Even if it took days.

Chapter 39
∞ Chu Lai ∞

It had been four, long, dismal days since Nora had heard the news about Steve. During those four days, she had not been out of her hooch. She had not taken a bath or changed her clothes. Other than to use the john, Nora had not gotten out of bed. The blinds to the hooch were kept dark. If any of the girls dared raise them, she rebuffed them. Gruffly commanding, "No. I want them down."

In the darkness, Nora could evade the unequivocal pain of facing the reality of Steve's situation. Jamie had called the base chaplain to come and see her. But it was futile, she would speak to no one.

Robert had been flying continual missions. In between catching a few hours sleep, he poured over Intel reports to see if anything came across the wire about Steve having been taken as a POW. But there was nothing.

At least as a POW, he had a chance to stay alive. There were now over 700 POWs listed officially by North Vietnam. They were kept in several POW camps, many of which were near Hanoi. Records were sketchy, as the NVA would move their prisoners to suit their needs. The National Security Agency, NSA, was tasked with identifying and relaying the signals accounting for men downed in the conflict. Unfortunately, many times they didn't have the assigned escape and evade codes given to pilots to use in the event of their capture.

For the pilot, it was their only means to communicate. Using their SERE training in concert with the landscape in such a way to avoid detection from the ground, the aviator would transmit his signal. Little did anyone realize at the time, but the NSA frequently encountered difficulty with crossed radio transmissions and shadowed frequencies thus preventing them from identifying the downed GIs they were tasked to protect.

As Robert well knew, Laos was a dark hole which swallowed many Americans. He hoped and prayed that wherever Steve had gone down, that it was far from the Laotian border.

That afternoon, another visitor appeared in the doorway of Nora's hooch. "Captain Broussard. Nora?"

Nora recognized the voice as Woody, the Chief Petty Officer that had helped her get so many supplies for her girls and the club. "Go away," she mumbled.

"Nope. Not until I deliver what I came to bring ya."

"I don't want anything. From anyone," Nora moaned and pulled her sheet over her head.

Woody wasn't taking 'no' for any answer. He moved over to her cot, pulled down the sheet and thrust a letter in front of her face. "Well, Ma'am. I'm sure you'll want to see this."

Nora rolled over. It was a padded envelope addressed to her. Squinting, she saw it was a letter from Steve. "Where did you get this? But how?"

"Look at the date, Ma'am. It was sent a couple of weeks ago. Just took a while to get to ya."

Nora looked at the post mark. It was dated May 5. Her hands started shaking. She was almost afraid to open it. But she couldn't resist. Sitting bolt upright, she tore open the envelope.

Woody turned to leave. His mission was accomplished. At least she had gotten up on the side of the bed. "I'm sorry, Captain Broussard. For what you're going through. But you have to keep the faith. MIA ain't KIA."

Nora looked up. "Thank you," she managed.

Woody had become quite fond of her. They had shared many a glass of beer at the club, wheeling and dealing over supplies. He had been a lifesaver to her and the girls. Why he took an interest in her, he could not explain. She was just another dame. But to him, Nora was more than that. She was the most unusual woman he had ever met. He returned to his jeep.

Nora heard the jeep start up and drive away. She continued to sit on the bed. It took several minutes for her to actually summon up the courage to even take the letter out. It was written with blue ink on white paper with gold US naval aviator's wings embossed on the top. She immediately recognized the handwriting of her lover, Steve.

My dearest Nora:

The days that we recently spent in Saigon were bliss. Bliss amidst a senseless war. I feel blessed to have you back in my life, finally able to show the world what you mean to me. My beloved. It was simply destiny. A destiny for which we had to wait.

But now, there is no longer a need to wait. We are one. Eternal and forever. I love you with all of my being. As I take off each day from the deck and fly out over the ocean, its vastness no longer feels empty. For I know, that you are here with me in my heart and shall be there for all time.

Those few days are what I hold onto each day as we fly missions to protect and defend our troops. I have been flying non-stop it seems. Cats and traps seeming to never end. I never realized how much ammo was produced. But I've dropped thousands of pounds of it myself. I take out my rosary after each mission and kiss the cross in thanks for a safe return. As of late, there have been several of our crew shot down who did not return. The SAMs are rife.

Please be strong and know that I love you. I'm almost at the end of my tour. A few months to go. I tick off the calendar daily. I'm due for my R and R shortly. Maybe we could rendezvous and do Tokyo or Hong Kong this time.

I am committed to staying safe, for I long to do nothing more than hold you in my arms again. I want you to keep this lighter and hold it until I can hold you. It is with honor that I look forward to being your husband and lover for life.
All my love,
Steve

Nora read and re-read Steve's letter. Probably about a hundred times. She poured over each word. Then, she turned the envelope upside down and shook it. There it was, Steve's lighter with the naval crest. The strength in his request of her, to be strong, echoed. She could swear she heard his robust, sure, commanding voice. Be strong. Be strong.

For the first time since the news, Nora got out of bed. She walked over to the small mirror mounted on the Quonset wall. Her reflection in the mirror was simply frightful. There were dark bags and circles under her eyes. She had cried off all her mascara, but traces of her eyeliner were smeared at the corners of her large, brown eyes.

Enough. Enough wallowing. He was out there. Somewhere. Fighting for his life. She had to get herself together. To quit wallowing. She had to be strong for Steve.

Nora splashed some cold water on her face, lathered up her hands and washed away the self-pity in which she had been cocooned for days. She ran a shower from the rain water collected. The cool temperature of the water re-energized the cells of her body which had been in hibernation. She washed her hair, which was matted. Next, she put on a fresh set of clothes. Resolutely, she applied her make-up and trademark eye-liner. Even some lipstick.

Nora was temporarily blinded from the bright sunlight, as she opened the hooch door for the first time in days. Life and the war had gone on without her. The dust and sand of Chu Lai were waiting to greet. She put on a pair of heeled sandals and made her way down to the club. As she crossed the bridge, her best girl greeted her.

"Well, hey there. Aren't you a sight for sore eyes," Marsha put her arm around Nora and guided her to the club. The sights, sounds, and smells were all the same. Somehow comforting.

"It's so good to have you back, Captain Nora." the cook greeted. He obviously had something savory on the stove.

"I'm not sure I'm all here. But I'm trying."

"Well, I'll be damned," Woody called out from the bar.

"Woody, I want to thank you. For bringing the packet."

"Anything for you, Toots. Anytime. I missed your croonin' is all."

Nora gave him a smirk. It was good to see that she still had some spark. She had neglected the club for days and was not sure what to do or where to even start. But it appeared that Marsha had kept things under reasonable control. Except for the books. As she entered the cubby that was her workroom, she noted the piles of invoices on her desk. Time to get back to work. Time to get back to life.

Chapter 40
∞ June, 1968 New Orleans ∞

Try as she might, Kayce simply could no longer button the hip-hugger jeans that she had continued to wear, despite being five months pregnant. She had managed to conceal the pregnancy from almost everyone by wearing the loose, gauze, peasant tops that were the latest rage. Only Cathy and Nellie knew. But today, she had no idea how she was going to keep her jeans up, if she couldn't get them zipped.

As she struggled with the zipper, she didn't notice that the bathroom door had opened slightly. Just enough to give the approaching Charlene, over for a coffee with Nellie, a glimpse of Kayce's enormous baby bulge.

"Kayce Greenwood. What in tarnation?" Charlene pried the bathroom door wide open and gaped at Kayce's stomach. "You're pregnant," her shrill voice announced.

Kayce quickly covered her belly with her top. She could not look Mrs. Hebert in the face and defiantly turned her back away from her. But Charlene grabbed her shoulders and spun her back around.

"Just how pregnant are you? Exactly who knows about this and why in heavens didn't anyone tell me?"

"Why do you think? It's scandalous."

"That's beside the point. Kayce, have you even seen a doctor?"

"No. Not since San Francisco. Grandma Nellie was going to arrange it soon," Kayce fibbed.

"Good Lord," Mrs. Hebert exclaimed. "Nellie knows and hasn't taken you to see a doctor yet? We have to get you into to see Dr. Gorman today. Today, do you hear me?" Charlene strode down the hall and into the hallway to use the telephone.

Cathy appeared in the doorway. "Guess the gig's up now, huh?"

"Looks like it. Well, shit. She'll tell everybody."

"Maybe not. But she was going to find out sooner or later. I can't believe we've kept it a secret this long."

"We had too. Or at least try." But Cathy had told Grandma Nellie. Kayce just didn't know it. Nellie asked her to keep it quiet with Nora gone.

"Oh, God. Now Mrs. Hebert's probably gonna tell Mother." Little did they know, but Nora, too, was already aware.

"No doubt. But maybe it will make her wanna come home?"

"The feds aren't gonna let her come home just because her oldest daughter is knocked up. Get real."

"You know Mama. She'll find a way."

"Whatever. I don't think she would even care. She'd only say 'I told you so' and rub it in my face."

"Kayce, you underestimate Mama sometimes. She does have a heart."

"A selfish one." With that, Kayce stomped back to her room to try to find some pants that would fit. She opted for a pair of loose shorts instead. The heat and humidity of New Orleans were sticky during the summer months. At least her legs didn't look fat.

Charlene returned to inform Kayce of her appointment. "It's all set. You are to see Dr. Gorman this afternoon at one o'clock. It's about high time we got this baby the care it needs. And you too."

Hearing the commotion, Nellie came around the corner. "What is going on in here?"

Kayce turned around to face her and outlined the baby bump she had been hiding. She was further along than Nellie thought.

"Did you know about this?" Charlene said with her hands on her hips.

Grandma Nellie looked at Cathy, then at Kayce. "Well. Yes. Yes I did."

"You told her?" Kayce glared at Cathy.

"I had to, Kayce. Someone had to know."

Kayce was almost relieved that the secret was out. But she was still unsure about her future. "Grandma. You're not gonna send me away are you? To one of those homes?"

"Heavens to Betsy no, darling. What on earth would make you think that? I'm not happy about this. But it is what it is. I just got you home. The last thing I'm gonna do is send you away."

"You all can deal with what to do about it later. Right now, we're gonna make sure you and this baby are okay." Charlene assured. "Nellie, you should have told me."

"I should have. But with Nora gone, I just didn't know what to do."

"I'm sorry, Grandma. I'm sorry to embarrass our family," Kayce apologized.

"Now, now, Kayce. You're certainly not the first person to ever get pregnant out of wedlock in this line of women. I believe your mother takes the cake on that one. At least I know about it this time."

Kayce hugged her Grandmother for the first time since she had been home. She openly wept. All the pent up anger and rebellion was released in a flood of tears.

"Come on, Kayce. Let's not cry over spilt milk. We are better than that. Somehow, we'll figure out what's the best thing to do."

"Are you going to notify Mother?" Kayce asked nervously.

"Nellie, does Nora even know?" a startled Charlene asked before Nellie could answer Kayce.

"Yes. I wrote her to let her know. But at that time, I didn't have many details to fill in."

"Maybe that will get her home," Charlene encouraged. "Go get some shoes on, Kayce. I'll go around and get the car."

Nellie was glad that she now had another adult to help her manage the unwed mother situation. She hoped that Charlene was right, that it would make her wayward daughter want to come home.

Chapter 41
∞ June 27, 1968 Laos ∞

A dark, dank smell startled Steve into consciousness. The minute he was cognizant, his spirit was crushed. For he knew he had been recaptured. Excruciating pain radiated through the tendons attaching his arms to his shoulders. His hands were strung above his head. He was sure his right shoulder had dislocated for a second time. Steve was suspended from a bamboo peg, his feet a mere six inches from the ground. Not high enough, however, to prevent the rats from taking a nibble at his rotting toes.

Escaped prisoners, who were almost always re-captured within a day or two, were beaten severely. Steve had been on the run for several weeks. The pain in his arms was superseded momentarily as Steve felt the strike on his back with a cat-o-nines. He was being beaten by an American deserter. He knew it because he could hear English amidst broken Vietnamese. Another Viet Cong guerilla, one who seemed to be giving orders was shouting at the GI to strike Steve again. But the army GI was resisting.

Up until this moment, Steve had been unconscious and couldn't even understand the questions they were screaming at him.

"Nơi bạn nghĩ bạn đi, ngu ngốc viên? Những người bạn sẽ? Bạn sẽ có được những gì bạn xứng đáng," screeched the gook. 'Where you think you going, stupid officer? Who you going to? You get what you deserve.'

"Dù, đủ." the GI screamed back. "Enough. We'll end up killing him. That'll be no good for trading."

The Army deserter's selfish protestations probably saved Steve's life. Steve knew they were not meant on his behalf. But officers were worth a hefty ransom to guerilla fighters. Steve swallowed hard and purposely kept his eyes closed shut, to make his captors think he was still unconscious. In doing so, he could try to make out what was happening. He wanted to determine if he was with the NVA or the VC. From what he could tell, he was still in the hands of the Viet Cong, but a different group.

Suddenly, the rope holding Steve up was slashed with a machete. Steve's bruised and beaten body fell to the ground. The deserter and the gook locked the bamboo gate above his head. Steve was in solitary. A small, dark, dank hole below ground. The only thing he could see was dirty feet and worn boots out of the six inch hole.

Steve was sure he could count his every rib. Many of which were now broken from the torture he had just sustained. It was hard for him to breath, as one of his lungs had collapsed. But he was alive. He was still alive.

The air hung, heavy and still. The humidity inside the small hole was made worse because of the poor ventilation. Steve could not tell if it was day or night due to the dense jungle flora barely visible from the small hole. He knew he was a physical mess. A vertebra in his back was broken. He had a wound on his ankle from having stepped on a knife-life bamboo trap. He faintly recalled having stepped on it with his borrowed boots during his escape attempt.

The wound had filled his boot with blood that was now dried solid. Steve reached up and felt his face. He could tell his unshaven beard had about another four days growth since he last remembered being alert. Yet again, while out of it, he had no control over his bowels or bladder.

Every few hours, Steve was taken out of the hole only briefly for interrogation or sustenance. He was questioned, beaten, and further threatened with the cat-o-nines. His blood soaked boots had been yanked off his feet. The wound was near gangrenous. There was talk about cutting it off. Thankfully, the Viet Cong decided against it, knowing he would need it to walk to where they were taking him. He was given some foul smelling soup and putrid water. Guzzling it down, he knew that it would probably worsen his dysentery. But at least it was some form of caloric intake.

Finally, the interrogations ceased and Steve was marched for four days to a jungle prison camp that was just across the Laotian border in northern Cambodia. He was given his boots back, but they had no laces. He, of course, had no socks. For two more days they walked. By the time he limped, in much pain, up to the entrance to the next prison, Steve's feet were like raw hamburger.

The camp was typical of the images he had imagined and heard about. It was carved out of the jungle and built from pieces of bamboo. Surrounded by a bamboo wall, it was reminiscent of an old cavalry frontier fort in the American West. There was one wall concentrically within another, with a moat-like ditch dug between the two. In the ditch were many punji stakes, which were pieces of knife sharp bamboo, dipped in human waste and stuck in the ground.

Steve knew if he fell on those, he'd sustain a wound to a vital organ or bleed to death. At the very least he'd die of infection if not killed outright. Across this ditch was a log that one had to balance across to gain entry to the camp.

Inside the walls were many bamboo cages that housed the prisoner population. There were South Vietnamese military and indigenous mountain people referred to as Montagnards or "Mountainyards" who had allied with U.S. Special Forces. In addition, there was one other American, a helicopter pilot captured a month earlier. At least a couple hundred prisoners altogether.

Conditions in this camp were deplorable. They were forced to live like animals. As captives kept in those cages, they did not have enough space in which to stand up. Even if they wanted to, they couldn't, because their feet were kept in wooden stocks.

With Steve's broken back, he could not lie back either; so he slept sitting up. Every night more rats scurried through the cages to nibble on his ankle wound. Unable to move his feet in the stocks, he couldn't keep them away. Steve had come to hate rats.

The only time the prisoners were allowed out of the cages was for a daily toilet call at the camp latrine. The time never seemed to be the same on any given day. Most of the prisoners, like Steve, suffered from dysentery. If a prisoner's internal biological schedule could not wait for the appointed time, they miserably went all over themselves in the cage. When the captors did let them out, it was to walk to the make-shift latrine in one corner of the camp.

On Steve's first visit, he discovered that the latrine was merely a couple of holes in the ground that one squatted over to relieve himself. The problem was that many of the sicker prisoners were not able to hold themselves until getting all the way to the holes. Their waste was left in piles all around the area. Some of the very sickest prisoners, near death, were placed in hammocks right next to the latrine. Pathetically, they would lay there and soil themselves, time after time. Some would summon enough strength to roll out of their hammocks, take a couple of steps and go there on the ground. The result was a substantial accumulation of human waste all around the holes that served as facilities.

Those able to control themselves were forced to walk through that waste field and squat over the holes. On return to their cages, the prisoners had no way to clean themselves. Shitter hell. Steve now understood the many fires he had seen from shit holes burning. He'd give anything to be seeing it again only from the air.

In this camp, water, although foul tasting, was not a problem. It was delivered in pieces of bamboo and there seemed to be sufficient quantities. Supposedly the water was boiled, but most still came down with bloody dysentery. Food continued to be a problem. The diet consisted exclusively of more horrid cabbage soup and rice.

Prisoners got one grapefruit sized wad of rice mid-morning and another mid-afternoon. Occasionally, they would get the treat of a tuberous root called manioc. Steve recognized it from JEST training. It tasted very much like yucca from Latin American countries. Steve's weight plummeted from around 180 pounds to something near 120 in just a few weeks.

He was skin hanging on bones with a beard that grew very long over time. He was never offered the opportunity to shave and received no medical attention for his wounds at all. No one fared any better. The ARVN next to Steve in the cage had a severe chest wound that had been bandaged long ago. But Steve never saw the dressing changed. The hole in the poor fellow's chest wall was never repaired. He was young and strong, but did not survive.

Living like animals, under those filthy, starvation conditions and without medical care; it seemed that someone died almost every day. Their bodies were carried out and buried on a hillside just outside the camp.

On July 4, Steve was taken outside his cage and lined up with a group of prisoners. There were about twenty-four ARVNs, the one other American, and a South Vietnamese Air Force pilot. Steve would soon learn that the pilot had been shot down the same day he had. The fellow had flown an A-1 Skyraider at Polei Klang. His name was Lieutenant Nguyen. Steve would never forget his name. Never.

The Communist camp commander addressed the group in broken English. "GI go to new camp. Happy Independence Day. Better camp. It is place of better food and medical care. GI's get packages from home. Trip to take eleven days. GIs should try to make it." Then he screamed some orders in an unrecognizable dialect to the rest of the guerilla guards.

Steve envisioned another jungle camp, somewhat better situated, staffed, and supplied, somewhere not too distant in southern Laos, or just across the border in Cambodia. The comment about trying hard to make it did not register in Steve mind at all until some days later.

The trip began with all barefoot and tied loosely to one another. After a few days, there was no longer need for this, because all of the prisoners struggled to just keep moving forward. Steve was weak from malnutrition, sick with untold disease, and suffering from wounds that were infected and worsening with the aggravation of the journey. Crossing muddy streams, he soon became plagued with more leaches, on top of everything else. They'd suck his blood. Steve was worried because he knew they could cause infections of their own. He must have been a site.

Lieutenant Nguyen was suffering the same conditions. He was fighting his own personal demons. Every step of the way, those demons threatened to destroy their physical ability, or derail the sheer mental will needed to continue. Both pilots knew that if they did not continue to march, they would most surely die.

In normal life, one had to take some overt action to die. One would have to commit suicide. As a prisoner of war, under these circumstances, that truth was reversed. Each of them had to reach deep within and struggle each day simply to stay alive. Dying was easy. They had only to just relax, give up and peacefully surrender. Many did. Death was a sweet and merciful relief.

They died in that first jungle prison camp and they died along the trail. Some would complete a day's journey and then lie down to die. Others collapsed on the trail and could not continue. The group was continuously marched ahead. Occasionally rifle shots were heard and the pitiful suffering prisoner was not seen again. The trip was not an eleven day hike to a new camp in the same vicinity as the one they had departed, as the VC had explained. It turned out to be a journey lasting over three months, taking them several hundred miles all the way up the Ho Chi Minh Trail into North Vietnam and then on to the capital city of Hanoi. The prisoners were to be ransomed and turned over to the North Vietnamese. During the trek, they lost at least half a dozen of the small band of twenty-seven captives.

Chapter 42
∞ July 1968, Chu Lai ∞

Robert had been pouring over intelligence reports with every chance he got in the office. One day there would be none. The next, an onslaught in no particular order; a plethora which required sorting the details of battles, missions, casualties, and MIA reports piecemeal. Despite the massive amounts of data that came through, there was simply nothing about Steve.

On the one hand, no news was good news. But on the other, Steve could be like the hundreds of missing military whose bodies would never be found. Intel reported mass graves near the Vietnamese and Laotian border. When VC units came close to being caught, they simply executed their prisoners, threw them into shallow, make-shift graves and scattered into the jungle. This atrocity made it impossible for rescue teams to save the missing. Soldiers became simply lost and virtually untraceable.

It was something Robert was going to do everything to prevent Nora from understanding. There was no way he was going to extinguish her last flame of hope. Without hope, she had nothing.

"That's some intense research you're doing there," remarked Robert's commanding officer.

Robert stood and saluted. "Yessir. It is, sir."

"Someone you know?"

"Yessir. A downed A-4 pilot. Over Laos."

"Sorry to hear, Captain. That border's a mess out there."

"Yessir."

"You're a good man, Lathrop. Lemme know what I can do."

"Thank you sir. I will."

It was good to know that Robert's extra work in searching for Steve was supported. Although, it was pretty unlikely that the commander could do anything specific. Robert planned to keep that endorsement at the ready. He had already used some of the commander's assistance in another matter.

The telex machine was ticking and sputtering. The message to the USO Robert initiated on behalf of Nora had received a reply.

> *Capt Lathrop stop Request on behalf of Capt Broussard to have USO terminated due to domestic stress rec'd stop Will notify Chu Lai Commanding Officer of decision stop*

Robert was determined, before he was transferred to some other type of service, to see that Nora was out of Vietnam and home with her family. He had come to know her well. He figured that if Nora stayed, she would resort to any means to try and find Steve, putting her own life in danger.

Since hearing of Steve's MIA status, Nora had changed. On the outside, she appeared to be defiantly confidant. Putting on her mask, she would cheer up the GI's and sailors at the club on a daily basis. But he knew, deep down inside, she was completely devastated. He saw it in the number of cigarettes she was smoking. The number of empty bottles of whisky in the rubbish bin in her make-shift office at the club. Thin and not eating well, she was bordering on a complete meltdown. It was time for her to go home. This crazy-ass, twisted war, with no clear agenda, was no place for a woman in her fragile state.

He planned to talk with her about it that evening. Robert was concerned about the turmoil with her family at home. Her cavalier reaction to Kayce's teen pregnancy was just a show. Nora tried hard to hide her grief and frustration, but it didn't fool him. Thousands of miles away, Nora felt she was not being the mother she needed to be to her own children. Although her efforts to support the GI's and sailors were admirable, Robert believed she was needed at home more.

When Robert himself was deployed to Nam, he had a wife and a three year old child. Married only four years, his second child was born while he was away. Robert had been notified about the birth by the Red Cross. In fact, on the same day that Roy Schmidt had been captured, the pilot he was relieving.

Initially when he received letters from home, often in bunches, he poured over every word. He had placed pictures of his wife and children on the wall above his cot. But soon the local news seemed meaningless. It was from a world that scarcely seemed to exist. It was a world he could no longer identify with, for Robert had become numb to things which seemed to exist in a land far, far away.

JEANETTE VAUGHAN

Once Robert had learned to live in the moment, the stress of war didn't bother him. What was in the past didn't matter, because it was over. What was in the future didn't matter either. The crises of the past were so horrific and things changed so rapidly in the present; that what was to happen in the future seemed not to matter because it couldn't get worse. Even if it did, there was simply not time to worry. One had to live and survive in the current moment.

In a mere seven months of living day to day, hour to hour, amidst the atrocities of a chaotic war, one became unable to think about the past, or the future. To think about life in a utopian, middle class society was like thinking about life on Mars when viewed from the daily routine of flying, flares and fatalities. Bombing, napalm, and the trauma that occurred with combat annihilated thoughts of life at home. He knew re-entry into that world would be hell.

Robert wanted to do anything he could to prevent that from happening to Nora. Watching her buffer reality, he knew some of it already had. As he always did, after reading his letters from home, Robert tore them up.

SOLO VIETNAM

Chapter 43
∞ September, 1968 New Orleans ∞

Word had gotten around the aviation grapevine that one of New Orleans' own, Lt. Commander Steve Novak, was MIA. Charlene had been beside herself ever since his name appeared on the VA's War Casualty list. She spent her time in one of three places, Lakefront Airport, The French Quarter, and Nora's home on Dante St. They were Nora's stomping grounds. Ubiquitous and quintessentially Nora.

Charlene took coffee with Gia a couple of times a week. She brought *beignets* from Morning Call to Nellie and Nora's children in uptown. She hung out on the flight line with Chet. But there was no solace to be found. Only speculation. Questions. Endless questions.

Where was Steve? Was he still alive? Did Nora ever see him? Would the USO let Nora come home? Would she get there in time for the birth of Kayce's child? Why did Steve have to be victim to such a ridiculous cause? When would this stupid, meaningless war end?

Charlene poured over news reels and news articles. She reviewed POW and MIA reports that she gained access to through her junior position at the VA. She was becoming obsessed and found it difficult to concentrate on her school work. She nearly made a "D" in Pediatrics and another in Community Health which would have caused her to flunk out of school.

On a blustery, rainy afternoon, Charlene found herself again walking the streets of The Quarter. She missed Nora so much. That day, she tightened her jacket and scarf around her shoulders, put up her umbrella and walked and walked and walked. She found herself, yet again, at The Ryder Coffeehouse where Gia worked.

It was Gia who finally helped her find peace and acceptance among the realities of what was happening within Charlene's stressful life. What had started out in America as the stylish Kennedy years, full of style and promise had disintegrated into turbulent dichotomies. Kennedy shot. Jackie now remarried. Anti-establishment vs. establishment. Black vs. white. Freedom vs. communism. Charlene just wanted it to stop.

Gia poured Charlene another cup of *espresso*. In times of trouble, Gia turned to her Tarot cards. Charlene hadn't given them much credence in the past, but she had simply run out of coping strategies.

"Life takes strange twists and turns, my dear." Gia comforted as she shuffled the cards. "Sometimes we just have to let go. Let da powers dat be take over, you know?"

"I'm willing to try anything. My mind has just been fraught with worry. All this just wasn't supposed to happen," tears began to run down Charlene's immaculate make-up.

"Now, 'chile. Dry doz tears. Let's see what da future holds." Gia said some incantations and then got out her Tarot cards.

"I have to tell you. Like Nora, I just don't understand all the meanings of cards," Charlene nervously explained.

"I will explain. Da Tarot tells of big events in one's life. Dere are major cards, da Arcana. If cards dat are turned over are mostly Arcana, dere are life-altering events. Tings dat will change one forever. If many Arcana cards are reversed, dere are important lessons to which da spirit must listen. You see?"

"Sort of. I think I understand."

Slowly and surely Gia began to turn over the cards, one by one. "Da first card is dat of da fool. A risk taker to be sure."

Charlene wondered if that was Nora. She certainly was the risk taker. But then again, so was Steve. Leaving his family to go serve in Vietnam.

Gia turned over the next card. "Da next card is strength." Charlene looked down and saw a lion with a saint-like figure guiding it. Gia then turned over another card. "Next is da tower card, but reversed. It means avoidance of disaster."

"Well that's good right? Nora and Steve. Maybe Steve is staying safe. Even though he's being held captive?"

"Could be. Could be," Gia swirled her hands over the cards. The incense was making Charlene a bit giddy. Then Gia turned over the final card. As she did, her eyes glistened. "Ah, da wheel of fortune. Dere will be change. Life will be better."

"But what does that mean?" Charlene's shrill voice was filled with anxiety.

"Now, now 'chile. We have to believe dat it means survival. We must look at da whole picture. You see? Da cards tell us much. For

Nora and Steve, dere is danger. But dere is hope dat da strength and love dat dey share will see dem tru."

"Oh, Gia. Are you sure? Is that what the cards are saying?"

"You must believe. Put your faith in what you know. Tis de only way."

"I will. I will, Gia. Thank you so much." For the first time, Charlene felt hopeful. This underworld faith was foreign to her. But if Gia, Nora's birthmother, believed it; so could she. Charlene took a deep breath. "I really appreciate you taking the time to do this, Gia. It has given me hope. We just have to keep the faith and have hope. I can do that. Yes, I can."

"My dear, tis da most important ting in da world. I am hopeful in dis reading. We must do more." Gia scooped up the cards and carefully placed them in a deep pocket within the long, black gauzy skirt she wore. "I am glad you came by. It does my heart good. She is part of me too, you know."

"Yes. I understand. Again, thank you so much. We will both hold close to hope," Charlene professed, grabbing Gia's hands in hers. She knew better than to draw Gia close to her in a hug. Gia's boundaries had to be respected.

Chapter 44
∞ September, 1968 Ho Chi Minh Trail, North Vietnam ∞

Each step for Steve marching was a nightmare. A horrid, soul-wrenching nightmare. Every footstep, every day wracked his body with pain. His infections became worse; disease was quickly setting in. Steve was quite near death. His leg swelled at least double in size, darkened in color, and filled with puss. Steve's calf swelled so much, long cracks formed in his skin. Beige, gooey puss and bloody, stinky fluid oozed from the crevasses.

Steve dragged his leg along like a pendulous, sodden club. Every movement lashed his whole being with the most excruciating pain. Pain that kept his face contorted and a cry shrieking within every corner of his consciousness. Pain that was burning a blackened scar deep into the center of his very being. He just didn't know how much more he could take. He had reached the point others had. The possibility of death seemed like mercy.

The bloody dysentery worsened and in addition, Steve got malaria and several intestinal parasites. Hovering perilously close to demise, he desperately tried to reach the end of each horrible day's journey. Eight to ten awful, grueling miles. Each morning he would begin a personal battle to stand, moaning loudly or screaming to himself through clenched teeth and pressed lips. Gravity brought a surge of new agony as blood continued to run down into his leg. The pooled, bodily fluids in the carcass of the leg caused increased pressure which pushed against his decaying flesh and failing vessels.

But there was Lieutenant Nguyen, suffering badly himself, yet always encouraging Steve, always helping as he could. They'd eat paltry morsels of rice for dinner, and he'd make a joke and tell Steve this was not how Vietnamese dined.

"Dis not representation of fine Vietnamese culture."

"You don't say," Steve grunted.

"No, navy man. A Vietnamese meal is a delight. Don't judge my native cuisine by the crap we are given to eat. Please, my fellow officer." Lt. Nguyen described the many fine foods in Vietnamese culture.

Steve believed him, and did not. Lt. Nguyen was right, of course. "So rotted cabbage soup is not part of it? Dim Sum?" Steve tried to maintain a sense of humor. It was hard, but it was necessary.

They both knew that maintaining the spirit was the most important factor in survival. A sense of humor, even under the very worst conditions, helped maintain spirit. Within spirit lived hope. Again and again, Lieutenant Nguyen helped. He was always concerned about Steve, and did all he could to encourage him to remain positive. To be hopeful. As bad as things got, Steve never gave up hope, not even the day he would have died, had it not been for Nguyen.

Steve mustered all his will each day just to wake, stand, and take a step. Then he fought hard for the remainder of the period to just keep going; to keep moving along the trail. He could barely walk, but somehow he continued, and thus survived each sunrise-to-sunset, to open his eyes in the morning to the gift of one more dawn.

On what was the worst day of Steve's life, he fought so very hard. He faltered. He dug deeper and staggered on. He faltered again, struggling, yet he reached even further within himself. Steve prayed for more strength. He collapsed, and then got up and moved along. The guard saw him crumble again, and yet fight with all he had in his body, heart, and soul to get up.

The final time, he collapsed and could not get up. He could simply not will himself up. He felt he was at the end of his life. The enemy guard came over and looked down on him, ordering him up. He yelled louder at Steve and threatened him with the cane. But Steve could not. It was done.

Nguyen, however, was not going to let that happen. Looking worried, he bent towards Steve. The guard was yelling at him in Vietnamese to discourage his efforts. But Nguyen persisted in moving to help Steve. The guard yelled even louder. Nguyen's jaw was set with determination, and in spite of whatever threats the guard was screaming, Nguyen pulled Steve up onto his own frail, weak back. "Navy man, you not giving up now," he whispered to Steve. Grunting, he pulled Steve's arms around his neck, clasped his wrists together, and pulled his fellow pilot along with his feet dragging on the ground behind him.

Nguyen drug Steve along all the rest of that day. Occasionally, he was briefly relieved by another prisoner, but it was Nguyen who carried the burden that juncture. It was Nguyen who lifted Steve from death, at great risk to his own life, and carried him. No matter how exhausted and weak he felt himself, he cared for Steve, until they completed that long day's journey.

The next morning, Steve went through the normal agonizing ritual of waking up, standing, and dragging his leg through those first determined steps. It was more of a struggle than ever before. Steve thought about Nguyen, mustered the will, and went on.

At the edge of the encampment was a broad log that spanned the rapids of a river. Steve started across, trying to balance. Pain awful, he was very weak. His equilibrium gone, he had no sense of balance. The worthless leg was throwing him off. Steve began to slip off the side of the log falling onto the rocks in the rushing water below.

Nguyen and the other American moved back off the log and came to his rescue. They pulled Steve from the river and onto the bank. Nguyen pleaded in Vietnamese for the group to remain at this camp until Steve was able to travel again. Although the rescuers were ordered away, they would not leave his side.

The guards dragged them away and forced them across the log bridge at gunpoint. They were marched forward with the rest of the prisoner group. Steve never saw Nguyen again.

As far as Steve's fellow prisoners knew, he was left at that camp to die, as others had been. But for some reason, the Viet Cong decided to give him penicillin injections for several days. After a week, he began to show some improvement. After a time, he was able to stand. As soon as Steve was able to walk again, he was put back on the trail. This time he was traveling with groups of North Vietnamese soldiers moving north and accompanied by his own personal guard. It continued to be an agonizing trip, but the worst was behind him.

Ever determined, Steve found another opportunity to escape once when he got one turn ahead of the guard on the jungle trail. It wasn't the best decision. But Steve was determined not to die in the hands of the Viet Cong. He had been tortured long enough. By virtue of the terrain, he knew he must be very close to the DMZ.

However, the VC guard quickly tracked him down. Resolved not to lose his ransom, the guard decided not to shoot him, despite his rage. Steve was recaptured again, his arms tied ever more securely behind him and the journey continued. Eventually, the NVA and guard joined Steve with another group of South Vietnamese prisoners as they entered North Vietnam, and ultimately reached Hanoi. By the time the journey was finally over, the other American that had pulled Steve out of the water was dead. He never made it to the city.

Steve knew that their travels had covered a tremendous distance. After what was his final escape attempt, he was beyond exhaustion. He was very sick and in need of medical attention. On a balmy, hot day, Steve was marched from the jungle to the outskirts of a city. Once there, Steve was logged in and placed into North Vietnam's prison system. He ended up at the infamous Hanoi Hilton.

Chapter 45
∞ September 1968, Chu Lai ∞

Whenever Nora was not at the club, she volunteered at the 312th Evac Hospital. Over the course of the war, the hospital went from tents, to a full on triage hospital complete with operating rooms and an ICU. It consisted of several large white Quonset huts. Almost everything inside was white. White overhead florescent lights. White-beige metal beds lined up one after another. White shelves and white air-conditioners mounted into the walls.

Not wearing a uniform, Nora added a bit of color. No matter what unit she worked, she felt useful there. She assisted the staff, most of which were medics. There were a few young, single RNs. Most of them were barely twenty-one. Nora wondered how they coped with what all that they saw.

Many of the injuries to the soldiers happened right on the base. The perimeters of Chu Lai could be dangerous. Shrapnel from sharp shooting snipers, burn injuries to aircraft maintenance crews, or general minor trauma from explosions of artillery stashes to name a few. No matter how major or minor, the staff was always shorthanded and busy. With several thousand people on base, invariably someone needed healthcare. The rest of the patients were some of the horrific traumas that occurred in the nearby jungle battles for this hill or that. More serious injuries were stabilized and transferred to the *USS Mercy* Naval Hospital ship when it came around. But some soldiers never made it out of the ICU.

By volunteering, Nora felt she was somehow doing something meaningful. In helping the GIs, she was hopeful that someone was doing the same for Steve, wherever he might be. Nora helped the medics and nurses change beds. She gently bathed the damaged bodies having survived the perils of war. She restocked supplies. She served food trays and fed patients.

SOLO VIETNAM

Probably the hardest thing she did, was read letters to the soldiers from home. In hearing the heartfelt wishes from their families, she was reminded of her own. It reminded her of the ill-thought-out decision to come to Vietnam. Homesickness loomed. But she had made a choice and needed to stick it through.

After word of Steve's capture, Nora found that she had to keep busy in order for time to pass more quickly. She wondered what ever happened to Dave Gillett, the pilot she had met at the Roosevelt. Had he been captured too? If she stopped working, her mind went to the same recurring theme. Fear. Fear, plus the nightmarish anxiety and depression that she might never see Steve again.

One of the nurses Nora knew from the club was Nancy O'Malley. She had gotten the idea to volunteer at the hospital from her. O'Malley was seeing Woody, the chief that wrangled supplies for the club. They became acquainted over a dare from Woody to see if O'Malley could drink a Hurricane and still stand up.

Over the course of the last few months, Nora and O'Malley had become friends. Watching O'Malley work and take care of patients reminded Nora of her own best friend back home, Charlene. She often thought about how Charlene was doing in school. Nora was so proud of her country club friend turned nurse.

One morning, Nora found out just what real nursing was about. She was assigned to work in the "expectant" ward. "Expectant" was a euphemism for those too injured to survive. They were almost assured of dying. Looking into the eyes of those men, crushed Nora's heart. Caring for the wounded in Vietnam wasn't like the cinematic portrayals of World War II. Thousands of young men lost limbs from land mines. Napalm burned many badly. Guerilla warfare reeked and ravaged bodies in horrific ways. High-powered weapon shells ricocheted through flesh, literally ripping through organs and tissue. This war had no boundaries.

Choppers brought mass casualties that would have died in other wars. Nurses were required to play God, triaging limited supplies and bed space for those who could survive. They eased the pain of death with Morphine for those who probably wouldn't. When surgeons were tied up with endless stretchers in the OR, nurses performed emergency tracheotomies, closed up surgical cases on their own, and gave the medications needed with total support of the physicians with which they worked. In Vietnam, rank meant little in the hellish circumstances where they provided care.

O'Malley asked Nora to get a couple of screens for an expectant patient. He was a young man, maybe only twenty. Badly wounded in a fragging incident, he circled death's door. The war had gotten ugly. Some soldiers were so strung out on drugs and shell shocked at what they had seen on the ground, a few turned on their own men. This young man had been injured by a grenade thrown into their tent by another GI.

His face had been mostly blown away. An emergency tracheostomy was in his throat. Nora could hear the sucking sounds of secretions that threated to block his airway. O'Malley was suctioning him almost continuously.

"Nora, I know you don't have the stomach for this, but I desperately need your help." She handed Nora the Yankauer suction tube.

"I don't know if I can."

"Just do it. Keep it clear. When you don't hear any air or gurgling, just suck. I have to get this poor boy some more Morphine."

Nora gritted her teeth and tried not to look at him in the face. There was massive amounts of blood oozing from the small hole and tube protruding from his throat. When she heard the deluge of noise stop, she touched the edge of the tube to the site. Loud, frothing, sucking noises occurred and Nora saw blood going up through the tube. For a brief moment, she thought she would pass out. But she carried on.

After a few minutes, O'Malley returned. "Thanks, Nora. You were a life saver. Literally." Nancy drew up a five milligram dose of Morphine and injected it into an intra-osseous line that had been drilled into the boys tibia.

"Is that going into a vein in his leg?" Nora asked naively.

"Eventually. Right now, it's going into his bone marrow. It'll be absorbed and get into his system. His arms were too mangled to start a regular IV line."

Within seconds, the young man's breathing was easier. Slower and more relaxed. His tense body more at ease. The Morphine was taking effect.

"It's about all we can do, to keep him comfortable."

"I guess that's true. Do you think he will die? For sure?"

"If he's lucky."

Nora made the sign of the cross. It was the most tragic thing she had seen of the war so far. She bit back tears. "I just don't know how you do it, O'Malley."

"Eh. It's my job. Buck up, girl. I can really use you today. We're getting slammed. The 99th lost a ridge just north of here. You probably heard the shelling last night. It's gonna be a bitch."

"I'll do what I can," Nora offered.

SOLO VIETNAM

* * * * * *

Later on that evening, O'Malley and Woody were at the club. They just finished a slow dance to a song Nora had belted out, *At Last* by Etta James. Afterward, Nora joined them at the table.

"Dang, girl. You've got a voice smooth as velvet," Woody proclaimed.

"Ah, well. It's nothing. Nothing like what your gal can do," Nora said humbly. "Today I saw what nursing in Nam is really like."

"Oh, yeah?" said Woody.

"Yep. O'Malley has the heart of an angel, but nerves of steel."

"Aw, thanks Nora. But girl, you were pretty amazing too. There's no way we coulda managed without 'cha. Hey, where did ya ever learn to sing like that?"

"A long time ago. In a place that seems to exist in another lifetime. The French Quarter."

"Oh, man. I've always wanted to visit there. It sounds so exotic."

Nora laughed. "I'm not so sure how exotic it is, but it's full of some crazy characters." She thought of Gia and Big Daddy. What bliss it would be to again take in a cup of Community coffee with chicory. "When the war's over, you all will have to come visit. Take in a Mardi Gras."

"That would be cool," O'Malley gushed. "I'll get me some beads and one of those carnival masks."

Talk of New Orleans had gotten to Nora. Her nerves were on their last synapses. She quickly said her goodbyes and went to the back of the club to work on the books. Pulling out the letter that had come from Nellie, she mulled over the news about Kayce and the baby. Kayce pregnant. As a mother, she felt totally helpless about a situation another world away.

Chapter 46
∞ October, 1968 New Orleans ∞

It had been two hundred-fifty years since the Crescent City was established. The year 1968 was filled with remembrances of New Orleans' settlement. Unlike other cities which were established by puritans and pilgrims, New Orleans was founded by French adventures. Soon joined by Spanish, Dutch, Italian, African and English settlers, the city took on its diverse, heterogeneous patterns within its laws, architecture, and art. The vivacity of its people formed the essence of the city itself.

The mish-mash of cultures carried down through generations could be seen in the various neighborhoods. The Garden District. Magazine Street. The Quarter. The River Road and even uptown. On Dante St. a clash of cultures were flaring with the Broussard home. Nellie was the consummate, conservative, Catholic. Kayce, the wayward, left wing rebel, now pregnant. Cathy and Liesel seemed to be caught in the middle of it all. Iggy was preoccupied, wanting nothing to do with female anything. He was all about sports and The Saints, New Orleans' new football team.

Kayce spent her days donning black armbands in protest of the war. She marched in demonstrations, distributed anti-war leaflets and helped organize boycotts and moratoriums. Not in school due to her confinement, she had way too much time on her hands. She believed in the anti-establishment cause of the day. Committed that her activities would somehow hasten the end of the war. She participated in anything that promoted the vague, radical agendas captivating youth at the time.

Being a mother was the last thing on her mind. Yet, day by day her shape grew, much to her chagrin. She was now seven months along. It was hard for her to look in the mirror and acknowledge the life now growing inside. Despite the fact that the baby kicked incessantly.

"Good golly, Kayce. Your belly is a big as a barn," Leisel exclaimed.

"Just shut it," Kayce said slamming the bathroom door closed. She had forgotten what little privacy a three bedroom duplex with only one bathroom offered.

"Can't hide from the truth," Leisel argued back. "You'll never fit into your hip-huggers again."

"Shut up. Just shut up," Kayce yelled through the door. She worried that Leisel was right. She couldn't imagine how her body would ever return to its normal shape. The pregnancy had gone by quickly. Nellie dragged her to the doctor once a month.

The routine was the same. Blood pressure check. Pee in a cup to check for sugar. Doppler to listen for the baby's heartbeat. At the last visit, the doctor told her that future visits would involve weekly pelvic checks. She shuddered at the thought. Being pried open with a metal speculum was just the worst. At this point, Kayce never wanted to have sex again. Not if this was the result.

Nellie began to probe and question her about what she was going to do with the baby. She left pamphlets from adoption agencies and Catholic Charities on the dresser in the girls' bedroom. Kayce just wasn't sure. Although she felt the baby moving inside her, she couldn't imagine being a mother at seventeen. But at the same time, Kayce doubted she could do what her mother had, and give the baby away. It was a part of her.

In a way, she felt guilty about how badly she had treated her mother the year she had given up that baby for adoption in Texas. Out of all of Nora's children, Kayce was still the only one of them that knew the whole story. The others were still oblivious about the affair.

More than she wanted to admit, she wished her mother was home. There was just no talking to Nellie. She just didn't get where Kayce was coming from. To her, the decision was black and white. Give the baby up and get back into school as soon as possible. At the moment, Kayce just couldn't wrap her head around a return to nuns, uniforms and conformity.

Chapter 47
∞ October 1968, Chu Lai ∞

The 9th of October dawned unusually cool and clear, much like the climate in which Robert had always lived, the mountains of southeast Washington. It was a treat that his flight suit was not soaked with sweat by the time he got to the flight line, as it was during most of the humid days in Vietnam. Robert stood at the top of the sandy hill where his Quonset hut was built, looking over the South China Sea taking in the beautiful morning.

The squadron had flown almost constantly since January, when the Tet Offensive started, forcing everyone to operate to their extreme limits. Robert logged nearly three hundred missions during the last six months. As such, he was anticipating word of a transfer. Most pilots were taken off combat duty after six months to fill positions at the Wing level or with a Division in the field. Robert hoped for a position as a forward air-borne controller. At least he would still be flying. Every marine pilot dreaded the potential transfer to a battalion in the field.

Robert knew word was coming any day. He hated that he would be away from active combat flying. He had flown with some pilots who hadn't flown war zone missions for some time. He knew himself that when he didn't fly combat, his skills slipped. A fighter pilot had to remain qualified. During a rotation off combat, a fighter pilot was allowed to return each month to the base to fly enough missions to keep current.

Finding themselves in the cockpit after a period of absence, pilots reported feeling like strangers for a few minutes. Instruments were foreign. Bombing runs didn't pan out as expected for the first few goes. It surprised the hell out of the pilot, as much as those with whom he was flying. Mainly, because it was difficult to stay in formation and stay on target until the aviator got his wits about him once again.

SOLO VIETNAM

Robert had flown recently with a wingman who had been gone for several months. He dropped his load right on the friendly forces and not on the enemy. Fortunately, he missed any actual humans with his ordnance. The wingman had seen the smoke the troops had popped to show their position and had released his load on that instead of the correct smoke marker left to show the enemy position. It was a close call that Robert didn't want to experience himself.

This day was going to be relatively easy. He had one scheduled flight and then Intel duty. The squadron wasn't going to fly in the afternoon because they were assigned to take the hot pad at 1800 hours. Robert had the squadron quarters to himself, as most of the day crew were loading aircraft for the hot pad launch.

Robert briefed for an 0700 launch. The mission was to attack the only intact village Robert was to ever see. The rising sun caused the beach to glisten as Robert took off. They headed up the coast and turned inland. As they approached the village, Robert saw no signs of any enemy, only the appearance of peaceful Vietnamese countryside in the morning sun. To Robert, the quiet village was beautiful. Yet he knew, nothing was benign in nature for that area.

Robert and his wingman napalmed the village and left it burning, the flames nearly one hundred feet in the air. They flew to a hill above the village while the village was bombed by two Phantoms. Turning back to look as he rolled out, Robert then saw the Phantoms strafe what had been a peaceful country scene in one of the few areas previously untouched by war. It was now totally destroyed. To Robert, the routine mission made him sick to his stomach. He thought about the women and children there. Again, it was simply too pretty a day for war.

Upon his return to the base, Robert took his intel post. His wingman headed for the USO club. While shuffling through the piles of paperwork left for him to process, all of sudden the telex went off. No doubt more reports of KIA, MIA and POWs.

At first, Robert ignored them, shoving the piles aside preferring to enjoy his Spam sandwich and a Coca-Cola. But he was there for a job. He pulled the telex off the machine and gave it a brief glance. His eyes nearly popped out of his head when he saw Steve Novak's name again.

      NAME: LTCDR STEVEN NOVAK
      STATUS: POW
      LAST KNOWN LOCATION: HANOI, N VIETNAM

Robert couldn't believe it. There had been no word in months. This was the news he had been waiting to see. Steve was no longer MIA. He was formally registered as a POW with the NVA. It was the dim hope for which he and Nora had been holding out. There was no guarantee, of course, that Steve would not still die in captivity. But the fact that he was a high ranking officer and was officially registered, at least ensured that he had survived up until that point.

Without waiting another second, Robert grabbed Frenchy off the six by six, had him stand temporary guard, and took off for the hospital. Knowing she was pulling another medical volunteer shift, he wanted to get the news to Nora as soon as possible.

Nora had just finished handing out the last lunch tray in the med/surg unit. She rolled the cart down to the end of the row of beds for picking them up. As she did, an anxious Robert appeared in the ward.

"Nora, I've been looking all over for you. There's been word about Steve."

Nora dropped the tray she was holding, the utensils making a clatter. "Ohmigod." She suddenly felt like the wind had been knocked out of her and couldn't catch her breath. Her heart was racing. "Please, please. Go ahead and tell me."

"It was on the telex this morning. His status was changed to POW. He's at the Hanoi Hilton."

"What? Whatever do you mean?" she knew he couldn't possibly mean a hotel.

"It's the largest POW camp in North Vietnam. It's nicknamed the Hanoi Hilton."

"Is he okay? Is he hurt?"

"There's no way to know. But the good news is, he is alive. Intel gets reports when POWs are logged in there."

"But he's still a prisoner of the enemy."

"Yes. But now he is in a high profile prison. The NVA are using the Hanoi Hilton to show the world that they are treating our guys decently. It's all just propaganda."

"But that's good, right?"

"Hell ya. The conditions are at least humane. He'll get adequate food and medical care, if he needs it."

"When will we know anything else?"

"That's just it. We won't."

Nora felt her heart sink. "Why. Why not?"

"It's not like the NVA are giving us weekly updates. The only thing we would hear is if he didn't make it. If he died in captivity, they more than likely would report it."

"But how long will he be there?" Nora asked warily.

Robert looked down and fumbled with the telegram. He hated telling her bad news. He cleared his throat. "Well, that's just it. He'll be there until the war ends."

"God knows how long that will be. Months?"

Robert knew the next part was going to hard for her to hear. "Nora. I'm so sorry. It could be years."

"Oh, gawd," she sat down on one of the empty beds and burst into tears. Robert came over and put his arms around her.

"Nora. I'm sorry. You know I don't beat around the bush."

"I know. I know. And I appreciate that you don't. You've been nothing but a true blue friend to me here. I'm sorry. I know I should be elated. I'm so thankful to know that he's alive. I just don't know how much more of this war I can take."

Robert did know. Although he had numbed himself to it, he realized Nora had not been able to do the same. He felt that now was as good a time as ever to tell her what he had been up to in terms of intervening for her early release from USO service. "There's something else I've been wanting to share with you," he started.

She blew her nose and wiped away her tears. "What's that?" she sniffled.

"You know I am only telling you this because I care about you."

Nora had no idea what he was about to say. It sounded serious. "Go on."

"Nora, you've done an amazing job running the club. You've given so many people on the base a touch of home. Great meals. Great parties. You're pretty terrific."

Nora managed a small smile. "Thank you, Robert. I've tried." She knew he wasn't finished.

"But now. Nora. It's time that you go home."

"Home. But I can't. That's just it. I signed a contract for eighteen months. Hell, I'll be stuck here longer than you!" she rolled her eyes.

"Not exactly. There's a way for you to go sooner."

"But how, I don't have the money over here to pay my own way home."

"I've been working on something," Robert revealed knowingly.

"Robert, what have you been up to?"

"I called in a favor. With the CO."

"I don't understand."

"Look, the CO, Commander Henry. He knows some higher ups at the USO," Robert hesitated. "Well. He made some contacts and explained your situation. Steve. The baby Kayce's having."

"And so?" Nora nervously waited for his response.

Robert broke into a grin. "It looks like you may be going home sooner than you think."

"Hell's bells, Robert. Really? Wahoo!" Nora cried out. The patients in the ward that were able started clapping, whistling, and cheering. Many of them having been to the club to enjoy Nora's warm hospitality and sexy voice.

"Yep. Looks like it'll be right after Thanksgiving."

"But how? That's only a few weeks."

"They're gonna send over a contract. To let Marsha take over. The CO told 'em that you've trained her in all the business of running the club. He endorsed her."

Nora gave Robert the biggest hug. Public display of affection was not really kosher, but neither of them cared. "You're pretty amazing, Robert."

"Hey. This war sucks. I don't have control over what happens to me or my fellow jarheads on a daily basis, but if there's something I can do for someone else, I'm happy to do it. Besides, sounds like your family needs you right now more than we do."

Nora thought about that for a moment. The last few letters from Nellie had sounded a bit frantic. There was no way Nora wanted Kayce to go through a pregnancy and possible adoption without having some strong support. There was too much at stake. So many choices for her daughter to consider. Nora needed to be with her and help her make the right decision.

Robert helped Nora pick up the tray and utensils she dropped. One of the nurses came into the ward. "What's all the celebration about?"

Nora beamed. "I'm going home. I'm going home."

"That's wonderful news. But I'm sad for us. You've been a huge helping hand around here."

"Thank you, Major Evans."

"Anytime. I'm counting the days down myself. Mine won't be until after the New Year. Congratulations. But who's gonna make the Gumbo?" she laughed.

"I'll make sure I leave my special recipe."

"You'd better. The base might go into Cajun withdrawal."

The camp had come to love the once a month crawfish boils and Creole hospitality that Nora had infused into Chu Lai. She managed to make sure she brought a little bit of home to everyone. No matter where they were from.

Robert had to return to his duty station. After he left, Nora could hardly keep her mind on the task at hand. She finished picking up the rest of the trays from lunch. Then, she rolled gauze and re-stocked the dressing change cart. The very first thing she planned to do when she got back to her hut was fire off a letter home. Home. She was going home.

Chapter 48
∞ November, 1968 ∞

Flying as many missions as he had, Robert was way overdue for R and R. His wife had been pestering him via letters on exactly when it might take place. He had missed going on R and R to Hawaii twice and was now going to be able to do so. He had gone so long without leaving Chu Lai that he was now at the top of the list for the air group.

He dug around in his sea bag and found the dress uniform that he had taken into the country for just such a purpose. The bag had not been opened in so long, most of the things inside had to be thrown away because they had mildewed. The uniform was okay, so Robert took it over and had it pressed. Next, he found some ribbons that he qualified for at the Americal PX and attached them accordingly. Everything was ready to go.

At 0600, in the midst of a rainstorm, he was awakened by incoming. It was hitting close. Way too close. There were sounds of explosions, not just the sound of the rockets going over. It sounded like a roaring freight train.

Robert rolled out on the concrete floor until the rockets subsided. It was time to get up, so he walked halfway to the shower room. As he did so, a second rocket attack was launched toward his living quarters. It impacted less than fifty yards away.

In the middle of an open area, Robert ran to the cover of a sand-bagged Quonset hut a few feet away. However, he felt a burning on his foot when he got behind the building. He looked down and saw the ground covered with blood. A hot piece of shrapnel or a piece of a metal pallet the rockets had hit struck his right ankle.

The wound wasn't serious. It had taken off the bottom skin over one-third of his foot, but other than burning pain, it was something to be overlooked. There was no way he was going to miss out on his scheduled R and R.

Robert went to the corpsman medic. "Say, can you clean this up for me?"

"From the incoming?" the corpsman asked.

"Yep."

"Sure you don't wanna go over to Americal?"

"Hell no. I'm scheduled for R and R today and unless I'm bleeding from some artery, I'm going."

"Gotcha, man. I gotcha."

The corpsman cleaned the wound and bandaged it up. In a humid climate such as Chu Lai, leaving it untreated could be deadly, as everything left open abscessed. Robert winced as he squeezed his right foot into his dress shoe. Once he did, the foot began to swell, such that he couldn't get the shoe off. But he was determined to not look injured. He was going to walk far enough without limping to get on and off the plane.

If he didn't, his R and R would be cancelled for sure. The big wigs didn't want soldiers, sailor, or marines hobbling down the gangway off the aircraft at Honolulu Airport. Robert took the next flight out to Danang, a C-117 and the following evening boarded a Boeing for Hawaii.

Robert had put in for a seven day pass. It was near Thanksgiving and it would be nice to be with his wife during the holidays. There were perhaps two hundred military personnel onboard the DC-10. They flew to Anderson Air Force Base on Guam and had a two hour layover. Soon, they were on to Hawaii.

It felt good to be clean and going someplace other than Vietnam. Although Robert felt relaxed and rested for the first time in months, he felt like an old man with all of the young enlisted on the plane. Halfway to Hawaii, he saw an aircraft carrier. No doubt in route to Yankee Station.

Due to the holidays, there were few hotel rooms. Radio announcers had made this known to the population of Oahu and as such, private homes were made available to those on R and R who did not have accommodations. He would have used one of those, but his wife had family here.

Robert did not meet his wife at the airport. He took a taxi out to Black Point which was the location of his wife's cousin's home where they were going to stay. He had been up nearly two days straight.

Seeing her for the first time was awkward. "Hey, there."

She ran to him and throwing her arms around his neck. "I'm so glad you made it. Finally." Although she hugged him tight, Robert stiffened. It was more like meeting someone for a first date, than meeting his wife.

"What's wrong?" she asked, pulling back from him.

"Nothing. Nothing at all," he shrugged, putting on his mask.

"I'm so happy to see you. Tell me all about what you've been doing."

Robert had no idea how to answer that. Did she really want to hear about the villages with children he had napalmed? Did she want to know about the deserters and fragging? Or maybe about the pilots he had seen shot out of the air. "Oh. Just flying in a war. That's about all."

She reached into her pocketbook. "Here. I brought you pictures of the baby."

Robert looked down at the photographs of the son that had been born while he was away. He was now about four months old. "He's pretty cute," he managed. His heart was breaking as he thought about the time he missed seeing his son as an newborn. He didn't know him.

"You can keep one. I brought you a small one, so that you could take it back with you."

"Thanks. I will," he said flatly. He tucked it into the pocket of his jacket.

Luckily, the lush scenery was so beautiful; the site of it distracted her. Robert had been gone so long and had changed so much, that it took some time to get reacquainted with her chirpy, happy conversation.

Later, in the privacy of her relative's home, Robert prepared to take a shower. His wife let out a gasp when she saw the wound on his leg. "Good heavens. What in God's name is wrong with your leg? You're wounded." She clearly had not been prepared for that visual. She had turned pale and her hands were up over her mouth in horror.

"It's nothing. Just some superficial shrapnel."

"But Robert. Are you okay? Do you need to see a doctor?"

"Nope. Just need a shower and to re-bandage it."

"But you need medical attention," her face was still contorted in concern.

"Not no, but hell no. Do you want our R and R to be over?" Robert was adamant.

"But how can you even get around?" she worried.

"It's nothing. Now let's get going. Let's enjoy what time we have." His wife looked surprised at the intensity of his reaction. It was unlike him. Lots of things seemed to be. She wondered if she really knew her husband at all.

Her cousin had booked an endless array of activities and the week passed quickly. Robert and she were taken to see all the sights of the island. He had requested to eat out at restaurants away from the main crowds, finding that he was jumpy around a bunch of civilians.

It was during nighttime that Robert found himself to be the most uncomfortable. One would think that being away from his spouse for so long, the first thing he would want to do was jump her bones. After all, he was one of the pilots over there that had remained faithful. But he found himself uncomfortable to even be in bed next to her in negligees. He was so used to sleeping in a sandy cot, by himself.

Robert knew it hurt her feelings. On a couple of nights, she had reached out to hold him during the night, only for him to turn away. By the third night, he realized he had to make love to her. He knew she wanted to. Almost mechanically, he got into bed next to her and began to kiss her. Reaching down, he fondled her breasts gently. He noticed that she had remained slim, as he ran his hands down over her hips.

Robert heard her moan in delight as he quickly rolled on top and entered her. With a few strokes, it was over.

"I'm sorry. That I came so quickly," he apologized.

"No. No. It was fine," she explained. But she knew it wasn't. What had happened to him?

Except for the trip to the Punchbowl, a military cemetery in a volcano crater in the center of Honolulu, the sights were pleasant. On the day they visited, a military cortege was present. They were burying casualties from Vietnam that must have occurred just as Robert had left. It was more than Robert could take.

They celebrated Thanksgiving dinner with his wife's family. Afterward, they went to a party given by local Honolulu families. His wife looked pretty in her turquoise, sparkly party dress. Although she chatted and seemed to be having a good time, Robert found it hard to make small talk. He had lost track of current events.

On the last night, they went to a floor show in one of the big hotels on Waikiki Beach. Many of the military personnel on the flight coming over were there. Some of the young enlisted had wives that looked more like children. Robert looked over all of his fellow passengers. He felt sad that many enjoying tonight's festivities and lifestyle were going to be seeing it for the last time.

"Penny for your thoughts?" his wife asked as they said their goodbyes.

"You wouldn't want to know," he said remorsefully.

"Robert Lathrop. Maybe you underestimate me?" her lip quivered.

"I'm sorry." Robert again put on his mask and pasted on a smile. "I had a great time. It was wonderful to see you again."

"Be safe, marine." His wife blew him a kiss.

"Will do," he shouted back as he walked out to the tarmac. He could not make himself turn around to see her standing there in tears, waving.

It wasn't easy for Robert to return to 'Nam. The thought made his stomach turn over. He boarded the aircraft, went to sleep and woke up sixteen hours later as they approached the anarchic landing pattern of the massive Danang Air Station. Robert got off the plane, changed out of his dress uniform which wilted in the heat, put on his flight suit and went back to the war. So much for R and R.

Chapter 49
∞ Chu Lai ∞

The very next evening, Robert flew his last mission over Chu Lai. He had been up for most of the previous day, first with his flights, then his duty, followed by a party of sorts at the club. Nora was celebrating the news about Steve which Robert brought her just prior to his R and R. He had drunk himself silly, as he was lucky not to be scheduled to fly until the next day's afternoon hotpad.

Robert napped in the ready room in case something came up, rather than have to be called from the living quarters and have to make the two mile trip back. As he did, a hotpad launch came from a unit near Camp Carroll. Another pilot, a Captain he had known from Washington, was available. Despite still having some alcohol in his system, he flew.

They took the launch and flew in the twilight past Danang to a point just south of the DMZ. It was not quite totally dark when they turned inland and were skirting the DMZ in route to their target. It was a valley in which they had never flown before, but which was near the area Robert had seen the 144 helicopters on fire.

Just as they made landfall, all the guns in North Vietnam opened on something, though they could not see what. It was truly a spectacle to behold, as they flew some five or six miles south of what appeared to be the flashing lights of a large city. There were guns firing everywhere. Everything from small arms to 100mm guns shooting explosions in the sky, as high as one could see.

As the pilots approached the target area in their Skyhawks, an OV-10 controller gave them their missions, not unlike the many before. The target was an enemy position at the head of another blind canyon, with the main units halfway up the hillside. It would be necessary to run up the canyon bottom, with rockets and guns attacking the hillside; then quickly climb over the other long, low ridge to their left. Eerily, it sounded exactly like the mission Steve had flown when he was shot down.

Robert lowered the nose of the A-4 and started his first run well back into the valley, accelerating down the valley floor. Everything was black on both sides of him. As both of them approached the headwall, Robert placed his gunsight on the center of the hill firing all sixteen rockets. Seeing them hit, told him he was way too close and forced him to rapidly pull up and roll, banking sharply to the left in order to roll over the ridge and down the other side to avoid enemy ground fire.

On the second run, Robert armed his Hughes gun pod and ran again down the valley. Two solid red tracer lines tore into the hill and he could see them bouncing around after they hit. The plane slowed to seventy-five knots forcing Robert into the straps of his seat harness. He was in the deep in the valley. Pulling up the hill, Robert did a little soft shoe on the rudders, sending two, red beams back and forth over the lower one third of the headwall.

He was coming in slow this time. The ridge was not high, allowing him to quickly make another run and join the other pilot. They rolled climbing back in altitude. Both pilots could see the disruption the bullets were causing all over the hillsides. Tracers and bullets were flying in every direction.

It was the first time Robert had ever fired a gun pod in the dark. The number of rounds going out and coverage of them was astounding to see. A massive amount of lead had slowed the 14,000 pound plane. He would not have wanted to be on the receiving end of that firepower. Whatever had been there, was now gone.

Guns were still firing in North Vietnam, beyond the DMZ, when they flew back towards the sea and down the coast. His last mission was gunfire at mystery targets in the black of night. Strange. After landing and checking over the planes, Robert entered the ready room.

"Major." Robert saluted.

"Captain. At ease. You've got orders," the Major handed Robert some papers.

He had immediate orders to Okinawa for Forward Air Control School. Robert tried to beg out it. "But sir. I've already seen hundreds of air strikes and controlled them. I've even flown in control of the *New Jersey*," he argued.

"Sorry, Captain. Orders are orders. You know that."

Logic was never a cause to change pre-conceived actions, nor orders. So Robert made his way back to his hut to pack his B-4 bag for another trip out of the country with $200 to spend. For his final act at

SOLO VIETNAM

Chu Lai, Robert went in and checked on the Intel reports he would have to turn over.

The documents described a red-haired male, seen leading an enemy patrol near Danang with a group of Caucasians, probably deserters. They were operating near Hue, independent of any unit. There was also a report on the total number of deserters and from where they had deserted. Reading about deserters sickened him. It validated the insanity of Vietnam. As Robert skimmed the reports, the last he was to see, he wished now that he had been transferred one day earlier.

The timing of these orders sucked. He would be missing Nora's going away fete' at the club. They had become close friends and comrades in this maniacal war zone. Bags packed, all he had left to do was to say goodbye.

Chapter 50
∞ November 1968, New Orleans ∞

Charlene used the Thanksgiving break to do nothing else but study. The decorations she normally put up for Christmas still remained in the boxes her husband Max had brought down from the attic. After nearly flunking during the last term, she was determined to do well in her final exams. This was her last term. She was due to graduate and take the Board of Nursing Exam for the State of Louisiana in mid-December.

With her children home on school holidays, she was finding it hard to cubby-hole herself away in quiet. She was studying Advanced Medical/Surgical nursing. The formulas and medications were difficult. Charlene had never been stellar at math. Thank goodness nursing only required multiplication, division and some basic ratio and proportion. In addition, there were cardiac rhythms and code drugs to learn.

"Mama. Mama. The mailman came," one of her children barged into the study.

"Mmm, hmm."

"Do you want me to go get it?" pestered her little one.

"Mmm, hmm. Mommy is studying. Please darlin.' You do that."

"Okay, Mommy. Ssshhhh. We'll be quiet."

"Mmm, hmm," Charlene answered, trying to concentrate on her books. After another few minutes, the door opened again with a slam. "What in tarnation do you want now?" Charlene was becoming aggravated. She had to pass.

"There's a letter with funny looking stamps. It's from Miss Nora."

"My stars. Gimme that, my little munchkin." Charlene grabbed the letter and ripped it open. She hadn't heard from Nora in months. Her hand started shaking as she quickly read the contents.

Charlene grabbed her little daughter and swung her around in the room. "She's coming home. Golly Jesus. Nora's coming home!" she giddily exclaimed. "Praise God. Just praise God. And Commander Novak is a P-O-W. He's alive."

"Miss Nora is coming home?"

"Yes. Yes. Yes."

"Will she be here by Christmas?" her small daughter, Michelle, asked?

"It sure looks like it. Glory be. Michelle, go get the rosaries. We're gonna say a special one right this very minute. Our prayers have finally been answered.

Charlene closed her books briefly and gathered her children around the picture of the Sacred Heart that was hanging in the alcove. She lit the tall votive candle she had blessed from St. Xavier Catholic Church.

"What's a P-O-W?" her youngest asked.

"A prisoner of war."

"But why are we happy that he's a prisoner?"

"Because, because, because. It means he's still alive. Somewhere, somehow," Charlene explained.

"Can we order one of those copper bracelets? I've seen some of the other kids at school wearing 'em." her teenage son asked.

"Of course. Of course. But now, let's say our prayers in thanksgiving. This is a miracle to be sure." Gathering her children around her, they all knelt on their knees and began the Rosary.

"In the name of the Father, the Son and the Holy Spirit. Now and ever shall be, world without end. Amen." Her children all made the sign of the cross. "Father, we offer up this Rosary for the safe return of our dear, beloved Nora. God speed her to a safe journey home."

As Charlene began the Glory Be, each one of her four children dutifully answered the prayers, counting the beads within their fingers one by one. Some of the younger ones did not fully understand the significance of this particular rosary, but they did as their mother asked. Ten decades later, they carefully placed their rosaries back in their tiny cases and put them on Charlene's bedroom dresser next to the statue of Jesus. As soon as they did, Charlene ran to the phone.

"Chet. Chet. Chet. You are just never gonna believe it. Steve's now a POW." Charlene could barely contain her elation.

"How do you know?" Chet queried.

"In a letter that Nora wrote. It just came in the mail. And that's not all, she's coming home. Probably should be here in the next few weeks. Can you believe it?"

"That's wonderful news. Just wonderful, Mrs. Hebert. Thank you so much for letting me know. I'm just glad to hear he's not MIA."

"Isn't that the truth? At least they know those Vietnamese have him. I just pray he's safe and still alive."

"We can hope. Does it say where he is?"

"Her letter says Hanoi."

"Ah, the Hanoi Hilton."

"What the heck is that?" Charlene questioned.

"It's a prisoner of war camp in North Vietnam. The good thing is, news reports say conditions there are better than some."

"Chet, that is so good to hear. I'm so glad you understand all this military stuff. Sometimes it's just a foreign language to me."

"Now we just have to hope that he's able to stay alive in captivity. At least until the end of the war."

"God only knows when that will be."

"President Johnson's been working on it. But for now, there appears to be no end."

"Well, we'll just keep on praying that's all. This is a sign. Glory be. I just know it."

The next phone-call Charlene made was to Nellie. She too, had received a letter. It was an answer to the many prayers and masses she had offered up for the safe return of her wayward daughter.

"We'll have to make it a big Christmas, Mrs. Broussard. Just huge."

"Yes, my dear. I plan on making all her favorites. Crawfish Bisque. Oyster Stuffing. And the biggest turkey you ever wanna see. The children are all just beside themselves. Well, all except one."

Charlene could guess who that was. Kayce. "Don't worry. I'll try and get over there to talk to her. Right after my final exams."

"I think that's just what she needs. That and a swift kick in the pants from Big Daddy or Mabel."

"Have they heard the news?"

"Yes. Mabel's been coming by to check on us. I can't afford to pay her, but she comes anyway to help me out."

"Mabel has always had a soft spot in heart for Nora. Ever since she worked at the Woodvine house."

"She and Big Daddy. Charlene, I haven't even had a chance to tell you, but I'm ever so proud of you becoming a nurse. A registered nurse."

"Well, I'm not there yet. In fact, I have to cut our talk short and get back to my books. My final exams are next week."

"Just know I am very pleased for you. Study hard. You're a smart girl. Always have been. The steady one of the duo. I know Nora will be elated to see you carry it all out."

"She was my motivation you know."

SOLO VIETNAM

"That's my girl. Always wanting to do something outta the box. But I'm terribly glad, ya hear?"

"Yes, Ma'am. Thank you. I'm gonna finish it. If nothing else to make her proud." With that, Charlene hung up the phone, brewed a strong pot of Community, and returned to her books. The receipt of the good news motivated her now more than ever.

Chapter 51
∞ December, 1968 Chu Lai ∞

As the days to her departure counted down, Nora ticked off her last tasks in Chu Lai. She packed up the extra *ao dai* she purchased for her girls, the *nón lá* traditional Vietnamese straw hats for Charlene and Nellie and the teakwood chess set for Iggy. Although the presents would not make it before Christmas, the base FPO post allowed her to send off the items for transshipment at a reasonable cost.

Nora went to the USO office and sorted through a lot of papers and other junk to throw away. Woody had commandeered a .38 pistol and taught her how to shoot in order to protect herself. Nora turned that weapon and the recommendation to take shooting lessons over to Marsha. A girl couldn't be too careful on a base where the perimeter was surrounded by VC.

Marsha had done a splendid job transitioning into manager of the club. For that, Nora was relieved. The young girl had been running it for almost a week by herself, allowing Nora a few days to mentally prepare herself for re-entry into a world which she no longer felt connected. Nora finished organizing the workroom and returned to her hooch.

As she was packing her small bag of personal effects, O'Malley popped in. "I can't believe it. The day is finally here."

"Yep. It feels very strange," Nora admitted.

"Remember, what I told ya. Going home is great. But take it easy. After the hoo-hah and libations of you coming home wear off, it's gonna hit ya."

"I know. That's what I'm afraid of. At least I can get cigarettes anytime I want."

"And plenty of bourbon."

"Yep. But I had that here."

"I mean the good stuff. Be careful. Be kind to yourself. Don't go becoming an alcoholic."

"Nah. Everything in moderation." Nora put on her mask to hide her fear. She was a mess of emotions. Happiness. Anxiety. But most of all, a profound emptiness knowing she was leaving Steve behind.

"Take care, Toots," O'Malley hugged her friend.

"You too. I'll expect to see you and Woody at the Mardi Gras after next." Nora knew that O'Malley wouldn't be home in time for the one coming up.

"Righto. Will do. I won't ever turn down an invitation to party in 'da Quartah' my dear," O'Malley assured.

Woody drove up in a jeep to take her out to the flight line. She was to hop the next C-117 transport plane from Chu-Lai to Danang. From there, she would take a Boeing 707 to Okinawa to pick up more folks going home. Then, just one more plane change to stateside. At Travis AFB in Sacramento she would transfer to a commercial airliner back to New Orleans.

Several GIs and nurses at the club gathered outside her hooch to say goodbye. As they drove past the USO club with its white and blue sign, it seemed to Nora that she had only just arrived a few days before, following her USO tour with Bob Hope. But in reality, almost a year had passed at Chu Lai. She wished Robert had been there to say goodbye, but he was now at his new duty station.

Woody pointed out the new sign post attached to the others listing mileages home. Her crew had painted it pink. It read *Nawins 9,509 miles.*

Not much had changed at the base. She wouldn't miss the dust or stacks of artillery or barbed wire. At the flight line, Nora boarded the C-117 with the mixed load of other passengers. It was cool and damp outside, possibly eighty degrees, with of course 100% humidity. So much for her hairdo.

The airfreight NCO gave the flight mechanic the manifest. There were two soldiers carrying M-16s and flack vests who looked to be merely eighteen or nineteen year olds. They took back seats, threw their rifles and packs on the deck and lay down and went to sleep. The remainder of the passenger manifest was comprised of several floor shows that had entertained the marines several weeks before during the Marine Corps Birthday celebrations at various USO clubs. The event was celebrated every November 10 regardless of where and what was going on when it was time to do so. Gotta love those marines.

Nora looked over the young women, dressed as though they were flying from New York to Boston, rather than from the sand of Chu Lai and its red dust. They sat in the center seats and along the litters that lined the fuselage next to the rows of windows.

The pilot was a Sergeant and glanced at the passengers shaking his head. When he started the starboard engine, Nora heard it backfire. But it didn't blow a stack, so he fired up the port. The wind was too strong to takeoff on the main concrete runway. A call to ground asking to taxi back to the Air Freight building was refused. The pilot, whose glasses were so thick Nora wondered if he could see over the nose and the pilot tube, was told that the crosswind was available.

Nora knew from her rides around the flight line with Robert that the crosswind runway, which couldn't be seen from the mat they were on, was reached by taxiing down the perimeter near the overrun of the concrete runway down a narrow strip. It lay between two rows of barbed wire that marked the perimeter. A plane got there by heading down a matting strip, some 4,000 feet.

Because the wings were low and moved up and down as they taxied, the plane had wing walkers on each side. They'd either pick up the wings or step down on the concertina to assist the progress down the taxiway. As the plane moved bumpily along, the women from the floor show cackled and clucked in fear like chickens in a coop that had been invaded by a fox. At this, Nora found herself laughing out loud. Her days as a passenger were soon to be over. In a matter of days, she would be in a cockpit of her own again.

The pilot ran up the engines and checked the mags and props. Suddenly, he pushed the throttle forward. The plane veered, first one way and then another. Differential throttle movements were needed to keep the plane in the center of the runway. Halfway to the takeoff point, the main gear ran over the catapult and the plane bounced off the runway, then back on. With less than 500 feet to go, the pilot pulled back on the yoke and shouted, "Gear up."

The C-117 flew through the clearing between the trees that had been removed at the end of the crosswind and turned out sharply over the glistening South China Sea. They were merely twenty feet above the water. The sounds coming from the rear cabin compartment now bordered on the shrieking level.

Initially, the weather was clear as the plane climbed to 1000 feet. The coast was pretty and the ocean teal blue and peaceful. But about ten miles outside of Danang, the plane entered a squall. The pilot was going to have to shoot an approach over the harbor and into Danang. The squall was pouring rain into the cockpit from the escape hatch which was loose and leaked over the center console. This was concerning because it was over the throttles and mixture controls.

The pilot was handed a poncho by the flight engineer to put over the controls. The rainwater continued to fall onto it and drained back into the passenger cabin, presumably on its way out the back door. It was now totally silent in back.

"Holy crap," muttered Nora. "Military transport at its best."

The plane broke out nearly 1500 feet above Danang harbor. Nora knew that the plane was in an attitude for landing that she had never seen before. Flying with full flaps and trying to land, it was wing level more or less, but dropping straight down.

"Good God," Nora exclaimed. "After all this, I can't die on a lousy approach."

The floor show girls, previously silent, began screaming as they felt the plane make a major flare away from the runway. It circled around again to make another approach. Wobbling this time, but at least on the right slope. Bounce, bounce, scrape. Finally, touch down.

As the plane taxied to air freight, Nora wondered just what kind of pilot had nearly ended her life on a runway. When the plane came to a halt, the women unloaded quickly jumping to the ground and hugging each other. They had tears in their eyes and ran from the aircraft like it was some kind of monster. The two soldiers were still asleep, and the NCO had to wake them up to catch their next flight.

By that afternoon, Nora was ready to leave the Old French terminal at Danang. There were several enlisted men, a warrant officer, a couple of helicopter pilots that had two rows of ribbons, one with a purple heart. All were going home.

The Boeing 707 that they boarded looked so clean. In contrast to the previous flight, the loading of passengers occurred quite orderly. Not like the dirty, wet and tumultuous trip up in the C-117. As they taxied out of the terminal, Nora thought there would be some sort of cheer or verbal response by the troops returning home. But the plane was silent as they lifted off of Danang's south runway. Nora looked out windows and saw two Phantoms and an A-4 Skyhawk taking off to the north on the other runway. Helter-skelter Danang. It made her think of Steve and all of the stories he had shared about flying sorties.

As Nora heard the landing gear pull up, her heart sank, for she was leaving a part of it behind. She took one last look out the window at the dark green mountains and back down the coast toward Chu Lai. As they crossed the beach in a steep climb she saw the smoke of ground fire activity below. "God, Steve. Please stay alive."

She remembered the anxiety she had felt the first time she had seen the torn up countryside from unrelenting combat. Her patriotic concern for the men fighting an unpopular war. But there was no anxiety in looking at it now. Her experience in Vietnam was over. As much as Robert had tried to protect her, she was leaving Vietnam totally numb.

Chapter 52
∞ December, 1968 New Orleans ∞

Before Charlene had finished her last final, she met with Nellie to begin preparations for Nora's homecoming. Nora's house wasn't big enough for the grandiose affair she had planned. Charlene doubted Nora would want to celebrate at Metairie Country Club, but she thought she knew just the place. The Roosevelt. It was perfect. Elegant. Stylish. Nora.

Charlene rang up the manager the next day to arrange it. Normally at the holidays, the Roosevelt was booked up. But when the manager of the Blue Room heard it was Nora, he was more than happy to reserve some space. It wasn't going to be a huge party. From the tone of Nora's letters, Charlene had guessed correctly that Nora wouldn't want that. No, it would be simple, but elegant.

Nellie helped Charlene with the guest list. Chet from Novak Aviation. Wyatt Aviation. Big Daddy and Mabel. Gia, although Charlene was not sure she would come. Nellie even invited Mr. and Mrs. Arceneaux, whom she had gotten to know much better since living at the house on Dante. They politely declined however, mentioning something about company coming into town.

"Should we keep it to hors d'oeuvres and cocktails? Or dinner, Nellie? What do you think?"

"A dinner might be nice. In a private room. Then, we can enjoy some cocktails in the Blue Room and listen to the music. I think Nora would like that."

"Yes. I think you're quite right. That sounds splendid."

"It's going to be crazy busy before then. You know I graduate from Touro next week. Our capping ceremony is Tuesday."

"Is it open to guests? I would love to come."

"Of course. They are having it at the Loyola Chapel on St. Charles. I would be honored for you to be there. I had so hoped Nora would get to see me get my cap."

JEANETTE VAUGHAN

"She'll be there. In spirit. I'm not sure exactly when she'll be home." Nellie heard from Nora's last letter that her transport home depended on availability. It could be tomorrow, next week or the week after. They would simply have to wait for word.

When Charlene contacted Chet, he was happy to RSVP in the affirmative. There was something he had to give to Nora. It was a letter that Steve had written her, in case something had happened to him. He figured the party was as good a time as any. He kind of already knew what was inside, as Steve had told him.

It was going to be a party in true New Orleans style. Charlene had already begun shopping for a dress. She bought one for Nora, too, at Maison Blanche on Canal. She could hardly wait to hug her dear friend. She might even squeeze the life out of her.

* * * * * *

On the evening Charlene was to be pinned, she got the surprise of her life. Charlene was a bundle of nerves as she prepared to graduate. As president of the Student Nurses Association, she had been selected to give the graduation speech. For weeks, when she wasn't studying her nursing texts, she poured over ideas on just what to theme her talk. Somehow, she wanted it to reflect her own motivation for going to nursing school, Nora's independent spirit.

All of the graduates were to wear nursing whites. Starched white dresses, not above the knee. White nursing shoes. White hose. No jewelry or makeup. Hair up, off the collar. Charlene stood before her full length mirror, making sure she looked just right. It was the first time they had been allowed to wear all white. She genuinely felt like a real nurse. After tonight, she was going to be a real nurse. A graduate nurse, until she passed her boards. Then, she would be an RN.

Max poked his head in the bedroom. "Come on, Charlene or we're gonna be late." Then, his eyes set upon her. "My, my. Don't you look fantastic, honey. My wife, the nurse."

"Max, do you really think so?"

"Absolutely, honey. Like you're ready to go give some poor patient a shot."

"Max. Seriously."

"No really, honey. You look great. But come on now, we gotta go. I can only go so fast down St. Charles."

"Okay. Okay." Charlene grabbed her purse and they left for the chapel with three of her children. Her oldest son was driving over after picking up Nellie, Cathy and Leisel. Kayce, who was huge with child, chose not to attend. Iggy was at football spring training. On the drive over, all Charlene could think about was Nora. How she wished she could be there. But she knew, like Nellie said, Nora was there with her in spirit.

"Max, what you think it will be like when Nora comes home?"

"What do you mean, honey? I'm sure it'll be just fine. Just like old times?"

"Do you think? I mean, I've read stories about veterans who have come home. How they were shunned at the airports in their uniforms. Some protestors spit at them."

"Well, honey. You gotta remember that Nora won't be in uniform. So it'll be just like she was another passenger getting off the plane."

"Right. I almost forgot."

"I wonder. if and when, Steve will come home. Do you think ever?"

"I sure hope so, honey. For Nora's sake."

"Me too, Max. Me too."

They pulled into the parking lot of Loyola Chapel. Although it was called a chapel, it was quite huge. It had leaded glass windows, twenty feet high The exterior was an intricate design of white and brown quartz. Lots of stained glass. Huge oak doors. It was magnificent.

Charlene got out and directed her children where to sit. She advised them to keep a look out for her son, Nellie and Nora's girls. Charlene kissed Max goodbye and went into the anteroom beside the vestibule. She, along with the valedictorian, would be sitting on the front row with the nuns who were her professors. The graduate nurses were to process in. Her stomach was churning with butterflies.

Max saw Nellie, the girls and his son to their seats. The ceremony was about to begin. Some trumpets began a salute. Then, a string quartet began to play *Pomp and Circumstance.* Two by two, the graduate nurses filed in, each carrying a brass Nightingale lamp with a candle. In the ambient gas lighting of the chapel, it was a lovely site.

Charlene took her place on the front row. She couldn't help but smile when she passed the row with her dear husband, children, Nellie and Nora's girls. What she didn't notice was that Nora herself had arrived and was standing in the back of the vestibule.

Nora waited until the procession was complete, before moving up the aisle and taking her place next to Max, Nellie and the group. Nellie could hardly contain herself. She had tears running down her eyes. Dabbing them with a handkerchief, she tried to gain control.

"Ssssh, Mama. It's okay. I'm okay. Let's let this be Charlene's night."

Cathy and Leisel moved over in the pew to sit alongside their mother. Each one held one of Nora's arms tight. Nellie kept looking over at her daughter. Nora, although beautiful, was way too thin. Her eyes had dark circles under them. She looked a bit haggard.

The priest gave a benediction. The Dean of Touro School of Nursing spoke. Next it was Charlene's turn to give her address. As she rose, Nora thought she looked almost as white as her dress.

Charlene pulled out her notes and adjusted the microphone. She cleared her throat. Initially, her head was down. But as she began to speak, she remembered the Mother Superior's words of advice at the practice. Head up. Address the crowd. Project.

"Being a nurse is one of the most honorable professions a woman could have. In the words of Florence Nightingale, 'I think one's feelings waste themselves in words; they ought all to be distilled into actions which bring results.' My fellow nurses and I, like Florence Nightingale, 'attribute' our 'success to this' – we never gave or took any excuse.' This was a lesson taught to our class by our instructors. It was a principle that guided us to accountability for all of our actions. But personally, I learned to persevere against the odds from another strong woman."

At that moment, Charlene raised her head. She almost fell over when she saw Nora's face beaming from the fourth row. Charlene couldn't believe her eyes. For a moment, she stammered in her speech.

But Nora only grinned, and nodded her head, yes. "Go on," she mouthed. "You can do it."

"The . . . the woman who most inspired me is not a hero to everyone. In fact, sometimes her choices in life caused great consequence to herself and those she loved. But she never gave up. She persevered. Through thick and thin, no matter how rough it got, she kept going. I marvel at her tenacity. Her sheer will not to give up. When she set her sights on a goal, she pursued it. Whether it was singing on Bourbon Street to earn a living, or learning to fly a plane. In fact, to regain custody of her own children, she actually stole a plane." The crowd laughed a little. "No, seriously, she did. As hard as that is to believe." Charlene began to waffle. Nora just smiled.

"Sometimes, her choices were not understood, like when she decided to go over to Vietnam to volunteer. She was frustrated that the government wouldn't let her fly over there, in combat. So, in true style, she found another way. She went over using her beautiful voice. She served our nation and our GIs in a war that no one has wanted to support. She provided our boys with a little bit of home. Going to

Vietnam wasn't a popular choice, but she followed her heart to conquer that mission. I learned a lot from that."

"Principles which I shared with my fellow classmates. Never give up. Never stop believing in yourself. Never stop chasing your dreams. As we see our world change, and we certainly have, we need to stay strong, my fellow women. Remembering our core values, but striving to achieve and make a difference. I would have never thought about going to school to become a nurse. Never had the guts to try, unless I had met my own personal hero. I would ask her to stand." Charlene held out her hand and beckoned to Nora.

With that, Nora stood up in the chapel facing her dear friend. "As both Florence Nightingale and my friend, Captain Nora Broussard believe, 'never lose an opportunity of urging a practical beginning, however small, for it is wonderful how often in such matters the mustard-seed germinates and roots itself.' Thank you, Nora. Captain Broussard. For helping me believe in myself and in the power of women."

The chapel erupted in applause. Nora, who was now blushing, sat down. She was honored to think that she meant so much to Charlene. It was a sweet moment.

A short time later, Nora, Max, Nellie and the group watched proudly as Charlene walked triumphantly across the stage. She knelt in front of the Mother Superior and a white nurse's cap with a black stripe across the top was placed on her head. Then, the priest pinned her with the Touro nursing pin. She was simply glowing in pride.

All of the graduates then gathered on stage with their lit lamps. They recited the Nightingale pledge:

> *I solemnly pledge myself before God and presence of this assembly;*
> *To pass my life in purity and to practice my profession faithfully.*
> *I will abstain from whatever is deleterious and mischievous and will not take or knowingly administer any harmful drug.*
> *I will do all in my power to maintain and elevate the standard of my profession and will hold in confidence all personal matters committed to my keeping and family affairs coming to my knowledge in the practice of my calling.*
> *With loyalty will I endeavor to aid the physician in his work, and devote myself to the welfare of those committed to my care.*

Another round of applause erupted. The nursing students began to process out. As she passed Nora, Charlene glanced over. Nora just winked and gave her a thumb's up. As soon as Charlene got to the vestibule, she hurried back up the side aisle to Nora.

"I can't believe it. You're home. You're really home. I'm so happy that you made it."

In her classically silky voice, Nora answered "I wouldn't have missed it for the world. I'm so proud of you, Charlene. I'm happy to see you, but remember, this is your night."

Nora gave her a huge hug. That hug was followed by many others from Nellie and her girls. The girls, whom would not leave her side, would barely turn loose long enough for Nora to hug anyone. It was a glorious occasion.

"What a blessed Christmas this is going to be," Nellie remarked.

"Yes, Mama. It will be."

Chapter 53

The one person Nora was waiting to see with trepidation was Kayce. As Nora got out of the car with Nellie and the girls, she bit her lip wondering how Kayce would respond to her being home.

Initially, when the door opened and they all came in, Kayce didn't look up. Coincidentally, she was watching *Julia*, a show about a black nurse on TV and didn't expect to see anyone other than her sisters and grandmother. It startled her, when Kayce heard Nora's voice.

"Kayce. Hello, there. I'm home."

Kayce looked up pensively. "Mama?" She hesitated at first, then jumped up, as best she could in her whale-sized state, and ran to her mother. "Mama. Oh, Mama." Kayce buried her head in Nora's bosom and hugged her tight.

"It's alright, Kayce. Mama's home. It's gonna be alright." Nora could not help notice that Kayce was calling her 'Mama' and not 'Mother,' as she did when she was upset with her.

"Mama. I'm sorry I didn't write. I've messed up. Bad this time." Kayce looked down at her belly. "I'm so sorry. I . . ." she sobbed heavily.

"Now, now, Kayce. Just hush. No need to explain. I'm here now."

"Mama, I just didn't know what I was going to do. How I was going to manage."

"I know baby. I know. But we're gonna get through it. In a matter of days, it looks like to me," Nora noted, taking in the size of Kayce's stomach.

"I still don't know what I'm gonna do. I can't believe I got myself into this mess. But I just can't give it up. I just can't." All of her emotion spewed forth.

"It's okay, Kayce. We can talk it over. But just know this, I'm not going to force you to do anything you don't want to do. This is your baby. This is your choice. Whatever you decide."

"Don't leave me, Mama. Please don't leave."

"I'm home, Kayce. For good. I promise you, I'm not going anywhere. Ever again." They held each other for the longest time. Then, Nora sat on the couch with her children gathered around. She took a deep breath and took stock in how lucky she was to still have her family.

It was only then that Nellie noticed her ring. "Nora. Have you got some news that you haven't shared with us? What's that ring on your finger?"

"Yes, Mama. It was . . . well, it is still. An engagement ring."

"Well, I declare. Nora Jean. You never cease to amaze me."

"It's a long story, Mama. But, yes. I am engaged to Lt. Commander Steven Novak."

Nellie and the girls all looked stunned for a moment. "But how, Nora Jean? Mr. Novak is married." Nellie hated to dampen the moment.

"Lt. Commander Novak was married. His wife died, last year."

"I see. Well, I am sorry to hear that. She was a lovely woman. I used to see her at St. Mathias."

"Yes, she was Mama. She really was."

"And all of those children. Where are they?"

"They are living with her parents, up in the Chicago area somewhere."

"But it's complicated, Mama."

"Isn't it always with you, Nora Jean?"

Nora gave her one of her looks. Nellie just smirked. It was good to have her daughter home. Then, Nora looked serious. "It's complicated because Steve is a POW. He was shot down and taken prisoner shortly after we were together and he proposed."

"Nora Jean." Nellie put her hand up to her lips and covered them. "I'm so sorry."

"No big deal, Mama. I mean, I believe he's going to be okay. He has to be. We've waited so long to be together," Nora's voice cracked. For the first time in a long time, she broke down in tears. The flood of pent up emotions all came pouring out. She had worn her mask for months. It was the only way to get through it all. But with Nellie, she had never been able to mask anything.

It was Nellie who spoke first. "Now, now, Nora Jean. This time it's your own mother who's going to comfort you. You are strong, Nora Jean. You are going to get through this. We all will. Broussard women are a fortress of strength and resilience."

Kayce came over to her. "That's right, Mama. You and Grandma Nellie are the ones who taught us that. We'll stand strong and stand together. We'll say our prayers until he comes home."

"I thought you didn't say prayers anymore, Kayce?" Cathy questioned.

"Sometimes in life, things change," Kayce retorted.

"That they do. That they do, girls. Thank you. For still loving me and being there for me. I never meant to abandon you all." Nora dabbed the tears from her eyes and blew her nose. "Now, let me see this Christmas tree you all put up. I'm sure it isn't as good as what I would put up, but let's see it anyway."

Just then, the front door banged open. Iggy bounded in to hug her. "Where did you all come from?" a surprised Nora exclaimed. Nellie had told her that Liesel and Iggy had been living with their father. Nora was hurt, but understood.

"Oh, Mama. When I heard you were back, I just had to come." said Iggy.

"Yeah. If you're home. We're home," announced Leisel.

"Besides. Living with Dad? It wasn't going so good." Iggy candidly explained.

"He still drinks like a fish. Half the time, he was never sober," added Leisel. "All he did was yell at us."

Nora decided that subject could wait for later. "Iggy, you have grown into a young man. And a very handsome one at that," she hugged her son tight.

"Even if he does have red hair," Cathy teased him rubbing his head. And then, they all laughed. Smiling sardonically through adversity was how Nora had always managed to keep going.

Chapter 54

The welcome home party for Nora was a smashing success. But she had scaled it back a bit more than Charlene wanted. Just family and close friends only. Vietnam had changed her. She wasn't ready for the hoopla of a big New Orleans shin dig. It was a night of fine dining, fabulous cocktails and wonderful jazz. The perfect way to celebrate New Orleans style, albeit a bit understated.

At one point in the evening, there was a request for Nora to sing. But she found she just couldn't. Nerves had never bothered her before. But the thought of going on stage to belt out a tune on this particular evening, made her heart race. She politely declined.

"So my dearest Nora, did we do you homage?" asked Charlene.

"Absolutely. It was definitely a *fais do do* to remember."

"Good. I'm glad my nursing gig hasn't dampened my hostess abilities." Charlene laughed.

"Not in the least. Listen, I'm sorry that I couldn't sing. I know you wanted me to. It's just . . . so hard now."

"Nora. You don't have to explain it to me. I get it."

"It reminds me too much of Steve."

"Sugar. You don't have to explain anything. We understand. All in good time, okay?"

Nora had taken O'Malley's advice. Take one day at a time. She enjoyed the celebrations for Charlene's graduation and her small welcome home party. But other than that, she stayed close to home.

She had several talks with Kayce about the baby. Nora had even quit smoking in preparation for the birth of her granddaughter. However, she kept the lighter Steve had given her in her handbag in a zippered compartment. It was a memento for them both. A sign that to Nora that he would come home.

Knowing the due date was close, Nora gave Kayce her Lamaze book. At first, Kayce wouldn't even open it, but after talking to Nora, she thought she might better.

"Listen to me, Kayce. You don't want the kind of labor experience I had six years ago. It was horrific. They basically snowed me. I didn't get to participate or make choices about anything."

"But I don't want to hurt. I've heard about the pain of childbirth."

"That's why you will want to read the book. To practice the relaxation. The breathing." Nora started to demonstrate the hee-hee-hee, ho-ho-ho patterns that she had learned.

* * * * * *

Christmas was quiet, with Kayce due any day. By some postal miracle, Nora's shipments from Vietnam arrived. The girls were not sure what to think about the unique *ao dai* Nora gave to them. Cathy tried hers on and wore it to Christmas midnight mass. Nellie planned to use her Vietnamese cone hat to garden.

During the next few weeks, Nora practiced with Kayce every day and went to a couple of last minute child birth classes. When Kayce's water broke, they were ready. Nora took her to Hotel Dieu, as Charlene had gotten Kayce an obstetrician at the Catholic hospital.

But during this labor, Nora took charge. She was determined that her oldest daughter was not going to go through anything like the hellish experience she had in Dallas. Accompanied with their book in hand, Kayce was admitted in full labor, already dilated to three centimeters and eighty-five percent effaced.

Kayce came through the delivery beautifully. On December 26th, two weeks overdue, Kayce gave birth to a beautiful baby girl. It seemed that the Y chromosome ran strong in Broussard women. With Nora at her side, she delivered wide awake by using the Lamaze method. No drugs. No anesthesia. Just good old fashioned midwifery and Dr. Lamaze, of course.

Kayce decided not to give the baby up. After much discussion, it was decided that Nora and Nellie would help her raise the baby girl. That way, Kayce could get her GED and possibly go to college. She named her daughter Noelle, as she was born around Christmas.

Kayce felt odd, holding a tiny infant in her arms. Her baby. It was surreal. Suddenly, she felt like a child herself. It was hard to believe that this living, breathing, innocent thing had been inside her only a few hours before. Seeing the face of the baby girl, touching the warmth of her tiny fingers, scared her. Kayce was now a mother.

"Mama," Kayce began pensively. "Do you ever think about the baby you gave up?"

Nora looked her directly in the face with her jaw set. "Every day, Kayce. Although I try not to, nearly every day."

Kayce was silent for a few moments. She felt the baby's fingers grip and wrap around hers. She had tears in her eyes. "Holding Noelle. Looking into her tiny face," Kayce began to weep harder. "I'm sorry, Mama. I'm so sorry for how mean to you I was, during that time. I hated the thought of that baby."

"I know, Kayce. But that was a different time. A different circumstance. Sometimes, the choices we make are made within the circumstances we are given. There aren't any other options that seem possible."

"I just feel so terrible. For how I treated you. That poor baby."

"What's done is done. I hope she has a happy life somewhere. With parents who love her. I pray that she does, anyway."

"Do you ever hope to see her?"

"I can't live with that thought. I gave up that option," the discussion was becoming more raw and frank than Nora could bear. She rose and touched the face of Kayce's beautiful baby with her finger tip. Fair skin and red hair, just like Kayce. "Hello, gorgeous," Nora cooed.

Luckily, at that moment, Charlene arrived. Boisterously bubbly, she was carrying a load of pink boxes. "Well, I'll be," she exclaimed, coming over to the bed. "That baby is just the prettiest lil' thing I've ever seen, Miss Kayce Greenwood. She's just precious."

Nora was relieved that Charlene's appearance and affect overshadowed the previous few melancholy moments. Nora sighed briefly. She could always count on Charlene.

"Thank you, Mrs. Hebert."

"What an angel she is." Charlene touched the cheek of the infant. "Good work, girl," she patted Kayce on the shoulder.

"Mama helped. A lot. Mrs. Hebert? I was wondering if you would consider being her Godmother?" Kayce timidly asked.

"Well, I'm gonna be super busy. Working now, as an RN. But of course. I wouldn't want it any other way, sugar. By the way, how's the new Granny holding up?" She glanced over at Nora who now had the baby in her arms again.

"Mama? She's been great. Hasn't left my side. I think she kinda likes her."

"Hey you, watch who you're calling a granny. I'm certainly not old enough to be one."

"But 'cha are. Just think about how much fun I'm going to have teasing you?" sniggered Charlene. "You won't ever live this one down, honey."

Nora had lots of time to think while she rocked the baby. She tried to prepare herself for what she knew was inevitable. Pretty soon, the honeymoon phase of her return would wear off. It would finally be time to take off her mask for good. To face what she had experienced in Vietnam. To face Steve's ongoing imprisonment until the end of the war. Whenever that was. Nora knew herself. Patience had never been one of her virtues. She had no idea how or where she would summon up enough courage to get her through. Kayce and the baby had been the perfect distraction. But it was time to face reality.

When Kayce was discharged, Nora carefully loaded her daughter and her brand new, first granddaughter into the VW bus. To be careful, she had Kayce sit in the back seat belted in with the baby in the car seat. As she drove home, she thought about how crowded the house was going to be. But it didn't matter. She had her children home. They'd just have to rent the duplex and find a bigger place.

As she rounded the corner at Hickory, Nora noticed the red Cadillac was back at Mrs. Arceneaux's house. Driving by, she saw a couple of little girls playing in the yard. For a moment, she thought her eyes were playing tricks on her. One of the girls, who looked to be about seven, had a large, round face and huge, brown eyes.

She looked up briefly as Nora passed by. Chills ran up Nora's spine. No. Stop it, Nora. Nellie had mentioned the resemblance. It was uncanny. But that was Mrs. Arceneaux's granddaughter. Nora looked away quickly and put those thoughts out of her head. By the time she pulled into the driveway at the duplex, the little girl had gone back inside. Mask. Put on your mask.

As she rolled over the bump in the driveway, baby Noelle was jostled awake. She began to cry. "Swaddle her up good, Kayce. Sound like she's ready for a bottle." Nora would think about what she had seen tomorrow. On this very important day, she was bringing her granddaughter home.

Chapter 55
∞ January 1969 Lakefront Airport ∞

With the birth of Kayce's baby, Nora had not had time to go to Metairie. But today, she was headed out to Lakefront Airport to see Chet. Despite Chet mentioning that he had something to give her at the party, he changed his mind and told her to come out to Lakefront to get it. It was some plan that Steve had set into motion before he left, evidently. Nora had no idea what it could be. It was still strange being behind the wheel of her VW bus after not driving for so long. But she loved the freedom to go whenever and wherever she wanted.

Lakefront looked exactly the same, its beige stucco art deco adornments glimmering on the crisp January day. It was the beginning of a New Year. The beginning of a new era. Nora took a deep breath as she entered Novak aviation. She hadn't been in the office for almost seven years.

"Good morning, Chet. Good to see you."

"Great to see you too, Nora. I'm glad that you could come. I wanted to give this letter to you at the party, but knowing what was inside, I thought you would want to read it here."

"Oh?"

"Yes. Before Steve left, he told me that should anything happen to him, that I should give you this letter. I know he's no longer an MIA, and that chances are great that he will be coming home to us after the war. But I kinda know what's in the letter. Considering he's still over there, as a POW for who knows how long, it would be better if I give it to you now."

"Sounds mysterious, Chet."

"No, no. I think you'll like it."

"Okay, then." Nora trembled slightly as she opened the carefully sealed cream envelope. Steve's initials were engraved on the front.

My dearest Nora,
If you are reading this, it could only mean that things in Vietnam did not turn out for the best, meaning I did not return home as planned after my deployment.
As such, I wanted you to know, you are the love of my life. I have never met anyone quite like you. I am sure I never will again. Some of the happiest moments, were when we talked aviation. You fly and talk aviation better than most of the pilots I know. You love soaring through the skies as much as I do.
As such, I wanted to make sure that should something happen to me, while I was over there, that someone who appreciates it would end up with my plane, the Corsair.
It's yours Nora. Take it, remember me, and fly like the wind.
Love always, Steve

"Chet. He can't mean it. Me? Take the Corsair? But he loves it!"

"That's why he wanted you to have it. You know? He wrote this and told me about it before he left. I had hoped, I'd never have to give it to you. The letter I mean."

"But Chet. He's going to come back. I just know it."

"Maybe so. But in the meantime, someone needs to look after it. It's not doing anyone any good just sitting in a hangar. Take it, Nora. Fly it."

"Are you sure?"

"Steve was sure. Here are the keys and the keys to the hangar."

"But it flies so differently than what I am used to."

"That's okay. He told me to get you qualled in it."

"That's my Steve for ya. He thinks of everything. Oh, my stars. I just can't believe it."

"It would mean everything to him for you to fly it. I'll show you how. Heck, now you can open your own aviation service."

"Do you think so?"

"Sure. It'd be great to have your own business. The Corsair would let you do all kinds of maneuvers."

"Maybe I could get it converted. To crop dust."

"I dunno about that. The Corsair's a pretty powerful bird. Here," he said getting out some paperwork. "This is what you need to study. When you're ready, I'll take you up and get you qualled."

Nora was still a bit shocked. No one had ever given her something like this. A plane. Her own plane. "You know I'll take the best care of it, until he comes home."

"I know you will. He knows it too. When you're up there, reach out there and touch the hand of God. Ask him to bring Steve home safely."

"Righto. Roger that." Nora threw her arms around Chet and hugged him tight. Not used to such gregarious behavior, Chet blushed.

He walked her out to Hangar Two and slid back the door. There it was. The Corsair. The very one she had first flown in with Steve, some seven years ago. It still looked the same. Nora walked over to it slowly, still not believing it was going to be hers. Running her hand over the dark blue fuselage, she felt chills go up her spine. It was beautiful. It was part of Steve.

Chapter 56
∞ February 27 1969, Lake Front Airport, Metairie ∞

It was hard for Nora to believe that Mardi Gras had rolled around again. Fat Tuesday. Most New Orleans revelers were out in the streets enjoying the biggest, the best and the last of the parades before Ash Wednesday. But not Nora. This day marked her inaugural flight alone in the Corsair.

Over the past few weeks, Chet had indeed gotten her qualified in the plane. Nora consulted with an avionics firm to find out just what it would cost to get the plane converted. After the flight she took in the plane with Chet, however, she just couldn't bring herself to touch one rivet. The Corsair had to stay the Corsair. The plane was just too magnificent to alter in any way. It was licensed to her and cleared by the FAA the week before. What better day, Nora thought to take it up for a solo.

Nora stood admiring this work of aeronautical genius. She could only imagine this aircraft attacking the enemy with ominous aggression. Even at rest, the Corsair took on a look of intimidation. It was a beauty. She had kept its cobalt blue original color. The plane was no longer just an inanimate machine; it represented Steve and his passion for aviation. Alone with the it, she felt his ardor within her soul.

Nora tried to remove these emotional thoughts and handle the task of pre-flight. It was like Steve was there too, encouraging her to focus. This plane was far more complex and fast than what she was used to flying. A thorough check was necessary. She walked around the plane and checked the pressure in the tires. Verifying all the fluid levels and air pressure, she then checked the landing gear, pitot-static system, control surfaces, and empennage. Satisfied all was in order, Nora climbed in to the cockpit.

Testing the rudders and flaps, she scanned the panel for familiarization. Nora noticed a weathered picture she couldn't quite make out tacked to the bottom right side. Closer inspection revealed it was a picture of herself. Tears blurred the panel momentarily, but she fought them, staying on task. Once the pre-flight was complete, she was good to go.

There was no one else around the tarmac but her. She wanted it that way. This was her moment. There was something ethereal about it. She felt it deep within her heart.

She taxied the plane out to the runway which overlooked Lake Ponchartrain. She signaled the tower. "Lakefront tower Corsair six, three, three five Charlie requesting permission for takeoff runway two seven. It'll be a left turn out to the north of Lakefront. Over."

Nora pushed forward on the throttle revving up the engine, she was ready for takeoff. Twenty-five knots. Fifty-knots. The ground rushed beneath her as the engine came to life. Power resonated through her body. The sensations were overwhelming. She could feel Steve within the plane. He knew she was ready. She felt ready. As she applied power, the sensations were familiar, but amplified. The pressure against the seat was intense. Control inputs were almost violent as she tried to stay on centerline. My darling Steve, help me to manage, she prayed.

"You've got this!" she swore she heard him say. Yes. Finally, she was airborne.

Climbing at an alarming rate, continuing to accelerate, the nose still pointed skyward. Rapidly gaining altitude, clearing the runway, she was quickly out over the water. Up and up and up into the brilliant blue sky. The plane was commanding, much more than the Stearman. She flew over the lake and could see downtown New Orleans and the muddy waters of the mighty Mississippi. Tug boats were pushing barges of sand and coal upstream. She banked and turned over The Quarter.

She had filed a flight plan to Vacherie, planning to land the plane where she used to dust. She crossed the swamps of the Bonnie Carrie Spillway and before long saw the winding River Road. Passing the bridge at Lutcher, she then saw *Amelie*. Flying over the crops of sugarcane reminded her of the heritage of the Deep South. Those were the crops she had dusted so many months before.

She rolled and banked the plane into a steep descent, just yards above the sugar cane which was just in growth stage. Reaching the end of the field, she pulled up and over. Again, making intricate patterns of rolls, banks and chandelles over the rows of crops. A delicate, aerial ballet.

Soaring through layers and layers of clouds, within minutes she was in clear air. Continuing to climb like a homesick angel, she racked the stick to the left, the nose of the aircraft making three complete rolls before her reflexes could stop it. She was in sensory overload. Becoming one with the plane, she felt vigorous back pressure from the intense positive G forces pushing her deep into her seat. The nose pitched up sharply until the plane was vertical. The airspeed bled off.

Lost in thought and deliriously blissful in the splendor of the clouds, suddenly she heard the stall warning. The stick began to shake. At that moment she kicked a rudder and the aircraft swapped ends, the nose now pointing straight down as the airspeed wound up instantaneously. Looking straight down at the ground with sounds of the wind increasing over the airframe, she pulled the stick again to level it off. She was united with this incredible aircraft, pushing it to its limits. Nora was performing maneuvers she had never seen before. It felt so natural. There was no doubt that Steve somehow was coaching her to perform with amazing grace.

Nora remembered the first time she had been up in the plane with Steve on the stick. But this flight was different. This time, she not only was in Steve's plane, she was flying it on her own. Finishing her last pass, she soared upward into a spiral towards the sky. Circle after circle, upward until she flared out into the rays of the sun. Suddenly, she felt Steve's presence.

Somehow, he was there with her in the cockpit. She was sure she could almost hear him speak. "I'm here, Nora. Right here in your heart. I'm coming home. Just believe." In that moment, that blissful moment amidst the clouds, she did.

What Nora didn't realize, as she deftly maneuvered the Corsair, was that she had an audience. Raynaud Arceneaux Jr. had taken a guest out to show off his mother's ancestral plantation home. The spectator and Mr. Arceneaux stood out in back of *Amelie* watching the show.

"What the heck is that?" asked the guest. "Who the heck it that?"

"I'm not sure," answered Arceneaux. "Probably one of the dusters we hire."

"I don't think so. Whomever it is, isn't putting down any spray. That isn't any duster. Get in the car. I've gotta see whose flying that thing."

"Okay. Sure," Mr. Arceneaux was game to oblige his guest.
Getting into his Lincoln Continental, they followed the aeronautics of the plane. The guest hanging out the side craning his neck toward the sky.

"Looks like it's setting up to land. See?" the guest pointed out. "Over there, just right of the levy."

"Yep. That's the old Wyatt Aviation landing strip. I know it." Arceneaux pressed on the gas taking a right onto the River Road. Wyatt Aviation was only about a mile down the road.

Nora set up for landing. There was no need to wait for clearance, as there was no tower at the rural strip. She went through the check list. Gear, fuel, flaps, and prop. Her natural ability to handle the force of this aircraft was quite clear. The strip in site, she eased her slope, gently landing the plane into the red dirt.

As she taxied to the ramp, Nora noticed a tall, slender, older man standing on the red dirt runway straining to see who was seated in the aircraft. He was accompanied by another dark haired gentleman. The men walked over to the aircraft as she disembarked.

"Hello. My name is Doug Finley," he introduced reaching out to shake her hand.

"Should I know you?" Nora asked curiously taking his hand.

"I expect not."

"Nice to meet you. I'm Nora Broussard."

"I was just admiring your performance. I have to tell you, I'm quite surprised to see a woman pilot get out of that cockpit."

Nora raised her eyebrows. "Don't be. There's plenty of able woman pilots," Nora rebuked as she pulled off her helmet unleashing her auburn curls.

"Touché, touché. But not many that can handle a Corsair like that. I'm the CEO of Standard Oil for the Gulf Coast region. We support an annual air show. Would you be interested in a sponsorship to share your talents across the country?"

When he first began to speak Nora was nonplussed. But then, she thought for a moment. Her wanderlust kicked in. She was never averse to a business opportunity knocking. "Could be. What did you have in mind?"

"You. Performing in our air shows. That's what. Here's my card. Give me a call. Maybe we can discuss an offer over lunch."

Nora gave him a smile. "Maybe so," she answered remaining aloof. Vamp was her calling card. In her head, she was dancing a jig. The Corsair. Paid airshows. Where one door was closed, God opened a window. "I'll be in touch," she answered.

SOLO VIETNAM

Epilogue
∞ Spring 1973 ∞

During the early months of 1973, through a series of protracted negotiations with the North Vietnamese called the Paris Peace Accords, preparations were made to release the U.S. prisoners of war. On February 12, 1973 three C-141 transport planes and one C-9A were sent to North Vietnam. Each plane brought back forty POWs.

The prisoners' order of return was determined by their length of imprisonment. The POW held the longest, had been in captivity for nine years. In preparation for their release, the North Vietnamese gathered them at the Hanoi Hilton and told them that the war was over. They provided them with brightly colored sweaters and suits with ties. Knowing this was more propaganda, but not wanting to jeopardize their release, most prisoners declined the brightly colored clothing. Opting for more sedate options, they accepted dark colored trousers and windbreakers, Steve included.

None of them believed that they were actually going home until the first C-141 leaving Hanoi lifted off the ground without a Vietnamese in sight. Once it did, the liberated prisoners broke out in cries of freedom. They yelled, shouted and shrieked for joy realizing they were now free Americans. The plane in which they were riding was later referred to as the "Hanoi Taxi."

Even after the return of 591 Americans, the U.S. still listed about 1,350 as missing. In addition, they sought return of roughly 1,200 Americans killed in action whose bodies had not been returned.

Unlike the other wives of POWs and MIAs, Nora who was only engaged to Steve, not married, did not receive governmental telegrams from the Dept. of Defense advising updates on the progress of the return of the POWs. The mostly benign and meaningless briefs went instead to his oldest son, who now helped Chet run Novak aviation.

JEANETTE VAUGHAN

Over the many months of Steve's absence, Nora had begun to make contact with Steve's children starting with his oldest. At first, he had been a bit reluctant, despite having known her from the time Nora had lived in Tyler with the family. But they both shared a love of aviation and a love for Steve. Slowly but surely, a mutual bond was formed.

Steve was among the fourth group released home. On a balmy March day in 1973, Steve arrived at Clark Air Force Base in The Philippines. He had survived over four years of imprisonment. With the other POWs he was debriefed and medically tested. Emaciated and gaunt, all were thankful for plentiful, good American food. Once they were issued brand new uniforms, they boarded more USAF aircraft bound for Hawaii and then California.

All that was on Steve's mind was New Orleans and Nora. Lifting off from Hawaii and headed for the mainland, Steve finally felt free. He couldn't believe in a few short hours, he would again be on American soil. It was mind boggling.

Sitting in their VW bus, on March 6, Nora, her children and Steve's waited nervously on the tarmac at Travis Air Force Base, California. Clad in her favorite fuchsia mini-dress, Nora felt that she was in a dream. The months of post-Vietnam stress. The agony of hearing nothing. The depression and helplessness had almost done her in. Had she not had her flying as a distraction, she surely would have emotionally caved. Years of hoping and praying were now coming to fruition.

Five years of loneliness, advocacy, and frustration at misinformation, as well as the protracted, political negotiations were now over. She had been stalwart in her refusal to believe that he would not come home to her. For four years, she wore her heart on her sleeve for only one man. Upon seeing Steve in his sparkling navy whites, she could wait no longer. Throwing open the VW's door, she and the children began running across the concrete to greet him.

Although he was frightfully thin, as soon as he saw them, his weathered, hardened face broke into a grin. Within seconds, she held his scant frame tenderly, remembering their touch. Her heart soared with joy. Mardi Gras day 1973 was a magic moment; when Nora and all of their grandchildren and children, except the one given up by adoption so long ago, were there to welcome him home.

Glossary

ARVN: Army of the Republic of Vietnam
ASRAT: airport surveillance radar used to detect positions of aircraft
bird: plane
black shoe: shipboard or 'surface' officers and senior enlisted members, due to the black footwear worn while in uniform
brown shoe: aviation community officers and senior enlisted members due to the dark brown footwear worn in uniform
bunker: protected area within living quarters; reinforced hole or tunnel
BuNo: identifying numbers assigned to individual naval aircraft
CAP: combat air patrol
Carqual: carrier qualifications; test for landing aircraft on carrier
chopper: slang term for helicopters flown by the US Army
C-130: large Air Force transport plan for troops and cargo
CO: commanding officer
Dash 1: the lead on a mission
Dash 2: the second plane in a two-or-more aircraft formation; the wingman
eye on the meatball: keeping an eye on the gyroscope of the airplane
DMZ: demilitarized zone
G suit: anti-gravity suit
Gs: gravity forces
greenieboard: the rating scale posted for each carrier landing in the ready room
hawk circle: orbiting stack of aircraft waiting to land on the carrier
HC-1: squadron of helicopters
helo: slang term for helicopters flown by US Navy
hooch: living quarter for military personnel; tent or fixed facility
I Corps: South Vietnam was divided into four corps zones by the ARVN. I Corps was the northernmost region bordering North Vietnam
Jolly green: U.S. Air Force HH-53 Super Jolly green Giants were the primary search-and-rescue helicopter in Southeast Asia

KIA: killed in action
les bon temp roulles: let the good times roll
Lt: lieutenant
Lt. JG: lieutenant junior grade
LCDR: Lt. Commander
LSO: landing signal officer
MIA: missing in action
MiG: Russian fighter made by Mikoyan-Gurevich Design Bureau
MiGCAP: missions during Vietnam to take out enemy MiG fighters
miniboss: second in command aboard an aircraft carrier
Montagnard: primitive hill-dwelling people of Indo-China
NAS: naval air station
NOLA: New Orleans, Louisiana
NVA: North Vietnamese Army
O club: officer's club
POW: prisoner of war
PTSD: post-traumatic stress disorder
qual: qualify
Quonset hut: metal structure for supplies or living quarters
SA: situational awareness; is the pilot aware of surrounding threats
SAM: surface to air missile
SDO: supply duty officer
SERE: survival, evasion, resistance, and escape is a training program that provides U.S. military personnel survival skills in evading capture using the military code of conduct
R and R: rest and recuperation
ready room: where pilots gather for brief and debrief
shrapnel: metal fragments from an exploding bomb or grenade
scooter: nickname for the A-4 Skyhawk
Tet: the Vietnamese New Year
USO: United Service Organization a group which supports military
VC: the Viet Cong guerilla warfare
Vice: tactical radio channel

References

Aircraft carrier flight ops via A-4 Skyhawk Association. http://a4skyhawk.org/2e/flt-ops.htm. Accessed June 4, 2012.

Freedman D, Rhoads J. *Nurses in Vietnam: the forgotten Veterans*. Austin, TX: Texas Monthly Press, 1987.

Grant, Z. Over the beach: the air war in Vietnam. New York, NY W.W. Norton and Company, 1986.

Gray S. *Rampant raider: an A-4 skyhawk pilot in Vietnam*. Annapolis, MD: Naval Institute Press, 2007.

Klein R et all. Former American prisoners of war. Washington, DC: Office of the Assistant Secretary for Policy, Planning, and Preparedness, US Dept of Veterans Affairs, 2005.

Lathrop R. Eternally at War. Lubbock, TX: Texas Tech University Vietnam Center and Archive, 2004.

McCurdy J, Ed. *USS Coral Sea Cruise Book*. Toppan America, NJ: Toppan Printing Company, 1967.

Reeder W Jr. My friend Xahn. In Vietnam Helicopter Pilots' Association (VHPA) *Aviator Magazine*, 2009, vol 27, no 2.

Talley, R The Cubi cat. http://a4skyhawk.org/?q=2d/tins/cubi-cat.htm. Accessed August 2, 2012.

The History of VA, VAH, VAK, VAL, VAP and VFA Squadrons in Dictionary of American Naval Squadrons Volume I. http://www.history.navy.mil/branches/dictvol1.htm. Accessed July 7, 2012.

Jeanette Vaughan is well established as a writer and story teller. Not only is she published in the periodicals and professional journals of nursing, but also in the genre of fiction. Out on her sheep farm, she has written several novels and scripts. She is the mother of four children, including two navy pilots. She lives in a Victorian farmhouse out in the pastures of northeast Texas with her sheep, chickens, donkeys and sheep dogs.

Follow me online here:

Blog: www.jeanettevaughan.com
Email: jeanettevaughan@ageviewpress.com
Facebook: www.facebook.com/AgeViewPress
Twitter: www.twitter.com/VaughanJeanette
Goodreads: www.goodreads.com/Jeanette_Vaughan

Made in the USA
Charleston, SC
21 April 2013